The Blue Wolf

*The Epic Tale of the Life of Genghis Khan and
the Empire of the Steppes*

FREDERIC DION

Translated by Will Hobson

THOMAS DUNNE BOOKS
ST. MARTIN'S PRESS ⚑ NEW YORK

THOMAS DUNNE BOOKS
An imprint of St. Martin's Press

www.stmartins.com

ISBN 0-312-30965-1

First published in France under the title
Le Loup Mongol by Editions Grasset & Fasquelle
First published in Great Britain by Weidenfeld & Nicolson

First U.S. Edition: May 2003

10   9   8   7   6   5   4   3   2   1

To Marvin, Rousslan, and Lila,
their mothers, their Aunt Anne and Roussia

'real horse, real rider, real land and sky and yet a
dream withal'

Cormac McCarthy, *All the Pretty Horses*

'Thinking of those expanses where whole skies could
collapse in rain without anyone ever knowing made
me feel somehow hollow, a sensation I would gladly
have been spared, empty as I already was'

Nicolas Bouvier, *Le Poisson-Scorpion*

The Blue Wolf

My name is Bo'urchu. My bones are very old and my life has dwindled to a faint glimmer. Slowly I circle on my worn out feet and drink in this land that has always been mine, Mongolia: an ocean of grass which dances and writhes. All around me, the wind buffets the rocks and bends the trees. All is as it should be. Now I can lay myself down.

My eyes grow dim at the beauty of these familiar horizons, intense and wild. They are the image of my warrior's life and tears come at the memory of the days spent roaming them; at the memory of the women whom I pressed to my lips, milk-skinned, pink-cheeked, their breasts hung with sweet-smelling flowers – how often they slipped away from my embrace.

Listener, do not lose patience. Now that I must lie down for eternity, I am going to tell you my cruel story. Steel yourself, for I will take you up on the crupper of my horse and ride through what has been my life, wholly devoted to Genghis Khan, King of the Mongols, Tenggeri's chosen on earth, Emperor of all the peoples, the most ravenous of men. But first I must take off my old man's clothes. Naked, this is how Heaven wants me. Let the vultures feed on my scraps and scatter them to the four winds, what does it matter? My blood will set for all time, my bones will permeate the earth and merge with the humus. The rain and wind will gnaw at my body, the lightning burn my flesh and the sun fuse my eyelids, but I am a Mongol, brother of Genghis the all-powerful, and I know that my gaze will be fixed on the azure sky for the length of my bloody, radiant story.

There, now I am stretched full length in the shade of a red pine, whose branches sway out over a sheer drop, amongst its russet needles, surrounded by smooth ochre and grey rock. My burial place is in the heart of the blue mountains of the Mongol land, a narrow terrace that looks like a fetching scar on the ridged back of a drowsing monster. On the flanks of this my lair, amidst the solid masses of cliff, I can hear the giant larches moaning in the wind, a petrified multitude that still stand although blackened from head to foot. Since Genghis Khan's death, Tenggeri has struck these larches one by one with lightning, and sent flames leaping into the air in this the sacred place, where the leader of the Mongols used to assemble us before a campaign, his ferocious warriors and me.

There, I am at ease now. My sobs have died away.

The chill of the earth seeps into my back and the gusting wind pounds my ribs. My body is frozen, yet my spirit seethes with a thousand rides, impatient to relive the memory of them. It is now that I can tell you of my adventure at Genghis Khan's side.

I was sixteen, in the prime of my youth, and I had a fearsome appetite for destruction . . .

The First Part

Chapter 1

The sky's great cloth of grey felt stretched over the steppe, leaving not a stitch of blue. Crouched in the middle of the herd, I was stroking the teats of the black mare. The milk beat hard under my skin; throbbed under my fingers; ran in my veins. It quenched my thirst and, passing through my body, as hard and taut as a reed in spring, was released into the endless carpet of grass.

Suddenly the heavy, warm udder pulled away; the tilting flow was cut short, my pleasure with it. Mane knotted in the wind, the mare was staring at the bare crest of two hillocks. Her interest in this breast of reddish-brown earth was so keen that I could have lifted her with one finger without her turning a hair.

A few paces away my lead horse, a fine chestnut, stood quivering. Soon the whole herd was on the lookout. Near the camp the dogs had got to their feet and were barking questions to one another, their noses in the air. My first thought was enemy tribes. Several moons had passed since they had last appeared on our territory, but they remained a constant threat to my father and his herds.

The wind subsided and with it the intoxicating smells of the steppe fell away. Then I saw him on his horse. He was alone, motionless, and like the shadow of the eagle on the morning-born lamb; his tall, faraway silhouette against the sky dwarfed us. He was like the wind. How long had he been watching me?

He tore down the slope straight for me and pulled up a hair's breadth away, scattering the mares. My chestnut reared, only to move closer to him, snorting with pleasure.

The stranger's mount, a scowling-eyed gelding the colour of parched grass, tossed his head, the bit jingling in his open, foam-flecked mouth. Sweat poured from his breast to his fetlocks. His rider was tall and powerful, with a knife and scimitar in his belt

5

and a quiver full of arrows. 'Have you seen four men driving eight horses?' he asked.

I had indeed seen them at dawn and could not help but notice their steeds' broken-down hocks. No man should drive his string so hard; only great danger or the pursuit of an enemy could explain it, I had thought, but then decided they must be thieves.

'Do the horses belong to you? I'll help you get them back. Without his horses a man is nothing!' I said.

He looked away from the fugitives' tracks. 'Tell me which way they were fleeing; that will suffice.'

I pointed to the hill shaped like a ram's profile, then offered him a horse so his own could rest, saying, 'Let me ride with you. I am Bo'urchu, the pathfinder.'

Momentarily surprised, he stared at me; his melancholy, wild eyes softened.

My chestnut was harnessed. From its saddle hung a bow and three arrows and a leather bottle of milk and in my breast pocket I had a good piece of dried cheese.

'Can you follow them true?'

'As surely as I can show you where the moon will rise.'

'Are you ready?'

'I am a Mongol!' I said.

'Well then, scout, let's go.'

With a flick of my wrist I caught the fresh horse he needed and we harnessed it. The next moment we were galloping towards the night; he was at my heels, determined that our ride across the grasslands should only leave a single set of tracks.

We rode until dawn and on into the following day. He was silent, but I felt him watching me, observing how I tested a pile of dung to gauge how much ground lay between us and our quarry. We rode with the wind in our faces and we heard them long before we saw them; isolated snatches of conversation, shouts or laughter coming to us in fits and starts, like bubbles of spittle ricocheting in the air.

At twilight we were on them. We hobbled our horses and checked the tethers that keep their heads to the ground to stop them neighing, then crawled up to the camp.

The thieves had dismounted in the bend of a river, a strip of level grass flattened by old flooding and dotted with stands of willow. Two of them were tethering their horses while the other pair collected *argols* for a fire. We hung back and, as we waited

6

for night to fall, shared the piece of cheese and curdled milk I
had brought in a leather bottle.

My companion's long, agile body emanated great assurance.
Impassive, silent, a strange fire crackled in his eyes. I still didn't
know his name and I jumped when he said it. 'Temüjin!' My
surprise was twofold. Not only had he known what I was
thinking, but when I heard the name, it felt as if a horse had
kicked me.

Temüjin: the one who works iron. I knew only one blacksmith
in all the land and that was the son of Yesügei, chief of the
Borjigin, from the line of the former khans, descended from the
great Kabul Khan himself.

'What did you say?'

'Didn't you want to know my name?'

'Yes ... but ... are you the eldest son of the valorous
Yesügei?'

He nodded.

Immediately I knew who he was. How could I not? The
herdsmen never tired of relating his exploits. On the death of his
father, the most powerful of his father's allies, the Sovereign
tribe, had spurned Temüjin, robbed him and driven him and his
family from their land. They had survived the winters by digging
in the earth's belly, eating roots, bulbs and such carrion as
Temüjin could steal from those slower-witted than he. The
Sovereigns' chief, Targutai, who hoped to press his claim of
legitimacy to succeed as khan, grew furious and demanded that
Temüjin's head be brought to him. But Yesügei's son foiled his
every attempt. And these tales of prowess were told by men in
the evenings in their tents, and soon songs composed in his
honour rose up from the land of the blue mountains, travelled
down the rivers and spread to the furthest steppe.

We had seen the same number of springs – sixteen – but,
perhaps because of the perils he had faced, he seemed by far the
older and wiser. He was like a rock fallen from the sky: a dense,
vigorous mass, burning and fearless. His whole being quivered
with an intense energy and even his slightest gesture had the
suppleness and ease of a big cat: I had never felt such an
impression of force and mastery. So when he stood up and asked
me to wait behind, I protested hotly, 'All this time we have been
riding, there hasn't been a shrub, not even the smallest stone to
separate us. Look! Our hoofprints have left but one track.'

'True, but these men are Sovereigns,' he said, pointing. 'Be warned that if you become their enemy, they will plague you remorselessly like flies on old horses.'

'I have come here because they have robbed a brother and now could kill you. I will not hang back. Accept my friendship.'

He was adjusting his quiver; he stopped, gave me an appraising glance and then signalled me to follow. A vast swathe of blue sky had just rent the night.

The Sovereign, reluctant to be woken, mimed a show of irritation. Then he rubbed his eyes. Only when he opened them did I drive the stone from the riverbed down onto his forehead. His skull gave a cracking sound; blood spurted out of the bridge of his crushed nose and flooded his eye sockets. One of his companions gave the alert and immediately all three of them were on their feet. Crouching in the shadows, Temüjin cut down two with an arrow in the back, as the last one took to his heels. In a flash we closed in on him. He was within range of our scimitars, panting with exertion and whimpering with fear. He nearly went sprawling but righted himself, windmilling his arms wildly.

'Sovereign,' I shouted, 'I can smell the stench of your gut.'

He stumbled again but managed to brace himself and knock Temüjin off balance, who rolled over him. I had more luck. I grabbed his topknot, wrenched back his skull and slit his throat. Inflamed now, I cut off his head and laughed at the sight of his face in the first light. His bulging eyes wore a look of dumb amazement.

'Your liver reeks and your plaits are greasy,' I said, then hurled my trophy into the distance.

As the sun came up, we were heading back with the recovered horses at an unhurried pace, when my companion said to me, 'Half are yours. Choose the ones you like.'

'These are not spoils: you are their rightful owner.'

'Would I have got them back without your help?'

'I believe so. Besides, you should know that my father's name is Naqu the Rich and I am his only son. Keep your horses.'

He said nothing more until we reached my father's camp.

My father scolded me for disappearing without a word, then pressed me to his breast and thanked Temüjin for looking after his only child. The dogs came forward to greet me, but, catching the stranger's eye, they slunk back behind the tents and hung their heads, their tails between their legs, as if they had been punished. My father also seemed disconcerted by the unequivocal look in my companion's eye. Although he tried to hide it, I noticed his discomfiture and told him who it was.

'Valiant Yesügei's eldest son? Whose cunning has reduced Targutai's Sovereigns to butts of the steppe's ridicule?'

Temüjin nodded. A moment later he was taking his seat in the yurt on my father's right. A sheep was killed forthwith. Our guest was so distinguished that my reckless escapade was forgiven.

We shared the steaming offal, sticking our gleaming blades into the liver and the heart and biting into the stomach so that our platters ran with blood. Our arms were smeared with fat up to the elbow. We drank, draining barrels of *airag* and clear soup, and stuffed ourselves up to our ears.

When we had polished the bones clean with our teeth, my father said to our guest, 'Your horses look in need of feeding as well.'

'It's true, they are thin in the belly, but they are all the wealth I possess. And without the help of your son, I would never have seen them or their jutting ribs again. You can be proud of him, Naqu: he stood straight and true and in his eyes I saw the purity of his heart.'

'Enough of this praise, else Bo'urchu will see himself reflected in the sun's rays. Tell of your ride instead, since you seem to me like a pair of young wolves who have just made their first kill.'

'That's just what we were. Like two lone wolves, we joined together to defeat those who had robbed me.'

Temüjin described our adventure, to the great joy of my father. I had never seen him show so much interest in anyone, especially someone so young. He plied Temüjin with questions as the fire lit up our faces and above us, through the smoke-vent, the stars shone. It was one of those still nights when the family yurt seems alone on earth and every sound, the slightest glimmer of light, even the slowly unfurling moment itself, is to be savoured like the first milk of the year. And that evening Temüjin's confidences added greatly to our sense of privilege. He began to play out the thread of his story as follows.

'As you know, esteemed Naqu, my father Yesügei was of the princely clan of the Borjigin. A worthy grandson of the Great Kabul, Yesügei was an exceptional warrior who fought the Tatars without respite. The Borjigin tribe chose him as their leader like so many of the other Mongol clans who came to pitch their yurts in the shade of his banner. When the Sovereigns rallied to his cause, my father could marshal ten thousand men. His herds were fat, his women plump and smiling and his slaves numerous.

'He had, however, one failing: carelessness. He feared no one and would often venture alone beyond our lands. Seven springs ago, when I myself had seen nine, we set off together for Onggirad country, my mother's homeland, to find a wife for me.

'After three days' trek, we made a stop at the encampment of Dei the Wise, chief of the Onggirad. When he learnt the purpose of our journey, Dei exclaimed, "Mark this, Yesügei: a pure white gyrfalcon visited me in my sleep recently. As it flew, it held the sun and the moon in its talons. It alighted on my hand and there I was able to contemplate the two heavenly bodies. Can there be a better omen? You have carried off one of our girls in the past, so you know that they play more havoc with the hearts of men than fermented mare's milk." Here, the old chief was referring to my mother, whom Yesügei had kidnapped from a rival. "We reserve the most beautiful of them for the khans' descendants, the lords of the Mongol lands, and we put them to ride on a cart harnessed to a black camel. Yesügei, your son has fire in his eyes. Before you set off for other camps to find a daughter-in-law, let me show you my own daughter.'

'Then old Dei called, "Börte! Börte!" until a little girl lifted up the doorflap. She held herself straight, a belligerent expression on her face, her jaw clenched, her brows knitted. It was my wife.'

Temüjin broke off his account. He seemed troubled and there was a long silence until my father asked, 'She must be beautiful, this Börte?'

'Yes, Naqu, a true beauty. Despite the dust clinging to her face, the purity of her features shone out like the full moon amidst the shades of night. Her eyes were the most striking. A thousand pinpricks of light, a mixture of gold and emerald. It is said that water and fire may never hold each other, but in her eyes, they embraced. Yet I had only seen nine springs, and her four more, so I felt little at that first meeting – I was still a child. It was my father who was sure that she would make a good wife, and was able to judge her full-blooded and radiant. Old Dei said to him, "People despise you if you give your daughters away without protest. Yet a girl's happiness is not to grow old at the door of her father's tent but to be given to a man. Mine will go to your son but, in exchange, leave Temüjin here until he is old enough to marry." And after a moon spent at Dei's camp, I saw Börte's eyes as I have just described them to you. Now, kind Naqu, if my confiding fascinates you, you should know that I have grown and my body is ready to take her and appreciate her perfumes. I must go and find this woman.'

'Your desire has sprung up: Yesügei was shrewd.'

'Not in all things alike,' replied Temüjin. 'He left at daybreak the next day. He counselled me to serve my guardian Dei in every way and warned him to restrain his dogs, claiming they terrified me. I remember hearing him sing as he rode off. He sang of his horse, of his horse's eyes where the world hung as Tenggeri created it before the coming of men; burning eyes with no temperate place, truer than the flight of swans and more precious than his own life. That was to be the last time I saw my father alive.'

He fell silent.

Like all the Mongols, we knew of Yesügei's disappearance. The story went that he had feasted with some Tatars, who recognised him as the chief of the Borjigin and poisoned him.

'Pay no heed to the rumour which makes the Tatars my father's assassins. Those dogs are delighted enough by his death as it is. My father loved eating, drinking and chasing women, but he would never have shared these pleasures with our enemies.'

'They say he managed to get back to his camp.'

'True, Naqu. He was in pain, vomiting a black liquid and shaking so badly that he couldn't speak. His warriors came to find me at Dei's. For he had a secret that he needed to tell his eldest son, me and me alone. I got there too late. But I am convinced that for him to have feasted with Tatars, one of his acquaintances must have been present, one of our allies.'

'Which of our tribes had cause to poison that great chief?'

'The Sovereigns, Naqu. They are the only other Mongol tribe able to claim a khan amongst its members, and their chief Targutai, with this princely blood, dreams of his ancestor Ambakai's glory. But he is arrogant, ruthless and grasping, and he has neither the stature nor the honour to lay claim to the supreme title.'

Of all the warriors whose praises were sung by the story-tellers, Ambakai was my favourite. His cousin Kabul Khan, judging his own sons to be too young for the task, had chosen him as his successor. At Ambakai's death, the Khanate had reverted to the rightful Borjigin line and Kutula, Kabul's fourth son, had assumed the responsibility. Yesügei was Kutula's nephew and, on his son's testimony, he alone had the calibre to become khan.

'Each of my father's successes was an obstacle to Targutai's ambition. He may have drawn closer to Yesügei and the encampments that steadily swelled in number around his banner, but this was only so he could steal away all my father had acquired when the moment was right. That is the truth, Naqu, since today I am alone. Because of Targutai, the prince impostor, I was cut off from my tribe, abandoned and persecuted. I curse him. His thoughts reek; they are worse than vulture's dung. If Tenggeri one day arms my right hand, I will crush him and grind his liver under my boots!'

Though he looked at me, his eyes were far too clouded with trouble to see how much I desired the fulfilment of his vow.

Temüjin stayed with us to sleep. Feverish from the drink, we reeled out under the star-flecked sky, pissed, vomited and then slumped down onto the couches in my yurt.

As I slept, my spirit escaped and led me far away to an unknown place, vast, flat and utterly barren – no grass, not a stone, not even a pebble – the ground was ash stretching endlessly into the distance. The sole source of light was a silhouette which I galloped towards. How could I gallop on that earth? No horse should have survived it. The silhouette became Temüjin. He smiled. A man lay at his feet, his limbs bound. I had never seen him before and yet I knew it was Targutai. Tears streamed from his eyes, tracing long, colourless furrows in his face, and sank into the ashes with a hiss. Temüjin, wide-eyed, staring, crazed, silently challenged me. I took my knife, opened Targutai's belly, thrust my hand under his ribs and tore out his heart. As I held it aloft, Temüjin bit into it. I did likewise. We vied for it and where the drops of blood struck the ground, grass sprouted forth, transforming the wasteland into pasture. Horses suddenly galloped up, thousands of them, beaded with sunshine, bunching and then scattering, snorting joyfully. We watched them and tore the remains of the heart to pieces. His stomach gaped wide, but the man was still alive. He implored me to give him back his heart, but I said there was no point shutting the pen when the flock had fled. It was then that my spirit returned to my sleeping body.

It must have hurled itself back because I woke up, nauseous. In the distance dogs' barking echoed into the night. Unlike their usual selves, ours did not reply. A glimmer of light flickered on the yurt's wooden frame, the reflection of glowing embers perhaps. But knowing we had no fire, I turned around. Eyes glinted; they pierced the darkness like a wolf lying in wait.

'Don't you need sleep?'

'Yes, but I sleep like horses, little.'

'Ah. Tell me. Did Dei muzzle his dogs as your father advised?'

'Yes.'

'And if he had not?'

'I would have buried my knife in their guts.'

'Do you fear them so?'

'It is not fear I feel but loathing!'

'For what reason?'

'They are cowards. They beg for our attention and our leftovers. They waggle their haunches like women and babble senselessly. They bask in the sun, but when night comes and we try to sleep, their racket tells the enemy exactly where we are.'

'You don't believe they bark to protect us from the spirits that circle in the darkness?'

'No, not them; they are braggarts. They scatter like rabbits when there's danger, tails between their legs. Not one of them could disembowel his enemy in silence like a wolf.'

'But during the great hunts they raise the game and make the kill.'

'Some do, yes. But most are sly. If they were hungry, they'd eat their own puppies. I despise them.'

At that moment I heard my dog, which always lay outside the yurt, get to its feet and slink away, neck turned sideways, whimpering softly.

When Temüjin was ready to set off the next morning, the grass was still bathed in dew. His provisions, a lamb and three leather bottles of mare's milk, were tied at his mount's flanks; together we had rounded up his eight geldings; now it only remained for him to drive them in front of him. Yet he seemed to be at a loss: he was delaying, pulling his horse around, and appeared unsure how to thank us.

'Now I know this valley with its fortunate herds, the winters will be shorter.'

My father promised that he would always be welcome and

added, 'Bo'urchu and you have seen each other. Never forget him. In the future, take care that neither of you harms the other.'

His eyes met mine. Did he read there the vexation I felt at his departure?

'In two moons, on the day of the golden marmot, I will go to the Onggirad lands to seek my betrothed. Will you ride with me?'

I smiled in agreement and he said that he would come and find me. Then he urged his horse forward, calling out, 'Onggirad girls are numerous, as well as beautiful. Who knows if you won't catch the eye of one of them?'

Chapter 2

My horse slowed and turned its head. Five pairs of dark eyes were watching us above the tall, bleached grass. Five roe deer on the gallivant. They did not bat an eyelid, although I could sense their hearts beating. They had been bold venturing out into the open. They sniffed and ran off down the slope.

The previous night's dream was coming true. The daughter of the Forest Spirit had visited me in my sleep; a good omen promising game the next day. That spellbinder had slipped in between my eyelids and run naked under the forest's canopy, merging with the shade, skipping from tree to tree, vanishing in the shafts of light to reappear elsewhere, each time more voluptuous. Time and again I had raced towards her smooth body, her hips, her buttocks shining with beads of sweat, but she was always hidden in the heart of a flower, a leaf, or a fern. She had escaped me every time, but still my sap, the bitch's food, had spurted out, as I realised when I awoke.

She filled a good number of my nights and the days did not quench my desire to possess her. May Tenggeri preserve me. To fall under the spell of her beauty is fatal. Only shamans are supposed to satisfy the daughter of the Forest Spirit's appetite for flesh, and if they neglect their duties, her wrath will make all the game disappear. Well, I was no shaman, nor had I ever wanted to be one.

This was to the great displeasure of the Arulat, my clan. As a very young child, the shaman and the elders realised that I showed unmistakable signs of a gift. But I had refused to pursue it and later this spread discord and resentment amongst the tents, so that when my mother died giving birth to her second son, himself stillborn, everyone blamed me for such misfortune. My father quarrelled with them and left the *ayil*. But the daughter of the Forest Spirit still visited me in our new, solitary life. Better still, she came twice as often.

I was not far from the forests of the Blue Lake, one of the most beautiful jewels in the daughter's kingdom. Reaching a narrow plateau, I rode to the lake's banks and put my horse to drink. I walked round him three times, prayed to the wolves to fetter any baneful animals and, leaving him there, plunged into the forest.

My father did not like me hunting alone. 'Be careful,' he would say. 'If you face the bear without your horse, you'll be like a bird without its wings.' He was right, but just as I secretly hoped to taste the delights of the daughter of the Forest Spirit, so a hand-to-hand with the Lord of the Caves excited me almost as keenly.

Alert, I walked forward, the breeze in my face. The trees were golden in the sunshine, their tops swaying gently in the blue of the sky. Soon their high peaks would be clad in pink and purple. A young, four-point stag leapt in front of me. It ran off, disappearing instantly into the chequerboard of sloping trunks. I gave chase and quickly came across the fresh tracks of an adult wolf. Other prints were embedded in the broadest pawprint. They were heading for the marshes and followed the line of silver birches amongst the larches. The stag's flight showed that the wolves were about to reach the oxbow lake. I chose an arrow, took cover behind the stump of a rotten pine and waited and waited in the silence until a cold fog had settled on the forest. Was I to go home empty-handed?

I was resigning myself when I saw him, enormous, coming down the path, casting quick looks around, his muzzle down, his shoulders rolling, his yellow eyes piercing the gloom. The pack followed in silence, each wolf placing its paws in the preceding tracks, creating the illusion that only one animal had passed: cunning leader and submissive pack. If I had shot my arrow, I would have been torn to pieces in an instant.

I watched them disappear into the shadows and was getting to my feet when another wolf, as powerful as the first, appeared from the shadowy path. He moved differently, his head held high, as he took stock of his domain. I pressed closer to the stump, but soon he bore off between the trunks, only to reappear opposite me on a hillock of moss and stones surrounded by three silver birches. He lay down facing west, sniffing the pack's scent. His fangs glistened in his half-open mouth. In profile, his heart exposed, he was my target. The breeze had dropped, so if I did not act immediately he would sense my presence. I stood up, drew my bow, inhaled deeply to fit my arrow and was about to release it when he fixed his eyes on mine: two incandescent knife blades. An old white scar ran the length of his muzzle. That I was about to shoot did not shake his confidence. Uneasy yet enthralled, I recognised Temüjin's eyes in the steady, serene brilliance of his gaze; then I saw his wolf's features melt away to those of Temüjin. The dog laps noisily, my friend had said, barks with fear, and whimpers when beaten. But the wolf drinks silently, bays his love under the moon and faces death uncomplainingly. He will never allow a fetter to be put around his neck and would sooner die than give up his freedom.

Temüjin's face faded and a woman's body took his place, smooth and savage, skin like the moon, her eyebrows like a double-arched bow, black and distinct as the sheath cutting across the top of her thigh, over which her long hair fell in twists and turns. Was it the daughter of the Forest Spirit? But I did not recognise her, so perhaps it was one of her sisters.

I lowered my bow and immediately the silhouette resumed the form of the great carnivore and padded into the night.

I am a Mongol of the Arulat clan. Although our elders say that to kill a wolf once in a lifetime is good, I had been paralysed by the vision of our first ancestor and unable to let fly my arrow. I remembered the stories which sing of the birth of our people and I was glad:

From the Sky came Blue Wolf. From the waves came Fallow Doe. Meeting at the source of the River Onon, in the forests of the Celestial Mount, they begat mankind. They coupled like demons and, as they ran across the steppe, they dropped their seed in the undergrowth, the riverbeds, the wild grasses, on the brambles and the fruits, letting the birds drink and scatter it to the four winds.

At the sources of the three rivers, the wolf and the doe made love day and night. Blue Wolf must surely have hesitated whether to devour his mistress but always, on seeing her tawny coat and her eyes like two great lakes, his love stopped him.

Such an unlikely union is perhaps why today we, their children, never cease to quarrel and steal each others' women and horses when we are not killing each other. But, be that as it may, Blue Wolf and Fallow Doe created the blue Mongols at the source of the three rivers. You only need to lift up the felt doorflaps of the yurts, those little moons with their roundels of smoke dotted across the steppe and the forest clearings, to see inside the same weatherbeaten faces with their fierce eyes that never flinch. They eat, drink and produce sons as if they are starving. Like wolves they hunt and kill. Protected by Tenggeri they fear nothing, neither hunger nor cold, and death, their enemy, cannot touch them.

My wolf of the Blue Lake had not feared my arrow, nor had he torn open my throat. He recognised my blood as his.

Numb and shrouded in darkness, I heard the pack returning. For a moment there was a sort of whispering over by the rock, like a secret assembly of hushed voices. Then the rustling of needles and again silence, only broken by the distant call of a cuckoo. They had regained their lair.

I made for the rock from which the lone wolf had observed me. As I groped my way forward, something wet touched my cheek. My blood froze. He was there, right beside me, the breath of his maw on my neck. I closed my eyes.

When I reopened them, I could not say after how long, sticky and bathed in sweat, I was alone.

I found my horse, and so as not to agitate him further with the musky smell on my clothes, I sang in his ear:

> You graze under the stars
> My horse of the night
> Your hitching rail is the steppe
> Your roof the glittering light
> Proud as the cold wind
> You wait for us to reunite.

Above the mountains of the Blue Lake, the russet moon rose with its velvety light. A wolf's howl shattered the silence.

Chapter 3

Our teeth sheared away the meat and scraped clean the bones. We were celebrating our reunion in Temüjin's yurt, fat up to our ears once again.

As promised two moons previously, he had come to find me. In token of friendship, and to help his marriage be sealed, my father had given him twenty sheep, including a white ram. With this bleating, obstinate escort, it had taken us three days to reach his camp.

Now we were finally sitting around his fire, our joyous scrabble for the feast lacked nothing. Cross-legged to my right was his half-brother, Belgütei, and beyond him his full brothers Qasar, Qachi'un and Temüge, aged fifteen, fourteen, twelve and ten springs.

In their own part of the yurt, the women busied themselves in silence over the cooking pot and the trays, casting curious looks at me all the while. There were four of them, one a child, Temulun, eight springs old and Temüjin's only sister. The other three were Hö'elün, their mother, Suchigil, Belgütei's mother, and an old servant with a parched face and a limp.

Yesügei's two wives displayed a different sort of beauty. Dark-skinned, Hö'elün had strong features, an aquiline nose and a firm mouth with thick lips, while Suchigil's face was softer, unassuming. The former held herself erect in the yurt, which accentuated her haughty bearing; whereas Suchigil's shoulders were bowed, her gestures tentative, her wrists slender. She seemed fragile, intangible, like a pool of water in the sand, and her large, perpetually watchful eyes showed fear. There was none of that in the fiery gaze of Hö'elün, whom everyone, out of deference to the fact that she had been Yesügei's favourite, called Mother Hö'elün. No doubt at all: one was milk, the other flame.

Hidden away in a small, stony valley, Temüjin's camp presented a pitiful aspect. The three worn yurts of blackened felt were proof of the trials suffered by this banished family, once so prestigious. But the sons were robust and ate with the gusto that befits princes. The sheep had come from their meagre flock. I was flattered by this mark of attention and responded in kind, emptying my platter and setting it back down with alacrity.

Suchigil was replenishing it when the women began to argue. Their sons' foreheads furrowed as they bent over their helpings. Suchigil held a steaming platter of delicious chunks of meat but Mother Hö'elün was crackling like fire, accusing her of giving Belgütei a greater helping than this, the guest's, to whom the choicest cuts must always fall by due. She grabbed her arm; the meat spilled to the floor. In a flash, Mother Hö'elün seized her by the throat and threw her outside, calling her a worthless cur.

They fell to the ground at the foot of a low mound of *argols*. I saw Mother Hö'elün pick up a bone which had had time to turn white, since there were no dogs. Jumping to her feet, she battered the unfortunate woman who screamed and tried to protect herself. Inside the sons did not move. Only Belgütei threw a distraught look at Temüjin, whose imperturbable expression seemed to say, 'My mother is beating yours. So. She is the dowager.' Mother Hö'elün finally dropped her weapon and came back into the tent, where she served me another platter as if nothing had happened.

Temüjin left suddenly. Belgütei followed close behind, going to his mother who, furious, pushed him away. Then he untied his horse, mounted, and we heard him galloping away to the north of the yurt.

Although the meal had lost its joyful atmosphere, Temüjin's three youngest brothers invited me to continue eating. The incident was not to be dwelt on. On the pile of *argols* two heavy crows squabbled clumsily over a blood-stained tuft of hair.

Once we had eaten our fill, Qasar, Qachi'un and Temüge offered to show me the lie of the land, a ride skywards to the high peaks which protected their camp. Bent forward over the necks of our mounts, we climbed the slopes to the ridge where, Qasar told me, they took turns to keep watch. From there one could see a half-moon valley so vast that it would take a morning's trot to reach the necklace of mountains on its other side. Two lakes like shields covered in blue silk and a serpentine stream adorned this carpet of grass. Far away to the right, an arid, perfectly flat steppe gradually vanished into the heat haze. Young Temüge pointed towards it.

'Can you see the River Kerulen? It's over there.'

One only had to follow its course to reach the Onggirad lands. I could make out its dark seam running along the edge of the steppe. As if terrified by the shimmering desert, it cowered, sluggish and chilly, at the first fold in the ground and, like a grass snake around an outsized stone, wound its way past the pyramid-shaped hills, the last sentinels of the mountainous escarpments.

Qasar told me the strengths and advantages of their camp. An enemy could only come through the valley, either by the south, crossing the Kerulen, or by the east where, in the crenellated rampart of sharpened rocks and snowy overhangs facing us, he pointed out a pass. There was another possibility, to the north, where the chain of mountains sealed off the valley. But to come by that way he would be forced to trek for three days along the endless cliff where we stood.

'You see, we'd have time to strike camp and lose ourselves in the deceptive maze of the mountains. We call them the Red Mountains.'

'But they're blue!'

'At dawn, they flush like a girl's face when you catch her squatting.'

We took the path back to the camp as the sun was setting and turning the kind-hearted faces of my guides amber. Unlike the cheerful Qasar and Temüge, Qachi'un's jaw had remained clenched.

As they hobbled their horses and I was turning mine out to graze, Temüjin advised me to follow their example. I had not seen him because the camp was hidden by slanting shadows and his silhouette was indistinguishable from that of a rock.

'Seeing my puny geldings, he might suddenly feel the urge to return to your father's well-fed herds.'

I told him that my horse would never inflict that humiliation on me; we were joined as the grass is to the soil.

He nodded and ordered Qachi'un to take up the post above the Seven Hills. Then he told me that since Yesügei's death, his wives had been behaving like barren sows.

'The merest trifle irritates them. It is time I went back to old Dei to find my betrothed. Her arrival, if her father permits it – and nothing could be less certain – will alleviate the tensions here. Are you still ready for this journey, even though the outcome is doubtful?'

I understood his trepidation about Dei the Wise. The Onggirad chief could so easily repudiate this son-in-law, no longer the heir of noble lineage. After seven seasons' absence, he would find him an orphan, disinherited, without herds or allies. What would he gain from giving him his daughter? He would have no shortage of reasons to renege, not least offers of alliance from lords of neighbouring lands. But if he was an honourable man, he would not go back on his word.

I told him that my friendship would not fail him in the trials ahead.

'Good. We will leave tonight before the dew.'

Chapter 4

We crossed the great valley in darkness. Temüjin was in front, I followed him in step, Belgütei was at my back and Qachi'un brought up the rear. Skirting the fallen rocks, we were winding our way along the foothills when to the west the Red Mountains grew pink and then abruptly flared up like a crimson cloth unfolded in the wind. Veined with water, their slopes became tinged with gold and, with the speed of a galloping horse, that gold filled the whole space of the darkness under which the valley was drowsing.

My three companions said nothing. All Temüjin had told me was that our climb would gain us half a day and that we would strike the Kerulen downriver. We rode on for the better part of the day, our mounts overcome with heat, toiling towards the high plateaus encircled with ridges and summits between which shone deep valleys and snow-covered ice caps.

We halted when dusk fell, making sure there was no firesmoke in the sky. The grass was good, the Kerulen was in sight and the landscape soothed us. On the opposite bank, a mountainous cone reared up, as if contemplating its solitude in the bends of the river.

While his brothers tethered the horses, Temüjin accompanied me to the riverbank, which was hemmed with tamarisk and bars of shingle half-buried in sand. A throng of birds squabbled in the branches. A pair of reddish-brown ducks beat the waters with their wings and flew off before us, quacking with displeasure. We could have brought them down with a single arrow but decided first to fill our leather bottles, then hide among the shrubs and wait for their return. There was time to follow the flight of a swan slowly skimming the grass on the other bank, before our two ducks came back, mistrustful and circling high in the air. Our two arrows ran them through. Each hit his own target although we had made no plan. Life was beautiful and the night, which was lighting its small stars one by one, promised to be the same.

The buzzing of a fly woke me. It was drying the dew on its wings in the sun's first light. I wanted to go back to sleep but the prying calls of a hoopoe would not allow it. I opened first one eye, then the other. In the distance a mirage seemed to float over the steppe. In the middle of the dawn sun, that furnace of light which blurs the sight – and sometimes, if you look too deeply into its brilliance, the mind – I glimpsed a myriad of swift-moving, shimmering lines that seemed to melt into one. Suddenly this tide stopped. I stood up and saw that it was an enormous herd of white-rumped antelope: *saiga*. Their tawny coats merged with the yellow grass. Then they were on the move again, skipping, light and anxious, towards the heights. At first I counted them in their hundreds. But the further the herd pushed forward, the more animals came up behind in their thousands, surprised in the low-angled light. I had never seen so many. Sometimes they came to a standstill on their frail limbs and displayed their moon-faced rumps.

What a pity Qasar was not with us. Temüjin had told me that he was the most skilful archer of the five brothers. We could have cut off their flight, forced them onto favourable ground, chased them down and shot them . . .

'We will hunt when we come back.' Temüjin was next to me, observing the herd's progress.

'But we will miss Qasar's arrows.'

'Qasar is always missed,' he answered, crouching down. 'His sight and speed are prodigious. He far surpasses you and me in strength and dexterity although he has seen two springs less than us. If two stallions were at each other's throats, he could lift up one with one hand and stun the second with his other. When we wrestle together, I know he could break my back if it wasn't for his restraint and control. But his artistry and power are at their most perfect in his bowmanship. His shooting is so precise that he never needs to refill his quivers. He will be an exceptional warrior . . . he is an exceptional warrior.'

'Why did you leave such a brother behind?'

'There must be a strong man to guard the camp. I trust him, although I know he has his impulsive side. He takes after our father. His heart is as spontaneous as a child's.

'As for him,' Temüjin added, indicating his half-brother,

Belgütei, 'he is no talker. He saves his words for the horses; he knows how to look after them, that is his gift.' He stood up and aimed a kick at the sleeping Qachi'un's back. 'But Qachi'un doesn't speak at all. Mother Hö'elün might as well have given him an arsehole instead of a mouth. No one knows what he's thinking. No, I do: he's not thinking at all; he's not capable of it. Enough talk; let's go.'

The steppe rose and fell beneath us in tender waves, soft as velvet and chequered with flowers. The Kerulen glittered and the air was heavy with the scent of wild thyme. Moving at a good trot, our horses drank deep of the aromas. They snorted and flared their nostrils and clamped down hard on their bits, straining after every possible intoxication.

'Do you see the peak of that purple-hipped hill?' Temüjin asked.

'With the flowering clover splashed over it?' I said.

'Ah, you are knowledgeable, Bo'urchu, but are you quick enough to reach the hill first?'

He put his heels to his gelding and his brothers instantly followed suit. I was slower, but it did not worry me because my horse had the heart and the spirit of a charger. As the grass flew past his sun-flushed muzzle, he lengthened his stride as if to bring the horizon under his hoofs. He reached full gallop and we flew past Qachi'un's mount so fast it was as if they were riding through heavy sand. Temüjin and Belgütei were surprised in the same fashion as they battled it out flank to flank. Then the boundless azure sky and its verdant garland, the steppe, all sweeps and curves, voluptuous and fertile, were ours alone. We cleft the air, the wind whistled and moaned at our back, and pounded by my horse's hooves, the earth and all its mysteries drummed the most beautiful of songs into my temples – togo-dou, togo-dou, togo-dou, togo-dou – until we reached the hill of clover. Stroking his neck, I congratulated my sweet mount, my silky, ardent-hearted twin soul. He slowed, allowing our companions to catch us.

'Bo'urchu!' shouted Temüjin.

I turned. He smiled and gestured at the ground with an open hand, the palm turned towards me. I swivelled the other way, not knowing what he wanted to show me. Almost immediately I was thrown out of the saddle. I had sensed Belgütei coming alongside but had not expected him to yank up my stirrup so brutally. Too late. I hit the ground – a smooth outcrop of rock in particular.

I promptly picked myself up, annoyed at having been caught out by such an old trick. They all pointed at me and burst into laughter. Belgütei held his sides, Temüjin roared, tears in his eyes, and Qachi'un, slumped forward on his mount, slapped him heartily on the back. My face was the source of such uproarious amusement. My cheek hurt, and when I touched it, my hand came away covered in blood. This only increased their joy.

Temüjin promised me that my cheekbone would swell up in less time than it had taken me to dismount. I wiped it with my sleeve and, claiming that I could not see, asked Belgütei to fetch my horse.

'Don't catch him by the rein, he'll buck and roll over. Jump on him!'

Belgütei heeded my warning and leapt straight from his saddle into mine. My beloved comrade's reaction was instantaneous: he flew off like an arrow but then just as smartly dug in his four hooves and, with a drop of the shoulders that would have shaken off the shrewdest horseman, hurled Belgütei head over heels to the ground.

I joined in the uncontrollable laughter that time, as Belgütei rubbed his head and my chestnut nuzzled him and sniffed his hair. Belgütei looked up and complimented him: 'You are a true Mongol horse. You avenge your master.'

My three friends wanted to know my fiery-hued steed's story. I was only too happy to reveal our secrets so long as they sang his praises when I had finished.

They promised. And so I entertained us on our journey with the story of my colt.

Afraid of Bears, as he would later be called, was born in the Moon of the Lark's Mating Display. Our camp had moved to spring pastures in the dale leading to the Red Throne near the Valley of the Giant. A thin layer of snow covered the hills and Afraid of Bears was the first of the newborn. With his downy, russet coat, his great bright eyes and his tufted mane like squirrels' tails, he was truly a fetching sight. Warming himself in the sun, he looked like a lion cub dozing on an ermine fur.

One night we were woken by the herd of horses passing close to our tents. They seemed agitated: some were kicking, others whinnying. It was an icy night when the faintest noise carries into the far distance and winter has given a last surge to freeze the ground and set bark and stone groaning. I went outside with my father. In the glow of our torches, we saw the herd huddled together, anxious, heads up and ears cocked towards the Red Throne. Something was wrong.

We took our weapons and ran. In the middle of a clearing, animals circled on the luminous snow. The mare and her colt were being chased by something massive: a bear. We knew it was a she-bear since two cubs, still timid, kept their distance, waiting for the colt to come within reach of their claws. The mare was wounded. She moved haltingly, exhausted by protecting her little one, until she was caught in the thigh, her hindquarters gave, and she sank to the ground. Instantly the she-bear was upon her, slashing her flanks and mauling her back.

My father fired two arrows. Growling, Mother Bear released her prey and, with an arrow in her left buttock, rounded up her cubs to take them under cover of the forest.

Terrified, the colt could not move. His mother called to him. She was panting, her body steaming, her flanks in shreds. But there were no tears in her large eyes where the moon bathed. My father calmed her with whispers of *xaya, xaya*. He built a fire to shed some light on the clearing and keep away predators. Then he returned to the yurts to collect sour lime and birch bark, which he applied to her wounds and to the gashes on the colt's shoulder from the bear cubs' claws. It was nearly dawn when he left me to watch over them.

As dawn broke, blood began to seep through the bandage, but the valiant mare remained calm, her faraway eyes fixed on some mournful, frozen world. With her little one pressed close to her breast, she stared at that invisible beyond, heroic and upright in the receding shadows, and made no protest.

The sun was cuffing the highest peaks with light when my father returned to check the mare's wounds. The dressing on her right flank had sheared away to reveal a wound as deep as a man's head.

When he told me we had to take the colt and try to feed it, I asked him if he was going to relieve its mother's sufferings. He said he did not have the right; now she belonged to the Forest Spirit who, by giving so much game to our arrows, could in exchange choose its levy from our herd. To interfere would only visit bad luck and evil spirits upon us. Stroking the mare's forehead, he cradled the colt in his arms. The mare did not flinch; she knew this was the end. As blood dripped from her stomach, I wished her a beyond where the flowers never withered.

At first the foal refused to suckle the teat my father had made from mare's skin. In the middle of the day, I saw three vultures circling in the blue above the sheltered grassland. Crows flew low in the sky, or turned the branches at the forest edge black, cawing and bickering.

I went back to the clearing before sunset. The two bear cubs had bloody heads. They were playing in the snow, while their mother was still busy with the torn flesh. Through the leaves I glimpsed wolves pacing back and forth.

We had to make Afraid of Bears take his first bottle, so I mounted my black mare and galloped to the Valley of the Giant. There were few families on the vast grasslands in that season and there was little chance that I would find a mare that had given birth to a stillborn foal. Guiding myself by the firelight rising from the smoke-holes, I rode from camp to camp. To no avail. At last, at the northernmost end of the valley, an old grazier gave me hope. He had two she-camels and one was suckling two colts. We separated them and, despite her deafening cries, milked her. The old man told me to add water, otherwise the milk would be too rich. I put the two leather bottles under my fur pelisse against my skin, and, my heart beating, I urged on my mare to fly towards our hearth fire. Nostrils flaring, the brave steed struck sparks off the snow. When I arrived, I leapt from the saddle and rubbed my hands on my black horse's dripping thighs, thanking her with a kiss before dashing into the yurt.

Afraid of Bears was drowsing at the foot of my couch, his limbs folded under him, his head with its glints of hazel nodding gently in the heat of the fire. I prepared the bottle, then tickled his lips with my foam-scented fingers. He licked, he nibbled, then he sucked . . . I slipped in the teat. It was this first bottle that made us inseparable.

One moon later, I received news that a foster-mare had been found in the Valley of the Giant. Slinging Afraid of Bears across my saddle I took him there, singing my joy:

> My foal is lighter than the goose's down
> Afraid of Bears needs milk
> More restless than the mountain torrent
> Afraid of Bears needs love

Nuzzling against a mother's flanks
Nevermore will he know fear.

The mare was yellow-dun coated, with deep-sunken eyes and a melancholy air. Her newborn had stopped breathing. The men took the dead foal's blood sac, laid it across Afraid of Bears' back and chanted *youri-youri-youri* to encourage the nursing, until the sound of sucking was hearty and distinct.

I was content; Afraid of Bears had a mother. But when I left my benefactors, my golden colt followed as if glued to my mount's hocks. No matter what tricks I tried – dismounting, hiding – he still trotted after me, his little hooves stubbornly drumming the ground as if to say that he would not be abandoned, he'd rather my bottles of camel's milk. So the yellow-dun mare's owner told me to take his mare, promising that he would fetch her before the summer.

The job of wet nurse was easy, with Afraid of Bears regularly butting her teats with his nose. But he never lingered at his adoptive mother's side and instead followed me everywhere, frolicking nearby and coming in and out of my yurt as the whim took him. Those first bottles of camel's milk had made him well built and strong. His joints were supple, his bones sturdy, his sinews lean and his tail thick. On his left shoulder this proud, muscular little warrior bore the gleaming scars of four claws.

He played with me like a puppy. If I ran, he would gallop at my heels and knock me over with a firm butt of his nose. Sometimes I would pretend to be wounded with my face buried in the grass, and wait for him to come up and sniff my hair. Then I would jump to my feet, grab his neck and pin him to the ground. One day when we were playing, unthinkingly I started running towards the clearing of the Red Throne. But I could not feel his breath on my back as usual; he had not moved. '*Xa, xa, xaya,*' I called to encourage him to jump the invisible pen. Nothing worked; he just pawed the ground, racked with fear. From that day, whenever I took the herd to graze in the fateful clearing, I tied a cloth over Afraid of Bears' eyes and led him to the middle, where I restored his sight. In this way, little by little, he was able to rid himself of his fears and the first time he grazed was on grass where his mother's blood had spilled out.

I hung an amulet in a purple pouch around his neck to protect him from evil spirits and make him grow up to be the herd's stallion. And to fortify him, I used to sing his praises:

Swift as the arrow,
Lighter than the wind,
My Dragon, my foal,
Bestrides the young grass,
Like a mighty chief.
I call, he takes flight,
To unleash tempest,
To cleave, like pure light,
The blackest forests.
Now my Bee, my foal,
Has no fear of the great honey-eater.

I rode him before he had seen two springs. And because we had always been together, I could steer him with my voice alone.

My companions had listened avidly to Afraid of Bears' story. But when I claimed that he knew what I wanted just by my tone, without me having to shift my weight, Belgütei demanded I prove it.

I let go of the reins, sat straight in the saddle and declared that Afraid of Bears would now turn towards the Kerulen. He made for the river. I asked him to go to the east, which he did; then to complete a loop, starting at the north. He went full circle. As a finale, he set off at a trot and came to a halt after nine strides, just as I had predicted. The demonstration was perfect but Belgütei, who was held to have great knowledge of horses, was yet to be convinced.

'Seeing you don't use signs,' he speculated, 'surely you'll be able to do what you've just done from the ground?'

'A horse is made to be ridden,' I told him.

'Then take my horse, I will mount yours and tell you where I'd like to go.'

'Do you want to meet the ground again?'

'As your horse can hear your heart and read your thoughts, tell him to be docile.'

I refused, claiming that a Mongol allows no other hands, even those of noble lineage, to drive his lead horse.

Temüjin cut in, 'Enough! Belgütei. You are like the horsefly on a stallion's balls.' Then he gave the order to proceed, but at a leisurely pace.

We rode for four days. On the evening of the fourth, we crossed the Kerulen. We had barely climbed the opposite bank when a dozen horsemen appeared. Temüjin recognised them as Onggirad. He explained the purpose of our visit. A scout was despatched instantly. Flanked by our new guides we followed in his tracks until nightfall, when we arrived at a lake thronged with wading birds. We ate some of their eggs and fell asleep under a starlit sky, amidst the chirping of numberless crickets.

The next morning we awoke to a thousand silhouettes framed against the fiery glow of the rising sun.

'It's Dei,' said one of the Onggirad.

Temüjin's chest swelled.

I did not know if this display of men augured well for the marriage of my friend but, seeing the look in his eyes, I profoundly hoped so. They were ablaze.

Chapter 5

Precious fabrics were being laid out to dry on the domed tents of the Onggirad camp which, like an anthill, was alive with activity. As ever, women were setting the work's rhythm. Some shook out their fine silks or beat the felt carpets, polished cauldrons, bowls, dishes and platters, ferried trunks, bags, leather bottles and utensils from yurt to yurt and dragged along heavy fur coats or squealing kids, constantly reprimanding the youngsters playing under their feet. Others were squatting amongst the mosaic of ewes bunched head to tail, milking vigorously, and the youngest were carrying the pails to the great leather bottles which they took turns to churn. Piled in pyramids on broad gilt trays, the *aaruls* were so plentiful it was as if they were falling like rain. The men seized the sheep, forefooted the plumpest, forced them to the ground and, spreading their legs, cut under their breastbone and, with one thrust of the arm, severed the heart from its arteries. They cut the dead animals into pieces, as the children looked on greedily, and those who had already dipped their fingers in the blood sucked them, laughing and shutting their eyes with pleasure. The women drew off the vital red fluid and cleaned the viscera, the old men lit fires, purifying them with spices and different types of bark, and the dogs flew at each other, driven into a frenzy by the smell.

A constant tide of families was arriving from the neighbouring *ulus*. Hanging at the flanks of their horses were quarters of kids and antelope, bunches of hares and partridges with dead eyes. They brought young boar, jerboa, ducks, marmot, wild goats, geese, and I even saw a badger, two mongoose, a handful of grouse and pigeons with blue stomachs and a white swan hanging off one pure *zain* crupper. Others drove calves, camels and ewes and their bleating added to the uproar.

The countless aromas enhanced by thyme and mother-of-thyme tantalised us, all the more so because we had only eaten a few eggs in the past six days. We dismounted before Dei's tents. He stood waiting for us in a crowd of old, austere faces, his eye still quick and keen. Sixteen men surrounded him: Onggirad nobles, warriors and a few cousins and nephews. The shaman was there too, toothless and wizened, smelling of high, goatish meat and closer to, of the garlic he rubbed into his gums.

Dei came forward to Temüjin, proffering a silver bowl. My companion took it, dipped his little finger in the liquid to sprinkle the four horizons, drank a mouthful and returned the bowl to Dei. Then it was passed from hand to hand in order of precedence. As ever in such circumstances, the elders were inclined to complicate the ritual. Their libations were accompanied by ever more extravagant propitiations to Tenggeri, to his icy azure sky, to his red skies, to his black skies. And as if that was not enough to protect us from his ire, they invoked the spirits of the earth, of the waters, of fire, of the ancestors, sprinkling liquid in all directions. They applied all their fervour to ensuring the blessings of heaven and its retinue of spirits, but none to soothing our parched throats and churning, impatient stomachs.

When each of us had wetted his lips three times, Temüjin said, 'Dei! I am no longer that child you knew seven springs ago. Then Yesügei's vast lands, his numberless herds, his proven warriors were all to be mine, his eldest. Now I have nothing. These meagre remnants I come with today are unworthy of the alliance that you and my father concluded.'

Temüjin took from his breast pocket a long strip of blue silk and draping it over his forearms, his palms turned to the sky, he gave it to the old man as Belgütei and Qachi'un stepped forward, holding out quivers filled with arrows and bows worked in wood, bone and horn.

'My son!' replied the Onggirad chief. 'Your stay here was so fleeting. After you left, fear of brutal times made me hide my daughter away as a butterfly hides its larva, and I protected this fragile chrysalis amongst my kin. But now the summer has come with your return. Seven springs ago, when your father entrusted you to me, there was fire in your eyes but it had not reached your breast. Today I feel a white-hot sun beating in your heart. Now it is my turn to entrust my daughter to you. But before that moment, let us feast.'

The boiled sheep were brought on long trays. Dei cut out the noses swimming in their juices and fed them to the fire. Then he plucked out the eyes. The first was for Temüjin. It was enormous, firm, round, bursting with whiteness. My mouth watered at the prospect of its pair being mine. But no. The elders were served first and I had to watch the choice bits pass under my nose: the skull and its brains, the shoulderblade, the tail, the breastbone and the upper ribs, the thigh bone and the shin bone. The only sound was that of chewing and swallowing, as everyone sucked up the juices and scraped away the flesh, their sleeves and collars smeared with fat, and the fire consumed its share of meat with a soft sizzling.

Dei chose a tail, white and fatty, and instructed that it be taken to his daughter: a rare privilege for a woman to bite into this noble cut. We had not yet seen the beautiful Börte, the one whose name evoked the brilliance of a sapphire. She was hiding, or spying on us perhaps. But absorbed in this feast which would last for three days, Temüjin seemed unconcerned.

When all that was left of the first sheep was bones, the singing began. The most beautiful, sonorous voices vied with each other in sweet competition. Two young, plump women, envoys of Börte, addressed this song in the form of a petition to Temüjin:

> From east to west, you have galloped
> To carry off your bride
> Our sister, the fair Börte.
> Crossing the steppe in one bound
> You have come for her rounded cheeks
> For the delights under her lock and key.
> Your marriage will be prolific, golden.
> But how will we, her sisters,
> Survive without our friend?
> With your brothers, your companions
> Your men, your chiefs
> Have you spared no thought for us?
> Will they not inhale our perfumes
> And dry the tears on our rounded cheeks
> With tender kisses.

Temüjin stood to sing his reply:

> My Isabelle horse is sulking
> I told him that when we return
> The most beautiful of songbirds would hold his mane.

34

Crupper to the wind, muzzle in the marsh
My Isabelle horse is sulking
He has not seen one feather of his songbird's beauty
You sisters who sing her praises
Who promise me mounts and delights
Lead me now to her branch
Show me her nest
Let me inhale her perfumes
For her spite has brought me to despair.

His chant was slow and halting, the tone almost indecisive. But it was poignant enough for everyone to join in. Transfigured with emotion, ramrod straight, their nostrils and veins quivering, the men carried us over the steppe and told of its sweet pleasures: the wonders of the Sky, the purity of the streams, the beauty of the horses and the women who opened wider the natural wound born in a manly heart. We hung on their every sweet-flowering word, and shivered. Their eloquence seemed infinite.

An old man with a silvery moustache sat down opposite Temüjin and said, 'You are wondering whether, after so many seasons, your betrothed has grown lovelier. Eat, Temüjin, drink, enjoy yourself and forget your doubts. I come to tell you, I whose great age has allowed me to see her as she is preparing to put on her ceremonial robes, that she is even more radiant than a crane with wings outspread in the wind. She has sent me to tell you that she too is impatient. Temüjin, her every attribute is that of a loving woman. She is the sun and the moon, and if my eyes shine, it is because they still reflect her luminous skin. You are wondering, my son, you are wondering. Her body is like the steppe, sinuous; horses' mouths would water because she smells of clover and must taste of it too. Her womb? A waiting chrysalis – what joy for your first blossom. Her throat is as white as a dove, her cheeks ruby-red and her eyes are like glowing embers. But she sighs deeply, her breast is heavy. She has sent me to tell you that she is still uncertain whether to marry. The thought of leaving her parents saddens her. But letting you leave without her causes her equal grief. There, I have warned you, Temüjin. She will have to be plucked and carried away. But take care, some of our valorous young warriors will certainly rise up to prevent the abduction of the most beautiful of our girls.'

The old man got to his feet. It was said that he was the most celebrated of story-tellers. As he bent down to cross the threshold of the yurt, I caught a glimpse, right by the lintel, of a sublime face: a young woman's. Long black tresses framed the charming oval and her huge, green eyes were streaked with fawn.

My heart leapt like a foal seeing the steppe for the first time.

Temüjin followed my gaze. 'Börte!' he exclaimed. The young woman disappeared.

He gaped open-mouthed, and my heart broke in pieces like a stone toppling over a precipice. Still, I was pleased for him.

'Every khan would dream of such a wife,' I said in congratulation.

'We must go and find her!'

He led me from tent to tent in search of this bride who was so afraid to leave her family. He had a plan: 'When we have found her, we will go back and continue the feast in Dei's yurt. I will tell of your charger, the wonderful Afraid of Bears, with such eloquence that the mud-splattered youngsters will start drooling and they'll have to pit their horses against him. So you will challenge them. But this cavalcade must take place before sunset. Exhaust them all, Bo'urchu, and in the meantime I will abduct my wife. Her father would gladly keep her by his side much longer. If I do not act, we will still be here at the next moon.'

The abduction of a bride was an ancient custom, but my friend was not even willing to wait for another opportunity. Seeing the old man with the silvery moustache, Temüjin asked him where Börte was.

'What do you want of her, my son?'

'To show her a budding branch beaded with honey which will calm her uncertainty and palpitations.'

'Give it to me, I will pass it to her.'

'But it is still growing.'

'Cut it then,' suggested the bard, his smile mischievous.

'Impossible, grandfather. To cut a tree is to rob it of all its powers.'

'I would like to help you, Temüjin, but I cannot betray her. She would curse me and her wrath would strike panic into the two doves cooing on her roof.' He slipped away, miming the flight of a bird.

We were turning over his words when suddenly I spotted two white doves atop a yurt from which came clear, pure laughter.

'We must be careful,' said Temüjin. 'It might be a trap.'

He pushed aside the felt doorflap to find four women. One was stirring the milk over the cooking pot, another was sewing, the third was kneeling, brushing Börte's hair, which fell, glinting blue-black, over her white *del*. Dei's daughter had high cheekbones that promised laughter and bravery, a radiant smile, finely arched eyebrows and green eyes that seemed spangled with stars. She was beautiful and although still young, she was ripe. A woman, wholly desirable.

Temüjin strode in; they jumped, their cries shrill; the doves took flight, a few of their feathers fluttering down through the open hole of the roof. He stood in front of Börte.

'It is true, you have become lovely!'

She stood up, her eyes never leaving him, both delighted and stunned. She was luminous.

Her companions had gone to the other end of the yurt, gesturing and calling for Börte to join them.

'Be quiet!' ordered Temüjin, his expression stern.

Börte stared at him and then smiled. It was a bold smile, mocking and thrilled, one of those smiles that casts a spell with its radiance. Her friends burst out laughing but the intensity of Temüjin's eyes riveted on Börte's awed them. Silent, we could not help but become their audience. Temüjin, with a sharp twist, opened Börte's *del*. His hand disappeared beneath the fabric; her companions squealed, fascinated more than shocked. The lovers were oblivious; we were invisible. Motionless, captivated, bound, they devoured one another, fiery-eyed like eagle-owls poised to swoop on their prey.

I heard the thin trickle of water, and then the sound became that of rain when it beats on the ground. Golden drops spattered their boots. The beautiful girl was emptying herself, pissing hard. Her nostrils quivering, mouth trembling, eyes half-shut, she was on the edge of abandon.

The noise ceased; Börte's features relaxed and her lips curled into a star-shaped smile. Temüjin withdrew his hand, sucked his fingers, one by one, brought the back of his hand up to his nose, and then left.

As he had predicted, my friend's tales of Afraid of Bears' prowess whipped Dei's guests into a frenzy. After the meal of lamb and fritters stuffed with curds, a kid garnished with herbs and some well-hung woodcock, we went out under a pumpkin sun and the many competitors gathered their horses, determined to shower me with their dust.

They flew off, winking conspiratorially at each other and striking the skittish rumps with their whips. The race was long. Those who took the lead early squandered it. Laughing and singing, they had cried victory too soon. I sang to Afraid of Bears of my happiness and pride at riding him, as the horizon undulated beyond his forehead. As the pace of the front-runners began to slow, their cruppers growing heavy, their limbs sagging, we passed these exhausted horses one by one, their thighs numb, their breathing broken. In the bloody light setting the yurts aglow the Onggirad people were assembled, ready to welcome the winning horse. Afraid of Bears raced, shining with sweat. How beautiful he was, flowing over that steppe as he caught and passed our final rival, a piebald with ivory hooves.

'A chestnut! It's Bo'urchu's chestnut. He is coming in alone ahead of all of yours,' cried Belgütei, who was the race's scout. The crowd rushed forward, waving their arms and shouting.

They pressed round us, applauding Afraid of Bears, gazing at him and telling him that I was blessed because, on his back, I became a bird. Then the bards sang his praises:

> He is fire, he is stone
> This chestnut of light
> He challenges the winds
> They lose him from sight.
>
> He is fire, he is blood
> This chestnut of light
> He bounds across the steppe
> It yields to his might.

Amidst the rejoicing, I spotted Temüjin making for the yurt with the doves. He entered; the birds rose into the air, as the bards kept up their verbal jousting to the glory of Afraid of Bears:

> His eyes are gems, his hair a river in spate
> His thighs are bronze, his backbone a necklace
> His crupper is rock, his ride is without end

Börte was first, Temüjin at her heels. They ran between the

tents and wagons, a darting, white figure with long hair whipping behind her, and a wiry, powerful man shouldering the shafts aside, pursuing her as she threaded her way between the startled kids, the ungainly calves and the hides drying in the sun. Börte made for the wood. Temüjin leapt on his horse and at a furious gallop followed those tresses disappearing up the slope.

Once the first moment of surprise had passed, the Onggirad men flew off after them in a cloud of dust, yelling and swearing. Thrilled, I did not miss a moment of the unfolding spectacle. Börte ran out of breath halfway up the slope, then Temüjin slid down his horse's shoulder, clasped her around the waist and lifted her like a leaf caught by the wind to clamp her against his torso. They disappeared into the wood. Their pursuers likewise, but without conviction, and they soon began to turn back one by one.

The couple headed towards the heights the other side of the wood. I thought I saw Temüjin, never loosening his grasp, take off her *del* and let it fall to the ground as they reached the summit of the pass. Then their silhouettes merged with the blue of the sky.

In my mind's eye, I saw them rolling in the grass, frenzied, passionate, caught up in a spiral like Blue Wolf and Fallow Doe.

Old Dei smiled. 'I am sorry I have no other daughter. I would give her to you, because I would be proud to call you my son-in-law. You are made of the same mettle as Temüjin.' Laughing, he beckoned me back to the feast.

In his tent I bit into the flesh, juices spurting everywhere, even through my nostrils. But though this calmed my appetite, my arousal, that heaving sap throbbing in my bud, was greater than ever. Deep into the night, feverish, awash with fermented mare's milk, I stretched out on the grass, only lulled by the sound of Afraid of Bears grazing next to me. Eventually I fell asleep under a breathless sky, flecked with many-pointed stars. It was a wedding sky.

Chapter 6

After three nights the lovers returned. Rocked by their horses' swaying gait, they rode down from the hills, Börte leaning back against Temüjin.

I saw them first. I had been waiting for them. Just like the day before . . . and the day before that. They passed by me without a word, their pulses beating as one, their cheeks ruddy from the three nights together, a faraway look in their eyes. Perched on a halter rope, a bird with a bright-red throat greeted them, singing passionately to the azure sky.

At first I was ashamed to have watched for them, but then I realised that my senses had been awoken. The waiting had shown me how I might find abundance. Suddenly I could see the point of life and how it was to be recognised. I was dazzled. To find my own Börte, that was my goal.

She looked exactly as Temüjin had first described her in my father's tent, with her crumpled *del*, her cheeks smeared with earth and catkins in her tangled hair. She slid to the ground holding on to his arm and disappeared into her mother's tent. Temüjin went to where the horses were tied up and dropped his gelding's reins at the post, before going to Dei, who invited him to share his meal.

On the fifth morning we set off west again, the sleeves of our *dels* covered in grease, our faces full of delight. Dei escorted us with fifty of his men to the Kerulen where he unstrapped the thin cords of horsehair holding a pack on his mount's back. He unfolded the felt blanket to reveal a sumptuous fur coat, which he held out to Temüjin. 'You are taking my daughter away from me. Watch over her. On dark days, throw this fur coat over your shoulders and it will banish all doubts.'

The fur was precious, the most beautiful sable. Lined throughout and with a high collar, the coat must have needed at least eighty hides. At the slightest movement, blue glints rippled through its shimmering folds.

The old chief went to his daughter, nuzzled her hair, took a deep breath, his eyes shut, and then turned away. He left with us his wife, who could not bring herself to part from Börte, twenty warriors, two heavily laden camels, a white horse, an ox with a piebald rump and four servants for his daughter.

We were a modest convoy under Tengri's luminous sky, patiently making our way across the waving grasslands. Temüjin led the train. Belgütei followed, gazing at the bands of cloud which topped the distant mountains. Just behind, Qachi'un and I escorted the black cart in which the bride and her mother rode. Temüjin's brother stared in fascination at his new sister-in-law, this flower of our return journey, whose dark locks played about her temples in the wind.

Suddenly Temüjin came to a halt. Twenty paces away the silhouette of an eagle guarding its eyrie emerged from the brushwood. Two grey, clumsy-looking eaglets huddled against her breast.

'We'll take one and rear it to be our ally,' Temüjin said, approaching them.

The eagle lowered her head, spread her wings and screamed plaintively. This mother's pathetic attitude filled Börte with compassion.

'Look, Temüjin, her eye is like the sun!' she said.

Temüjin agreed. He knelt before the bird, never taking his eyes from her, with his arm protected by a blanket. 'Give her some meat. I'll just take one of her feathers to hang in our yurt so that it will give us protection.'

I beckoned to Börte and held up a leg of lamb smoked over ashes. She ran over to me, clutched the quarter of meat to her chest and rewarded me with a smile, brimming with light. Her teeth were like pearls and her eyes like two emeralds set with topaz crystals. I was struck dumb.

She turned away.

Temüjin stretched out a hand towards the eaglets, snatched it back immediately as the mother went for him with her beak and talons, and while she was distracted, plucked out one of her feathers with his other hand.

Then the convoy set off again and continued on its way until evening.

As we pitched camp on the heights above the Kerulen,

Temüjin pointed out a great herd of antelope. They were heading towards the river, their figures crimson in the setting sun.

'Fill your quiver, Bo'urchu; tomorrow we will pit ourselves against them,' he promised. We watched them until the sun dipped behind the chain of purple mountains.

Temüjin ordered fifteen of Dei's warriors to go to the west, keeping to the lee of the hills. Before sunrise, they would reach the crests and fan out to drive the herd towards our hide.

Then he took me, Belgütei, Qachi'un and the five remaining Onggirad to find a grassy hollow amongst the mass of tall rocks where we could all wait. There we lit a fire. There was not a breath of wind; its flames flickered gently amongst the blocks of granite and rose straight into the air, accompanying our invocations.

Custom demanded that on the day before a hunt women be sent away to conciliate the spirits. That night we called on the daughter of the Steppe Spirit who, like the daughter of the Forest Spirit, was lustful and jealous. So no women stayed with us, and we swapped obscene, lascivious stories that we hoped would excite the daughter and win us her prize: a successful hunt. The size of the herd we had seen inspired us. We told of loins besieged, bodies writhing on the steppe's undulating breasts, rubescent scrota, wondrous, impossible members and ferocious couplings which fed the hungry earth her share of sap and scents.

Our storytelling quickly found its own rhythm, set by our Onggirad companions. One of them told this strange story:

Many, many moons ago in Jürchen country there lived a family of herders. The mother was considered a great shaman. She was no taller than a newborn colt and her name was Scampering Steps; her husband, who was practically a giant, was called Dry Dung. She had borne him twenty-one children, until she was gaunt and shrivelled with age and unable to give birth again. But when the next spring moon rose, Scampering Steps suddenly recovered her appetite. As a good husband, Dry Dung fervently embraced this renewal. But not the man he once was, he was unable to quench the fire in her and the poor woman was left taut with desire. Every morning she awoke sluggish, her face drawn and sombre, her cheeks hollow. Although her torments faded at the end of the full moon's cycle, they would only return, increased tenfold, at the start of the new moon.

At first Dry Dung refused to admit defeat. He gorged himself on plants that were reputed to harden the member and pounded at his bony wife for nights on end with loins powerful enough to break larches. Finally he had to beg the men of his *ayil* to take a turn with their pleasure.

Scampering Steps exhausted each one of them, until a day came when there was no one hardy enough to sate her. Every full moon she would roll her eyes, wriggle her buttocks and vanish, naked and furious, into the sleepless night.

It was time to call the greatest shaman. He divined that a sour, vengeful animal spirit had come to torment his sister shaman: physical pain alone could prevent it continuing to occupy her body. Therefore Scampering Steps was tied to a larch and her nipples nailed to the trunk. But when the full moon returned, the possessed woman thrashed about so hard that she ripped off the tips of her breasts and fled.

Her eldest son, Scatterbrain, followed, only to see the unspeakable. Splayed on the Stone Egg, a solitary rock in a clearing, Scampering Steps was writhing and neighing like a mare. Suddenly the stallion of their herd emerged from the night, neck arched and hooded in the moonlight. Stamping, snorting and pounding the ground, he approached the Stone Egg, looking at her sidelong. Scampering Steps stroked his nose, writhing even harder. The stallion blew noisily. He curled up his lips and stood sniffing the fragrances coming off her scarlet vulva. His rod swelled and he jammed it into her ribs. Then with a jump he dug his forefeet over the woman and spread himself along her length, impatient and brutal, his hindquarters jerking up and down. Although Scampering Steps struggled and complained, she still grasped the giant mushroom head and guided it between her thighs. The stallion entered her up to the hilt. His hooves and jaw scraped against the stone, but his haunches kept rising in sinewy contractions. His back arched, he plunged in and out, his lathered dark scrotum slapping wetly against the rock.

Dumbfounded, Scatterbrain watched his mother crushed beneath the stallion, her face distorted in rictus.

The stallion spilled himself with a lash of his tail. And then froze. Short of breath, his eyes wide with surprise as if he had seen some shadowy creature, he stood motionless, with only his flanks heaving. At last he withdrew, releasing a flood of seed and moved away, panting slightly, his cock glistening.

Her eldest son saw how Scampering Steps had been transformed. Her body had grown tall and supple and vigorous; her breasts, usually so flaccid, were swollen; ample and heavy from the mating, they swung like curds in leather bottles.

He was making for her when he saw two young colts at the edge of the forest play-fighting with their hooves and teeth.

Scampering Steps called to them, whinnying like a joyful woman.

Days, then moons passed with no change, and everything would have remained the same if the woman's unquenchable desire for the Mongol horses had not had unexpected consequences for Dry Dung's herd. Bewitched by their mistress, the stallions deserted their mares. There were no more births and so no more milk. Other males were introduced, but they were driven away or torn to pieces. At last, in a fury, Dry Dung took up an axe and strode to Stone Egg, where he found the lovers, his wife impaled, chuckling merrily. She was like a teenage girl frolicking in the mountain spate, offering her porcelain fruit up to the waterfall. He lifted the axe against the round face of the moon, performed a full swing, and split the horse and the woman in two.

By sunrise the herd had disappeared. Dry Dung followed their tracks. They led to the heights of the Great Khingan Mountains and by evening he was trekking through snow, baffled by what had driven his stock this far, up amongst the clouds. He thought he would catch up with them on the other side of the mountains, on the Tatars' grassy plains. But they drew him on on into the Gobi Desert.

He often glimpsed them. But every time they fled, disappearing into dunes, a swirl of sand, a mirage. His strength drained away. But still he went on. He walked and walked as he had never done before, despite his cold, hunger, thirst and grief. He became more and more unsteady on his legs and, at every step, the pain reminded him that horses are more important than anything on this earth. He had killed his wife, but he would have killed any woman, even the most beautiful, his sons too, if only he could recover one of his wretched horses. At last he fell, never to rise to his feet again, and in his madness he was aware of his herd surrounding him, trampling him, and he wondered why he had not been able to spare the stallion.

Today Dry Dung's herd roam the Gobi. Wild and untameable, sometimes they raid the mares reared on Xixia land. Their stamina is matchless. Their hides have become the colour of sand to make them invisible. Their full, thick manes are cropped short, as if an invisible hand clips them. And the only thing that equals the depth of their grudge against men is their ferocity.

We had listened avidly to the Onggirad warrior's story of the wild horses of the Gobi. It was exactly the sort of tale the daughter of the Steppe Spirit enjoyed and we had every reason to believe that the hunting next day would be good. Temüjin lay down and concluded our assembly with this prayer: 'O Daughter of the Steppe! Visit our sleep, watch over our horses and set our bulbs throbbing purple!'

Chapter 7

We waited in an arc, hidden by the waving grass. A warm breeze ruffled my horse's mane as he drowsed in the soft sunlight, with his head bent and eyes closed. Already the flies were buzzing around us tirelessly, aggressively – it looked as if it would be a hot day.

At last the herd of antelope appeared in the hazy folds of light, almost like a mirage. They were trying to reach the heights. They stopped, hesitant, then flowed towards us. At their rear their number kept growing and soon their panic shook the steppe.

Afraid of Bears looked up. I told him to keep still. Shifting his weight onto his other leg, he sank back into his reverie until the heads of the first antelope appeared on the ledge that was hiding us.

When they realised our trap, the herd exploded in a maelstrom of dust, milling fawn hides and scared eyes. Some fell, horns clashing, others ran along our flank, cowering, muscles like whipcord; still others, borne along on this wave of terror, leapt over our mounts. One antelope smashed into Qachi'un's horse, felling the young warrior. In that hail of panic-stricken limbs, I only had room to slash wildly with my scimitar. Afraid the herd would escape us by splitting, Temüjin yelled the order to break into a gallop. The saiga were faster than us but their herd unfurled endlessly over the steppe like a standard, and so every time we let fly an arrow, one fell, its eyes round, its heart quietened. It was pure joy witnessing their headlong flight – the thunder of hooves, the grasses mown flat, the carcasses smashing into one another – and in their exhilaration our horses pushed themselves hard enough to tear their every muscle.

Too soon our quivers were empty. Temüjin gave the order to drive straight through the flank, causing the beasts to scatter into bewildered groups. Two more antelopes fell to my blade, bringing my trophies to twelve. In all we slaughtered seventy, and we opened them up immediately to bite into their warm livers and hearts.

The women returned and Temüjin handed a bowl of blood to Börte, then to her mother. They drank while the servants skilfully drew off the precious fluid and collected it and the entrails in skins and leather bottles. We laid out delicacies for the daughter of the Steppe Spirit and continued our trek.

The horses had begun to struggle, overcome with the heat and their burdens, too weak to shake off the swarming flies. We had finally left the banks of the Kerulen, climbed a long hill of scorched grass and reached a plateau crenellated with peaks. A mountain stream flowed into it and there was a smell of clover and fresh grass. We still had a good day's trek before we would even see the Red Mountains. We decided to stop and make camp for the night.

I was watching a lone antelope wearily climbing the green incline, wondering what had driven it to make such a difficult journey, when Temüjin exclaimed, startling me, 'It is the end! The end of her earthly life. Though she has spent it on the steppe, far from high ground, now nothing will stop her returning to Tenggeri's blue expanses, not terror, not exhaustion. Let's follow her!'

So we shed our weapons, slung our belts around our necks and began to climb, our destination a stark outline against the azure sky. Neither the highest nor the most imposing of the mountains, it was sheer nonetheless and soon we were gasping, our calves aching. Above us the antelope laboured across the mountainside. We meant nothing to her.

At last we stood on the summit, with the setting sun in front of us, and to our left the mountain ranges that look like an ancient, slumbering camel. The antelope had vanished, as if into thin air. Unsurprised, Temüjin said, 'The mountains are Tenggeri's stepping stones, his mistresses. His breath is always caressing them, his storms hollow out their slopes and fashion white crowns for their brows. By their embrace the earth becomes fertile. Blackened with desire, he cups their breasts and with a single shaft of light illumines their wombs and drops his seed to fatten their haunches and bathe their feet. If the whole earth were to become a desert, an open wound, life would live on in the mountains, which not only safeguard souls, like jewels, but also reveal his pronouncements. Isn't that why the old climb up here when their time has come – to decipher his will?'

He was silent. Glaciers flashed in the distance, as their ice-blue ramparts were illuminated by the disappearing sun. It was a perfect moment. I praised Tenggeri and implored him always to water his beloved, the earth, whom he had made so plentiful. And in my heart, I thanked him for his bounty, and especially for bringing Temüjin and me together, when I had always wished for a brother to make my happiness complete.

'Bo'urchu, you need search no longer,' he said. 'I am your brother.'

I was sure he could see into my mind and this transparency both alarmed me and made me glad. I said nothing.

He continued, 'You rode with me to help me reclaim my horses. You shed the blood of those traitors, the Sovereigns, who robbed me. You raced against the finest Onggirad chargers and drove your horse as if your life depended on it to win over my father-in-law. Dei could see I wasn't that orphan, that outcast the steppes' gossip-mongers would have me be. You have dealt with me better than any of my brothers. You are without guile, Bo'urchu, upright, and your heart is unswerving. I have seen the silent way you approach the enemy, as one with your horse. I have seen how you lull your prey, your harmony with the steppe, the wind, the animals and the sky. I watched you when we hunted the antelope; you too became an antelope. When you shoot a duck, your arrow becomes a drake. In the name of that wolf of the Blue Lake whose life you spared, in the name of that wolf who did not slit your throat, you are the wolf I have been searching for! You are the Arulat, I am the Borjigin, by our ancestors we are of the same bone, and the blood of the Mongols gallops through our veins. One day we will seal our friendship with that blood. When a Mongol speaks, his words are always made good.'

His eyes shone, his face was resolute. He looked away and his profile was silhouetted against the darkening sky. As the stars came out, its matchless indigo canvas seemed to bloom with immortelles, the glacier flowers that never wither.

After a long silence, my companion addressed the sky, 'O Tenggeri! Do not abandon me. Send your sons, my brothers – brave and pure men – and arm my hand! By your command, I am the firstborn, but my family have been stripped of all they possessed, and now I wonder if my fate is not a punishment, whether it would not have been better for me to be the youngest.'

I wanted to assuage Temüjin's doubts, but knew I must not interrupt.

He continued, 'I want my clan to return to me like these stars massing in the sky. But what should I do? What will it take for them to recognise my name? Will I need fifty Bo'urchus at my right hand before they can overcome their fear and break away from the Sovereigns?'

'Did your father not ally himself with other tribes?' I asked.

'Yesügei? That brigand. His whole life was spent fighting. He never asked for a woman's hand in marriage; he kidnapped his wives, all of them. Even Mother Hö'elün. Newly wed, she and her Merkid husband were returning to his family when my father and my uncles hunted them down. For him there was no difference between a woman and a battle as long as he triumphed. Being such a man, he rarely concluded alliances and, if he did, discord quickly broke out. The reason I set up camp in the Red Mountains is their distance not only from the Sovereigns but also from the Merkid, who are still waiting to exact vengeance for the wrongs done them by my father.

'But you are right, he did have one ally with whom he didn't have occasion to quarrel. A Kereyid, whom my father had freed from slavery to the Tatars. He was called To'oril and he was in fact a prince. They became friends, like brothers. And later my father even helped him rally his people and claim his throne. As far as I know he is still Khan of the Kereyid.'

'Do they live in the great Orhon valley?'

'Yes.'

'Then these are the allies you have been seeking to help reunite your clan and defeat the Sovereigns. They are said to be even more numerous than all the Mongol tribes together.'

'I have thought of it . . .'

'So why do you hesitate?'

'Because To'oril is a rogue who will only risk his troops in battle if he thinks there is profit.'

'So, the Sovereigns have gold, felt tents, herds, women.'

'You are forgetting one thing, Bo'urchu: the Sovereigns helped my father restore To'oril to his khanate. He's not going to turn against old allies for me, with the promise of nothing.'

'If he is as greedy as you say, I think he will. His spoils will be the Sovereigns. Just take care the Borjigin don't join them.'

'But he and my father were blood brothers.'

49

'They swore fealty? Then they were *anda*! Now Yesügei is dead, you are To'oril's son.'

'That's no guarantee of loyalty. He slit the throat of two of his real brothers.'

'They must have given him cause by conspiring to oust him from his throne. But you have no designs on his position; your only interest is to persuade him to help you as Yesügei helped him.'

'And what shall I give this bird of prey whose appetite for riches is said to be boundless? Mother Hö'elün once told me she thought he'd stab his own shadow if he saw the faintest glimmer of gold in it.'

'There is only one gift which could satisfy him. A treasure which in the eyes of such a man is equal to any number of thoroughbreds.'

'Go on.'

'Dei's sable coat.'

'Except it is in the women's hands and I don't think they are going to part with that fur as soft as silk once it has warmed their bodies.'

'Börte intends giving it to your mother,' I said. 'And the only thing that could truly warm your mother's heart and appease her anger is if you were to make the Sovereigns vomit out their tongues and yield their fetid entrails.'

Chapter 8

The horses stopped alongside one another at the crest of the hill. At last the Red Mountains towered overhead, and before us lay the steppe, swollen with dew and caressed by the breeze. In its cradle of ruddy cliffs, the Island of Grass, as Temüjin called it, undulated as if it was breathing deeply. It sloped down to the vein of the Kerulen and, in its middle, two lakes sparkled like violets set in their rosette of leaves.

'They are the Island of Grass's tears,' said Temüjin, turning towards Börte. 'They may look identical, but one is clear water, good to drink; the other is muddy and salt. We drink from the first and watch its fish as long as a man's arm; in the second we heal our wounds with the leeches' kiss.'

On the promontory running alongside the two lakes, the dark silhouette of a horseman was streaking through the light. He seemed to fly over the grass like a bird, his face flat against his horse's cheek.

'Who is that rider?' asked Börte.

'A young, harebrained bull. From the look of him, it can only be my brother Qasar. He is impatient. Watch: doesn't he remind you of a great tiger who has just smelled his tigress's spray?'

Moments later, Qasar brutally pulled his lathered horse up short a few paces away from us. In his dark clothes with his red belt he was as broad as he was tall, the tips of his arrows and his bow barely showing above his powerful shoulders. His face was aglow, glossy like an apple. His brigand's eyes swiftly assessed our baggage, the state of our horses and the look of those who made up our convoy. After an appraising glance at Börte, he stared at his elder brother and said, laughing, 'By almighty Tenggeri, you have arrived! I know the Onggirad lands are strewn with flowers, but to come away with the most beautiful is quite an achievement. Marriage must make a man thirsty – let us go to the camp.'

We descended to the Island of Grass, jolted by the step of our weary horses. We drank at one of its cool streams, which left a taste of sulphur in the roof of our mouths, then crossed the steppe, making for the long stony pass which led to my hosts' lair in the maze of the Red Mountains.

The women received us in silence. They were standing in a line. Temüjin's young sister Temulun was between Mother Hö'elün and Suchigil, Belgütei's mother, and the old serving woman, Fart Walking, was at the end. Three paces from them, dressed from head to foot like the warrior he was to become, stood Temüge. He was the only one smiling, his child's face radiant and adoring at the return of his elder brother with the most breathtaking of sisters-in-law. Börte stepped down from the cart and took from her mother the cow's horn filled with the flickering embers of her father's hearth which had been brought with her belongings. The young bride walked forward, shielding the base of the horn with her hands, and when she was facing Mother Hö'elün's ultramarine *del*, she gave a low bow full of grace and humility. Mother Hö'elün observed the young girl for a moment, then invited her into the yurt. Temüjin dismounted and signalled to us to follow him inside.

Mother Hö'elün was standing near the fire. Her long plaits braided with gold thread hung in two gleaming curves over her breasts, higlighting the vividness of her dress, which was already enhanced by a long, sleeveless brocade tunic. After Börte had tipped her embers into the fire, Mother Hö'elün knelt beside her and offered her meat, which the young woman hastened to eat. By this ritual, Börte confimed her willingness to share in the destiny of her new home and accept its thrall.

Börte served the broth, to her husband first, under the scrutiny of the two mothers. We men watched our chief's wife as well, our eyes following her above our steaming bowls, but our gaze was more forgiving. Her assurance, her attentiveness, her youth – everything about her moved us.

Her mother broke into a beautiful song that explained why she had not been able to resist following in the golden steps of her daughter, her jewel, Temüjin's wings. By the end, Dei's wife's eyes were wet with emotion. But it was Suchigil who was truly distressed and biting her lip, her face clouded. Although she stood in the shadows, I could see the furrows of vexation across her brow, the dark fold between her eyebrows. The lines around her mouth seemed deeper since our departure as if she had not stopped crying while we had been away. The purplish marks bruising her nose and the dark rings around her eyes only intensified the fragility of her face. Her eyes met mine and I sensed that if I had thrust a sabre through her body it would not have hurt her more.

Luckily Qasar decided to sing and we were all captivated by his deep, unerring voice. Then he handed a bowl to Börte and invited her to continue, saying that he could not contain his impatience any longer because he was convinced that her voice would equal her great beauty.

Flushed by the compliment, the young woman took the bowl and from her throat came a sound as clear and effervescent as a spring:

> May my husband's mother be eternal,
> May the eyes of her children be ever radiant.
> Your eldest has carried me off, seized me round the waist,
> May ashes never smother our fire,
> Drink, laugh, dance, sing,
> Like the suckling lamb, the sunlit colt,
> The swimming fish, the sky-borne bird.
> Here, far from my father, make my heart glad.

Contemplating her I shivered with pleasure – I longed for the time my wife would press herself to my chest.

When everyone had sung we went out to put up the married couple's immaculate yurt, which had been part of the dowry. It was new and smelled of willow and young fir. When we had tied the last straps of plaited horsehair securing the walls of felt, each of us sprinkled the floor and the threshold with milk and walked around it three times, chanting prayers for happiness and everlasting life. Then we helped the Onggirad pitch their worn-out tents and the two mothers-in-law prepared the newly-weds' couch, kissing each of the blankets so that they would be blessed with bright-eyed children.

Once the tents were up, Temüjin called together the family. He had hung the sable coat from one of the roof poles behind him and, addressing his mother, he said, 'This coat is for you.'

'It is a present fit for a prince,' replied Mother Hö'elün, 'and great would be my happiness if it covered my shoulders. But, meaning no insult to your wife's family, I think we could put it to a different use.'

Börte looked up and said she would agree with whatever Mother Hö'elün decided.

'You are wise, my daughter,' she congratulated her. 'A coat so valuable can be exchanged for livestock, horses and armed men to guard them.'

'Bo'urchu has had a better idea,' said Temüjin. 'As you know, To'oril, the King of the Kereyid, is powerful. In exchange for this coat, would he raise his men against Targutai and his accursed Sovereigns?'

'Be careful, my son,' said the dowager. 'This To'oril is cut from the same cloth as Targutai. Always tempted by easy prey, he is the sort of man to ally himself with the strongest to strip the weakest.'

'Is he not my father's *anda*?'

'He was.'

'And still is, because death cannot break the sacred bond of mingled blood. At the next moon we will go west to find him in his kingdom. Why this reluctance? Since he was my father's brother, aren't we his sons?'

'I fear for your lives,' answered Mother Hö'elün. 'To'oril is a bird of prey. Who do you think he will help – you the orphan with just a fur coat or Targutai with two armies' strength?'

'Me! Because I will be the first to ask for his help.'

'Take care! Never forget that he killed two of his brothers.'

'Is he alone in having done such a thing?' an angry voice cried out.

We all turned to look at Suchigil, who had been silent until then.

'Didn't your sons kill Bekter, my eldest, their brother?' she said accusingly. 'Did you cut off their hand for all that?' She jumped to her feet.

'Stay!' ordered Temüjin. 'We are hungry.'

As if paralysed, she stared at him for a moment, her eyes bulging, and then said ironically, in a choked voice, 'You want to eat? But you are married now . . . Wasn't the serving woman part of the dowry, or are you afraid that she'll tremble as she serves you – the fratricide looking to ally himself with his double?'

Temüjin, his face black, cut Belgütei a furious look. We all understood his silent order: keep his mother quiet, unless he wanted Temüjin to. Belgütei obeyed, seizing Suchigil's waist and carrying her out. But not quickly enough; her tirade reached us:

54

'How dare you touch me? I gave birth to you, I am Yesügei's first wife. Conspirator! You let Temüjin kill your brother, Temüjin who is nothing but the bastard child of a mistress stolen from a Merkid. Bekter was the true heir . . .'

Mother Hö'elün wanted to intervene but she knew from Temüjin's frown to stay where she was. We could still hear Suchigil accusing Belgütei of being a traitor and a coward and crying out that she had no more sons; then came the sound of a dull thud and the silence of dusk returned.

Near the tent Afraid of Bears sighed noisily, his nostrils buried in the grass. My horse was telling me his desire for new horizons to open up before his slender hooves.

Chapter 9

The remaining stars were fading in the dawn sky when Temüjin woke me. The horses were already saddled and we set off towards the heart of the Red Mountains, climbing swiftly on the wild sheep's paths. From his yurt far below, a column of smoke rose up, steady in the early light.

'Already your wife is bent over the fire.'

'She is hardworking,' he said. 'She is a real woman.' He dug his heels into his horse's ribs.

We rode all day up the slopes and through the valleys, where the flowers were a mosaic of colour. Yellow, blue, red and purple lilies stretched as far as the eye could see, broken only by the bold shades of orange poppies or violets, and bees were everywhere gathering pollen. Plagued by horseflies, we silently cut through forests and forded rivers bordered with grass and rustling young silver birches. Temüjin wore a scarlet *del* fringed with black, a present from Börte. Buckles and studs inlaid with turquoises glinted at his belt. A lock on his forehead almost touched the arc of his eyebrows. That burst of hair from his fox-fur cap intensified the wild flash of his gaze. He guided his horse with a firm, light hand and the feathering of his arrows rippled in time with its step.

Once we had reached the highest peak of the Red Mountains, we dismounted. To the south, the green, brown and ochre grasses merged into a bluish veil. In the opposite direction, far to the north, a snow-clad mountain-top soared above a chaos of peaks, outlining against the sky a vast, mirror-like promontory the colour of milk. Tenggeri lit every part of his beloved earth with a shaft of silver light so bright that we were dazzled.

As I squatted down, the ground was alive under my feet, rippling with a thousand muscles, both incredibly strong and gentle. These faint pulsings made me feel I was at the centre of things, absolutely there, in the very heart of that never-ending love which binds the sky to the earth.

We, two of their children, had climbed one of Mother Earth's high shoulders to be as near as possible to Tenggeri for the mingling of our blood. With this sacred exchange we would become allies, brothers – far more than that, we would be *anda*!

We took off our fur caps and hung our belts around our necks, then Temüjin looked at me.

'Before we cut ourselves, I must tell you of my life since my father died. Then, if you still choose to be my *anda*, there will be nothing about me you do not know.'

'The bravery and honour in your eyes are all I need to know,' I replied.

'No, you heard my aunt Suchigil say I killed her son Bekter. I want you to know the truth of what happened.'

'Then I will listen.'

'When my father died, the Sovereigns and the other clan chiefs under his banner gathered in secret to sacrifice to the ancestors. Despite her pre-eminence, Mother Ho'elün was not told. But when she chanced on the other wives going to the place of sacrifice, she followed and sat down in the front row with the other widows. The shaman, a Sovereign, ignored her, even when they began to share out the meat. At that, she stood up and, glaring at the assembly, admonished them: "How dare you treat me like this? I am the wife of the dead man, Lord of you all." She ordered them to divide up the meat in the traditional way, only to be challenged by the widow of Ambakai, the former khan who, believe me, Bo'urchu, was so ancient that a heavenly reprieve must have been keeping her old husk alive. Her pallid face shook under the weight of her heavy headdress and a steady, piss-like trickle seeped from her grey eyes. She looked like a diseased liver, but still she spat out her venom. "Who are you, O Abducted One, to tell us of our customs? The true wife is the one who has been pledged since childhood. Do you need reminding that Yesügei plucked you from a Merkid's saddle? Look, all around you are his brothers. These Borjigin princes and their clans all want Targutai's protection. You can agree to this alliance or you can leave our tents.' "

'Mother Hö'elün retorted that she would assemble her people and leave the Sovereigns. The old hide just sniggered, "Go then and take down the poles of your yurt. I will help you count how many of the Borjigin, the Mangkud and the Urut are with you."

'That night the *ulus* was restive. First came the sound of whispering, of secret consultations, the noise of galloping hooves, messengers sowing rumour and discord, then the racket of dogs barking and quarrelling amongst themselves. By morning the Sovereigns had yoked their oxen, folded their tents, harnessed their teams and were driving their herds before them in a cloud of dust, followed by those we had thought of as allies. Worst of all, the Borjigin were with them.

'Faced with this disaster, her eyes ablaze, her hair loose, her rage awesome, my mother climbed the hill where our standard stood. But when she tried to lift it, it would not move, too firmly driven into the ground by my father. I saw her brace herself and push and pull with such force that one of the nine yak's tails was shaken free from its iron ring. Her breast spilling out of her shirt, she bent over the shaft and, in a final effort which tore one of her sleeves, she wrenched it out with a terrible cry. Staggering under its weight, her arms outspread, she yelled, "Where are the warriors who swore to defend this standard to the death?"

'Our departing kinsmen ignored her, so she charged into them, grabbing the reins of one, striking another's back, abusing them all: "Sons of dogs, dung, traitors . . . "

'The troop continued to withdraw in silence and my mother halted in their midst, breathless, ragged, her mouth open, as if she had been run through by a spear. She was risking her life challenging them like that and Charaqa, our venerable shaman, went to her aid. He draped a sheepskin over her shoulders to cover her breasts and was threatening the deserters with the wrath of Tenggeri, when Targutai and his brother pulled their horses around and advised the old man to be quiet and return to his yurt. He harangued them all the more, only to slump to his knees, Targutai's lance buried between his ribs. Clasping the shaft, he prophesied, "By Tenggeri, Yesügei's wolf cubs will tear off your balls."

'The Prince of the Sovereigns burst into laughter and pulled out his weapon. I ran up to help my mother support the shaman. When Targutai ordered me to let go of the helpless man, I spat at his horse's hooves. "When you are old enough to hold a bow, brat," he said, no longer smiling, "I'll nail you to the ground as well."

'Charaqa's agony lasted three days and three nights, Bo'urchu. Three days and three nights when I never left his side – his own children had followed the Sovereigns. He was a good man. I

58

loved him, considered him my grandfather. In the happy days of my childhood he had always watched over me. He had taught me the stars, the moons, the sun, the art of tracking animals, of communing with the trees. Whenever he stayed for long spells in the forest or on the steppe, he would bring me something: stones fallen from the sky, roots or dried fruits without a name which I'd suck in secret at night, my head buried under the fur blanket. I had never shed even a single tear, yet I wept like a lamb for those three days. I knew he was lost, but what made me truly despair was the lance wound out of which his blood, his very soul, was leaking. In killing him, Targutai had enslaved him for ever in the beyond. I could not accept that a man so loyal could not join the good spirits in the blue of Tengri's sky. When the opaque veil was drawing down over his eyes he whispered that my father's death had rekindled the Sovereigns' old desire to see one of their own become khan. "They're greedy for the glory of their ancestor Ambakai and will shrink at nothing to recover it. Be on your guard: of all the heirs of the Mongol khans, you, Yesügei's eldest, are the chosen one. Targutai knows the legitimacy of your claim and he dreads it. He sees the fire of our ancestors burning in your eyes. Be like the wolf, Temüjin, go to earth, slip through the shadows of the forest and watch for Tengri's signs. Only they can tell you when to fight. Until then hide with your family, gather your strength for that day . . . Go, my son, and leave me now, because nowhere is it decreed that in my new dwelling place I will not be able to make Targutai spew out his liver . . . " These were the shaman's last words.

'Mother Hö'elün, my brothers, our old servant and I carried him to the heart of the Blue Forest and laid him to rest on the top of a rock surrounded by silver birch. Sometimes I can still hear his voice. I go to him on the threshold of his new home for guidance. I felt that it was he who led me to you, Bo'urchu. There in that sacred place, you appeared to me in my dreams, protected by a pack of great wolves.'

I was speechless. This confession had disarmed me. Temüjin knew this, but continued his story:

'Charaqa's death was a bad omen for the Borjigin families who had stayed with us, a hundred of them at most. In less than a moon they had folded their tents and joined the Sovereigns. We were alone, adrift. All that was left was my father's wives, Mother Hö'elün and Suchigil, the two sons the latter had born him, Bekter and Belgütei, my young brothers, Qasar, Qachi'un and Temüge, and my little sister who had not yet seen two springs and was still called by a man's name, the Terrible, to deceive the spirits that lust after newborns. There was also our old servant, Fart Walking. That was all that remained of our *ulus*: three women and a handful of children, a paltry flock without a ram, eight geldings and a barren mare. Even the dogs had followed the Sovereigns, except one, a mastiff as black as he was sly, which had been raised in Suchigil's tent and was as attached to Bekter as the calf is to the udder.

'Our first task was to collect up all the camp's *argols* into a huge mound. At least we had something to keep the fire alight through winter, but my mother would say, kicking the dried dung furiously, "What's the use of being warm if our bellies are empty?" Only Bekter and I could handle the bow, so Bekter taught Belgütei how to shoot, and I showed Qasar. Our first spoils were thin: a few birds, wood pigeons or squirrels, but more often marmots, field mice and other burrowers, which we soon became expert at hunting. In the meantime, when the women were not nurturing our little flock, lavishing care on a particular lamb in the hope that it would grow into a prolific ram, they were doggedly scouring the valleys and high grasslands, gathering blueberries, scratching for roots and grubs and digging up garlic and onions. Her many years had taught Fart Walking to find the apple or cherry tree, the juniper's violet berries or the pink spikes of the great burnet no matter how deeply hidden away in the lee of cliffs. In the marshes she was swift to unearth the bullrushes' tubers and many other plants. She was renowned for her gifts of healing and she would set aside a share to treat our ailments. In this fashion the moons and seasons passed, and we were still caught up in their dance, whether Targutai liked it or not. By the autumn of my twelfth spring, I could shoot foxes, lynx, stags and boars. The following winter I killed a bear sleeping in its lair, delivering the final blow with my sword.

'However, the melting snows brought Targutai and twenty of his men. They appeared one day, looming against the horizon. We had made ready for this visit and prepared the ground – hidden, staggered rows of trenches, broad and deep enough to bring down any attacker. At the edge of the wood, Qasar had built a barricade of spikes as a bluff from which he could fire his arrows. Leaping onto my gelding, I made for the heights and Qasar, Belgütei and Qachi'un covered me as we had planned, since we knew that Targutai sought me alone. But as I raced towards the Celestial Mount the Sovereigns posted on the bank of the Onon river saw me and sped off after me. I managed to reach the sacred mountain before nightfall and was swallowed up by its deep forests. I hid for nine nights and the Celestial Mount protected me. Each time I attempted to return to my camp, Tenggeri sent me a message of caution. First my gelding's saddle slipped, then a rock blocked my path where none had stood before. But on the morning of the ninth day I ignored Tenggeri's warning and the jays' strange calls. As I crossed a clearing I found myself surrounded. The Sovereigns pulled me off my horse and, grabbing hold of my plaits, dragged me to Targutai, who sat sucking clean the bones of a young partridge at the forest's edge. "So, here we have Yesügei's cub," he said, seizing me by the throat, "All grown up. The time has come to deal with you, young Temüjin. Your milk teeth have become fangs, and those aren't just sparks gleaming in your eyes but two suns."

'His *ulus* was three days' ride. As soon as we arrived, he put the *cangue* round my neck and told me that I would be paraded around all his camps so that his people would have the chance to humiliate me. Then I was dragged round the scattered tents of his *ulus*, my neck bowed under the heavy collar, and the Sovereigns crowded round, their children taunting me and their dogs snapping at my bare feet. So many of those faces were familiar to me. They brought back memories of my childhood, of my father's glory . . . Some shrank back into their tents after a quick glance, others showed themselves in broad daylight, full of vengeance, arrogance and disdain, while others came and told me of their discomfort – believe me Bo'urchu, the scars on my back were nothing to those on my soul.

'At last I was brought back to Targutai's tent. It was summer's first moon and the men were feasting in honour of its flushed face. Like an animal waiting for the sacrifice, I sensed that at the end of that lunar cycle, it would be my turn to die. That night my guard was changed and although the new one was almost the same age as me, he had a drunkard's face, the bovine smile of a halfwit and his arrogance made him think I was less trouble to watch over than a flock of sheep. Guided by the sound of laughter, he dragged me from tent to tent, begging for food and drink, until he grew weary, sat down and complained that he was a prisoner because of me. I said that nature's urgent desire was piercing me. He ordered me to do it in my trousers, an idea which must have amused him because he put down the arrow he was absent-mindedly whittling and stood behind me. I asked him to take down my trousers. He refused, saying I was just a bag of shit anyway. He sniggered, looking at my buttocks. I suddenly span round, so that the end of the *cangue* hit him in the temple. He didn't make a sound. To be certain and also to vent my fury I crushed his dullard's brain until the muscles of my back tore. Then I left him to rot like the scum he was.

'The great full moon was rising milk-white now she had shed her russet coat. By the time the dogs started barking I had reached the Onon. I stepped into the water and let the current carry me downstream to a bend of the river where I was able to dig my feet into the mud and come to a halt, my face and the *cangue* hidden by the reeds. The Sovereigns were already combing the banks, slashing through the thickets, shouting to one another. Mosquitoes swarmed over my skull, gorging themselves. There was a rustling – I had been seen. The reeds parted, a man crouched down and whispered, "Do you recognise me? I am Sorqan Shira, I was your guard for one night. Don't move, I'm going to throw them off the scent. Then run, flee, go so far away that Targutai will forget you ever existed." He got back to his feet. Moments later, I heard him persuading the others that the *cangue* would prevent me getting far and that it would be better to resume their search in daylight. Sorqan Shira was a member of the Suldus tribe. The night I had spent in his tent had been the sweetest of my captivity. His two sons had remembered the carved larch knucklebones I had given them many seasons before. They had loosened my bonds, fed me until I could eat no more and we had talked until morning as they beat the mare's milk.

'Flight didn't seem the best course any more. I waited for the voices to die away before clambering out of the river and making for my protector's tent. The Suldus were a small presence in the Sovereigns' *ulus* and I easily recognised the tent of Sorqan Shira and his two sons. They were startled at the sight of me; Sorqan Shira asked if I was mad – the Sovereigns would kill him if they found out. But his sons said it was a good omen to have a visitor while the milk was being beaten, which made me smile because in their tent it seemed that milk was beaten day and night. "It is wrong to hack off the squirrel's branch when the wolf is waiting open-mouthed below," they reminded him. "Or dismantle the yurt where the swallow has nested." This seemed to calm their father. He cut off the *cangue* and burnt it, then hid me under a great pile of wool in a cart next to the yurt. The following night he came bringing a chestnut horse with a white cloud on its nose and told me to ride it until it was exhausted, then abandon it. He also gave me a boiled lamb, two leather bottles of milk, a bow and two arrows. I thanked him and slipped away like a snake in the grass.'

An eagle circled, drawing its shadows around us. Temüjin mopped the beads of sweat from his forehead then continued, 'I found my family. They were unharmed. The Sovereigns had contented themselves with knocking down our tents and stealing our only ram. My family had all thought me lost so our reunion was joyful. Only Bekter, who had assumed the position of head of the family in my absence, seemed piqued. By evening he and I were arguing about my decision to strike camp at dawn, because I was sure that Targutai would come looking for me. Bekter accused me of being the cause of all our troubles. "If it wasn't for you," he said, "we could live among our people in peace. Why should we quit our ancestral lands just because of you? You should go on your own." However, the family council upheld my decision and as we left the banks of the Onon for the Red Mountains, Suchigil's son whittled his resentment to a point.

'You should know, Bo'urchu, that there is a chance I am not Yesügei's eldest son: Bekter could have been older by perhaps one or two moons. But what I know for certain is that my father had not yet spread Suchigil's thighs when he abducted my mother from the Merkid chief she had just married. Mother Hö'elün never complained, only Suchigil, who is very skilled at stirring trouble. Yesügei may have quieted Suchigil's snivelling by giving her a second son, Belgütei, but he never neglected Mother Hö'elün, whom he thought of as his first wife, his sun, the fallow doe who would bear him his blue wolf cubs. It was with us that Yesügei chose to live; Suchigil and her sons had a separate yurt.'

Temüjin's eyes bored into mine as he spoke – his voice clear, emphatic, without the faintest hesitation. Suddenly, behind him, the silhouette of an eagle tore across the vast sky, its wings beating like a standard. I glimpsed it, then it vanished, swallowed up by the slope.

'The sky has found its prey,' he said without batting an eyelid.

Far below marmots whistled in terror. 'Whatever my father's true preferences, he treated all his sons with the same consideration. But Bekter always set himself up as my rival. He was like the worm in the apple, sly and with no equal when it came to sowing discord. Arrogant and loud-mouthed, he could not speak without scaring the birds, eat without ogling his neighbour's share, move or even breathe without drawing attention to himself. Like a snake, he was always slithering in search of trouble. How could I have deferred to him, that arse without a head? Our life was so precarious that we had to scratch the earth for food, but Bekter spent all his time scoffing, upsetting my young brothers, following after me and erasing my tracks. If we came home empty-handed, he was overjoyed, forgetting that his belly was empty. From the very start he was like a lash in my eye.

'Our dog accompanied him everywhere and listened to no one but him. One day when I was fishing, the mastiff snatched up my catch which I had laid on the ground behind me and took it to Bekter, looking pleased with itself. That night I slit the dog's throat as it slept and tossed its head into the river. Bekter set little store by my warning. The very next day, when I was teaching Qasar on the river bank, he stole a gleaming silver fish and threatened to kill me, "the Merkid bastard". His mother only aggravated the insult. "That is the truth. You are a Merkid's son," she said, claiming that I was already conceived when my father kidnapped Mother Hö'elün. I could have torn out that magpie tongue, but what she said made me dizzy.'

'Didn't you . . . ?'

'Ask my mother? Of course, but she didn't listen to me. She just said, "Stop stabbing each other. Save your blades for the Sovereigns."

'Like a famished louse, Bekter kept on goading my patience with his thieving. One day Qasar and I brought down two skylarks, but we could not retrieve them. That evening Bekter proudly entered the yurt carrying them, with our two arrows in his quiver. The next day, as he was watching our meagre flock, Qasar and I climbed to his lookout point. When he saw me bend my bow, he turned to my brother and asked with an ironic smile, "So, what have the Merkid bastard and his slave flushed from cover this time? A butterfly?" My arrow struck him in the liver, Qasar's in the heart. Before he died, he begged us to spare

64

Belgütei so that his bloodline could continue. I felt then as if a thorn had been pulled from my foot.

'Suchigil was the first to realise that we had killed her son. When she saw our faces, Mother Hö'elün cried out that we were like dogs fighting over an afterbirth, pikes swimming against the current, jackals devouring their young, ducks eating their brood. Turning to me alone, she said I was like the snake that bites its tail, the falcon that flings itself at its own shadow. Even the rutting camel that bites its colt's heels was gentler than her eldest son. Still the truth was revealed in the end.

'Not long afterwards, perhaps because she realised she had been remiss, she assured me that I was Yesügei's child. "As the cub is the son of the wolf, so you are the son of Yesügei, the great Kabul Khan's ninth grandson. You were born between two silver birches, opposite the largest of the Three Lakes, whose waters heal all ills. The setting sun was playing on the mountains and your eyes bore the colour of its last rays. Your right fist was clenched and I couldn't prise your little fingers open. Your father was far away, putting the Tatars to the sword. On the ninth day of your life he lifted up the felt doorflap and took you in his arms. Then you opened your fist and a blackened clot of blood was stuck to your palm. Wasn't that a sign from the heavens? Your father had returned victorious, having torn out the heart of a Tatar chief, and he decided to call you by his name, Temüjin, the Blacksmith, the one who is as strong as iron. You are a Mongol, my eldest son, the son of Yesügei, the chosen one of the Borjigin, the khans' descendant. The eagle," she said in conclusion, "does not reach for the duckling that has strayed into his nest."'

'Why did Suchigil lie?' I asked.

'Mother Hö'elün said never to listen to her malicious gossip. Suchigil is like the cuckoo in the forest. You must never let yourself be deceived by that call which leads hunters astray. She could not control her eldest son and now her mouth is rotten with bitterness. If she cannot hold her tongue, I will tear it out.' He fell silent.

The wind ruffled our horses' coats, bringing the smell of the valleys which was as sweet as that of the first milk of summer, when the foals are young and with their mothers.

The sun was well advanced in its round. We watched it sinking gently towards the glittering necklace of mountains in the west. When it was spreading out its purple sheets, coppering

65

the lakes and our horses' eyes, Temüjin asked, 'Do you still want to become the brother he could never be?'

I quivered like a herd of a thousand horses galloping over a sheet of water.

In the twilight, Temüjin took a silver birchwood bowl out of his breast pocket. He filled it with milk from his leather bottle, put it on the ground and cut my veins. I cut his in turn. The blood spurted out, flowing over our fingers, splashing merrily on the surface of the milk. We grasped forearms. From that moment on we were *anda*, allies for all eternity.

'Our two bodies are now but one,' he said solemnly. 'More than my brother, Bo'urchu, you are my blood. Side by side we will walk, hunt and vanquish our enemies. If a third person whispers evil thoughts in the ear of one of us, let the other run him through the middle. If a snake comes between us, let us crush him and only believe the words of our own mouths. We are *anda* and I pledge my oath by Tenggeri that no plot and no person will ever separate us.'

We sprinkled the earth, the four points and our horses, circling their hindquarters three times. Then we fixed our eyes on each other and drank deep. When our downy moustaches became pink with the nectar, gales of mad laughter overcame the gravity of the moment. We fell on one another, struggling to see who could spatter the other's face with the most blood.

We rolled about until we were breathless, then we lay on our backs, pressed our wrists into the ground to seal the wounds, and waited for evening to give way to sparkling night, intoxicated by the pungent, heady smell of the blood smeared over our faces.

Chapter 10

We rode at a leisurely pace, three abreast, Temüjin, Qasar and I, and Belgütei followed with two packhorses, the sable coat wrapped in felt on one.

Thanks to Qasar, the journey to To'oril's camp passed in a flash. His was the sort of joyful nature that could find jokes and interest in everything. He had not yet seen sixteen springs but he seemed far older. His shoulders were as broad as the hindquarters of two horses and I knew no hands big enough to span that massive neck which rose from his shoulders like a granite cliff. Bright-eyed, always alert, he raced towards anything that caught his attention – marmots, swans' nests or distant white domes. Thanks to his affability, he accumulated news and friendships wherever we went.

It was on the fifth day that we saw the dark fringe of the Black Forest, famed as To'oril's *ordo*. Before we reached its edge we were surrounded by Kereyid.

They wore ash-coloured reversed hides, some lambswool caps as well, and all were adorned with pieces of finely worked silver. The precious metal gleamed on their horses' heads and breasts, saddles and cruppers, but still more on the men's belts, on their quivers and their boots, on their fingers, or hanging from their earlobes in half-moons. They led us across the winding River Tula with its willow-covered banks, then through the alders and tall silver birches to the heart of the forest, a vast clearing which contained nearly two hundred tents but could have held four times as many. From one of them a Kereyid chief named Nilqa told us that the king was at his summer camp on the banks of the River Orhon. He offered to take us there, saying it was a journey of at least two days' hard trot.

Temüjin agreed.

'What will you give me in exchange?' asked the Kereyid.

'All I possess I am giving to your king,' said Temüjin. 'So only he can say what shall be your share.'

'Every service deserves a reward, young whelp!'

Having seen no more than twenty springs himself he had no right to call us brats. Temüjin and Qasar seemed easily his equal in age. Bare-chested, he sat on a coffer, his hands on his thighs, wearing a pair of baggy trousers, and a short scimitar and a dagger were hooked through a broad finely detailed silver belt at his waist. Three silver rings adorned his muscular body – a delicate one at his ear, another through his left nipple and a third, broader one clasping a lock of hair plaited with red and gold thread which hung down to his shoulder blades from the tip of his freshly shaven skull. Two guards squatting on their heels at his right burst out laughing like fan-bearers.

'Then we won't use your warriors,' retorted Temüjin.

'While you are on our land? No one rides here unaccompanied. What do you say to that?'

After a moment's thought, my *anda* suggested giving him one of the packhorses when we returned.

'That is a small price. Don't forget that by killing you I'd get them all, quite apart from To'oril's reward for killing a spy. Well?'

'Well!' said Qasar, hurling himself at him, 'we are not frightened of dying.'

He grabbed Nilqa's plait, pressed his knife against his throat and shoved his knee hard into his balls.

The two lackeys froze for a moment. Temüjin and I seized the opportunity to level our blades at their bellies.

'You won't leave this camp alive,' groaned Nilqa, his face purple.

With a broad smile, Qasar assured Nilqa that he would be the first on that journey to the beyond.

We left the Black Forest in darkness and by dawn it was far behind us. The heat rapidly grew more intense and progress more painful, especially for Nilqa, who was riding beside Qasar with his hands bound. We had brought along his two guards. Reflections glinted off the silver studs in their reins and cantles onto their dark shirts. Other sparks, of anger, flashed in chief Nilqa's eyes.

Afraid of Bears found it easier going than the other horses. At times his golden neck and silken mane were silhouetted against a succession of gentle, pale-green hills, at others they blazed

68

against the azure sky. I sang out all my pride.

'He has a fine stride,' remarked Temüjin.

My training had paid off. Even on the coldest days of winter and in the full heat of summer, we had ridden, roaming the steppe and climbing the sheerest slopes. Now the horse was well muscled, sure and slender, with strong shoulders and an open chest. Afraid of Bears had never gone short of anything, least of all love; we were two of a kind, motherless.

As it grew dark, we decided to continue on our way, taking advantage of the cool of night, which drifted in as we crossed the eroded base of a massif. The crescent moon illuminated the brows of the frozen peaks as sharply as if it were full. The peaks sparkled, pale and sharp-edged above the chasms, and their silence weighed heavy on us.

Afraid of Bears led the way with a confident step, his neck perfectly aligned with his shoulders, casting furtive glances from time to time at the shadows. I could feel his longing to expel the wind from his nostrils, a longing made keener by the constant effort and exhilarating pleasure of this night ride. I had taught him mastery of all his desires so he held his sigh in, awaiting my consent.

I loved becoming one with him, slipping into the hollow of his back, letting my spirit run under his skin, pulse through his body like blood, reach into his four skimming hooves which drummed the rhythm of the grass and the wind into my heart. I was a horse, as free as a bird and, as I knew in those moments of perfect unison, he delighted in my joy. Thus attuned, we made our way into the heart of the Kereyid lands, I conscious of my friend's every need and feeling, he hoping for our agreed signal, some nocturnal animal's call that would drown out his snort.

Finally I whispered my permission in his ear, and Afraid of Bears released his breath, flattening the grass at his feet, five great bursts of air erupting in the silence, his neck bucking and falling.

Temüjin followed behind on our right, his shoulders luminous with frost. Although his face was partly in shadow, the radiance of his eyes betrayed an intense jubilation like that of tigers when the mating season has come.

At dawn the great Orhon valley appeared before us. The river was split into many branches and amidst their intricate patchwork tents stood like a chain of islands. There were thousands. Nilqa told us that we had reached To'oril's royal ordo.

When we arrived at the heart of the great city, we were surrounded by guards and made to wait. Around us the valley was waking and the chorus of bleating animals was deafening. We saw countless shepherds in dark *dels* bent over white and black fleeces or galloping through the light, and the size of the flocks they were tying head to tail took our breath away. The children were helping to round up the animals; the youngest enjoying themselves catching runaways with lassoes while those as yet unnamed crawled out of the yurts on all fours looking dazed, bare-arsed and snotty-nosed. Qasar kept Nilqa bound, within range of his knife, and Belgütei held the horses.

Once the milking was finished, the ewes turned loose, the sun high in the sky and the flies buzzing, we were given permission to enter To'oril's tent. Hung with golden silk, rectangular in shape and supported by thick horsehair ropes, it was vast enough to contain six of our yurts.

Gathered beside the throne, men on the right and women on the left, some eighty austere figures fixed their eyes on us. The gold of the hangings gave their impassive faces a patina like old parchment. Sitting above them To'oril studied each of us in turn, until he came to Temüjin. He had one sharp, keen, black eye, and the other was blue, half-shut and split by a waxy gash.

'Who are you?'

'I am Temüjin, your son.'

'In the name of Tenggeri! Since when has any son of mine appeared before me with a weapon in his belt?'

'This man tried to rob us. He says his name is Nilqa. If we were going to reach you, it was his life or ours ... '

The king thought for a moment and then said, 'By not being able to outwit you, this archer has shown he is little value to me. Kill him!'

Without knowing why, the order rang false to me. I whispered to Temüjin to ignore it. He ordered Qasar to sheathe his knife and free the prisoner.

To'oril clapped his hands and we were surrounded by guards, their swords at our throats.

'Tell me, young Temüjin,' resumed To'oril, 'who is that who whispered in your ear?'

'He is Bo'urchu, my *anda*.'

'Would he make a shield of his body to protect you?'

'Just as my father did for you.'

'You presumptuous young upstart. We will see which of you

four is prepared to give his life for the others because my true son, my only son, whose name is . . . Nilqa . . . is going to put one of you to the torture.'

Guards pushed us outside as the man we had just set free knelt at To'oril's feet. They stretched us out on the ground in quartered star-shapes and lashed our limbs to thick wooden pegs.

There was a naked man near us in an identical position. His body was nothing but bruises and abscesses. Nilqa went over to him.

'Look what happens to spies. He was a Naiman. Now he is a treat for the maggots.'

He put a foot on one of the man's purplish forearms and, kneeling down, cut into its mass of pustules and drew out a white maggot, as broad and fat as a thumb. As he held it up, he explained that these worms fed and grew only on rotting flesh, then lay dormant in the putrefying body as they pupated. Three hundred could gut a man in a matter of days.

'So? Who is going to be your volunteer?' inquired To'oril.

Temüjin, Qasar and I immediately began to argue, each of us wanting to protect the others. Qasar claimed that he was the fattest, I that I was the leanest – the maggots would make short work of me – while Temüjin said he wanted to pay personally for having led us into this death-trap. Only Belgütei, who was having trouble swallowing, was silent. King To'oril watched us with that slightly crazed look an osprey has when drying its feathers, and his convex nose, long and hooked as it was already, extended even further to catch what we were saying.

'Are none of you frightened of death?'

'No! But you should start to be,' haughtily challenged Temüjin. 'Because in killing me you are breaking the oath you gave your Mongol *anda*, Yesügei. Heaven will avenge us.'

To'oril laughed so hard his headdress fell off. His court followed suit. Finally he gave the order to untie us, saying, 'Look at this ring. See the wolf it bears!'

He had on eight rings, all in silver; only his thumbs were bare. Temüjin nodded.

'It is the Borjigin wolf. Your father gave it to me, your father Yesügei, my *anda*, who saved me from the Tatars and returned my people to me. Come, my son, come to my heart . . .'

Once we had got to our feet, To'oril stretched out his arms and, looking at us sidelong, added wilily, 'I use this ruse to

71

discover the intentions and true nature of strangers. I can read it in their eyes. Yours are full of fire. You are like the bull-calf, full of pride. I like that!'

He took Temüjin by the shoulders and sniffed his forehead. Then it was our turn and, dumbfounded but delighted to be still in one piece, each of us was tickled by his goatee beard.

Three days and three nights passed. Three days and three nights of eating, wild celebrations, singing, wrestling. Three days drinking, telling stories, warming ourselves at the fires, hazy stares on our faces as we smelled the perfumes of the Kereyid women.

To'oril spoke of his rides at Yesügei's side. His stories painted the picture of a luminous man who loved to laugh, fight and carry off pretty women. As we listened, we felt that he could equally well have been the subject of this portrait.

Temüjin and Belgütei were reserved, but our host was captivated by Qasar's good humour. Qasar was never to be outdone in the pleasures of conversation and he and To'oril established a friendship based on alcohol, which they drank without interruption, and smutty stories of purple keys unlocking the dark padlocks under women's *dels*. They drank far more than anyone else and yet were far from being the drunkest.

For three days men came from all over the Kereyid lands to join in the revelry. Wrestling bouts were held and Qasar proved himself supreme in strength, speed, and subtlety. Jaws were shattered, arms broken and murderous gleams flashed in the eyes of the defeated. As furious as he was entertained at the sight of his wrestlers' shoulders pressed to the ground, To'oril sent for his most famous fighters, three illustrious waist-crushers.

The three of them strode to the wrestling ground, bare-chested, shaven-headed, their massive torsos brushing aside the crowd pressing round them, while a bard sang their exploits:

> With his arms, Musa repulsed an army,
> With his shoulders, Baian hefted his enemy,
> With his chest, Kebek suffocated the multitude,
> Musa, Baian, Kebek,
> Three as strong as the bear,
> Three as swift as the tiger,
> Three as cunning as the wolf,

Quick-eyed like the eagle
Musa, Baian and Kebek are invincible.

Their chests were like a cedar's trunk, rounded, dense and rough. Their shoulders curved in a perfect arch and their thighs were so broad they had to swivel their waists at every step.

Kebek was the most awesome. I had never seen a man so tall. He was two heads higher than Temüjin, whose own forehead towered over most men. A giant, a living giant. The ground echoed with his tread. We looked at his body, which was mightier than three of ours put together, and wondered how anyone could stand up to such a suit of armour. The crowd whispered that he had knocked a rogue camel senseless with the back of his hand when taking it to fight bulls, that his mother had not survived his birth, that he was without wife because no woman could endure his embrace, that he found relief on the backs of mares . . . There seemed no end to the rumours about him and when Temüjin announced that he was quite willing to take on these three colossi, I was amazed to hear him nominate me to wrestle Kebek. He chose Musa, the narrower of the three, for himself and Baian for Qasar.

I was no mean wrestler but even if I had been excellent, it would have made no difference. Temüjin saw my downcast expression.

'Is that the fierce countenance of a Blue Wolf? Aren't you honoured?' I mumbled my concern that I would only be able to offer a paltry resistance. He told me with a roguish smile that it would not be seemly for us to win every bout. Instead he was counting on my cunning tiring out Kebek, so that he could set Qasar against him afterwards. I took off my *del*, trying not to look at my nightmare. The sight of his boots alone made me feel dizzy. He was sweating profusely and he tore up a great handful of earth and rubbed it on his shoulders so that I would be able to grip. How thoughtful.

Then he spun me round and made as if to go into a clinch. Bewildered, I surprised myself by grabbing his wrist, although my fingers couldn't reach all the way around. I was the one meant to be holding him, but I felt myself being pulled off my feet. He lifted me by the throat and threw me into the air. I landed face-up on his knee and all the breath shot out of me. When I came to again, I was head down in the vice of his legs. He was squeezing me so hard I could not moan, let alone shout –

it was as if he wanted to grind me into his body. My back was broken, my face contorting under the massive pressure of his thighs; I felt I was about to shatter like a walnut under a heel. He was going to kill me, I was going to die, mouth open, gasping for breath, as helpless as a worm cast. Suddenly an overwhelming smell of rutting camel told me that my nose was pressed against his testicles. I bit them, viciously, filling my mouth. He howled and let me go, but I didn't let go of him. Enraged, he grabbed hold of me again and smashed me into the ground and scrabbled for my eyes before I could rip off his bulbs completely.

I have no memory of what followed, but when I regained consciousness, I was vomiting out blood and dust, and shreds of cartilage blocked my nose. Temüjin told me that Kebek had slammed me from his full height. 'You must have become well acquainted with his arse!'

Temüjin himself had been worsted by Musa. However, Qasar had carried the day against Baian, and, after quenching his thirst with a jug of *airag*, he had challenged Kebek, who was finding it difficult to walk. A lucky knee in the giant's tenderised balls knocked him off balance and Qasar was able to unman him for good by forcing his backbone to the ground. In honour of the great victor whom everyone had renamed the Mongol Tiger, King To'oril decided there should be another feast. I could not enjoy the delectable dishes of mutton which were paraded past: even attempting to chew made me feel my jaws were cracking right through my skull. While the others stuffed their faces, I drank broth, milk mixed with butter, milk mixed with fat and plenty of koumiss (their name for the fermented mare's milk we called *airag*) and, like them, I drank far too much.

Other boiled sheep arrived along with pails of *airag* and more sheep and goats baked over stones, then does and patridges. Everyone ate, drank, went out to vomit and reeled back in, ready to stuff their bellies anew. Soon – and it was not just the gleam of the firelight that made them more desirable than the day before – the men started teasing the women. They tugged at the bottom of their *dels*, grasped their wrists or plaits and pulled them close. In the middle of the night most of the men began to leave the banquet for other pleasures. Couples frolicked near the tents, others ran and chased one another or fell into the arms of the river, laughing, shouting, even weeping. An occasional bare breast shone in the pale moonlight like a trophy, and everywhere bellflowers garlanded the curves of expectant buttocks.

A beautiful Kereyid woman came to find me by a rock. I inhaled the scent of her hair as she told me about an ardent-hearted warrior who had deserted her for more fragrant paths. She said her name was Gerelma and lowered her chin. I took it in my hand as the moonlight caressed her face, and turned it to me. My head spun, the ground fell away beneath my feet. I was about to nuzzle her cheeks when my stomach heaved terribly. I turned away and vomited. She stayed at my side and seemed to stare at something in the distance. With the sleeves of my *del* spattered, I did not dare repeat my attempt. I waited for a moment in silence, reeling slightly, and then fell asleep like a boat high and dry after being battered too long by a storm.

We were saddling our horses when To'oril came out of his tent swathed in the sable coat Temüjin had given him.

'Wait, my sons, this sable deserves recompense.'

Temüjin refused, saying that a father's protection was worth all the treasure in the world.

'That may be so! But these three slobbery-mouthed companions of yours mustn't leave without some show of gratitude on my part. They need a wife to pluck the lice from their heads, two arms to tend their hearths and warm their beds.'

So the three of us found ourselves married to To'oril's great-nieces. Metekna was matched with Qasar. Despite her youth, her body was already ripe and Qasar had discovered in the course of the night how welcoming she was. She burst out laughing at his every joke and her face had beautiful, fat, full, laughing cheeks. Qasar fell in love instantly. Much thinner, with a wan complexion, Mandra's face lacked charm. Self-effacing, awkward and tongue-tied, she seemed constantly troubled. She became the wife of Belgütei, who showed no emotion at this event.

I, meanwhile, had put forward Gerelma's name and she was sent for. In the sun's embrace, her face was even more alluring than seen by moonlight. Gerelma was mine. I had no inkling then that she would prove to be the coldest-hearted of To'oril's three great-nieces.

We had been riding for three days and still she refused herself to me. Why such an attitude? I did not understand. She was deaf to my advances, indifferent to my desire, which grew at every stride of my horse.

Each of her features was ravishing. A small narrow nose,

rounded cheeks, determined chin and a mouth with a perfect line like a double-arched bow. There was only one drawback: she never smiled. Her look was black, cutting, and her face was locked in perpetual dissatisfaction. Qasar and Metekna had set an example on the very first night of our return journey. Since then they kissed and caressed constantly, and galloped towards the hills to frolic there out of sight when the passion became too much. Belgütei and Mandra were more reserved, because Temüjin's half-brother was still only a child. But his young wife finally entwined herself around him.

'The man does not need the woman's permission to claim his marital rights,' Temüjin counselled me. 'To'oril has given her to you, so put her to use.'

Against my better judgement, I took my friend's advice and lifting my wife out of the saddle, I carried her off at full gallop. Her face slapped against Afraid of Bears' shoulder and her headdress came loose, bejewelled plaits spilling out. She protested. In a small valley, I harshly reined in my horse, released my grip and threw myself on her, tearing the collar of her blouse, uncovering her brown, sweat-drenched shoulders.

She struggled, giving off a powerful smell of musk, which drove me wild. With a head-butt to the bridge of her nose, I silenced her and ripped off her clothes. I had never seen a naked woman before and my eyes lingered on her breasts, her narrow waist, the half moons emphasising her cleft, forgetting that feasting your eyes without the woman's assent could bring bad luck. I rushed in. She let out an oath and tried to shrink back; I sank my fangs into the blue vein that follows the line of the throat and brought her down on the grass watched by my horse, who was grazing near us.

After a violent shudder had left me gasping for breath, Gerelma gave me no time to recover before hurling abuse: 'You are like the Tatar, a ravenous flea that feeds on the newborn, the venom in the wound. Are all Mongols like dogs to their wives?'

I stopped myself from slapping her, buckled my belt and mounted. When we rejoined our band, I told Temüjin how I had sabred my wife's dark lock and how she had upbraided me.

'Women are like wildcats, sometimes they need to use their claws.'

'I hoped to soften her and I have only made her harder. I dreamt of a union and I have reaped an enemy. Perhaps I acted like a blind boar?'

'*Anda*! Clear the mist from your eyes. You raped her? What of it? As the warhorse must obey his warrior, so the woman must yield.'

Chapter 11

Two winters passed.

Our camp was now on the upper reaches of the Kerulen, just before the great curve, where it was hidden on one side by a copse of willows and on the other by a cliff. On that stretch of the river, the water barely reached a horse's shoulder and it was easy to spear the fish basking on the white pebbles.

I was fond of that camp. We came there in summer and called it the Magpie Cliff because of the great colony of black-and-white birds nesting on its face. Every evening, in a final blur of feathers above the willows' ashen leaves, the magpies would return, chattering noisily, to settle for the night. Our lookout post was at the top of the cliff. From there we were able to see the whole Kerulen valley, a vast, predominantly marshy expanse which was all but uninhabited. The few familes who did graze their herds nearby preferred to pitch their yurts in the valleys amongst the hills rising in tiers to the north-east. To the south the view ended at a narrow gorge, the last obstacle the river set its travellers.

I would take up my watch just as the sun was sinking, coppering the hills and transforming the Kerulen into a vast golden snake uncoiling itself. I savoured those moments when the layers of burnished light slanted over the land, turning the orange marmots into blazing torches as they stood on their hind legs in front of their burrows, and I knew exactly what was to follow: first the return of the squawking magpies, then Qachi'un and Temüge crossing the river in a heave of foam. They were setting off to bring back the herd and would look up so that I could point them in the right direction.

It was in this light that two men approached our camp one evening. Their mounts were wretched and they said they came from the Blue Forests. The older carried a blacksmith's bellows on his back. After drinking the bowl of coypu broth which

Mother Hö'elün gave him, he told us he was an Obligee, one of the clans formerly in the service of the khans whose duty was to guard their burial places high in the mountains.

'I bring you my eldest son,' he said, fixing his eyes on Temüjin. 'At your birth I pledged him to you, but he was too young then to be of any use. You are the same age. Now that he has grown and broadened out, he is yours. Jelme is hard-working, skilled and brave, and his heart is pure. He will saddle your horse, forge and polish your arrowheads, guard your door, carve your meat and be as a bulwark to you. Even though he is my son, I would say that one couldn't hope for a better servant.'

Temüjin promptly invited Jelme to sit at his right. The new arrival was not tall but he was sturdy, with broad hands which told of his blacksmith's trade. He had an open gaze, eyebrows swept up in crow's wings, hair hanging loose at the nape, and thick sideburns that curled up towards his cheekbones and brought out the fine proportion of his face. He wiped away the milk beading his thin moustache with the back of his hand and, with an intense look in his hazel eyes, came and sat at Temüjin's side without a word.

Our visitors told us that the Sovereigns regularly rode up the Onon in order to patrol the source of the Three Rivers. This could only mean that their chief, Targutai, had not given up hope of catching Temüjin.

Jelme's arrival brought the number of men to nine if we counted Temüge, Temüjin's youngest brother, who had seen only twelve springs. With Temulun and her ten springs, the women were one more. Our flock of sheep was thirty strong, since my father had given us two rams and several ewes, and we also had the two camels and the oxen with the piebald rump left by Börte's parents.

Our *ayil* was composed of six yurts. The married men each had one. Suchigil slept next to her son and his young wife; Qachi'un with Qasar and Metekna; Mother Hö'elün, Temüge and Temulun shared theirs with the old serving woman, Fart Walking; the two other Onggirad couples, Börte's servants, occupied the last yurt. Jelme set up his couch at the foot of ours.

After a few days Temüjin asked me if the blacksmith's presence was disturbing our married life.

'His arrival has brought no change in Gerelma's ways. When she invites me between her thighs, we make love, as always, like hedgehogs – that is, very cautiously and, above all, in silence.'

'But surely she cries out like the field mouse when it's being throttled?'

'No, she buries her face beneath the covers and only re-emerges when my assaults are over.'

'Do you stroke her, sniff her belly, her gourds of milk, all the jewels that stir one's ardour?'

'I've told you we mate like hedgehogs. She thinks both our souls will be in peril if I venture to touch her more than she thinks is allowed. She is not happy with me; she thinks our yurt cramped, dark and empty; she wants it full of chests, carpets, embroidered fabrics. My wife talks constantly about the thousand felt homes of her childhood encampment with a light in her eyes which is absent from her heart. I am going to send her back to her family.'

'Do not think of it, To'oril might take offence. We need him.'

'So what do you suggest? Bite my tongue?'

'Don't let a wife make you lose your way, my friend. Look at Belgütei – do you think Mandra has changed him? Yet she is hard-working, tends his hearth, has good red cheeks. But he does not speak to her, asks her nothing and is always with the horses.'

'Belgütei is no example. He is young and prefers his horse to his bride. Speak to me rather of Qasar and Metekna. Are they not like two colts on the steppe?'

'Do not try to love a woman more than your horse, because that way you will lose not only yourself but also the most precious of your possessions, your chestnut stallion.'

I stroked Afraid of Bears. My horse switched my hand with his tail and I read in his great eyes how dearly he loved me.

We trained every day: wrestling, bowmanship, swordmanship. But, although we made good progress in the arts of hunting and combat, nine men did not make an army, especially since Qachi'un and Temüge were so young.

We had to flee our first skirmish. We were surprised as darkness was rolling towards the west. Fart Walking sounded the alert: 'On your feet! On your feet! The earth is rumbling.'

In a flash we were running for our mounts.

'To the Blue Forests,' Temüjin shouted, adjusting his belt and quiver. He disappeared behind the willows, followed by Jelme, Qasar, Qachi'un, Temüge, and Börte's two freedmen.

Above us, several dozen silhouettes were trotting along the

crests, seeking easier slopes by which to reach our camp. They seemed to be clad in thick furs.

'Merkid!' said Belgütei. 'Quick, Bo'urchu, let's go!'

The women had gathered together and were watching us, dazed and shivering. Apart from our two mounts, there was only one horse left. Belgütei told Mother Höelün to take it and she mounted up immediately with Temulun on the crupper.

Suchigil broke away from the others, crying, 'How dare you choose her over me?'

'It is her they are looking for. They have come to avenge her abduction by Yesügci.'

'She is the cause of all our troubles. Her and the scavengers she has given birth to. Let her pay!'

Seeeing Börte's rounded shoulders peeping out of the blanket wrapped round her waist, I was tempted to take her. But Temüjin himself had not taken her up behind him and she would slow me down.

'Flee,' I shouted. 'Make for the cliff and hide amongst the rocks.'

They all did so, scattering like a flock of birds, apart from Suchigil, who continued her rant: 'How can you leave me to follow your brother's murderers? It's Temüjin's fault that your father is dead; your brother was killed by his hands, now he's abandoning me and you obey him like a slave . . .'

Belgütei did not know what to do, so I struck his horse's hindquarters. Behind us Suchigil screamed, 'Because of him you will all be killed!'

Chapter 12

Afraid of Bears' pounding hooves shattered the stones of the ford, and in that racket and shower of water my heart leapt. It may have been flight that had set us galloping, but what did our direction matter to me? This affront called for revenge and was leading us toward stirring days.

I saw our two camels lying in a dried-out ravine, looking at us disinterestedly. It was a pity they hadn't been tethered near the tents as Börte and Suchigil could have used them to escape.

Our horses were feisty and quickly reached the rallying point on the heights, one of a collection of large hills broken up by deceptive valleys which we called the Wind's Pillow. There was no room for mistake in that swell of hills because, within ten paces, the ground could change as easily as a smile into a grimace. It was fortunate we had already scouted it out in anticipation of such a withdrawal. There was nothing easy about our route so I took Temulun in my arms and we hastened towards the Blue Forests. The narrow little valleys nestling at the summit of the foothills were waterlogged and slowed us down. Then we followed the animal tracks winding between the close-packed trunks which forced us to bend low over our horses' necks. I was leading and whenever I hesitated Qasar thrust himself forward, impatient to take over, but Temüjin, with just a look, ordered him to hold his peace because this was my favourite hunting ground. Despite the tangled maze of paths, the play of light and shade which became blinding when we tried to peer through it, and the ground that was so unchanging it made us think we were going round in circles, Temüjin had confidence in me.

In my arms little Temulun gazed at me intently. Every time I bent over Afraid of Bears, I gave her a wink. Her doe eyes were hazel and in her face one could see both her mother's features, though much less pronounced, and those of Temüjin. These made a subtle combination, soft and serious.

'Are you angry?' she asked me.

'At being made to flee like a rabbit?'

'No, at being separated from Gerelma. The men will take her, they may even kill her.'

'If they can find her,' I replied, 'yes, one of them may carry her away to his yurt.'

'Don't go and look for her! Ever!'

This outburst was more a command than a warning. I was silent, but secretly the idea of Gerelma's abduction appealed to me and the thought of avenging my cuckolded honour didn't even cross my mind. We were both quiet for four strides, then she added, 'And then you will take me as your wife.'

Her nerve made me smile. Her brown locks brushed against my lips, smelling good of wool fat and hot ashes.

'This is a poor moment to imagine our future,' I instructed. 'Keep quiet and let me get us out of this forest.'

There was nothing appealing about the approaches of the Celestial Mount – thick brush, deep, black bogs. Every rock, every tree, even the smallest rise seemed to assume the form of an evil spirit and soon we were surrounded by an impalpable, rustling throng. Throughout our flight, the sky had been low and uniformly grey but here, dark clouds massed strangely in the greyness, as if all the storms of the earth, all the darknesses were hatching their wrath in this region. Temulun huddled a little closer to me. I ruffled her hair. We watered the horses. Temüge was feeling ill, his forehead as burning as a pot on the fire, his back drenched with sweat, his legs unsteady. Qachi'un made fun of him, and as a quarrel broke out, Temüjin stepped in between them to point to a pass which made a beautiful softening of the bellicose clouds in the distance. A dozen silhouettes stood there.

Holding our horses on the leading rein, we regained the shelter of the forest, moving discreetly like herons, and pushing on until we reached the flanks of the Celestial Mount where the clouds suddenly split open.

That night only Temüge lay down, under a holly bush with his mother crouching beside him. We stayed on our feet next to our horses, who had not even a blade of grass to keep their boredom at bay. The rain pelted down with such force that all we could hear was its music. We were as drenched as snails and even though we bunched together, we still couldn't see each other.

Sometimes I laid my cheek against Afraid of Bears' neck or pressed my belly against his nose, affectionately cupping his lower jaw. We would remain like that, waiting, dazed by the downpour.

At last daylight gradually restored our silhouettes and the pallid outlines of our faces. Then I saw us all, men and horses, faces contorted, as plant-like as the weary-branched firs, the peat underfoot and the long festoons of silvery moss trailing sadly all around. Temüjin's eyes were those of a cornered beast, flashing wildly like claws slashing into empty space.

'We will wait as long as the rain lasts.'

His irrevocable decision earned us three days under a downpour that was as hard and unrelenting as a waterfall. The rain erased our tracks and quenched our thirst, but it could have been fatal for Temüge if his fevers and delirium hadn't suddenly vanished, as if by magic.

The rain itself stopped on the morning of the fourth day. Temüjin sent me to scout ahead with Jelme and Belgütei. The shadow of the remaining clouds sped across the hills now bloated with water. We picked up our pursuers' trail on the pass where we had last seen them. It turned back to the north towards the Merkid lands. In the middle of the day, as we were descending between two wooded hills into a long valley, I saw a flock of sheep watched by their shepherd. In the distance smoke rose lazily above a few rings of yurts. The sky had drawn across its radiant sheet of blue silk.

I made for the shepherd, leaving Jelme and Belgütei to hold the point. A lamb was slung across his saddle and when he turned, I was dumbfounded because I saw that the shepherd was a shepherdess of about sixteen springs and incomparable beauty. Her *del* was of the same azure blue as my shirt and the way it hung open at the neck only increased my confusion. Was she a young mother who had just given the lamb suck to relieve her breast? Mesmerised, I wondered at the purity of her face, her long, lustrous hair, her large dark eyes that were brilliant and deep, her clear forehead and the swallows' wings that were her eyebrows. Two dimples in her cheeks brought out her cheek-bones and her bilberry-coloured lips were as fleshy as that shrub's fruit.

'What is your name?' I asked in a hoarse voice.

She looked away. I urged Afraid of Bears closer.

'I am called Bo'urchu.'

84

'I, Queen of Flowers.'

The sound of the stream in the grass could not have been sweeter than her voice. Her long eyelashes fluttered.

'I don't suppose you have a stream of strangers distracting you from your work.'

'What are you doing?' she asked mockingly.

'Just that . . . and glad of it. I meant there can't be many men who visit your *ayil* because it is isolated.'

'No, what you meant is, who were the last strangers here and when did they pass by? And why would I tell you?'

'As a way for us to get to know one another,' I answered, shaken by the assurance of the beautiful stranger to whom I was so clearly transparent.

She brushed back a lock of her hair and with a bored air dug her heels into her gelding's ribs.

'Wait!' She sullenly carried on her way, stroking the lamb in her arms.

I trotted up to her and surprised myself by declaring feverishly, 'Don't go! Now that I've seen you, I'll never be able to forget you . . .'

She stopped her horse and looked hard at me. All the breath gone out of me, I hung on her words.

'That sounded sincere.'

'I want to see you again.'

'In that case,' she said solemnly, 'you must first meet my father.'

I galloped like the lightning in the sky to fetch my companions. In Queen of Flowers' tent her father confirmed to us that it had been the Merkids. As a youth, he had been a slave of their three great tribes and knew them well. When he had been freed, his masters had permitted him to marry a Merkid girl whose mother was a Mongol. The couple had settled near the Celestial Mount and started a family. So Queen of Flowers had a quarter Merkid blood and this mixture only made her more beautiful. But even had she been pure Merkid, she would not have seemed any the less bewitching.

The father of the fairest of all the flowers told us that fifty Merkids had crossed his pastures two days before. They had exchanged a few words and he had noticed an ox with a piebald rump pulling a cart carrying two captives. From his description we knew it to be Börte and Suchigil. So, the Merkid had come to avenge Yestügei's old affront. Although a long time in coming, their retaliation was little surprise because to be robbed of one's wife or one's horse deserves reprisal, even if many moons after the event. But what had they done with the others, our three Kereyid wives, the two Onggirad serving-women and old Fart Walking?

Queen of Flowers and her little sisters kept looking at me and bursting out laughing, the younger ones teasing their elder sister. Watching them, I began to wish that Gerelma and I would never be reunited.

Knowing that Temüjin was still waiting in hiding, we could not tarry any longer. As we rode away, I turned back. Queen of Flowers was pouring the libations of departure, her young brothers and sisters pressed against her hips. Her complexion was as pale as a lily.

From that moment onwards, despite my joy at the prospect of seeing and releasing Temüjin and his family, I had only one obsession: to smell her perfume one day, caress her velvet petals and taste her nectar.

We were passing close to the herd of horses when Afraid of Bears spotted a white filly. He slowed and whinnied softly to her. Ears pricked up in our direction, but it was the white horse that stepped away from the herd and, gracefully tossing her head, set the blue-grey tints in her mane flashing in the evening light. My horse's neck swelled, his nostrils quivered, he neighed . . . and the stallion, the herd's master, cantered up immediately to shoo away his mares from us. When the white filly kept on staring at my chestnut mount, he bit her in the hock to make her move.

I gave Afraid of Bears three good slaps on the shoulder and made him a promise: 'We will return, my friend, should we have to trace a path of blood to do so.'

Chapter 13

Our women had strung a piece of patched-up felt above their heads as a makeshift tent and not moved from the Magpie Cliff until we returned. The camp had been pillaged and all that was left was torn yurts and scattered piles of *argols*.

Metekna rushed to Qasar and he clasped her tenderly in his arms. Mandra was at a loss. She fiddled with her hair, smiled shyly and then lowered her gaze.

Gerelma looked at me stony-eyed.

Börte was nowhere to be seen.

I was relieved that Temüjin had stayed behind with his young brothers, his sister and his mother. As talkative as the magpies whose nests she had shared, it was Metekna who told us about the Merkid raid.

The three of them had been able to hide amongst the boulders, but Fart Walking had still been making her way round the base of the cliff when the Merkid were upon her. They interrogated her – was Temüjin one of those who had escaped? How many women were with him? The old woman, whose ears were sharper than a Mongol's horse's, feigned deafness and claimed she lived higher up the valley and was only here to collect the fleeces Temüjin owed her master as tribute.

After endless discussions, shouting, jostling and blank incomprehension, it was Suchigil, already slung across a Merkid's thighs, who gave us away: 'Look under that wool and you will find Temüjin's treasure.' The warriors did as she said and discovered Börte under the fleeces. As punishment, Fart Walking had wool stuffed down her throat until she suffocated.

The crows were feasting on her corpse. We carried her to the top of the hill, where we gave her humble offerings: a marmot, a leather bottle filled with camel's milk and a few of the grasses whose healing powers she knew so well how to use. Then we built two fires and took turns walking between them, in order that Fart Walking's soul would not seek to follow us or be in danger of losing its way, but instead go straight to join the birds in the sky.

By chance our two camels had escaped the looting. Mandra and Gerelma each took one while Metekna climbed up behind Qasar, laughing happily. Belgütei rode out in front. Mandra seemed grieved by his distance; her *del* in rags, head bowed, shoulders jolted by the gait of her mount, her rainy eyes remained fixed on her husband's back. I kept my distance as well, because I could feel the full weight of Gerelma's reproachful stare boring into my neck.

After riding for half a day, Qasar carried Metekna off to the top of a hill, planted his lance and disappeared. Mandra and I sighed. Driving your lance into the ground told all in the vicinity that a couple were doing what all couples do when they want children. Shepherds generally plant their *ourga*, but if one does not have this tool for catching horses, the lance is just as good at prompting any unexpected passers-by to make a detour, unless they are curious about what is afoot the other side of this symbol, this discreet invitation to a woman to shed her modesty and reticence.

From then on our journey was hard to bear. Afraid of Bears was full of energy, so I decided to scout ahead and soon we were surrounded by the silence we both loved so.

We set up camp beside the Blue Lake, where we found shelter from the violent winds. I knew the place intimately. There was not a tree or a rock among the dark forests and hills that could surprise me. Had it not been there that I had seen my *anda* in the great wolf's stare?

The more I scrutinised Temüjin's eyes, the more certain I was that it had not been a dream. And yet those same eyes were growing darker with every passing day. Even Qasar's good humour made no difference. The row of shelters we had erected side by side in the Merkid way, frames of branches covered with humus, horsehair, pine needles and parmelia moss, seemed to give him no comfort. He spent whole days alone in the forest, and long spells at the shore staring into space.

At each sunrise and sunset the master of the place, a fishing eagle, came to catch his meal from the black waters. Temüjin never missed this unchanging kill, always executed with the same insolent precision. After describing a broad, high circle to find his prey, the raptor would make a sudden dive, break the surface of the water with a muffled splash, disappear for a moment, plumage submerged to the base of the wings, then struggle back into the air, a fish as long as a man's arm in his claws.

One evening when we were waiting for this ritual, Temüjin said, 'I want to swoop down on the Merkid's camps like that eagle and snatch Börte away before they can even shift their backsides. I'm going to find her. Will you ride at my side?'

'Do you want me to be your spy and discover where Börte is being held? I'm willing to. But even if our mission is a success and we carry her off, how will we survive the journey home? The Merkids are numerous, their lands are vast. Only with the Kereyids' help is an attack possible. Aren't you under To'oril's protection? What is making you hesitate so?'

'Mother Hö'elün. She says he speaks with a forked tongue, that his skin is so thin an alliance is never safe. Under his leadership, anything could happen to Börte.'

'But without him . . .'

'You are right, Bo'urchu. I have no choice. I will climb the Celestial Mount to ask for Tengri's blessing. When I return, I will announce my decision.'

Afraid of Bears leapt from peak to peak, crossed plains and valleys in a bound, and sailed through the densest undergrowth, sending startled blackbirds into the air. We knew where our hearts were leading us and this intoxication only increased our speed.

Our arrival at Queen of Flowers' valley set the herd of horses stepping restlessly, their ears pricked curiously in our direction. The stallion came forward, ready to chase away his mares. Afraid of Bears stopped. Neck arched, nape full and quivering, drawn up to his full height, he observed the stallion's manoeuvre.

The white mare that had pleased him so broke away from the herd. My chestnut mount whinnied softly to her, making the black stallion bite the air to restore order amongst his mares. With his broad back, long, waving mane and thick, ragged forelock, he looked every bit the tyrannical, jealous little brute.

Sensing my consent, Afraid of Bears launched himself at the herd. Surprised by this sudden onrush, the black stallion panicked for a moment and half-turned, swinging his head from right to left as if he was counting his mares and didn't know what to do. But any action would have been too late. Afraid of Bears swept up the pretty fillies in a great welter of raised tails, clashing rumps, furious farts and hooves clattering on stone. At his side, galloping nose to the wind, was she who had first guessed his wild intentions – the white mare.

We passed a few hundred paces from the yurts, and I took care to hide myself behind Afraid of Bears' shoulder. The felt doorflaps lifted and children, then men came rushing out. I led the many-coloured pack to the edge of the forest, and slipped into its shadows. Moving along the line of trees, the herd slowed and then scattered, their sides heaving. The pure white mare was the first to stop. She turned her milky face to us, but the stallion had caught up and was already hurling himself on her and biting her at the base of the thigh. Meanwhile Queen of Flowers's family had scrutinised the area, seen that there was no danger threatening their holdings and returned to their tents.

I stayed for a moment under cover of the forest, allowing Afraid of Bears to get his breath back. At last Queen of Flowers emerged from the yurt, holding a little leather whip. She walked towards the horses' rail, untied a gelding which was still in a frenzy of excitement because the stampede had rushed within a hair's breadth of him, mounted and set off at a walk in my direction, serene, straight-backed and pink-cheeked. Two locks of hair, each threaded with a turquoise bead, formed a dark shape like an arrowhead on her white *del*. She rode into the forest, but the sun followed her, picking her out before anything else under that canopy of leaves – it was as if a thousand fires crackled around her silhouette. Her mount came to a stop a few paces from me and my heart was thrown into turmoil.

'Is this the only way you can announce your arrival, by tormenting my horses?'

'My stallion was stamping its feet with impatience at the prospect of seeing one of your mares again.'

'Is she the only reason you're here?'

She was delectable; my voice grew hoarse. 'No . . . I couldn't wait to return either.'

She lowered her eyes. I rode towards her and put my hand on hers. Under her thick *del*, which was too warm for that season – teasing, perhaps? – her breasts heaved. A shiver ran up my spine. Blushing, she furtively glanced up at Afraid of Bears' head.

'Which mare is it?'

'What?'

'Which of the mares is able to cause such urgency and commotion in your horse's heart?'

'Ah. Look into his eyes. There you will see a mane as white as your dress.'

'White Moon!' she exclaimed, breaking into a broad smile studded with mother-of-pearl.

I brought one of her hands to my mouth. She withdrew it gently, a wary look on her face.

'You have nothing to fear from my lips – they are like the down on a bee's back.'

'I have no wish to be stung, because once his dart is spent, the bee dies. Look at your horse, he is not rushing at White Moon.'

'That is because he has done so already.'

'Because you encouraged him!' she cried indignantly. 'Still, your horse has good taste. White Moon is my favourite. She was born on the night of a full moon. But sadly she is barren.'

'Promise her to my horse: he will cover her and fill her womb with golden colts.'

'Why not?' she said laughing. 'But if he is to have her, I want to see no other manes in his eyes than hers, because she is my jewel.'

'And what can you see in mine?'

She looked up and my fingers encircled her chin.

'Something disquieting, red – the red of desire. Come, let us ride on.'

'Wait, look at me again, tender queen. It is the red of your smiling lips.'

'See that it is always so.'

Her tone was meant to be threatening, but it felt like a cool breeze playing on my back.

The peaks were sprinkled with the first snows when my *anda* reappeared.

He held the Borjigin standard in his left hand and, in the icy light, the trident's flames rising above the nine yak's tails seemed to cut into the clouds racing across the sky.

'Let us go and see if To'oril has a tongue,' he said, not even dismounting. His eyes were sharper than the cutting edge of a sabre, but their yellow gleam would have dispelled the shades of night.

Before Jelme could fetch provisions, Qasar and I were in the saddle. The good blacksmith handed me the meagre saddlebags and our horses sped off, breathing hard at the ground, as Mother Hö'elün hurried after us, miming the libations because she had neither pail nor dipper to perform this propitious rite.

Before us the Blue Lake was flecked with white caps but no complaint could dent my elation, not even the squalls of wind moaning amongst the hills.

Chapter 14

On his knees in front of King To'oril, his belly as rounded as a
new cushion, the slave stared at the ground without moving.
Tufts of hair poked out of the hollows of his ears. One of them,
sliced to the bone, had no shell.

The retinue of malevolent faces which made up the king's
court, mainly intriguers and decrepit old women who seemed
half-asleep, stared at him with cold, bitter contempt. There were
candles arranged all around the tent and their light reflected off
the silver jewellery everyone wore in the flash of a thousand
fireflies.

To'oril's voice boomed out, 'Temüjin is like a son to me. Your
people have ransacked his tents and made empty his bed and my
anger is great. You Merkids have your heads lower than a dog's
arse. Show me your tongue!'

The Merkid raised his head and opened his mouth slightly.

'Stick it out further from that putrid mire!' ordered To'oril.
He stood up, drew his dagger, seized the man's tongue and
yanked it towards him.

'Don't cut it out!' cried Temüjin.

'What's that you say?'

'He will be a sorry spy without a tongue. How will he be able
to tell us where my wife is and the layout of the Merkid camps?'

'You are astute, my son. But there it is, this slave is mine and I
have many scores to settle. That missing ear is recompense for
what the Merkids made me suffer many moons ago, when,
having been foolish enough to seek their aid, they enslaved me. I
had brought my daughter to seal our alliance. They took her
from me. For that further treachery, I have torn out this piece of
dung's balls.'

'I understand your anger better now, father. Cut off his
fingers.'

'They are no match for the tongue,' said the king, in an aggrieved tone.

'The tip, then.'

To'oril's knife sliced off a half-section of the purple organ, far too much for him ever to prate again. Blood welled up and flowed over the slave's torso.

'Let us see if he can still talk.'

A guard handed To'oril a hatchet and he cut off the Merkid's hand at the wrist. Although his face contorted in a rictus of pain, the prisoner did not make a sound.

He was taken away and the king declared we should feast to celebrate his reunion with his adopted Mongol sons. He clapped his hands and a host of slaves, servants and cup-bearers instantly took up their positions.

To'oril asked if his women were good wives and we answered that, proud to have us as husbands, they were hard-working and pleasant. Then his jagged vulture's face became grave.

'From the moment you came to me, I have thought of you as my sons. Every night, kept warm by your sable fur, I puzzle over how best to help you reunite your people. It is a bad father who does not suffer when his children are wounded in their very flesh. The Merkids' crime will be avenged in blood, Temüjin! We will find your azure one, she who goes by the name of Börte, that I promise you. But I cannot raise my whole army for this expedition. At my back the Naiman are attacking my lands.'

'How many men do you command?' asked Temüjin.

After a moment's thought, the Kereyid mentioned the figure of ten thousand.

'Far more than are needed!' Temüjin exclaimed in delight.

'Don't be fooled! From milling their grain and doing their most menial jobs, I got to know the Merkid well. Their clans are larger than the Mongols' and make up three great tribes. Thanks to this spy I have just schooled, we will find out which of the three Merkid chiefs is holding your wife captive. But believe me, after crushing one tribe we'll find ourselves facing the other two. We need that orphan your father gave a home. What has become of him?'

Temüjin turned pale. 'Jamuka!'

'Yes. They say he has gathered together many scattered clans and camped on the upper reaches of the Onon. Go and seek his support.'

'Never! Jamuka and I were raised in the same tent, we were

like brothers. Until the day the Sovereigns abandoned us, then he too turned his back on us.'

'Calm your rancour, my young wolf. Something tells me he was in no position to oppose the Sovereigns' decision. He has become a chief now and, if my information is correct, his tents are not allied to the Sovereigns. He is a Mongol and you cannot avenge the wrong done to your honour without the help of your people.'

'I'd have to cross Targutai's lands!'

'Send Bo'urchu. He has nothing to fear from the Sovereigns.'

So that was how I found myself galloping into the night with mutton chops in my saddlebag, which were not enough to banish the aromas of the banquet from which I had had to take my leave.

To'oril had instructed me to accompany the Merkid slave to the banks of the Kerulen, but, as I hoisted myself onto Afraid of Bears, Temüjin discreetly gave me a different order, convinced that after the slave's treatment at the Kereyid court, he could never make a good spy. The maimed prisoner was pissing mournfully in the middle of the steppe, the stump of his arm wrapped in a bloody cloth, when I slid my blade across his throat. He slumped heavily to the ground and the light in his eyes guttered like a candle. I felt a stab of remorse. Not because of the reward he hoped for – I doubted To'oril would be generous enough to release him from slavery – but at the thought that he and Queen of Flowers might have shared ancestors.

I rode on towards Jamuka's camp. Since bringing together several clans under his banner, this name was known beyond every hill. He was of the Solitaries tribe, and his tribesmen had journeyed up the Onon to join him.

To'oril thought that Jamuka would be able to marshal ten thousand men, which would make a solid left wing to complement To'oril's own forces.

I rehearsed Temüjin's message to him. The earth's rhythm under my horse's hooves, the silence, the cold, the starry firmament as domed as a yurt – all this would usually have had its place in my inner song. But there was another voice in my head, the voice of a woman who danced before my eyes, under my skin . . . I was happy, too ecstatic to concentrate.

In a single day's ride through Jamuka's *ulus*, I had counted more than three hundred tents. The same number comprised his camp.

But in the darkest part of his yurt, I could only see the essential saddles, harness, and quilted leather breastplate beside the *airag* pail and beater. Otherwise there was a yak hide stretched on the floor, a plain chest and a fur tossed in a heap on the rope matting. That was all. A simple shepherd would have possessed more.

I had just announced myself and was starting to give him Temüjin's message when he almost yelled, 'Your *anda*, you say?'

Taken aback, I looked at him. He was tall and broad, with a gaunt, smooth-shaven face. He was staring at me suspiciously, his eyes black and sharp.

'I only knew him to have one *anda*. Who are you?'

'Bo'urchu, as I said.'

'I am Temüjin's *anda*,' he growled. 'Continue.'

'He sends me to tell you that the Merkid have destroyed his camp and made empty his bed. At his side, the Kereyid king is marshalling ten thousand warriors. He asks whether, in memory of those happy days when you swore allegiance, you will lead your warriors to form his left wing.'

Jamuka thought for a moment, then turned his head and called out, 'Kököchü! What say you?'

From outside the yurt a man's voice replied, 'It is a sign from Divine Tenggeri. The two shoulder blades that burnt in the fire last night did not lie. Temüjin asks for your help? Then fix the meeting place, for the spirits favour you.'

'You will tell my *anda*,' resumed Jamuka, scrutinising my face, 'that I too will perform libations to my standard, set the drums beating and marshal ten thousand warriors. Let Temüjin sharpen his arrows, his lance and his sabre, for heads will be severed for our pleasure. I will lay the Merkid waste for their wrongdoing. I will rescue his wife, quench his thirst for vengeance, and thereby merit recompense. The three Merkid chiefs are cowards – one jumps if the sweat flap of his saddle slaps his horse; the other takes to his heels if he sees more than three quivers uncapped; the third trembles if a bush so much as rustles. Before the sedge is high in the marshes, we will be on the march. On the first day after the third white moon let him and the Kereyid king be waiting at the foot of the Celestial Mount, in the clearing where as children we saw a wolf and her cubs bring down a roe deer and tear it to pieces.'

As I was gathering up Afraid of Bear's reins and remounting, a man came up, staring at me with interest.

'So, Yesügei's eldest has not wasted away?'

I knew by his shrill voice that this was Kököchü, that eavesdropper crouching outside Jamuka's tent. He carried a shaman's drum and in the depths of his eyes flickered an ironic smile.

'Shaman! Throw another shoulder blade on your fire and you'll see Temüjin's strength. Take care he doesn't launch himself at your throat!'

I made Afraid of Bears rear. His golden mane flared up and, before Kököchü could respond, I urged on my horse towards the ragged clouds fraying in the dusk.

Chapter 15

The Kereyid came by the pass of the Hanging Marshes, their quivers bristling with arrows, the handles of their hatchets slapping against their flanks, their lances cross-hatching the sky and their standards emblazoned with ravens snapping in the wind. The lead horses were caparisoned with dark leather and their columns stretched out like long strings of beads against the snow. But no matter how many times Temüjin counted, he could still only see two thousand men, five times less than expected. To'oril explained himself by saying that the Naiman, neighbours to his lands, had become bolder by the day. 'I am lucky to have been able to bring this detachment,' he added, slapping Qasar hard on the shoulder. 'But I was determined to help my *anda* Yesügei's sons in person.'

With these words, he established his *ordo* close to our camp. Temüjin and I, meanwhile, had managed to gather three hundred fighters, mostly Arulat Mongols, simple shepherds of my tribe. With their patched, reversed furs, their threadbare caps that reached to the nape, and their humble panoply of arrows, axes and short sabres, they had none of the orderliness of To'oril's battalions. But the eyes of these three hundred men were steadfast, determined and loyal. Whether Arulat, Borjigin or Suldus, they were above all Mongols, hungry for riches and a new leader. I could not wait to see them loping into battle at the side of Jamuka's warriors and To'oril's Kereyids. However, the Kereyid king thought that we would be outnumbered by the Merkid.

'My men are easily equal to those you have left behind,' said Temüjin.

'When I knew your father,' replied To'oril, 'he commanded more warriors than I ever have. Where are they? Do the Mongols hibernate like marmots? Let us go to their burrows to test their loyalty.'

The next day we scoured the country to enlist other men. But it turned out that To'oril preferred hunting, eating, drinking, playing and teasing any women he met to the business of enlistment, and although a further three hundred men joined our columns, we reached the meeting place three days late.

Jamuka's eyes flashed as he sat astride his black charger. Ten thousand warriors were drawn up in battalions at his back.

'I thought nothing was allowed to delay us,' he said, holding his horse harshly on its hocks. 'Had we not agreed to banish from our ranks anyone whose word was not to be trusted?' He stared fiercely at Temüjin.

To'oril spoke: 'You are right, young Jamuka. Blame me. Your patience deserves reparation.'

'Temüjin will know how to make amends when the time comes. But let's go now, we have wasted enough time on idle talk.' He struck the hindquarters of his horse which bounded forward. We followed at his heels and the troops swung into motion, their step in time with the muffled drums.

Of the three great Merkid tribes, our attack was to be directed against chief Tokto'a's. As Mother Hö'elün had been kidnapped from one of his relatives, it was most likely that he was holding Börte captive. The journey had been difficult – sheer ascents, precipices, steep-walled valleys, seething rapids. But after two weeks' march, we made our way under the cover of the forest to encircle our prey, and sent out scouts. One of them was caught by sable-trappers, but the others returned as the light was fading. We gave the order to attack immediately so that the advantage of surprise would be ours.

The Merkids' defences were so unprepared that we breached them in no time. Heads rolled like falling hailstones and soon their camp offered nothing to our swords but women and children. Our attack moved up the valley and not a single *ayil*, whether of three or a hundred tents, escaped our arrows.

Qasar and I were at the head of two hundred horsemen, and he always led the charge. The fervour with which he slashed, sabred and ran the enemy through spurred on our men. Hooves and blades clashed, arrows whistled, tent frames shattered like splintering bone and nothing but bloody carnage lay in our wake. Night was about to fall and the fighting died down. But none of us was sated. I felt a strange pleasure hewing into Merkid flesh. They may be reputed good archers, but their thick furs make them stiff and awkward – easy victims. If my blade became embedded, hitting but not slicing through the bone, my shoulder shuddered in protest. But when the thrust was true I felt pure elation – the body fell away, split in two, trembling, convulsing, gurgling, sometimes even with the sound of a death rattle as its spirit flew into my arm as fast as the wind.

To'oril and Jamuka's elite pushed on ahead and we followed their progress by the fires blazing up over most of the valley floor. They left few men for us to kill. If we happened to find one, it was most often the sullen silhouette of an old man creeping away, stupefied amongst the crackling flames. An arrow would have been enough, but we could not resist our desire for swordplay.

Finally I caught sight of a group of runaways trying to reach the crest of a hill, whipping up a pair of yaks. I pulled around my horse instantly, his coat pink with foam and blood. When they saw me, the women leapt down from the cart and scattered, screaming and dragging the old men and children after them. Only one remained standing on the yoking. She faced me, proud and beautiful amidst the turmoil. My whirling sabre did not alarm her. She stared at me unblinking and when I recognised her, I pulled up Afraid of Bears so brutally that I was almost unhorsed. It was Börte.

I gave her my hand.

'Where is Temüjin?'

'Further down. Come.'

'No,' she said, recoiling. 'I want him to find me. Go, tell him.'

I seized hold of her, lifted her off the cart and carried her away. Temüjin was pulling one of his arrows out of a Merkid's neck when I called him. He turned, dropped his bow and the furrows of anxiety darkening his brow dissolved. Börte slid to the ground. They ran towards each other and embraced, sniffing the tips of their noses, the folds of their necks, the locks of their hair blowing in the breeze. The crescent moon rose from the forest and hung itself behind their silhouettes as if Tenggeri wanted to crown their reunion with a halo of fine-grained sand.

Qasar and Jelme were instructed to carry a message to To'oril and Jamuka: 'My beloved has returned to my arms. Let us cease the hunt and spend the night in our positions. We will resume battle before sunrise.'

At dawn it was clear To'oril and Jamuka had paid no attention to Temüjin's message. When we caught up with them in the first light, the steppe bore the marks of a night spent settling old scores. Tokto'a's *ulus* had been destroyed. Although they had not been able to find the chief, his brother Darmala was now captive. He confessed that Suchigil was a servant in his tent. His *ulus* was further to the north and Qasar, Belgütei, Jelme and I set off at the head of a thousand men, with Darmala tied by his wrists to two horses. By the time we reached his camp his knees had been crushed to a pulp. After we had slain or routed the inhabitants, he pointed to Suchigil's sleeping place, a heap of old clothes on the edge of a wood.

Belgütei was making his way there when his mother, deathly pale and emaciated and dressed in rags, leapt out of her wretched shelter.

'Don't come near me!' she cried. 'Keeper of horses, who couldn't find one for me.'

Vermin had eaten away her scalp and her few remaining strands of hair hung sadly on either side of her face, bringing out even more the crazed look in her eyes.

'You think yourself a nobleman, but it is by your hand that the Merkid have dishonoured me. Go away from here!'

She ran towards the forest, her son after her, but then turned suddenly, tore at her rags and screamed, 'Look at the body of the woman who carried you, look at these breasts like a battered sow's udders that once fed you, look at this rump exhausted from so much abuse.'

She bent over, pulled up her clothes to show us her behind, that secret part that if sighted brings great misfortune. We looked away, giving Suchigil the chance to flee.

Belgütei scoured the forests and tramped the hills for days on end, but could not find his mother. At last she was discovered at the foot of a cliff, damned for all eternity by Heaven, which does not permit anyone to take their own life; she was broken into pieces, her flesh black and hard as stone, an army of woodlice burrowing clean through her corpse.

Her son gave orders for Merkid prisoners to be brought to him, mostly women and old men. He chose the youngest and most beautiful girls, raped them, then buried his sword in their hearts. As Belgütei went on this savage rampage, Darmala grimaced, not at his clansfolk's lamentable fate but because, as he hung by his feet, his purplish skull was bloating like the stomach of a drowned sheep. When he had ceased to be anything but a foul, shapeless mass of contusions, Belgütei slit his throat. The Merkid chief's blood rushed out like a river breaching its dam.

Our raid may not have snared Tokto'a, but his other brothers, Red Head and Spirit Rabbit, did not escape Jamuka's net.

Spirit Rabbit, a great strapping fellow, threw himself at Temüjin's feet, wailing like a woman, 'Forgive me my wrong-doing, Yesügei's son. Forgive one who, weary of feeding on scraps, wished to taste the flesh of swans, of white geese and the blue-bellied turtle dove. Like the boar I spread myself on your noble wife, but I did not hurt her. These hands have caressed your sweetheart's down. Here,' he said, holding them out, 'they are yours.'

Temüjin slit his throat. His head rolled to the ground, the trunk of his body twitching until Temüjin kicked it over with the tip of his boot. King To'oril meanwhile had asked that an old acquaintance, be left to him – Red Head that same blotchy, shaven-skulled Merkid who had enslaved him and taken his daughter.

After tying him spreadeagled to the ground, To'oril said, 'The difference between us is that you regret not killing me when you could, whereas I always dreamed of watching you rot like a fruit, and now I can. Do you know where the rot sets in on a fruit?'

The red-faced chief said nothing, too busy following the long dagger in To'oril's hand. The glinting edge of the blade was so sharp one could imagine the patient grinding that had been needed in order to fashion it.

The Kereyid king tore down Red Head's trousers, seized his parts, and cried out, 'The stalk!' Then he cut them off and jammed them down his throat.

He took his time dying, so To'oril dragged him behind his horse.

We tallied up the spoils. As we left the battlefield, the slopes grew black with waggons, herds and the conquered bent under the weight of their burdens. I let Afraid of Bears graze on one of the promontories surrounding the great valley so that I could watch the spectacle.

I was enchanted by the piercing uproar composed of the plaintive creak of waggons with stray wheels buckling and loads crashing to the ground; the crack of lashes on oxen's meaty rumps; horsemen galloping back and forth amongst the columns; children weeping, mothers boxing ears, ewes bleating and camels roaring their fury at being girthed so tight under their loads.

I could not help but relive the memory of our charge, the first shock, the flash of sabres in the fading light, the whistling arrows, the terror in our enemies' eyes as we cut into their midst.

Temüjin vainly tried to hide his contentment behind a mask of impassivity, but magnified by victory, he was as euphoric as I was. After making sacrifices to Tenggeri and our glorious ancestors, he had thanked To'oril and Jamuka, the first for being true to his word, the second for acting like a sworn ally, and then added, 'Heaven chose you to come to my aid. It sent us its strength and opened the abyss under the Merkids' feet. Their livers are torn out, their beds empty, their bloodlines at an end. Let us distribute the prisoners and return to our own lands.'

The greatest share of the spoils went to Jamuka, who was sure to compensate himself for our delay. However, To'oril still had reason to be satisfied and he left us, light-hearted and laughing loudly.

Jamuka asked Temüjin to set up camp with him. 'We will share everything, just as when we were children.'

Chapter 16

It was one moon after our victory that Temüjin pitched his yurt next to Jamuka's on the steppe of the Spreading Tree. His decision may have made us safe from the Sovereigns, but it held little appeal for me. Jamuka's overbearing arrogance did not inspire trust. From the moment we arrived he made plain his desire that he and Temüjin should become blood brothers to strengthen the ties formed in childhood.

'Our two lives will then be as one,' he said, his glance to me full of contempt as if I was a pile of dung.

Sensing my resentment, Temüjin confided to me that he was wary of the Chief of the Solitaries' desires. Not content to have been sheltered by Yesügei, the orphan Jamuka had done everything to be treated as the eldest son, creating a constant rivalry, which luckily had not influenced the adults. He still dreamt of inheriting a share of Yesügei's authority.

'When my father died, Jamuka could have established himself as his legitimate son if he had stayed in our tent, and then he would have been my brother. But he leapt onto another perch – he took advantage of the Sovereigns' departure and the clans' discord to set up his own *ulus*. I don't know how he managed it, but I will find out, you can be sure of that.'

My *anda* also explained why it was necessary for him and his family to join Jamuka's camp. Great changes were afoot on the steppe. Once again the Mongols wanted a khan to unite their tribes and he needed to have access to the assemblies where the noblemen drew up their plans of conquest.

'Aren't you afraid that being at his side will put you under an obligation? That your hands will be tied and he'll force his will on you?'

'He may have guessed that I thirst for vengeance, but he can never know how hard that thirst will be to slake. Besides, my friend, he would never have forgiven me refusing his invitation. It would have meant the death of us all.'

I did not doubt his words, but I was only partly reassured.

The Spreading Tree was a great, flame-red pine rising haughtily above an ocean of grass. Fiery branches supported fiery branches and it seemed to embrace the whole landscape. It should not have been possible for it to grow, let alone survive in that spot, but the elders said that it did so because it was the vessel of the winds. Like the birds in its thriving crown the horses vied for a place in its shade, but never rubbed against it in case they damaged its bark.

'Ambakai's spirit resides here,' Jamuka declared shamelessly, as if the spirit belonged to him. 'This was where the last, great *quriltai* which elected Kutula supreme leader of the Mongols was held. Let us mingle our blood before this sacred tree, Temüjin, then nothing and no one will be able to part us.'

The young grass rippled gently, flushing pink in the setting sun. Temüjin absentmindedly stroked the hairs of his goatee beard between his thumb and forefinger, but in the fire of his slit eyes I saw an extraordinary sight – birds, stones, horses, wolves emerging from the Spreading Tree and sliding the length of its trunk. When they assumed human form, I knew them to be our ancestors. They retrieved their armour, their faces rubbed with blood, their eyes wild. A blazing sky at their back, smiles needle-sharp like fangs, they gathered together in Temüjin's gaze.

'Kutula was my father's uncle,' Temüjin reminded him. 'He was a good khan. I like this place.'

So, at the foot of the Spreading Tree, they cut each other's arms and drank from each other's veins. Jamuka gave Temüjin a horse with a coat like goatskin and a calloused brow. Temüjin gave Jamuka a yellow-dun, black-maned stallion which had been part of his share of the Merkid spoils. A white mare was sacrificed to the ancestors and impaled by the tree, while plenty of sheep were set aside for the banquet.

The foaling season came and the earth received its share of the year's first milk.

Temüjin and Jamuka never left each other's side. They ate and drank together, danced, laughed, wrestled, and hunted together, feasted often and even shared the same couch in Temüjin's yurt.

As for me, my spirit rode through the clouds to Queen of

Flowers' tent. I dreamed of her. Everywhere. Every moment. I longed to hold her in my arms, especially now Gerelma was colder and harder than a stone to me. 'Give me a son,' she would say with bitter reproach when she wished us to couple. She never came to find me in the hills to show her desire like so many of the other wives, not once did she hold out her arms to me. It always happened in the yurt, in darkness. I felt no passion, yet the thought of Queen of Flowers sharing my couch supplied my ardour. But, try as I might, her belly would not swell. Full of treachery, she mocked me, saying a healthy Mongol was no match for a Kereyid, not even a mutilated one. Again and again she said that a woman without sons grows stooped and has to wait in line to fill her pails at the river.

Was I sterile, cursed by some evil spirit, or banished by the daughter of the Forest Spirit? Was she jealous of the dreams I now dreamed? When doubts overwhelmed me, I clung to Afraid of Bears' mane and we escaped to Queen of Flowers' valley and its echoing laughter. The journey took several days' hard trot, but the sky was always cloudless, and the nights full of stars, speeding us on to our hearts' destination. Afraid of Bears cut through the grass like a sabre through flesh, straining at the bit and, to show his joy, playfully lashing out and swaying his rump, the wind ruffling his mane and tail.

Queen of Flowers' little camp was where we both felt happiest. The children ran to greet us, shouting gleefully, and on the thresholds their parents broke into dazzling smiles. Only the stallion of the herd snorted with displeasure at the sight of Afraid of Bears.

From the moment I arrived, I would work constantly, helping until nightfall. Then on the second day, Queen of Flowers' father would ask me to sit with him in his yurt. We would stay there musing a long while, under the hung venison and its whirl of flies, drinking cold milk and warm alcohol in turn and winking to each other – our substitute for conversation. Finally, when he saw the flock of sheep framed in the door, he would say to me, 'If she lets them graze there any longer, they'll be eating mud.'

'Isn't the grass on the mountain better?'

'Yes, it is excellent . . . and so high.'

That was our signal for me to be able to join Queen of Flowers.

'Shall I take the calves?'

'Yes, otherwise they will low for their mothers.'

Then I would go to my ray of sunshine and we would climb the slopes, our hearts beating, our ears ringing with the bleating of ewes and goats.

One of those days when we were lying high up there in the flowers talking, we heard neighing. I recognised it immediately – it was Afraid of Bears. He was climbing the slope rubbing his jaw against White Moon's flank. Their tails were switching against their hocks in excitement and happiness at knowing that they had defied the law of the herd, a wonderful fit of madness they intended to take full advantage of. They grazed near us for a moment, making eyes at each other and Afraid of Bears steered his beauty to where the grass was sweetest, giving great sighs of contentment.

As the sun moved across the sky, their silhouettes receded further and further, but lying amongst the crocuses, buttercups and scorpion grass, I quickly lost interest. Queen of Flowers let me close to inhale her perfumes. My mouth gathered the honey from her nape and the tips of her collarbone, which fluttered in the shade of her clothes like twin doves. She smelled deliciously of pine, moss and ewe's milk, and the taste of her skin made me dizzy.

Realising we could no longer see our horses, she took my hand and led me higher. In a ravine I found a flattened horse's hoof. It was the colour of dried cheese and still contained the first toe bone. Perhaps it had been a chestnut's with a pure white stocking. I gave it to Queen of Flowers, saying it was a sign that Afraid of Bears and White Moon's conspiracy would result in the birth of a colt as white as snow. She tucked it into the opening of her *del*, reminding me with an amused smile that her mare was barren.

'The moon is also said to be barren,' I replied. 'So many stars have dashed themselves against her. And yet each evening she climbs the sky, speeds through the night and hastens to let the sun illuminate her with his light. And when her round face is hidden by her lover's hair, she blesses us with her fertility. Colts are born, the grass springs up and the lambs rise to their woolly feet in the dew. You will see, White Moon has found her sun and he will cover her with his rays.'

Their silhouettes reappeared on the peaks, very small. They gazed into the distance for a moment and then disappeared into the last of the sunlight. The air was warm, heralding a beautiful night.

'We can't go down without our horses.'

'That suits you very well,' she said, poking me in the ribs.

'Only because you are with me.'

'Then let's return to my father's tent.'

'Why disturb him? He can find you if he needs you.'

She pinched my lips affectionately, saying that I was more brazen than a cuckoo.

I led her under the shelter of a copse where we lay down again on the grass dotted with orange poppies and, holding hands, gazed at the sky.

As the stars came out, an owl alighted on a branch and tore into the evening's first field mouse. I held Queen of Flowers. She trembled, pale and luminous. I undid my *del* and partly opened hers, letting my lips glide lazily over her eyebrows, her forehead, her eyelids, the wings of her nose. I drew breath, captivated by her adorable face, her throat, her shoulders emerging from her pool of hair. Her fingers fluttered on my chest and her lips formed a silent phrase.

'I love you too,' I whispered.

My hand ventured to her stomach, then along her hip. A newborn's skin could not have been softer. A whinny sounded out of the darkness, from high up the mountain.

'Our horses! I want so passionately to do as I know they are. Be the mother of my first child.'

'Oh, Bo'urchu, my radiant Bo'urchu,' she said, clasping me, 'it cannot be. Not yet, not yet.'

'Why not?'

'Because of . . . Gerelma.' She pressed her mouth against my neck and bit it.

'But she is nothing to me! I loathe her as much as she hates me.'

'I know,' she said, putting her fingers to my lips. 'So you must part from her and return her to the Kereyid or give her to your *anda*. The wolf always drives away the jackal. You are the man I hoped for, as gentle on my skin as the tread of your horse on the steppe. I would love to be your wife and perhaps I would agree to you having others, but I will never be the one that sleeps on your threshold. I will only be your favourite. When that day comes, my womb will bear your children.'

I picked her up, carried her down the slope, and under the starry vault we slid to the ground as I removed her *del*. Embracing, mouth to mouth, we tumbled over like children,

Queen of Flowers asking me, 'Will you do it? Tell me! Will you do it?'

'Yes, I will do it. Without children a man is a desert.'

There was one worry. Could Queen of Flowers give me this child? Was I not to blame for Gerelma's empty womb? Was it not my scrotum that was arid? I spoke my concerns.

Queen of Flowers reassured me, 'How can you doubt yourself when you are so convinced of your horse? If his seed takes root in her, then yours will bud in me.'

We were soaked with dew and I licked its beads from her face.

The marmot's burrow stirred with life in the first rays of sunshine, but its occupant had no time to give its morning greeting. The smooth stones I had heated were burning hot and I crammed its entrails up to its face. As it cooked, Queen of Flowers looked at the valleys in the distance, pensive, hugging her knees to her chest. I contemplated her. More still, I devoured her as, sitting facing each other, we feasted on the marmot's fragrant, tender flesh. She blushed when her *del* slipped from her shoulders. And that pleased me. Just before the sun reached its peak, Afraid of Bears and White Moon came down from the mountain, backs bowed with exhaustion. They grazed below us, breaking off to exchange looks, sniff or rub against each other. Their coats shone so brightly one could have seen one's face in them and in their eyes there was such joy, gleaming like silver, that it was as if they had drunk the moon's reflection from every stream.

Chapter 17

The news of our victory over the Merkids caused a great stir. Spread abroad by bards, shepherds and warriors, Jamuka's and Temüjin's exploits were sung throughout the land, and in the passing the story swelled and twisted into different forms. One rumour had it that the two orphans had suckled at the same breast, although that could not have been, Jamuka being already ten springs old when Yesügei and Mother Hö'elün adopted him.

Little credit was given to To'oril and his Kereyid, something of which Temüjin and Jamuka cannot have been entirely innocent, since their main concern was to spread the news of their feats of arms and alliance so as to muster the greatest number of men. This they managed without difficulty. Day after day fresh domes joined our number. Families came with their arms and livestock from all around to swell and strengthen the *ulus*.

Talking to the new herdsmen and sentries I began to realise the extent of my *anda*'s renown, with most claiming they had come over because of Temüjin, the dispossessed, not Jamuka, the prosperous. Yesügei's eldest son had been abandoned, he had been stripped of all he possessed, he had been hunted down, and yet it was this outlaw who had defeated the Merkids. He was becoming the chief most likely to revive the Mongols' power. That his lineage was nobler than Jamuka's had certainly played a part, but the force of will and the powers of persuasion he had revealed in recovering his wife were what had decided it for these Mongols. The woman is the keeper of the hearth, man's counterpoise, the radiance of the yurt, the elders had said. By snatching Börte away from the enemy's grasp, Temüjin had proved that he would not only protect but enrich any who placed themselves under his standard.

Squatting around the fire, the shepherds described Temüjin's eyes – they were those of a big cat or a wolf, but greater still and more terrifying; undoubtedly the mark of Tenggeri. Moreover, didn't the events of Temüjin's life, from his birth holding a clot of blood in his fist to the recovery of his wife, bear witness to Heaven's favour? Who could doubt it, when he had overcome so many perils? 'He will avenge his father and our ancestors,' the voices had said, 'and he will drive the Tatars from the great steppe. Those plunderers and their table companions, the Chin, had better be on their guard.'

Weapons were polished and although nine white tails still flapped gently on the Borjigin standard, the loyal Jelme was beginning to plait black ones, a sign that battle would soon resume.

Temüjin's renown made me proud, but it also distanced me from him. I would have liked to tell him my joy at everything I heard but with Jamuka always at his side, he was becoming unapproachable. The Solitaries chief never went anywhere without his shaman, Kököchü, who in turn was always accompanied by his six brothers. These eight clung to Temüjin like ticks to a horse's neck.

My lack of affection for the arrogant Jamuka was nothing compared with my hatred for his shaman. Affected, conceited and scornful, he was credited with great powers and therefore revered and feared in equal measure, and it annoyed me that even Temüjin treated him as someone of importance; it was as if he was indebted to him in some way.

The days were growing shorter and still there had been no chance to discuss my constant disappearances and the fact that Queen of Flowers was as essential as Gerelma was unbearable.

I now no longer even touched my wife. One evening when I had spurned her, she flew into a rage. I threw a blanket over her head and left. The night was thick and heavy. Afraid of Bears was grazing. He stared, astonished that I was naked. I raised my hands to his jaw and pulled his nose to my chest. Suddenly a tiny, cool wing fluttered against the small of my back. It was Temulun. 'What are you doing here?" I asked. 'You should be asleep.'

'Not when you are with us,' she said with an affectionate, mischievous smile.

'Why is that?'

'I want to be near to you. I heard everything. Get rid of her!'

'Quiet. What would Temüjin say if he knew his baby sister listens outside yurts?'

'Nothing, because I am to be your wife and so I am watching over you.'

I pushed away her small hand which was by now stroking my buttocks. 'Enough! Go, quickly!'

'Shhh! Listen to me. Your arms were not meant for her. Tell Temüjin it is me you want to marry and we will be rid of Gerelma.'

'You must stop this. You are only twelve springs old . . .'

'So? Temüjin already has plans to marry me to a prince to strengthen his alliances.'

'That is beside the point.'

'Mother Hö'elün says that now I am ready to have a child.'

'The young warriors who follow you everywhere obviously agree.'

'They're silly. Only you interest me.'

'Listen, Temulun, there is something you should know . . . No, go, come on, go now.'

'What, what should I know, Bo'urchu?'

'Nothing, go!'

She took a few steps, before turning to me.

'Do you love another? Is that it? I am not blind. You haven't touched your slaves yet.'

She meant the two Merkid women Temüjin had given me and it was true what she said, the adorable leech. I had not lifted the hem of their *dels*, although they were desirable, especially the one whose ample breasts seemed to clothe the rest of her; because, although far away, it was Queen of Flowers who, claimed all my attention, a fact that made me wildly happy.

'Do you love her very much?'

I almost answered yes, more even than my horse. The darkness prevented me seeing her clearly, but I could make out two fat tears falling from the corners of her eyes. I did not have time to take a step before she disappeared into the night.

The next day I went to find Temüjin. He was holding council with Qasar, Belgütei, Qachi'un, Temüge, the inseparable Jamuka and Kököchü and the latter's swarm of brothers. He invited me to sit at his right. I declined, requesting an audience in private.

'You are free to speak here,' said Jamuka. 'My *anda* and I have no secrets between us.'

'This matter does not concern you.'

'But we would like it to, and we would like to hear you speak here more often,' Kököchü interrupted. 'Your name, the Path-finder, is a shaman's name. What matters is not why you refused this divine office, but that when the clans rally, there should be more Arulat amongst our warriors.'

'Do not worry on that score, shaman. On the day of battle, when the drums sound the attack, I will be there to shield my *anda*, stouter than a bulwark and all the assembled Arulat.'

I left, telling Temüjin that he would find me with Börte, as Jamuka complained that he was shown less respect than a stranger.

Wreathed in steam, ladle in hand, Börte was stirring the milk in the great cooking pot. She greeted me cheerfully and brought me a bowl of milk and a platter of dried cheese. I studied her as I sipped the hot liquid. Oiled, perfumed and impeccably braided, her plaits had grown long, but her wild, shy features, dominated by her panther's eyes, had lost none of their freshness. And yet something about her shape had changed since her return. It was more rounded, even more alluring, and her ruddy cheeks shone like two ripe fruits. When I saw the care she took crouching down and standing up, I understood. Her womb was full. This swell enchanted me, but I was careful not to ask her any questions lest they attracted the attention of the spirits that prey on vulnerable souls.

She asked after Gerelma.

'She lashes out over nothing, like a barren mare.'

'But you know that if a stallion neglects his mares in summer, they will be thin in the belly and full of bitterness when he returns in autumn.'

Stung by the allusion, I did not reply. Eventually Temüjin appeared, hung up his whip and sat down beside me.

'Jamuka and Kököchü annoy you, don't they?' he said, picking up the bowl that had been placed in front of him.

'You're like a dog, the way you trot at their heels.'

'I knew Kököchü when he was a child. He is the grandson of Charaqa, the brave shaman who was killed by Targutai when the Sovereigns abandoned us.'

'So why didn't he stay?'

'His father Münglig was afraid and moved their tents to join the Solitaries. A good shaman, but it is Kököchü, his eldest son, who is the greatest of all. He can raise the blackest storms and cause snow to fall in summer. I have seen him mate with the earth, and where he buried his seed, a birch sprang up next season. I can take you there; the tree's vigour is matchless. It stands alone on top of a hill, no other tree or rock in sight, on top of a hill, yet lightning never strikes it. Kököchü's power is great. Look how Jamuka has benefited from it. He rides at the head of twenty thousand warriors.'

'Some of whom used to fight under your father's banner.'

'True. And some have now sworn allegiance to me. They use their ears to keep me informed.'

'So, do you still need to bow your head before Jamuka and his shaman and let them always be between us?'

'Yes. Until I have united the Borjigin I need them. Be patient, my friend.'

'What about To'oril?'

'Involving the Kereyid in our quarrels would only cause more division. The alliances of the Mongol tribes are not his business.'

'So will you then agree to me separating from Gerelma?'

'What are you saying, Bo'urchu? That is quite another matter. What is happening between you two? You should know that she has come to complain about you.'

'And I have had enough of her. So let's be done with it!'

'Do not even think of breaking that bond,' he burst out virulently. 'To'oril gathered together his warriors for me, he offered his nieces to you, my brothers – and you would now have me be an accomplice in your betrayal? Did we not swear to protect our shared interests?'

When I did not reply, he put his hand on my arm.

'Do you want another woman? Chose the most beautiful of my Merkid slaves.'

'No. I have not even looked at those you have already given me.'

He was aghast. If I had told him that I had ridden Afraid of Bears into the ground, he could not have been more shocked.

'That is no way for a warrior to behave! Go and see the shaman, he knows how to restore a man's potency.'

'I have no need for his plants, his potions of rutting stags' urine and white dogs' droppings! I am haunted by a woman! There, the truth! I am as taut as a bow, my head swims, I am dizzy and Gerelma is at my back, turning my heart black.'

His face darkened. 'I warn you, I cannot dispense with a single ally. Leave them be and make pregnant any of your women you choose, but make them pregnant, because there is nothing more full of bile than the liver of a childless woman.'

The felt door flap pushed back and Jamuka appeared.

'Very true,' he said.

'I did not know you were a father,' I said, getting to my feet.

'My sons will not be long in coming,' he replied, sneaking a glance at Börte.

Eyes to the ground, Temüjin said nothing. I went out.

Behind me Jamuka called out, his tone ironic, 'You're supposed to be the pathfinder, but you don't seem able to find the path that leads to a woman's womb. Invite me under your roof and I will show you.'

Chapter 18

A sure measure of the cold and its ravages is the crows' death toll. Well, that winter the ground was littered with the frozen corpses of those hardy birds, and we suffered our share of many losses as well. None of our herds were spared and the wolves roamed near our camps. Temüjin and Jamuka often went on great hunts, but I preferred to go alone into the icy silence of the forests, until one day Börte's waters broke.

My *anda*'s wife gave birth to a vigorous son.

Swaddled in lambskins and belted with a fox-skin, the tutelary animal of newborns, the child was alert and quiet. From the moment he woke, he would silently and calmly watch the comings and goings until Börte unbuttoned her *del* and took her to him. The weaned lamb they were rearing in their yurt bleated more importunately. I had added a little bow, three round-tipped arrows and a golden lock of Afraid of Bears' hair to the charms that dangled above the baby, tied to a cord attached to the roof poles. A fox's paw, a feather, a claw ... venerable, diverting or protective objects.

I spent much of that winter contemplating him, bent over his face like the sleeping moon. I could stay staring for a whole feed, hypnotised by his mother's starlit hand supporting his head, my spirit soothed. But, in order to deceive the malevolent spirits, I'd be careful not to appear to congratulate Börte. I'd speak of her son in the harshest, most contradictory language, saying that a fouler grub had never been seen, and she would reply that her Ugly Duckling was indeed loathsome, all her pride clear in the tender smile playing about her lips.

Then Mother Earth sucked up the snow as if she was dying of thirst. I saddled Afraid of Bears and returned to the Pass of the Ash-Grey Birches, Queen of Flowers' family's wintering place. And at each visit I would stay a little longer.

Her rounded shoulders, white in the moonlight, her shivers in the chill of dawn, her lustrous hair running between my fingers, the scent of honeysuckle when she moved, her fits of anger when her throat quivered like a roe deer flushed from cover – everything about her overwhelmed me and sometimes, like a fruit gorged on sunshine that splits open in the heat, I would overflow, too happy even to speak. I could not sleep when I lay down with her brothers and her fathers, as agitated as a worm on hot coals from knowing her so close, just separated by two felt curtains. How many times on those nights did I roll over, imagining myself creeping like a dog to her couch to intoxicate myself with her breathing? When dawn turned the inside of the yurt blue, I would hear her get up and fasten her belt, and I would wait, my heart beating, for her to kindle the fire in our part of the yurt. Moments later she would be there, kneeling down, her beautiful oval changing from blue to amber as she struck the flint. She would linger over the embers and I would devour her with my eyes until she raised hers to mine. Then she would lower them instantly with a faint smile of amusement and embarrassment. I would get up and follow her outside. There she would stop and turn and smile full at me, her face pale apart from a pink flush on each cheek, before carrying on to the stream to fetch water, the white steam of her breath circling about her hair.

It was on one of those mornings that she took me upstream to see White Moon, and, stopping a little before the place, her eyes alight with excitement, told me to go and find her. As I approached the mare, I saw that her tail and hocks were spattered and that she seemed exhausted. Then, immediately, I saw the one whose arrival we had been expecting so impatiently lying a few paces away, his head nodding. A colt the colour of happiness, white as a swan. He was catching his breath, his limbs folded under him, slightly dazed and twitching occasionally from the cold.

Coming up behind me, Queen of Flowers laced her hands round my waist and pressed her face into my plaits, whispering, 'He is yours.' My head swam. I shut my eyes and when I opened them, I spotted Afraid Of Bears on the top of a hill, his mane and tail raised, his silhouette merging into the transparent glow of the rising sun. He was watching over his family.

The colt had strong withers, fearless eyes and four black hooves. He had one other distinctive feature: a tawny patch on his left shoulder. As his mother licked his hindquarters, he unfolded his forelegs, spread them out and waited for a moment. Then he jerked out his neck, half-straightened his forequarters, drummed his hooves on the ground, tottered and quickly hauled himself upright. Carried forward by the momentum, he toppled over and rolled in the grass.

Straightaway he tried again, struggling valiantly on his trembling legs and this time managed to stand and proudly steady himself, his ears bolt upright as if they were a part of the distant, glittering cloud.

Queen of Flowers nibbled the nape of my neck and murmured, 'Meet White Cloud.'

Sometimes we slept in a hollow on the slopes or by a tree, curled up under a bearskin blanket, our breath playing on our faces.

One night when the stinging, glacial rain eased, Queen of Flowers stroked my cheek and stood up. I brought our boots and slippers under cover and when I looked again, she was naked, rising from the pool of her clothes, head thrown back and arms outspread, offering herself to a thousand crystal kisses. She slowly spun around, her long hair plastered to her body like black foliage. Dazzled by her divine impulse, I did not dare move. She came towards me and, defying the taboo, straddled me. She took the nape of my neck and drew me towards her thighs and her delicately displayed silken bush. I gripped her calves. They were firm, icy. The rain ran down her body and met at the porcelain cleft. I drank straight from this lubricious stream, fragrant like no other spring. There was a gust of wind; she pressed me harder to her and moaned softly, her body jerking and shuddering.

I knew from having discussed it with them that Queen of Flowers' brothers wanted to join Temüjin's camp. But every time I raised the idea, she opposed it stoutly. 'Throw Gerelma out of your bed and then we will fold our tents. What are you waiting for?'

I tried to justify myself, speaking of the danger to Temüjin if the Kereyid king turned his back on him, but she remained adamant.

'Who do you want to marry, Temüjin or me?'

She flicked milk at my woebegone face and warned me: 'Otherwise we will never go further than that night in the rain.'

This cost her as much as me, because that wonderful,

audacious night, after I had slaked of my thirst at her rift, she had taken my taut bow in her hands and kissed it, sobbing.

At least I liked to think it would be painful for her, because she added, threateningly, her shoulders dropping, which, for her, was the equivalent of a sigh, 'And we will surely never start again.'

A full cycle of twelve moons had passed since we had joined Jamuka. It was the moon of the Cuckoo's Dance, when the steppe put on its coat of flowers and Temüjin and I, another spring older, had now seen twenty.

I was in front of my yurt, contemplating the beauty of the horizon, as Gerelma busied herself inside. My mind was on the tiger, whose year it was. I had never seen one, but my father had and his description still set my thoughts racing.

The more I imagined him, the more I wanted to hunt him, track him until I was breathless, catch the scent of his urine, spot his fur snagged on the dry moss, mark his acrobat's progess, discover his lookout posts. With his paws like felt, his rough nose, his deceptive markings, the tiger pads his vast domain with an infinite softness, as meticulous as a maze-builder. His lightning springs are saved for the kill. Of all the big cats, he is the quickest and the cleverest. Next to him the lion appears a clumsy, hulking lout and wretched tactician. Unlike the wolves who hunt in packs, the tiger is a loner. Stealing up on his prey, he rolls in their dung to mask his scent and my father had told me that even standing in his fresh tracks and hearing his snarl is no guarantee that you will see him. He vanishes into the background. He mesmerises his victims, numbs their reflexes, crushes their will. With one swipe of his paw, he can kill a horse and drag it into his jaws. Like a cloud in the sky, he moves without a sound and after nightfall, his flashing eyes witness murder and lovemaking of every kind.

I saw myself skinning that princely fur to drape it over Queen of Flowers' shoulders, when Gerelma's voice cut short my reverie.

'Are you deaf?'

'I was thinking about the coming hunt,' I said, stretching.

'Your tongue lies. You were thinking of leaving again.'

'Yes. And for a long time.'

'You are going nowhere until I have a son.'

'Nothing blooms without love.'

'Stay, let's try and make one,' she grabbed my sleeve, suddenly begging. 'The moon is round and rising. Kököchü has promised that tonight you will make me with child.'

I shook myself free. 'So, you blow your nose on the shaman's clothes as well?'

'Be warned, Bo'urchu; he has told me that if a Mongol neglects his wife, she can take another husband.'

'So what are you waiting for?'

'Look at yourself, with your dumb expression like a dog mooning over his mate. I'm not a mole; I see your eyes when you come back to me, they're dull as a castrated bull's. Your balls are rubbing up against some bitch's arse. Your ears are full of her moans and the stench of her vulva reaches to here.'

I left her still venting her spleen and went to find Afraid of Bears before fog covered the plain.

'Go on, try to leave, you might find it a slow business,' Gerelma threatened as I walked away.

I met some watchmen returning to camp in silence who had seen my horse earlier that day near Temüjin's herd. I sent a herdsman to find him, then went to Qasar's tent where, as ever, friends were congregated, laughing and drinking with abandon. Their good humour was contagious. Metekna was bustling about, her belly rounded, smiling constantly at her husband, who could not resist touching her whenever she came within reach. These two still loved each other as much as the day they met, and attracted swallows and friends to their home.

By the time the herdsman brought back my horse, the night was already well advanced and my head aflame. I asked him to saddle Afraid of Bears because at dawn I planned to ride to Queen of Flowers. Then I went back inside to carry on drinking and singing.

The frost-covered plain crunched under my boots. My head was heavy, I wanted to retch and my legs felt as if they would buckle beneath me. Afraid of Bears was lying down, his golden nostrils pressed to the ground.

I rubbed his jaw, studying him. His eyes were clouded, full of a strange melancholy. 'What is wrong, my friend?'

He whinnied faintly. It was a greeting, but full of affliction. Unable to see any wound, I checked him over. One of the camp guards came to tell me that he had found him like that just before the sky grew light.

'Why didn't you tell me?'

'I tried. Your wife told me not to wait. I offered to look after Afraid of Bears but she said you'd kill me if I dared touch him. I didn't insist.'

His upset seemed sincere. I signalled that he could go.

I tried to lift Afraid of Bears to his feet. It was impossible: his cold, stiff legs did not react. In his eyes I saw White Moon and her colt gambolling in the grass under the benign gaze of Queen of Flowers. Then a sudden, frenzied rage swept over me. I ran back to the yurt and threw myself on Gerelma, lifting her bodily and holding her upside down over the cauldron, ready to plunge her into the boiling milk.

'What have you done? Tell me or I'll kill you!'

'I haven't done anything . . .'

'Who then? Who?'

I plunged her into the scalding liquid for a moment. Her screams alerted the camp. Men threw themselves on me. I split the skull of one and broke the noses of others before I was overpowered and taken to Temüjin. He came out of his tent, quickly followed by Jamuka.

'Release him,' ordered my *anda*. 'What has happened, Bo'urchu?'

'Get them out of here! All of them!'

A look of Temüjin's and everyone was gone, even Jamuka.

After I had explained the reason for my fury, he tried to reassure me. He said that my companion would recover as quickly as he had sickened. He would ask Belgütei, who was without equal in curing horses, to look at him, and if he was confounded, he would call for the shaman. But first of all, he wanted my bad blood with Gerelma to stop.

'Listen, Temüjin. Even with a broken leg, a horse never lies absolutely still. Only an evil spell can turn him to stone. Kököchü is a powerful shaman. Gerelma and he have conspired together to stop me leaving. Don't let them near Afraid of Bears.'

'You may suspect her, but do you have any proof?'

'She knows where my gallops lead. She threatened to hamstring me if I continued to visit Queen of Flowers.'

'Sometimes a threat said in the heat of the moment is enough to unleash evil spirits, but that does not mean a person's prayers have been answered.'

'That viper is gloating. She hates me. Leave her to me, I will make her talk.'

'Impossible. You must think of her as untouchable. In time, she will confide in Börte or Qasar and Belgütei's wives, and then if she is at fault, she will be yours to deal with as you see fit.'

'She will blind you.'

'Enough, Bo'urchu! You are the one who is blind. You have let bitterness dwell in your tent. Before you ran after other women, you should have first made yours pregnant.'

'Her womb is stony and arid.'

'Maybe it is your fruit that is parched? Tell me at least that Queen of Flowers is with child.'

'She will only surrender her maidenhead when Gerelma goes.'

Temüjin made a long face, his slit eyes opened wide. 'You are the leader of the pack, not a wolf cub. Behave as such. Never submit. Master your women, bite them if necessary. Go to her, force her dark lock, spill the blood on the ground and bring her straight back.'

'I did that with Gerelma. Look how she thinks of me now.'

He gestured irritably.

'But there is a difference between your wife and the woman who is driving you mad. If things are not right, you can be rid of her. Gerelma, you cannot. I am watching.'

It was then I realised the gulf that separated Temüjin and me in matters of the heart, and I knew that nothing could bridge it.

'Robbed of Afraid of Bears I am like a bird without its wings. He is still alive and I will not abandon him, even to deflower the one who holds the strings of my heart.'

'I know how loyal you are. It is why you are able to see what is most important to a man, because no woman will ever be worth such a horse.'

The hypocrisy, after all he had done to recover Börte! His words rang hollow, but I made no comment.

Chapter 19

The elders came with their remedies. Afraid of Bears was entitled to all they could offer: plants, bulbs, berries, stones, mud, bark, even quail's gall and the mating crane's droppings. But neither poultices fashioned in the greatest secrecy nor bloodlettings nor powdered volcanic rock had any effect. Day after day, he grew worse. His jaw resting on his forelegs, his eyes were sad like those of a guilty dog begging forgiveness.

His legs swelled, then his guts contracted in violent spasms. I resigned myself to Kököchü's intervention.

The shaman appeared in full regalia, a metal band across his forehead adorned with eagle's feathers and stag's antlers. More magnificent still was the complete hide of an adult stag he wore, hung with the furs of nine scurrying creatures, a squirrel, a marten, a sable, a fox, a polecat, a dormouse, a jerboa and a mongoose, each the finest of its kind and offered by our most skilful hunters.

He approached Afraid of Bears, shaking his costume and its countless metallic pendants, miniature weapons and human and animal figures. His whirling brought no response from my stallion, not even the twitch of an ear. The families pressed closer, holding their breath, watching the shaman beating his drum and jumping from foot to foot. Suddenly he stopped, his elbows spread and eyes open wide, as if the wind had caught him. He rose up among the spirits and mimed the swallow skimming over the grass, the bumblebee's clumsy flight when it is drunk with pollen. Then he speeded up the rhythm of his drumming and the transformation was clear: Kököchü was a stallion. His right hoof pawed the ground, his lips splayed. He rose up as if he was covering a mare and rode his drum, furiously thrusting his pelvis and biting his shoulder as if it was her withers. His face streamed with sweat and whinnying rose from his throat. At last his back arched and he began singing and talking incomprehensibly. Then he was a foaling mare, giving birth in the time it takes an insect to emerge from its chrysalis and dry its wings.

The spirits were speaking when suddenly he began to run in all directions, maul imaginary trees, scrabble in the dirt and rub himself against invisible stumps, growling. His dumbshow was so expressive that we soon recognised the animal. He was playing out the events of Afraid of Bears' life. I recognised the poignant calls of the she-camel separated from her colt, the indecisive, agitated dance of the wolves, the cawing of the crows ... Quicker and quicker the cries and incarnations answered each other until everything merged and it seemed as if the whole forest was competing before us.

The possession reached its climax when, his mouth filled with foam, he screamed like ten men plunged in boiling water. He collapsed, convulsing violently. Everyone rushed forward, the women lamenting that he was lost, but Kököchü rose to his feet and came towards us, burning-eyed.

'The spirit of a she-bear has taken possession of your horse,' he said. 'A long time ago you came between her and her due. Now his time on earth is over and she is come for him.'

'Is this the limit of your powers?' I replied mockingly. 'The spirits are clever; they treat you as a toy. I have heard that the shamans of the Gobi are unrivalled; I will go and find the greatest of them.'

The crowd muttered, indignant.

'I can still save him, but it depends on you.'

'Why would I refuse?'

'Because you have pitted yourself against invisible forces.'

'What bargain are you proposing?'

'The bear's spirit demands compensation, a human soul dear to you.'

'I will sacrifice Gerelma.'

'No, Bo'urchu. The spirit is demanding. In your sleep you call this soul Queen of Flowers.'

My chest heaved. 'Who can vouch that this will appease the spirit?'

'No one. I will have to make haste to fight the demons of the nether world and then perhaps your chestnut horse will recover the use of his legs and his taste for grass.'

It seemed a terrible price to pay. Seeing me hesitate, Kököchü added, 'Do not think too long; the passing of time provokes the spirits. Their anger could sweep away everything, the horse and the woman.'

I spent the night with Afraid of Bears. His breathing had dwindled to a thin, hoarse rasp. Stabbing pains coursed through his body, making his head jerk up abruptly. After a while he grew resigned to the contractions hammering at his ribs and suffered without flinching. We looked at each other and he seemed to be telling me that it was time for him to return. The moon shone at the corner of his eye and suddenly grew fuller, taking on the shape of a tear. My stallion was crying. I took his jaw and drank the salty pearl before it sank into the ground. He blew on my neck to console me, when it should have been me comforting him.

My father had told me that when a horse sits like that, his guts tied in knots, he will never rise again. The moment was near. I beseeched Heaven, 'O Tenggeri! It is I, your son, conceived by Naqu the Arulat and Tana in the moon of the Rutting Stag and born in the moon of the Cuckoo's Dance in the Year of the Horse. O Tenggeri, spare my friend's life . . . You alone can do this . . . '

Dark clouds born of blackest night rose in the sky and veiled the moon. Afraid of Bears shook in terrible spasms. I thought the pain would bring him to his feet, but realised otherwise as his neck fell back on the ground. He was defeated, his eyes haggard and seeping death.

In the early light, I watched for those eyes to gleam again. Browns and bronzes, old gold, the retina's misty blue: all their colours had faded. Only a dull, uniform tint remained, like a grey rock when the clouds block out the sun.

He was in pain and neither of us could endure it any longer. I was going to end his suffering without shedding a drop of his blood, so that his soul could rise free and unharmed into the beyond and never be at the mercy of Kököchii or the spirits down here again.

Gripping him by the neck and the withers, I managed to rock him enough to slide my knees either side of his ribs. Understanding what I intended, he did not resist. With my knife I cut a hole the size of a man's palm in his chest, pushed in my hand and then my arm up to my armpit. My fingers felt around, found the artery and followed it to his still beating heart. Afraid of Bears had seen me cut off a sheep's breathing in this way many times.

He was trusting, perhaps because he knew no death was more peaceful.

Our pulses beat in unison, renewing our pact for one final time. I cut my shoulder. The blood ran into his wound and sealed our brotherhood for eternity. His pungent smell filled my nostrils as I stroked his chest with my other hand.

He twitched. I took it as a sign of encouragement and severed the artery.

The sky was an endless expanse of grey felt.

'O Tenggeri, watch over my friend and preserve him in the blue of your skies.'

He slipped away under my fingers without a tremor.

'My precious steed, the spring is dried up. Now you are a firebird.'

I had squeezed him so hard that pins and needles were shooting through my hand as if someone wanted to strip it to the bone. I slid towards his neck, brushing back his mane and tail. A cold, blue film drew down over his eyeballs. A film that reflected nothing. I set about skinning and gutting him.

Qasar's wife came to help me, bringing two slaves. I sent them away, asking them only to leave their vessels.

When Afraid of Bears was ready, I whittled a stake out of a fence pole, drove it into the Spreading Tree and arranged his skeleton and hide upon it, his forehead raised and facing south, leaping towards the sky. I circled nine times, sprinkling milk and chanting praises and prayers to Tenggeri.

Returning to my yurt, I barred the door with a lance wrapped in black felt and made an *ongon* out of horsehair, twigs and stuffing, with black pebbles for the hooves and eyes. My miniature Afraid of Bears emerged and took its place in the northernmost corner of the tent amongst my ancestors. Looking at it, in my mind's eye I was seeing my companion in the first days of his life, his coat dazzling against the snow, golden as honeybread in the sun.

At his feet I laid a handful of tender grass and flowers picked from the heart of his favourite grasslands.

I needed another lead horse. There were five or six animals among my herd fit for the task. I picked a palomino taken from the Merkid, which we called the Blind Man because of his blue eyes.

I saddled him. The camp was barely out of sight when I

realised I should have ridden him before. Astride him, everything oppressed me. He had grazed for too long and I knew from the sway of his neck that he would find it hard to set, then keep, a rhythm. But he was brave and, despite his rounded belly, he rode on, alert and anxious not to do wrong. The sensible thing would have been to break up our trots with long spells of walking and let him catch his breath. But, overcome by my desire to reach Queen of Flowers, good sense had deserted me. The more so because I had made my choice – to carry her off and declare that from now on she would be my wife, my only wife. I was desperate to tell her my great resolution, impatient for our shared elation. Queen of Flowers would perfume my yurt and I would fill her with children. Ah! I could see them already, crawling on the threshold, tugging at the puppies' ears or climbing onto the lambs' backs, sucking at their mother's breast, clinging onto her *del* or clambering onto my knees. I had already waited too long.

No matter how hard I tried not to compare the Blind Man to the charger that had carried me yesterday, his every faintest hesitation stirred my pain. I should have given him time, but the more he slowed, the harder I forced him on. If he stumbled fording a stream, I savagely pulled up his head and lashed him. His coat was covered with foam like churned milk, he trembled at the knees. The inevitable happened: he fell. Despite the fear I inspired in him, he couldn't get to his feet. I flogged his hindquarters until he righted himself. He took a stride and staggered stiff-legged, exhausted. I saw the distress in his blue eyes – not a flicker of hatred, only utter bewilderment. I despised myself and, unable to bear this feeling, banged my forehead against a rock. When the blood spurted out, I slumped to the ground, as the first drops of rain beat on my shoulders.

Night came and went without bringing sleep. In the murmuring downpour I had gone over to him and clasped his neck to beg his forgiveness.

We walked all the next day, part of the next night and the morning after until finally we reached Queen of Flowers' summer camp. Clustered next to the stream, the four yurts raised their crowns towards a sky heavy with trailing clouds. But no smoke rose from them, no dogs lay at their thresholds, no herds cropped nearby. A desert.

I jumped from my horse and ran into the first tent. Two

stripped beds, one of them Queen of Flowers', a floor littered with half a dozen bowls.

Going to the other yurts I noted the saddles and harness, the *airag* pails. Nothing was missing, except ... the *ongons*, and seeing that empty space, I knew the owners would not be coming back.

The tracks merged round the tents and elsewhere. They had clearly been obscured. I followed different sets and each led me back to the camp. They showed about fifty horses, at least ten without riders, but no sign of the goats and sheep.

For three days and nights I scoured the region, stopping at every *ayil* to question the shepherds. One of them had seen thirty Merkids driving a herd several head strong. Yes, he thought there had been women with them, but he could not describe them, his sight was poor. Why had we not slaughtered the Merkids down to the very last man? I retraced my steps to where my search had begun and fell asleep in her bed, drinking in the fragrance of its covers like a drowning man.

As day broke I found a bone stuffed down between the mattress and a tent pole. I recognised the white hoof from the ravine, which I had given Queen of Flowers, and remembered telling her that Afraid of Bears would cover White Moon. I was stroking the toe bone, dreaming of those moments of happiness, when I sensed a presence. I lifted a corner of the felt and saw the silhouettes of White Moon and her colt at the edge of the forest. They were cropping the grass and staring at the Blind Man, clearly delighted to see a fellow creature, even a stranger.

The next day I checked that there were no other horses nearby, rounded up the few goats and sheep on the mountain and drove them back to our camp by the Spreading Tree, my heart grieving and bled white.

Chapter 20

At the start of the summer of the Year of the Tiger, the steppes seethed with agitation. Tribes and clans were perpetually on the move, meeting up and concluding or sundering alliances. Tempers flared in an instant and blood was shed, sometimes in the bosom of families. To the east, the Tatars were rallying beside the Kerulen and the elders, confident from past experience, did not think it would be long before they attacked. If my father had been there, he would have said, 'It is the will of the Year of the Tiger. There is nothing that can be done. Might as well try to catch the snow on the tip of a cow's horn.'

The scourges accompanying the great cycle of the striped cat were legendary and the sages told how Tengri's rage could split the earth in two, engulf plains and forests in fire or flood over a span of thirty days' trek, decimate herds, stuffing them with maggots and frothing blood, set men at one another's throats, provoke conspiracies and unnatural alliances, and bring forth children without arms or brains. The Year of the Tiger brought upheaval of every sort and although our misfortunes were not yet of that order, the sky was heavy with fatal portents. And so it was that a rumour spread to the four corners of the *ulus* like fire across a dry plain: Jamuka was the true father of Temüjin's son.

Everyone dreaded each coming day and suspected the man who yesterday had been his brother.

I as much as anybody.

With the disappearance of Afraid of Bears and Queen of Flowers, I had paid a heavy tribute to the Year of the Tiger. Temüjin had promised to march against the Merkid, but he kept on deferring the day for the same reasons, 'Patience, Bo'urchu. The moons exert an evil influence. Kököchü insists that no new enterprises should be undertaken.'

'So, we must hibernate then, must we?'

'Don't forget that my father was poisoned and that I was abandoned by my people in the last great cycle of the Tiger.'

'I will go and look for her alone . . . '

'And get yourself killed. This is no time for us to turn away from each other, Bo'urchu. We will march on the Merkid . . . but the cycle of the Tiger is not the only thing against us. There is Jamuka, as well. A rift has opened between us.'

'Oh!' I exclaimed, feigning dismay. 'Is your sworn ally growing tired of you?'

'He is afraid of losing his power. Many men have sworn allegiance to me and the balance of troops in the *ulus* is tipping in my favour. We have agreed to attack the Tatars and, for this purpose, he wants us to ally ourselves with the Sovereigns. But, as you know, I want to fight the Merkids first. We brought them to their knees once, now we must make every last one of them submit. We can use the prisoners against the Tatars, driving them ahead of our squadrons. But Jamuka thinks this is the time to be reconciled with the Sovereigns because Targutai's authority is weakened and his most important allies, the Jürkin and Borjigin, are talking about breaking away. Jamuka's schemes do not fool me: he wants to put me at a disadvantage and sew discord.'

If the Jürkin and Borjigin did break away, the lie of the land would change completely. They were the two senior clans amongst the descendants of Kabul Khan and without them Targutai's claim to the khanate, as great-grandson of Ambakai Khan, would lose its legitimacy. Where would they go? Would they establish a separate *ordo* or would they join us? Their chiefs were Temüjin's uncles and cousins who, at his father's death, had turned their backs on him to wipe their noses on Targutai's collar.

'They will come to me,' my *anda* pronounced, as if he had guessed my question. 'As surely as the lamb finds his way back to the manger when the first frosts come.'

'Jamuka could win them over and set them up in your stead. Your position is not so secure – let's be honest, you are a guest.'

'Mother Hö'elün and Börte agree, Bo'urchu. There is still the Kereyid . . . '

'You said they must be kept out of any conflict amongst the Mongols.'

'Yes, but I will not be pushed to one side. If this goes badly, I will appeal to To'oril.'

'But will Jamuka give you time? You have shared everything with him, even your blanket. Take care he does not drag it with him, leaving your back bare.'

He looked hurt. My remark let him know that I had heard the rumour that Jamuka had fathered Börte's child.

'You as well? Such a remark should not even be thought and if you were anyone else I would rip out their eyes and tear out their tongue.'

'Who are these rumour-mongers? Jamuka, Kököchü, their brothers? Such insolence must be based on a grain of truth. Is it?'

'If you share the lion's kingdom, sometimes you have to play with his balls.'

'That sort of answer will be no help in quashing the rumour!'

Discomfited, he finally said, 'I do not know for certain whether Ugly Duckling is mine or the son of that stinking Merkid, Spirit Rabbit. But of one thing I am certain: Börte's belly had begun to swell before we joined Jamuka's camp.'

'So, he is a liar. And yet you do nothing?'

'The Mongol tribes will never accept as their supreme leader one whose eldest son is a Merkid's bastard. Jamuka's slanders make trouble, but they do mean my son is a Mongol.'

'You forget that to lay claim to the rank of leader, one must be able to name one's ancestors for at least nine generations. Jamuka cannot because he is illegitimate. So your son will never succeed you.'

'I am only thinking of myself.'

'That's as may be! You thought you were playing with his balls, but Jamuka has got yours in his mouth. What are you going to do?'

'Mother Hö'elün and Börte think we should break away from him, so we can move faster.'

'A river of blood is set to flow.'

'Better to die than suffer humiliation.'

My herd of horses had accepted White Moon and her colt without protest, but even so Queen of Flowers' mare kept to herself. She may have been afraid for her colt, but I preferred to think she was waiting for Afraid of Bears. This secret hope stopped her joining the others, as if she knew it is better to remain unattached if you plan to leave one day. I had tied blue ribbons and silver bobbles in White Cloud's mane and tail and, as final protection against baneful influences, I had hung a silk pouch containing a milk tooth that I had been given by Temulun around his neck.

Temüjin's little sister persisted. She never stopped talking about marrying me and smiled more and more prettily to show that her adult teeth were just as fine as those she had had as a child.

One evening when I was holding the mare's head and she was milking, she said, 'Bo'urchu! You are alone now, free of Gerelma and abandoned by your sweetheart. Why are you waiting to make me your wife?'

'Can't you keep quiet, little girl?

'I am of age now. You can see for yourself.'

'You know one should never start anything new in the Year of the Tiger. That's what your brother believes.'

'Plague on Temüjin! That's just the elders' nonsense. But still, I'm happy enough to wait, as long as you marry me when the snows end. The first day of the spring moon, you will rap at my yurt door and carry me off like every young warrior who has won what his heart desires. Now don't say you didn't know.'

'Slow down, little swallow! When this pure white colt has been broken in, then, maybe, we will discuss it again.'

'What! And wait another two winters?' she cried, playing up her frown.

'Three. I will not ride him before. Afraid of Bears' only son will be stallion to my mares.'

'And I will be a grandmother! If that's what you want, I will take back my lucky tooth.'

'Touch that amulet and I will cut your hair off and feed it to the camels.'

She laughed, then heaved a deep sigh of resignation.

Chapter 21

We had been travelling for two days in search of new pastures when our convoy came to a halt in the middle of a valley. It was ringed by high, banked hills and its mouth was choked by two granite cliffs, which heightened our feeling of being at the bottom of a bowl. On the Blind Man, I was riding with Qasar and Jelme near the waggons carrying Mother Hö'elün's yurt, when Temüjin, who had been at the head, came to find us.

'Jamuka wants us to set up camp here.'

'This place is not safe,' said Qasar, 'and there will never be enough grass for all the animals.'

'He insists. He is giving us the meadows by the river, while he has the slopes.'

'We must be careful,' warned Mother Hö'elün. 'What do you think is afoot?'

'I am not sure what idea lies behind his words.'

'I know,' cried Börte, dropping the piece of blue fabric she was embroidering with white clouds. 'Jamuka is easily bored and the moment has come when he is tired of us as well. Do not dismount. Let him set up camp and let us take this chance and part company.'

'Your wife is as sharp as a she-wolf,' Mother Hö'elün said approvingly.

'Qasar, Jelme!' Temüjin ordered immediately. 'Ride back along the convoy and tell our people that we are not stopping. Close up the ranks! Bo'urchu, come with me.'

We trotted to the head of the caravan.

Jamuka's mount was drinking from the river, blowing through its nostrils. At its side, his rider was crouching down, also satisfying his thirst. He invited us to join him. 'A virgin's lips couldn't be cooler than this water.'

'We are carrying on past this valley to find other grazing grounds,' said Temüjin not slowing his horse.

'My *anda*! Look, my people are already pitching camp on the inclines.' It was true: the Solitaries and their associates were scattering over the slopes.

'We will ride on, as our horses need to learn adversity and privation.'

'These are my lands,' said the chief of the Solitaries, standing up, full of menace. 'I decide who camps where.'

'Then I will leave them. Have we not sworn that neither of us may give the other orders?'

He dug his heels into his horse as Jamuka threw down his cap. We heard his mocking cry: 'True enough. But nobody said that your women would be in charge. What army is going to follow a prince who is deafened by the lowing of a mother and a wife?'

That night saw us crossing the *ulus* of the Besut, a clan allied to the Sovereigns. The order was given: our arrows were to stay in their quivers. These potential rivals followed suit.

Next morning we dismounted in the valley of the Spreading Mulberries. When the waggons were drawn up in a circle, the horses hobbled and the camels knelt down, horsemen began to appear – not only Besut but also Solitaries who had taken advantage of the darkness and confusion to leave Jamuka.

'The two *anda* have broken their bond.' This rumour was spread through the valleys like dust on the wind and brought with it a dilemma for many families. They now had to choose a camp, and quickly – the two wolves' parting of the ways could slide into open conflict. Some may have feared this possibility, others – and I was one – desired it.

In three days the rings of our tents were swollen by almost two thousand men who had come from the Mongol clans – the Jalair, the Tarkut, the Barula, the Baya'ut, the Suldus, the Ganigas, the Undjin, the Sakayit and many others.

Three hundred Obligees joined us, led by Jelme's younger brother, Sübetei, a peerless warrior. But the biggest surprise was when Qorchi presented himself along with his entire *ayil* of thirty tents. He was Jamuka's half-brother. He undid his belt, dropped his sabre, quiver and knife on the ground, took off his helmet and knelt before Temüjin.

'I did not want to leave Jamuka, for we were sheltered by the same womb, but your destiny was revealed to me in a dream.'

'What dream was this?'

'A reddish-brown cow was circling Jamuka and as she tried to butt him, she broke a horn. Furious, she pawed the ground, raising a cloud of dust and bellowing, "Give me back my horn." But Jamuka ran away with it. Then the cow harnessed herself to a wagon carrying the khan's great tent, and despite the rutted ground and that heavy load, Temüjin, you managed to make her pull what twelve oxen could not have moved.'

Qorchi's dream was so powerful that everyone fell to their knees before Temüjin: they knew the reddish-brown cow represented the Earth and the yurt the kingdom, our people triumphant.

Impassive, Temüjin finally said, 'If you speak the truth, I will give you a thousand men to command.'

'When the day comes for the Mongol tribes to be united under a single standard, you will be their khan. On that day, if you wish to complete my happiness, and as a reward for what I have foretold, let me have thirty of the most beautiful prisoners.'

Trenüjin gave his word.

Nine days later, messengers came saying that the princely clans, the Jürkin and Borjigin, were approaching the *ordo* we had established at the Blue Lake. Temüjin asked if the princes, his uncles and cousins, were at the head of the columns and was told that their standards had been seen flapping in the wind. Half a day passed until the lances and banners arrived, criss-crossing the stretch of sky framed by the pass, and Temüjin spent this time savouring his victory in complete silence. All his skilful manoeuvres, his patient calculations, were now bearing fruit. No need to climb to the top of the tree; it was falling into his hands.

He brought out his family, his brothers on his right, his mother and the other women on his left; all stood so straight, they were like an armful of arrows in their quivers.

He recognised his uncles and cousins by their spiked helmets and broad neck shields as they rode flank to flank down the slopes. He listed them.

'Here are Daritai, Quchar, Altan and Sacha Beki.' His slit eyes gleamed like the cutting edge of a sabre. 'Daritai, our father's younger brother, is our uncle. Quchar, our father's nephew, is our cousin. Altan, younger brother of Kutula, the last khan, is our father's cousin. And Sacha Beki is his nephew and he is the heir, his line, the first born of Kabul Khan's.'

'But the council of elders will never elect him,' scorned Mother Hö'elün. 'Nor any of the other good-for-nothings. They left us for Targutai, and now, look, they are breaking with him.'

Temüjin did not take his eyes off them and almost seemed to be purring. At last the princes' mounts were before us, snorting joyfully.

Altan, the oldest of the four, was the first to speak: 'In all the directions . . .'

'Who are you?' Temüjin interrupted.

The prince started and looked to Daritai before answering, 'I am Altan, son of Kutula Khan.'

'Youngest son, keeper of his hearth? Strange, I do not remember your face.'

The last khan's youngest son cleared his throat. Daritai broke in, 'You were young, Temüjin.'

'And you? Who are you?'

'Come now. I am your uncle.'

'Daritai?'

'The same,' he said, half-smiling.

'Another youngest son, entrusted with looking after my grandfather's hearth? How could I have forgotten the face of the man who at my father's death became our protector?'

'Surely you know that before he died, Yesügei asked the shaman Münglig, Kököchü's father, to take care of you.'

'Münglig failed in his task. As keeper of the hearth, you should have taken your brother's wives and children with you. If you had done so, I would recognise your face today. But as absence erases the memory of a man's features, so time dispels old quarrels. You have my attention.'

'In all the directions,' Altan began again, 'men are like horses before the gathering storm. It is time that a khan came to bring them peace of mind. Targutai would love to be that man and so, it seems, would Jamuka, except the council of elders will never sanction a leader who is not a direct descendant of Kabul Khan. The council has reconvened and decided that the Mongol tribes will keep on tearing each other apart as long as Kabul's heirs are scattered. That is why we are here. We have come to ask you to draw tight the circle.'

'What evidence have I that you will be loyal?' asked Temüjin, but seeing Altan's offended expression, he immediately added, 'I want you to pledge your oath under this standard. It will be able to judge your candour, because it is home to my father's spirit.'

Altan swallowed, then began.

'In battle we will be your scouts, your front line. We will bring back the fairest captives for you, the horses with the finest rounded cruppers. In the hunt, we will be first to step out of the circle of beaters and drive the game towards you. We will do nothing which could cause you harm and everything to give you pleasure. If we break our word, then pull down our tents, take our women and scatter our blackened heads in the desert.'

'I accept,' said Temüjin, smoothing his brown goatee beard thoughtfully. He pierced them one by one with his murderous gaze. 'Be warned. No lapse will be pardoned,' he added.

Chapter 22

The steady tide of arrivals dried up once the cold had stripped the birches of their coat of yellow leaves. The frames of the yurts were covered with another layer of felt and the Blue Lake hid itself under a pallid, icy veil. At night we could hear it cracking, drawing mysterious sighs from the water's depths.

I could not wait for the dead of winter, when the great cycle of the Tiger would finish and yield to that of the Hare.

Queen of Flowers stole into all things – I would see a hill in the distance, and there was the curve of her hip; two hills, the contours of her breasts; a ray of sunlight in the undergrowth, her silhouette; a cloud flushed by the setting sun, her profile – and like a horse's hooves on the young grass, these mirages wore heavy on me.

Where was my swallow? Who was holding her captive?

I dreamed of her. But it was not Queen of Flowers in my dreams; she did not eat marmot cooked over stones, or offer her body to the rain and my kisses, or smell of tender moss, or, most of all, feel my rage that she had gone.

This is how the winter passed. In the Moon of the Rutting Ibex, the starving stags stripped the larches of their bark; in that of the Antelope hail fell constantly, then snow covered everything to a depth of five fists. In two nights it was swept away and the wind blew and howled for a whole moon, carrying off everything towards the frozen skies ... The Tiger fled, giving way to the Hare, who entered his year cautiously, furtively rolling his great, haggard eyes at the sight of this desolate land, polished and cold, as if dead. At last the geese formed up like arrowheads and crossed the blue of the sky, and soon the ashy cranes were calling over the steppe and the plovers, egrets and other raucous waders returned to the marshes. Now it was the middle of the moon of the Cuckoo and a smell of hot sand hung in the air, exhilarating the birds. I begged these messengers to bring me one lock of Queen of Flowers' hair. But in the constant beating of their wings, I found not a single answer to the mysteries that so haunted me.

Temüjin meanwhile presided over the nobles. It was not that he had a greater say than his uncle and cousins, simply that they agreed with all his pronouncements. He was careful that all his decisions and plans were made in their presence and if he nursed thoughts of revenge, he never let them show.

He established a code of iron discipline and put it to the test in the great hunts which punctuated that winter. He divided the troops into formations of a hundred horsemen, the *centuries*, and organised drives of four to five days' march, sometimes more. Despite the snow and hail, the cold, violent wind that cut into the horses' breasts and made them rear and struggle against their rider's grip, we always had to go on and never dismount. In a world without contours, some drowned in the relentless blizzards and were lost. Shame on those who did not reach the place of the final kill at the appointed time: no game, even scraps, was set aside for them. After listening to the commanders' explanations, Temüjin would list their mistakes and tell them exactly what they should have done. If they repeated a single one of their blunders, they would be stripped of their commands. Temüjin possessed an extraordinary sixth sense, that of a peerless hunter, a wily strategist. Whilst others conscientiously bent over the tracks studying every detail, he was able to take astonishing short-cuts, as if he himself was in the animal's skin. Time and again he was first to flush from cover the animal that had eluded our net, and tell us in which fold of the forest and on which promontory it would be found. He had an unerring intuition, coupled with an incomparable vision of the whole, like an eagle high in the sky. This profoundly impressed his entourage and many of the men saw in it Tengri's work. I thought it more likely that his skills had been learnt as a youth when he had had to be constantly on his guard and dig in the earth for the lowliest root. He had known fear and, rather than paralyse him, it had only served to sharpen his survival instinct.

It was very hard to know his feelings. No matter the situation, his expression was always impassive and watchful. But, although we endured the most terrible hardship on these manoeuvres, the sight of him at our head facing the unchained elements without blenching inspired us to ever greater heights.

How many times, riding at his side, did I see him ecstatic at the sight of such recklessness? Horses expired, men watched their limbs freeze and rot, some cut off their fingers to halt the putrefaction, others died, and yet always he pushed on, hunched over under the tempest, stiff-jointed like us all, his face blue, his cheeks split by the ice, his lips splayed not in pain but in joy. At those moments his name Temüjin, the Blacksmith, took on its full meaning. He was made of an indestructible metal, an iron mass that kept going and going, forging those who were able to keep up with him. He had no pity for those who gave up, the sniveller, the weakling, the doubter, the paralysed. He gave them only a look, and they either got to their feet or never did so again. And yet, to the man who struggled to the limit of his strength, who met pain with pain, wounds with wounds, he would give even his own coat lined with wolf's fur, which warded off the most bitter cold.

As generous as he was intransigent, he foresook the finest prizes, even those he had killed himself, when the moment came to share out the spoils, and always gave them to the most deserving.

That winter was long and harsh, but rich in learning and pleasure. Three thousand men took part in each hunt and not a single family went short of meat. Our blacksmith's fire never dimmed and our men warmed themselves at its flames, every day moving a little closer to its source.

Temüjin appointed quiver-bearers, cup-bearers, camp guards, scouts, messengers, tanners, ostlers, beaters and the commanders of the centuries, but, more important still, he instituted a system of lookouts across the *ulus* which were kept on permanent watch and connected to him like the links of a chain. Pairs of men were stationed on the highest crests. At the slightest alert they signalled with coloured flags according to an arranged code, so that any movement on the steppe could be communicated from hill to hill. At night they used fires. We were a hundred *ayils*, with a day's gentle trot between those at the Blue Lake and those furthest from it. Some were small, only ten or so tents, but most were of twenty to thirty yurts and Temüjin's, with two hundred tents, was the largest. In total we were fifteen thousand, with almost a third of fighting age.

An incident was soon to provide us with an opportunity to display our mettle.

One of our sentries was watching the Steppe of the Donkey's Back when he saw two men stealing his herd of horses. He mounted and quickly caught them up. With a well-aimed arrow, he stopped one of the thieves in his tracks and terrified the second; he then gathered his horses and went to recover his arrow. But the wounded man, a Solitary, was still alive, so he shattered his skull down to the very teeth.

Two days later, flags fluttered on the hilltops, informing us that the grazing land to the west of the Steppe of the Donkey's Back was growing black with horsemen arrayed in battle order. Temüjin gave the command to form up.

The women rounded up the herds and hurried through the forest towards the hills of the Wind's Pillow where we would meet them after the battle was won.

The sun was reaching its zenith when our troops took up position behind the hills. Temüjin sent three centuries forward to the highest ridge. At their back flew the clans' standards and the Borjigin's emblem, the nine black yak's tails topped by a trident. The enemy deployed a hundred centuries, twice our number, and sent a light escort flying the Solitaries' standard towards our lines. To prevent it appraising our forces, Temüjin rode out with his brothers.

'I speak as Jamuka,' said the messenger. 'One of your people killed my brother and so broke our oath and severed our bonds. I have come to demand reparation. Either give me the guilty man and one of your brothers as well or prepare to fight.'

'Tell my *anda*,' Temüjin answered, 'that apart from Qorchi, who rides with us, I know him to have only one other brother: me. Tell him also that his so-called brother, the Solitary, died while trying to steal our horses. His accomplice knows this full well and deserves to have his tongue torn out for his lies.'

As the escort rode away, one of our scouts reported a column of at least a thousand warriors outflanking us to the north.

'Jamuka wants to push us south,' said Temüjin. 'He must have three times as many men in reserve there. I'd wager that those scavengers, the Sovereigns, are with him.'

He stared for a moment at the Wolves clan. These warriors with their quivers full of light and heavy arrows, their tightly buckled belts, and their keen, imperturbable gazes made a fine battalion. They were light, lean, volatile as air, adept at harrying and skirmishing. Temüjin instructed them to block the troops to the north. As cover, he put Qachi'un's century at their shoulder.

Because of the enemy's greater strength, our only option was to withdraw to avoid falling into their trap. Our chief's plan was to lure them into the Seventy Marshes, leave them to founder there and escape to the north through the breach opened by the Wolves.

As he had anticipated the Solitaries pursued us into those mosquito-infested swamps which show no mercy to any who lose their way. We were formed up on the other side of the marshy ground when they flailed into the trap. Their charge was checked and put to the sword and, in a flash, we broke through their flanks and rained a volley of arrows on their centre.

The battle was turning: we were rolling up their wings and fighting hand-to-hand when suddenly our rear was submerged in a hail of arrows. We span round. The crests of the hills were fringed with dark silhouettes, the enemy was swooping down on our flanks in waves of a hundred and Jamuka's archers, cunningly stationed halfway down the slopes, were unhurriedly taking aim.

Temüjin gave the order to retreat. Caught in our own trap, our only means of escape was the hills facing us. We had to clear a path with our shields on our backs, smiting the enemy, slashing and hewing into their flesh with all our might like mastiffs locked on a stallion's balls who never release their grip, no matter how much the horse lashes out. It was a glorious melee and, despite our losses, we were reaching the slopes when the Solitaries were given the order to suspend their pursuit. So welcome was this turn of events that Temüjin feared it must be one of Jamuka's feints, but it proved not to be, although we were not to know the reason until a few days later.

When we were retreating, the Solitaries had drawn the Wolves into a small valley where three thousand of their confederates lay in wait, and fallen on them. By the end of this ill-matched contest, only seventy-one of our men, including Qachi'un, were still alive. Jamuka instructed them to be bound hand and foot and taken to his camp, where water was set to boil in seventy great cauldrons, one for each person.

The prisoners were boiled alive. As for Qachi'un, Jamuka cut off his head and tied it to the tail of his black charger. Then he considered himself avenged and ordered an end to the fighting.

We learnt all of this from Kököchü, whose witnessing of the events had persuaded him to join us. He was followed by two thousand families, which in part made up for our losses.

These weren't Jamuka's only acts of brutality either: for archers and scouts taken from our ranks, he ordered that the former's fingers be cut off and the latter's eyes dug out.

So while victory may have given him an indisputable advantage, his cruelty robbed him of many of its benefits. He scorned the way of the elders and many of the Mongol tribes thought his sole ambition was to destroy the princely lines.

Temüjin seemed unaffected by his brother's death. One evening when he was playing with his child, forcing his little finger between his gums to sharpen his milk teeth, he amazed me, as he often did, by guessing my thoughts.

'Qachi'un is dead and he is fine. He left life as he lived it, without a word. When he was alive he was like a shadow, without strength or character. Now there is more to him.'

I said nothing, but vividly remembered the sobs that had shaken Mother Hö'elün's yurt and risen into the sky.

'The *ordo* would be stronger if we had a khan.'

I do not know whether Temüjin or Kököchü was the first to voice this thought, but either way it echoed through the tents, met with unanimous approval and was quickly followed by the question of who that khan should be.

Temüjin emerged as the obvious candidate equally straightforwardly. His merits were listed, his courage, his honour, his generosity, the nobility of his soul, his princely origins and, of course, that clear-sightedness that had enabled him to escape every trap. Everyone was in agreement: he would make an ideal khan.

It was when the moon of the Black Grouse was waxing that matters took clearer shape at a session of the council of the elders. All the wise men attended, along with the blood princes, Kököchü and the commanders of the centuries. Altan was the first to speak.

'Temüjin, the council has chosen you to be our khan. We will arm your hand . . .'

My *anda* listened him out, stared at the assembly, then shook his head. 'I cannot accept. It is for you, Altan, son of Kutula Khan, to walk the white felt carpet that was your father's.'

Altan refused, claiming that he was no longer a young man like Temüjin, with his twenty-one springs.

'Granted,' Temüjin replied. 'Sacha Beki, then. Is he not of the first branch of Kabul Khan's descendants?'

'Yes, I am . . .' said the Jürkin prince.

'Then you will be khan!' broke in Temüjin. 'Nowhere is it decreed that the Borjigin should claim that honour. Have you ever seen a subordinate sit on the heir's throne? I am not like the cuckoo, stealing other's nests!'

'Listen, Temüjin,' Daritai interjected. 'For many moons now it has been our intention to elect you fifth Khan of the Mongols. All of us here are descendants of Kabul's bone and all of us approve this choice, Sacha Beki and Altan included.'

'I understand now, uncle,' answered Temüjin. 'But can Sacha Beki's tongue confirm what you say?'

My *anda* was steering the council to perfection. Nothing less than an unconditional pledge of allegiance would satisfy him.

'I do not covet the supreme honour,' said Sacha Beki. 'That is why I did not seek to oppose Targutai when I could have, something for which I have been reproached. But one thing is certain, I do not want Jamuka, the bastard, at the head of a great power. United, we can thwart him.'

'Good, now you only need to show such determination when we face him in battle. What about you, Quchar, my young cousin? Look, you are robust and, I've no doubt, as shrewd as the wolf. What say you?'

'I do not yet have the judgement to be the leader of the pack. For that I would need to have braved adversity, as you have. I am proud to ride at your side and I intend to convince you of my devotion.'

'You are wise, Quchar. In battle I will put you at my right hand. Now, since I must take your offer in all seriousness, I would gladly hear you swear your oaths of loyalty.'

Which they did, in turn, a heroic ring to their voices.

All that remained now was for them to keep their word.

Chapter 23

Along the winding valleys they came, bareheaded, jolting merrily on their mounts and, as far as the eye could see, carefree smiles displayed those strings of dazzling pearls that are the making of every handsome face. They rode in groups of ten, twenty or thirty, chattering in the first pale light and their booming laughter and ringing songs rose into the thin air. Lambs and brimful gourds swung gently at the flanks of their horses and calves, camels and other gifts for the Khan followed, gybing at the leading rein.

They climbed the slopes and massed on the narrow plateau of the Blue Lake, between the islands of yurts and the larch woods, their hair greased and plaited and hanging on either side of their necks in two carefully braided, matching locks.

As the sun rose in the sky, the plateau filled and soon not a space was left amongst the mass of horses' heads, that sea of manes and plaited forelocks.

The mighty clamour gradually subsided to a whisper, then silence, leaving only the buzzing of flies, the jingling of bits and the plaintive bleating of a few lambs.

An avenue had been cleared in front of Temüjin's tent and when the pure white felt was pushed back, the throng burst out, 'TEMÜJIN! TEMÜJIN! TEMÜJIN KHAN!'

Their throats hammered out this chant as arrows whistled into the sky.

Raising his hand, my *anda* stilled the jubilation.

'Pay heed, all of you!' he said, taking them in with a long, sweeping glance. 'I am Temüjin, son of Yesügei and Mother Hö'elün. My grandfather was Bartan the Brave, son of Kabul Khan and so, by the blood of my illustrious ancestors, I am the twenty-third generation of descendants of Blue Wolf and Fallow Doe, our creators. The council of elders, my uncles, cousins, brothers, princes and noblemen, has elected me. Look on me! I am your khan. Never forget this, just as I will never forget your faces on the days when the spoils are divided up. I will remember you, you who have been the first to serve and cherish my standard. You will obey me and I will see that all of you know the *yasak*, my law. You will lack nothing, I will watch over you, but woe betide any man who turns away from me. I am the Khan and your lives are mine to command. They are in my hands, your deeds are my deeds, your eyes are my eyes. You are in your thousands and yet you are one, because such is my will.'

Cheering erupted. Again he brought silence.

'Bow your heads and pledge your souls to me. Be warned. Treachery will never be forgiven!'

Like falling water, every bronzed skull bent low in obeisance. Kököchü stepped forward in his ceremonial dress at Temüjin's side and solemnly proclaimed, 'The Khan is Tengri's son, His chosen one. By His order, I raise Temüjin above us all towards Him.'

My *anda* bared his head, unbuckled his belt, hung it round his neck and walked to the centre of the thick white felt carpet. Then Qasar, Belgütei, Temüge, Jelme and I lifted him and carried him three times round his tent as the men cheered and tried to follow on horseback in a tangle of manes, coats and *dels* gleaming in the sunshine.

Then the Khan invited the princes, his brothers, the shaman and me to enter his tent.

'Before I honour the brave and embark on any enterprise as Khan,' he began, 'there are two men I wish to reward. When I was nothing, they wedded themselves to my shadow. They are as necessary to me as the rain and the sun to the flower. They are the roots of this flower – its support and vigour. Know you all that they are untouchable and if any one of you thinks of harming them, I will consider that you have affronted my person and I will flay every part of your body that touches the saddle when you ride.'

And that was how I became Keeper of the Horse and Jelme Commander of the Khan's Guard.

My duties were to select the horses and establish how they were broken in, in particular those who would face our prey hunting or in battle; to nominate the grazing lands, the routes we would follow in peace and war, and the men who would care for and train the horses. As a prerogative, Temüjin allowed me the pick of any women we seized from the enemy . . . once his own

146

appetite had been satisfied. I was exempted from tribute and free to choose any lands I pleased, which would be mine for all posterity, handed down through the line of my male descendants. Lastly Temüjin promised to redeem ten of my offences.

'That should give me enough leeway not to have to punish you,' he said with a complicit smile.

The blood rushed to my cheeks. I was by no means the only one to give him my unbounded admiration, but now he had become the master of all, he was notifying everyone that I was at his right hand. Henceforth no one would stand between us, most of all not Kököchü, the shaman.

And yet, as Tenggeri well knew, what did all these rewards and all this power avail me, when I could not clasp Queen of Flowers to my breast?

Chapter 24

.

The feasting was entering its third, starlit night. The fires lit up the tops of the trees and the men were downing the heady *airag* by the pitcherful, singing and laughing, their eyes aglow.

As the investiture celebrations reached their height, the first signs of hot-headedness began to appear. Sarcastic comments – disputatious or mildly threatening – squabbles and tussles broke out amongst the groups. The causes were generally innocuous: bruised pride, old clan differences not properly laid to rest, a wife's chin raised too high towards a pair of manly shoulders – trifles distorted by alcohol which would be resolved by the wrestling bouts.

But things suddenly grew more serious when the Khan saw two men squaring up to one another by our horses; they were rolling up their sleeves about to fight. One was Belgütei, who that night was guarding our horses, the other a strapping Jürkin called Giant, who was a cousin of Altan's and known to be in Sacha Beki's service. We saw him seize a sabre and strike Belgütei.

Temüjin leapt at them, grasped the Jürkin by the plait, threw him to the ground and jammed his knife against his ear. 'Move and I will slit your throat,' threatened the young khan.

'Leave him, it's nothing,' said Belgütei, his shoulder bleeding freely.

'Nothing?' repeated Temüjin, shocked. 'A Jürkin tries to cleave you in two and we're meant just to watch?'

'It's only a scratch, come . . . ' Belgütei forced his half-brother to let Giant go.

But Temüjin Khan's fury did not abate. He called his brothers to his tent and asked Belgütei for an explanation. Belgütei said he had found Giant near our enclosure, holding one of our horses by the bridle and about to go back for others.

'The Jürkin steal from us, they provoke us. This is insufferable!'

'The princes have rallied to our cause,' said Belgütei. 'Let's not fall out with them. I'm not going to be robbed of my strength by this wound.'

His brother did not agree. He was convinced that Sacha Beki's Jürkin were bent on challenging his authority.

'They must be punished. Now!'

He assembled the Borjigin in secret and, before dawn, armed with stout sticks, we fell upon the Jürkin as they slept. Giant was taken off and made to wear the *cangue*.

Called to come and explain himself, Sacha Beki knelt at the Khan's feet and promised henceforth to curb the Jürkin's animosity towards the Borjigin, Giant's in particular.

My *anda* was not convinced. After the Jürkin chief left, he confided his suspicions to me: 'Sacha Beki is like the glutton, so greedy that all he can see is the prey he covets. But that prey stands on the edge of a crude trap which will be his downfall.'

'No one should be drunk for more than three days at a time. Two would be more reasonable, one the sign of exemplary restraint.'

'No one should be drunk at all,' I said, draining my bowl of *airag*.

'Don't exaggerate, Bo'urchu,' Temüjin said mockingly. 'Drinking is necessary; alcohol and its fevers are cleansing. It is beloved by the spirits as an offering, and does honour to both Heaven and Earth. Three days seems a sensible middle course.'

'Each moon?'

'No, each quarter of the moon.'

The Khan was discussing the precepts of his *yasak* with us, his faithful attendants and members of his family. He planned to impose his law on all the blue wolves, as he called his warriors, so that they would beget the Mongols of the future – a strong, united people, respectful of the ways of the elders and observant of the Khan's code of honour. He listened to our opinions, but reserved the final decision for himself. When he had made his decisions and given his ruling, he called together the princes and champions to inform them. They in turn told the nobility, the heads of the *ayils*, the commanders of the centuries, the bards and so on, because no one was to be left in ignorance.

The first laws dealt with the customs and taboos concerning

water and fire. For instance, it was forbidden to lift one's *del* in a river, either to relieve oneself or to wash. One could not cut the flames of a fire with a sword or any other object.

When I pointed out that everyone must know these prohibitions, Temüjin looked at me and said, 'What is obvious to the Mongols is not to the tribes that live beyond their lands. On the day of their subjugation, they must know what they will incur if they defy our laws.'

He went on through the list of ordinances and the penalties that awaited those who flouted them. It was forbidden to step over or duck under the hitching ropes of a herd; to step over a man lying on the ground, or go through his legs, if he was standing; to sit so that the soles of one's feet were showing; to tether one's horse to one's yurt; to walk under one's horse's neck or stomach; to whip it with one's reins; to wound the earth. Death would be the punishment for anyone who stole a horse, raped a virgin, coupled with an animal or human of the same sex, committed incest, or killed a prisoner without having first consulted his superiors. (In this Temüjin remembered the lesson of the sentry who had killed Jamuka's so-called brother.) A similar fate awaited the inattentive sentry, whether he was guarding a herd, the *ulus* or the perimeter of the royal camp itself, and the disobedient warrior. Adultery was only permitted if the cuckolded husband gave his consent.

One morning when I was watching the horses being rounded up for the colts to be branded, Temüjin sent for me. The grass was white with hoar frost and crunched underfoot as I ran to the Khan's modest tent. He was with his wife and Ugly Duckling, their adorable child, who would be known as Jochi when he was older. He was approaching his second spring and already the beautiful Börte was filling out again.

Temüjin put his son on the ground. Bare-bottomed and plump-thighed the little crumb todled towards his mother, making his baby noises.

'How are the horses?' my *anda* asked.

'Sturdy. Their manes are supple and light, and their hooves shine like stones in the river. At dawn they look to the rising sun. All day long they sniff the breeze bringing summer from the south. And at night they continue to graze even though they are not hungry, their eyes full of mischief, their hocks quivering, and if one of them so much as breaks wind, they lash out hard enough to bring the moon tumbling from the sky.'

'So they are ready for battle!' he cried joyfully as Börte handed me a bowl. 'And what about you, my friend? Will you be able to draw them up in ranks, their ears cocked like featherings poking out from a quiver?'

Half his face was hidden from me by the lip of my bowl and the steam rising from it, but I could still see the smile whetting his eyes into dagger points. He gave me no chance to drink my broth.

'Be happy, Bo'urchu, because when the next moon rises we will leave this camp with six thousand men and you will command the right wing. It will be the first to hurl itself on what is left of the Merkids.'

My heart broke into a gentle trot.

'But first I have a favour to ask of you ... Take Gerelma back.'

It was the season of good resolutions, so I could not refuse, but I qualified my acceptance: 'Not into my yurt. She can pitch a tent in my *ayil*.'

That night I slept on the steppe next to my colt. His sleep was troubled and he started constantly. I had a dream: the earth was covered with decapitated Merkids and over them were swarming cohorts of woodlice, dogs, crows, vultures and men. In the distance, Queen of Flowers sat enthroned on a mound of torsos spattered with vomit and blood. Smooth and white as milk, my beloved was naked and calling me. The faceless bodies blocked my path, their arms wound themselves around me and I had to slash at them with my sword. But the more I severed, the more they writhed and grabbed at me and soon there were so many that my legs were pinned to the ground and I was paralysed. I shut my eyes to block out her mouth beseeching me to come to her, those cheeks wet with tears, and suddenly my fingers were touching her. Was it because I had desired her so much? Her pink lips glided over my skin, marking it with kisses, pecking with hungry little dabs until they reached my mouth and were swallowed up. Our teeth clashed. I devoured her, tasting her gums, the roof of her mouth, hunting her tongue, trapping it, sucking until I drew blood and felt myself melting into her. We were one being, bone against bone, wonderfully impaled, every pore of our skin a bud bursting into dripping flower, utterly indifferent to the scavengers digging into the stinking, disembowelled bodies, entranced by ourselves alone as we drank the pure nectar in great gulps.

Suddenly Queen of Flowers vanished. All around, nothing but a great valley of mire, a tide of waste stretching endlessly away under a pale, cold, lifeless sky. Gone the slaughtered Merkids, the plumes of blue smoke, even the flies. A face emerged from this foul vision and filled the orb of my dream: Jamuka. He laughed and laughed and the echo of his laughter hammered against my temples. Then the sun split with a terrifying sound . . .

I opened an eye.

White Cloud and his mother were tearing at the grass by my face, looking at me intently with their great dark eyes as if to say that this was the most succulent grazing place on all the steppes.

Chapter 25

The massacre happened, true enough . . . We marauded over the Merkid lands, throwing down their tents, killing their men and carrying off their herds, their healthiest women and their children.

But though I ransacked their camps, I found no trace of Queen of Flowers. Temüjin thought he had found her, but instead he gave me the most beautiful girl of the land.

She was called Mother of Pearl Stream, and though she thought she could disguise her womanliness with men's clothes and her hair with a filthy cap, her beauty was as plain to the naked eye as the scorpion grass-coloured reflections of a spring in the middle of the desert. I pushed her into a tent and ordered her to undress. She did not move. I stood in front of her, my eyes level with cheeks as pink and soft as May blossom. She was half a head taller than me and smelled of hot goat's cheese. Her sweat-beaded throat quivered.

I tore off her blouse. She stiffened, trembling, her lips pursed, her nostrils flared. She had slender shoulders and wore a large necklace of fine turquoise glass and coral beads which brought out the creamy swell of her breast. She inhaled deeply and stared at something past my forehead. My desire had no need of her eyes. I ripped away her laughable trousers, some sort of kaftan of coarse cloth, and saw, in the bright orange light of the fire, the jet black down on the plump mound of her groin. I seized her by the nape of the neck and with my other hand foraged between her thighs, seeking out their mystery. She went so rigid, an arrowhead would have broken on her. At last her opening yielded to my fingers. She cried out like a shrew mouse. Why, at that very moment, did I seek out her eyes? She was biting her lip and a tear was furrowing her cheek. My lust wilted. I summoned up the image of Queen of Flowers as I kneaded the Merkid's flesh, banging my head against her breast and crying out inside, 'Be like the wolf.' To no avail . . .

I pulled back, covered her with a fur and told her to go to the other captives, when really I wanted to dry her tears in the crook of my arms.

The next day the Merkid women, children and herds were sent back to our camps. The Khan decided to pay a visit to To'oril and drive any game we encountered before us. We set off south-west with three thousand warriors.

As we rode back up the course of the Selenga river, two messengers went ahead to inform the Kereyid king that we were bringing game, arms and precious gems by the sack full.

Flushed out by our army, the game – almost six hundred does, stags and antelope, fifty wolves, two bears and three panthers – was surrounded and killed by To'oril's men in his green Orhon valley. As was his wont, the Kereyid ruler clasped us in his arms with a great show of emotion and effusively welcomed 'his son's' investiture, expressing his astonishment that it had not happened sooner. 'How could the Mongols, my allies, have survived without a khan for so long?'

That same night the sheep were set to boil and the men drank, stuffed themselves and sang wholeheartedly enough to burst their guts and vocal cords. The women smelled sweet of sage and, either willing or fearful, gave themselves up to the men's merriment and the lascivious games that stretched out over the shadowy steppe.

I could have had my share, but I hadn't the heart for it, my desire hamstrung by pointless regrets. What was the source of this uneasiness stealing over me, Temüjin's lucky star? Had I not felt happiness cresting a hill at the Khan's side to watch our army pass, its squares black against the reddish-brown grass? Had I not felt exhilaration plunging my sabre into Merkid flesh and embedding my arrows in their backs? We had struck terror into them, slit their throats, raped their women; but all that was forgotten, past. Now the very moment oppressed me – Queen of Flowers's absence plunged me deeper into this sea of wearisomeness, and the memory of the Merkid woman and the way my purple standard had withered kindled my loneliness.

Who could I confide in? Which Mongol warrior would understand, when women meant nothing to them but a cause for celebration, and when the raids orchestrated by the Khan could be guaranteed to satisfy their ardour?

The gap Afraid of Bears had left was another reason for the strange feeling in my heart that I was lower than a horse's withers. My chestnut stallion's spirit would not leave me. It trembled under my fingers, ran in my veins, neighed in the hollow of my ear . . . Before daybreak, I rode away from the fires through a purple-tinged valley to try and distract myself. Following the whims of his appetite, the Blind Man led me from hill to hill and, to a degree, I was successful; then it grew light and everything shone, so blue and so green.

In the days that followed, To'oril wanted us to go hunting together and see the heart of his vast kingdom, a waterfall he called the Ancestor's Beard.

So, formed up in centuries, Mongol and Kereyid rode side by side along the Orhon, through a long, deep valley strewn with black rocks. The waterfall was two days' ride away. At places grass gave way to stony ground studded with dwarf stalagmites which required a tortuous, winding course. At others we had to hug the mountainsides to negotiate sheer precipices carved by the river. Anticipating this, To'oril had brought plenty of slaves, Naiman mainly, to clear a way through the fallen boulders. Some had barely ventured onto the paths of former avalanches before whole flanks of the mountains subsided and they were thrown into the roaring waters. Others the Turkic ruler pushed over the edge, not for our safety but simply to demonstrate the depth of the gorges. The prisoners fell, flailing their arms and legs, and if they did not bounce off the outcropping ledges, they disappeared straight into the foam, no bigger than ants.

At dusk, our labours were rewarded by the sight of the Ancestor's Beard. It was equal to seven men in height and its waters fell boiling into a round pool broad enough to hold forty head of oxen. From there the river swiftly traced a path between red cliffs, sparing a few small islands of pines that flourished out of the winds' reach.

Upstream from the waterfall, the shallow river caressed its bed of pebbles and reflected the red and blue garlands of the summits. All around grew grass as soft as velvet which made the horses' mouths water. We pitched camp.

In the glow of the firelight, Temüjin told us the sacred nature of this place.

'This is the burial ground of the ancestors of all the peoples. In the beginning this valley was lower than the vein of the divine Orhon. Then Mother Earth filled it with the slough of her womb. Look, up there, you can see her mound.'

We looked in the direction he was pointing, squinting to make out the faint, bow-shaped gleam in the darkness.

'At dawn,' continued To'oril, 'we will climb there with our belts around our necks to purify ourselves at her hips.'

The next day, as the beaters skirted the massifs, we ascended the steep slopes until we reached a long ridge where nothing grew. Our guide pointed to what he considered to be the origin of the world – a mountain, perfect in its curves, which was the Earth's vulva. Cylindrical in shape and adorned with a coat of blue ash, it reared skywards, towering disdainfully above its neighbours, unreachable, its peak fringed with snow. A glistening halo of mist cloaked its upper reaches, but through a broad rift one could see the beautiful giantess's inner walls. Dizzying chasms that were hard to make out, since even the sun's rays could not take hold there, but were instantly swallowed up by the phosphorescent blue of the enormous cavity.

'Long ago,' said To'oril, 'Mother Earth poured out the blood which replenishes all female kind. Rocks and molten waves flowed out of her sex, gouging away the soil and turning it inside out like a ewe's fleece. This valley became an immense inferno as the River Orhon wasted away in agonised convulsions. Only after two moons did Mother Earth's loins grow calm and more than two winters passed before her discharge set and grew cold. Those black, jagged rocks we rode through and these tall cliffs lining the Orhon like ramparts are the mark of that sublime purge.'

To'oril rubbed the scar on his cheek, then went on to say that, thanks to its stubborn persistence, the Orhon had managed to work its way under the solid lava, whittle it down and finally carry away the great sheets, one by one, that blocked its path.

Above us, a pair of eagles were calling their eaglet. Nilqa, To'oril's son, fired an arrow and hit one in the wing. His father yelled, 'You brat! Must I tie your hands behind your back? That female you just wounded could have taken us to her eaglet and gained us a precious ally. Go, retrieve your arrow, and don't come back until you have – I do not want it said that my son is clumsier than a woman about to give birth.'

Temüjin signalled to me to go and find the eaglet so that we could give it to To'oril. Seeing Nilqa unsure which direction to take, I advised him to follow me. He said he had no orders to take from a horseboy, so I set off on my own for the escarpment which the birds had been flying over.

I found the eaglet soon enough. It was below the ridge amongst a confused mass of rocks, its beak in the air. I took off my boot to carry it, then spotted the wounded female slightly higher up. Wings outspread, she was trying to pull the arrow out with her beak. I climbed towards her as her mate hovered overhead, craning his neck. When I was in range, I took aim and . . . Nilqa's voice rang out, ordering me to leave his prey. He was too far to have a hope of shooting true, so I finished her off, then went back for the eaglet.

Delighted with the gift, the Kereyid king waited for his son to climb down, then handed the bird to him, saying, 'You did not kill the mother, so he's yours to feed and tame.'

Nilqa cut me a murderous look, like that of an exhausted camel when he sees the camel-driver striding impatiently towards him, stick in hand.

Upstream from the waterfall, we formed up into a solid wall of archers, apart from a few gaps we left to add spice to the hunt and make it easier to surround our prey. Driven towards us by the beaters, they poured in from dawn to sunset.

The peaks were becoming wreathed in purple when we dismounted. The men set about cutting up the spoils and making fires, as the gourds of koumiss were passed from hand to hand. To'oril congratulated us on our shooting, particularly Qasar, who had been the outstanding bowman. With one exception – a lynx he had finished off with his spear – he had needed only a single arrow for each kill. Now he was laughing heartily and greedily stoking his fevers with the fermented milk that slurs words and makes a man unsteady on his legs.

It was then that To'oril told us that he had received a visit from the Jin at his *ordo* a few days before our arrival, 'Messengers of Prince Wan-yen Hsiang, a subject of the Golden King'.

'What, and you didn't cut their balls off?' Qasar asked, astonished, his face flushed with koumiss.

'No,' said To'oril. 'I left their little coins in their silk drawers because they had something very interesting to tell me. The alliance between the Jin and the Tatars has soured. The former no longer want the latter anywhere near the great stone serpent that bounds their kingdom.'

'My scouts reported a great gathering of the Tatars in the Uldja valley, not far from our lands,' Temüjin said. 'This must be the reason for it.'

'And there will be others,' To'oril assured him. 'Because this Wan-yen Hsiang does not want them as his guard dogs any more. What would you say to falling on their rear and slaying them like this game stretched at our feet? Their herds are large, their girls comely and the Jin will not fail to reward us – at least that was the promise they made me.'

Temüjin threw his koumiss into the distance.

'The Golden King's favours mean little to me. Nothing could match the pleasure I'd get from crushing those vermin and avenging my father.'

After long discussions, the two sovereigns agreed to gather on the first day of the Moon of the Hoopoe's Dance and give the Tatars a winter's respite. Their day of reckoning seemed far off, but Temüjin knew that this delay would allow us to observe them closely.

'The main thing,' joked Qasar, 'is that they won't have time to grow fat.'

Half a moon passed at To'oril's encampments. We hunted, matched ourselves in games of skill or wrestling bouts and feasted often, but above all we relished the sweet light of that autumn's end.

A few days before we were to leave, To'oril was amazed to find out that neither Belgütei's nor my wife's wombs had borne fruit. I tried to convince him that my return would correct this, but to be certain, he declared that I had to spend a night on the Fertile Rock.

This was a great white rock, half-buried in the ground and shaped like a man's sex and scrotum. Even more astonishing was its setting – a hollow in a hillside tenderly sculpted by the rains to be a perfect replica of a woman's loins. The rock's powers of fertility were such that it was reputed to make even old maids pregnant. Polished by the seasons and the buttocks of sterile women, apparently I needed only spend one night on it for Gerelma, five days' ride away, to conceive. To'oril was so convinced and insistent that I did as he wished. It was a perfectly still, moonless night. I had barely laid my fur blanket on the grass before I felt someone near. Hobbling my horse, I peered into the gloom and made out the outline of someone curled into a ball. In three bounds, I was on them, knife in hand. It was a woman. I smothered her cry. She tried to get to her feet, stumbled and soon her hands stretched out towards my forehead grew still.

She was the first of a long procession, because that night the famous rock was visited by women of all ages, many of them old maids and senile grandmothers. Of these, apart from their clumsy kisses, I still remember a strong smell of piss.

Chapter 26

The great Uldja valley lay at our feet, masked in darkness. Next to me, sitting side-saddle, elbows on knees and chins cupped in the palms of their hands, Qasar was chewing a twig and Temüge was sucking a piece of *aarul*. The Khan's youngest brother was barely sixteen springs, with a dark down on his upper lip, and this was his first major expedition. But like a true Mongol, he was perfectly calm before the start of battle. Temüjin had ordered him to follow Qasar into the charges. I was to cover him and see he did not become carried away like a young bee gathering pollen in the first days of sun.

Behind us, further down the slopes, our troops were formed up. With the Kereyid we were more than twenty thousand. Only Sacha Beki's Jürkin were missing. We had waited for them for three days until Temüjin had lost patience and ordered us to move out. To'oril, who was commanding the right wing, had set off to skirt the Uldja valley by the south.

A light breeze bore a smell of hot ash from the enemy's encampment. Clad in his dark armour, Qasar was looking at me, smiling, his eyes greedy, his hair wild. His good-natured, round face, his insouciance, the strength he emanated – all these attributes made him a magnificent companion. I smiled back at him.

'We're soon going to find out,' he said in a low voice, 'if Tatar girls' beauty is a match for their Merkid sisters.'

'You seem very starved for a young father of a family. I'll have to talk to Metekna . . .'

'And I to Gerelma about your night on the Fertile Rock. No, don't play the innocent. You left enough souvenirs in Kereyid wombs for them never to be lonely again.'

'I don't know what you mean,' I said, disingenuous and delighted.

'It would be the first time,' whispered Qasar, 'someone bit into a biscuit and didn't make any crumbs.'

After that we waited in silence until first light.

Our tactics were to send three to four centuries around their camp. The Tatar launched twice the number of horsemen. Ours then retreated behind the hills, drawing the enemy straight towards our reserve troops which surrounded and decimated them. By the time they understood the trick, they were outnumbered and it was too late. After that they did not dare make any forays beyond the triple row of stakes protecting their tents – their second mistake. It was easy for us to put them to the slaughter, like sheep in a pen.

After three days of fighting the Tatars laid down their arms. Five thousand of them were stretched on the ground; we counted them as we stripped their corpses. The same number surrendered. Unsure what to do with them, even more so because Kököchü had seen signs that they would be a source of trouble, Temüjin called a meeting of his council.

Belgütei and I thought we should keep them as slaves and share them out amongst the clans. Qasar thought there were too many and was inclined for us to be rid of them. Temüge said nothing but was not averse to the prospect of more heads rolling in the ground.

When each of us had given his opinion, Temüjin Khan spoke: 'Victory has made you blind. You are like hares in springtime. The steppe smells sweet, it's bathed in sunshine, the scamperer is happy. He hops from tuft to tuft. By evening he is sated; it feels like he has won a great victory. But as he grows fatter and fatter, the hare becomes forgetful. That shadow on the ground is so far away. Yet it is the eagle's that carried off his father last summer ... Have you forgotten the names of your father's poisoners?'

He raised his voice, which shook with anger and reproach. 'And have you forgotten the names of those who handed brave Ambakai over to the Golden King?'

We shook our heads in silence.

'Temüge! What were Ambakai's last words? ... Let me remind you who he was and how he was tortured, and then perhaps you will try to remember in the future. Kabul Khan, his cousin, had chosen him as his successor. Ambakai was tired of the constant fighting with the Tatars, fighting which only played into the Jin's hands who have always set the tribes against each other. So he sought to make a pact with the most powerful of the

Tatar chiefs. His daughter was among the gifts he brought with him and he took only a light escort. The Tatars fell on them, clamped them in heavy *cangues* and delivered them to the court of the Golden King. There Ambakai was thrown into a well of brackish, stinking water which sapped his flesh, as invisible parasites burrowed into him. When he was so weakened that he was nothing but a lousy, rotting puppet, they led him to the centre of a square where a wooden ass stood with a bristling strip of spikes along its back. The crowd pressed forward. The Mongols' leader was hoisted astride this accursed animal and impaled. He summoned enough strength to cry out, "I Ambakai, of the Sovereigns Clan, Khan of all the Mongols, vomit on you Jin pigs." The crowd pelted him with stones and excrement. From his high balcony the Golden King commanded that he be flayed alive with blades as fine as silk and as long as a pelican's beak.

'Husked like grain, Ambakai howled in excruciating pain and in a last agonised convulsion, his eyes two pits seething with vipers, he screamed, "Sons of Blue Wolf, avenge me, avenge me! Should you have to tear out the nails of all your fingers, should you have to tear out your very fingers!" There, Temüge, that is what he said before he died. As for his daughter, the Tatars raped her so brutally that she died on the second day. Well? Do you still think that we should spare our prisoners?'

'No, let us kill them! Let us cut off their heads and give them as offerings to Yesügei and Ambakai!'

Temüjin rose to his feet. 'Good. Tomorrow Belgütei will stay behind to divide them up. Any that are taller than the axle of my cart, women and children included, will be put to the sword on our return.'

In the meantime we were to catch up with Daritai, Altan and Quchar's troops. Temüjin had ordered them to hunt down the Tatars who had scattered to the west and we had had no news of them. Something was hiding behind this silence.

The Tatar camps we rode through to the west of the Khingan Mountains were charnel-houses. All the dead had had their ears and fingers cut off so that the Jürkin could take their rings. The men had been disembowelled, the women raped, and all the corpses stripped; apart from the inevitable scavengers marauding in packs, we saw only destruction and wavering plumes of

smoke. No trace of weapons, chests, cauldrons, bowls, dishes or
airag pails.

We rode for four days on the Jürkins' trail and each day
Temüjin's anger grew. Plainly they had paid no heed to the
yasak on the spoils of war, which he had ratified at the start of
the campaign. Once victory had been won, the Khan alone was
to supervise the sharing out of the enemy's possessions. Before
then no one was to take a part for himself. Whoever transgressed
this law would have to face the consequences.

'Perhaps the Jürkin princes have gathered the spoils together
to make their division easier,' Qasar suggested, to play down the
importance of the sights that met our eyes.

'They have ignored my orders,' the Khan flared up, striking
his saddle with his fist. 'I will teach them discipline.'

At dawn on the fifth day, one of our trackers found the
Mongol princes' troops making for the blue mountains of the
Onon river. Clearly they were not returning to the Uldja valley,
as had been agreed. We gave chase straightaway and outflanked
them by evening. Their long columns stretched like clouds across
a vast plain glowing red in the setting sun.

In their rear captives and herds of oxen and camels taken from
the enemy struggled forward, swaying under the weight of their
loads.

Centuries were deployed on the summits, as Temüjin, at the
head of a light detachment, took up position at the mouth of the
plain. The Jürkin scouts were soon before him.

'Tell your masters to halt their convoy. Altan, Daritai and
Quchar are to dismount and come here on foot!'

This was how, humiliated, the three princes appeared before
him.

'By what authority have you turned your back on the Uldja
and claimed these spoils?'

'They are ours by right,' Altan protested indignantly. 'This has
always been the way, since the time of our ancestors ... '

'Silence!' Temüjin broke in. 'You are not fit to speak of them.
You Jürkin, like so many of the other Mongol clans, think you
can ride more than one horse at a time. When will you learn
discipline?'

Then he disarmed them and compelled them to return to their
lands empty-handed.

The next day our caravan set off back to the Uldja valley
where To'oril impatiently awaited our return.

At the rear of the convoy was a cart carrying a black tent drawn by two white camels. A child with a freshly shaven head marched proudly at the animals' side, two gourds slung over his shoulders and two quivers filled with field-mice arrows jiggling at his belt. He had a gold ring through one nostril and wore a shirt of hides and silk with a fur collar. Temüjin asked him his name. He said he was Shigi, son of Cheren the Great, one of the Tatar chiefs we held captive in the Uldja valley. Turning to me, my *anda* gave instructions that this child should be given to Mother Hö'elün, saying that it was honourable to spare orphans.

I was more interested in the black yurt. I lifted up the felt flap and ordered its occupants to show themselves. They were slow complying; I lashed the yurt's wall with my whip and threatened to set fire to it. There was a sound of rustling in the darkness, then the face of the most wondrous of all Tatar women emerged into the light. I almost fell from my horse. She was kneeling, her head bowed, trembling slightly. Her face, framed by two long plaits richly adorned with jewels and brooches, was of that pure whiteness that in winter shrouds the steppe. A further set of jewels swung at her neck to the rhythm of the cart's progress. Her fluttering eyelashes looked as soft as sable and her mouth was as full as the lotus bud.

Sensing Temüjin at my shoulder, I let the doorflap fall.

'It's strange,' he said. 'These Tatars are ruddy-faced but their women have complexions like milk.'

Still dazed, I told him I'd like to take her as my wife.

'I granted you the privilege of taking the pick of the captives before the noblemen. But with one proviso: the Khan must first have taken his share. Well, this Tatar woman pleases him. Enjoy that Merkid woman I gave you instead. Mother of Pearl Stream. If her name is to be believed, she will bring you manifold delights.'

With that he galloped off to the head of the train.

I lifted up the felt again. The Tatar had not moved, except that now she was looking at me. O Tenggeri, I thought, what spirit of mischief prompted you to create such beauty?

I asked her name.

'Yesügen,' she said, trying to hide her faint smile with the tip of her shoulder. She was Cheren the Great's daughter and the little prince Shigi was her younger brother.

She in turn asked me who the man was who had just left me. I told her he was the Mongols' khan and that, to my great misfortune, he had chosen her to be one of his wives.

'Do not be sad,' she said gently. 'I have a sister whose beauty is so great that at her side I become dull and insipid. Everything I desire, she desires. Find her, kill her lover, and when she finds out that you love me and that I am wretched not to be yours, she will want to be your wife. Her name is Yesüi; she is my eldest sister and she will increase your happiness tenfold.'

I could not believe it. Was it possible that her sister could be more graceful than her, pure wonder that she was?

She reached out to the edge of the felt doorflap and touched my fingers. Then the yurt's flap fell and we were separated.

I reined in my horse and, paralysed, watched the cart move away. Yesügen's crystalline song rose up from the black yurt:

> The princesses are going to the kings
> And their fathers' hearts swell with joy
> But if they saw their daughters' tears
> Their sighs at the laughter of a horseherd
> At the sight of a nimble-fingered saddler
> Or the flight of a bird high in the azure
> Would they succumb to grief?
> I am the Princess Yesügen
> Brought to tears by a tender smile
> Barely glimpsed, vanished already
> The Khan has mastered him
> Driven him away
> For I was fated
> To take my place by the throne.

Chapter 27

To'oril received his share of the spoils. Well satisfied, he clasped us in his arms and then disappeared at the head of his black warriors towards his distant kingdom in the west.

That night, under cover of darkness, I slipped away from the revels to the prisoners' camp, which was guarded by six ranks of archers. I ordered that Cheren the Great be brought to my tent.

One of the Tatar chief's eyes was closed, bruised and swollen by a blow. The other was the merest slit, yellow as amber. I bade him sit.

'Where is your eldest daughter, whose name is Yesüi?'

'Isn't my youngest enough?'

'No harm will be done her.'

'You Mongols are cut-throats. You have kidnapped and raped my wives, slit the throats of a hundred of my people . . .'

'Listen, Cheren. Your daughter Yesügen has been chosen by Temüjin Khan. If our men find your eldest, Yesüi, they will mete out the same treatment to her as they did to your wives. Beauty drives them into a frenzy like wolves after a winter's privation. Suppose she survives and they take her to the Khan. He won't want her; he'll just hand her over to one of our ravenous chiefs. But I want your daughter as my wife. If she is mine she will be treated like a queen because I am the Khan's right hand.'

'What will you give me in exchange?'

'Your life.'

'It matters little to me whether I live or die. Promise me only to preserve my soul by seeing that none of my blood is shed.'

'I give you my word.'

'What will happen to my men?'

I told him that some would be sent back to our camp and the others suffocated, like him, without bloodshed. It was a lie and, as I saw his eyes grow dark, I thought he had guessed as much.

Yet still he told me where I might find his daughter, who had fallen in love with a petty king named Gold Ring.

Temüjin, his brothers and I were waiting to watch the prisoners' execution from the top of a hill when their camp was thrown into turmoil. Hand-to-hand fighting, shouting, men collapsing – to our amazement, more of our men seemed to be falling to the ground than theirs. The Tatars were wielding improvised weapons which they had taken out of their sleeves or boots.

Reinforcements arrived to stem the fighting.

'Which of you betrayed the council's secret and warned the Tatars?' asked Temüjin.

I confessed.

'We have lost many men because of your stupidity, Bo'urchu. You deserve to be punished, as you well know. But you are my faithful wolf. When I honoured you on the day of my investiture, I promised to redeem ten of your offences. There are only nine left. Try not to use them.'

The fighting came to a halt. The order was given to put the wounded Tatars, a hundred in all, to the sword. Cheren the Great was among them, blood pouring from his belly and neck.

Temüjin ordered me to disembowel him.

'We will not have died in vain,' the Tatar chief said. 'We have taken more Mongols with us than we could have hoped. They will be pillows for us in the tomb and you, forked tongue . . . '

He tried to spit but broke into a coughing fit and spattered my face with what remained of his lungs.

I cut short his death throes.

Temüjin decided to prolong our stay on that land stained with the enemy's blood, no doubt because he was susceptible to the charms of that newly won corner of the steppe, but primarily so that he could enjoy his fill of Yesügen, with whom he seemed mightily smitten. How could he be otherwise? Her beauty was past all comprehension. As the Khan stared at her with mounting fascination, I saw the same expression of dumb bewitchment I must have worn at Queen of Flowers' side. So, I was not the only Mongol to be laid low by a woman's face.

He gave orders for a wedding banquet to be prepared.

On the third night of festivities, when a young musician's love song rose up to the stars, the Khan's new wife shivered. She was dressed in a white silk *del* embroidered with intertwined, scarlet dragons and her headdress was exquisitely adorned with coral, silver and delicate kingfisher feathers. Temüjin called for his blue wolf coat to drape around her shoulders, but Yesügen shook her head.

Temüjin seemed to take this askance. The night air was warm. He scrutinised the princess's profile for a moment, then questioned her: 'A man is pulling at the strings of your heart, isn't he? Answer me!'

'No,' said the young woman, bowing her head respectfully. 'It is my sister.'

'Why?'

'I miss her.'

'Then we will go in search of her. Does that comfort you?'

'No.'

'Explain yourself.'

'Her beauty is greater than mine. You will spurn me the moment you see her.'

'Nonsense.'

My heart began to beat faster.

'Yesüi is more translucent than a spring,' she continued thoughtfully. 'And whiter than a swan's neck. The sound of her voice intoxicates any who hear it so profoundly that they cannot imagine living without her. When she sings, the nightingales are struck dumb. Many are the princes who have died because they have failed to win her heart. She is fit for an emperor.'

'Where is she?'

'Ah my Khan, you see how impatient you are?'

'Were I to possess the most radiant beauties on this earth, you would still be among my favourites. You have nothing to fear.'

'When your army fell on us, she fled with the man she is supposed to marry.'

'We will find her, and if I succumb to her beauty, then you will join us on my couch to distract my caresses.'

'O my Khan, I would be so flattered.'

Yesügen turned to watch the musician but as I looked at her, I realised her delight at feeling both the Khan and me gazing at her delicious profile.

Tormented, I stood up.

'Where are you going?' he asked, not taking his eyes off his adorable viper.

'To see the horses.'

'Take Temüge with you. And Belgütei and ten centuries. Ride

like the wind and find the princess Yesüi. I am impatient to know if what my dove says is true.'

So that was how I found myself at the head of a thousand warriors, most of them roaring drunk, riding towards the forests of Mount Khingan through the warm, sweet night that to me, despite all my efforts, seemed so cold and drab.

A band of five of these men flushed her out of a copse of young firs when we had thrown down the tents of the small encampment and were holding their occupants captive. The beautiful girl sped off down the slope, legs bare to the thighs, her *del* partly ripped away, with two of them at her heels. Two others started fighting and the fifth, who had seized hold of her for a moment, fell off his horse.

Although they knew she was forbidden fruit, the Khan's harvest alone, those two fools were still trying to tear her to pieces. Laughing, they threw themselves at her boots as she pirouetted and skipped out of their reach.

I put my horse into a gallop and was halfway towards them when they managed to bring her down. The one who had lost his stirrups had caught them up and was belabouring the first man he could lay his hands on. Only one lucky one, the most frenzied, was left – he violently attacked the princess, desperate to breach her waxy bastion. But his was a short-lived hope. I seized his plait, jerked his head back and slit his throat, taking care that the gushing blood did not spatter the fair Tatar.

The brawlers meekly got to their feet. I ordered that they be tied back-to-back by the wrists and taken to the Khan's tent on foot and under close guard. On horseback, this was four days' journey; it would take them at least five times as long. But they were in no hurry – once they stood before Temüjin, I knew it would be the end of their earthly lives.

I turned back to Yesügen's sister.

'Are you Yesüi, eldest daughter of Cheren the Great?'

She batted her eyelashes, and I felt the shock in the pit of my stomach. The horde of men pressed closer, every one of them staring greedily at her ivory thighs.

I told her to take one of the riderless horses and when she had mounted, I took off my jerkin and laid it across her knees. Then I went back to the corpse, cut off its head and hung it from her mount's saddle. My father had taught me that wolves delay the kill when they see what has become of one of their own.

Once we were under way, she wanted to know where we were taking her.

Belgütei answered. Usually so detached, it seemed as if he would never grow tired of looking at her. Temüge likewise.

Yesügen had not lied. Her sister was so beautiful that one could have followed her without one's feet ever touching the ground or one even feeling tired. She was as slender as a reed, and her long hair which gathered in folds on the saddle could have covered her like a cloak. Everything about her was glistening and undulating and I envied my *anda* who, provided Yesüi did not cause a revolt on the way, would be the lake into which this river flowed. She radiated light, casting such a spell over us that we started if she so much as parted her lips, and her voice lulled us like waves on the seashore.

'I don't want Yesügen anywhere near me.'

Chuckling, Temüge assured her that Temüjin would be nearer her than her sister.

'He is our eldest brother, the Khan,' he added, pride in his voice. 'When he faces the enemy, his warriors run up in their thousands to carry his standard. He has taken your sister as wife, but you are who he wants as favourite.'

'I want nothing to do with your khan,' said the gazelle sullenly. 'Let me go.'

'Wait until you have seen him,' I said. 'He is tall and strong and there is such a fire in his eyes that he makes the hardest frozen hearts burst into flame.'

She tipped back her head and shut her eyes tight. I assumed she was addressing Tenggeri.

The moment he saw Yesüi, Temüjin shut himself away with her in his tent and savoured her for nine days in succession.

Eventually he rejoined us and almost single-handedly devoured a Tatar horse which had been killed in battle. As he restored the strength drained from him by the caresses of love, with Yesüi and Yesügen pressed to his side, the festivities resumed and wrestlers, singers, dancers, musicians and virtuosos of every stripe sought in turn to entertain him.

The day before we were to strike camp, Jelme was singing the lay of a man whose woman and horse have been stolen from him, when Yesüi heaved a sigh of such melancholy that it set the pearls and jewels of her headdress jingling.

'Who is the man who casts a cloud over your eyes and my joy?'

She shuddered.

The Khan turned to Yesügen, and the younger sister jerked her chin in the direction of the musicians.

Quicker than the lightning striking the earth, Temüjin grasped the situation. He asked me to call the men together and when the army was arrayed before him, he ordered his warriors to group themselves by clan.

Then he commanded, 'Identify yourselves, each in turn, and cast out of your ranks any man you do not recognise as one of your own.'

When they had done so, a handful of Tatar children taller than a cart's axle stood apart; they had been spared because they were orphans.

In front of the Besut clan, however, stood a man. He must have been twenty springs and although he wore the scaled breastplate of a Mongol archer, the features of his face set him apart.

He was taken to the Khan. When he stayed standing, I forced him to his knees.

Temüjin's eyes had become like the wolf's – two slits aflame with blazing thunderclouds that contrasted with the pallor of his Tatar wives; sitting either side of him, they were as white as ermine, and Yesüi the whitest of all. She kept on glancing furtively at the man's face and every time she did so, she seemed on the verge of fainting. The depths of a lake could not have been more silent than that moment.

'Whose spy are you?' Temüjin asked finally.

'No one's,' the stranger answered hastily.

'To what do we owe your presence then?'

He darted a wretched look at Yesüi, whose head shook.

The Khan understood. He rose, approached the handsome intruder and asked him who he was. The man replied that he was the son of a chief responsible for the peace of thirty yurts.

'I am Gold Ring, son of Valiant Heart, chief of a small clan allied to the Onggirad. For Yesü's sake, I pledged my arrows to the Tatar cause. When your warriors found her, I followed them from crest to crest and slipped in amongst them. Noble Khan, let me serve you.'

Temüjin looked at Yesüi. She was shaking like a leaf and wringing her hands. Then he looked deep into my eyes and bit his lower lip. Our hunting signal was unequivocal: 'Cut his throat!'

I would have rather he performed the task himself. Was it not the honour of his favourite that was at stake? But I understood that he was loath to offend the Onggirads, Börte's and Mother Hö'elün's tribe of birth.

The handsome lover's head rolled to the ground.

Yesüi sobbed as Yesügen undisguisedly took a deep breath, a look of satisfaction on her face as if my sabre had relieved her of a great weight.

That night Temüjin made no change in his habits and slept with the two sisters.

At dawn the next day, we left the Uldja valley.

After ten days' ride, one of our scouts came galloping back, hell for leather, to the head of our columns. When we saw his desperate speed, a dark suspicion took hold of us.

Chapter 28

We had prepared ourselves, but still we missed the usual shouts and laughter of children running towards us and the barking of the dogs. A cluster of horses came to greet us as we descended the slopes, but the great reserve herds of many colours were nowhere to be seen. On the faces of the broken-down old men who slowly approached and the women wiping their cheeks grimed with dust and tears, we saw humiliation.

Temüjin reined in his mount in front of his yurt and, without dismounting, listened to his wife whose belly once again was rounded and curved down to her thighs.

'They stripped us and had their sport,' she said. 'Swarming like flies among the tents, they took what they pleased and beat our brave elders as they reached for their quivers.'

Temüjin asked me to bring him a fresh horse. 'A horse that can fight like a lion. One that, even when his coat is drenched in foam and blood, will gallop on and scythe through those unworthy descendants of Kabul Khan.'

Our scout's report had been accurate: the Jürkin tribe led by Sacha Beki had taken advantage of our absence to betray us and ransack our encampments. Double betrayal – premeditated, what's more – because Sacha Beki had not appeared as agreed to fight the Tatars.

Amongst the horses we had taken from these latter was Cheren the Great's, a magnificent black charger which we had seen hurling himself, mouth agape, at our archers. But when he was ours, no one could make him move and I had had to unsaddle him and lead him on the leading-rein back to our lands. We called him 'The Unridden', but when I mentioned him to Temüjin, he gave him a different name.

'Grey Ear? Harness him; he's just what I need.'

He was observant: the charger's right ear was indeed flecked with grey.

The Khan gave me no time to remind him of the horse's recalcitrance, because Börte had caught sight of Yesüi and Yesügen and he had to usher her quickly back into his tent.

Before any of us able to do so had changed our mounts and the rest had filled their saddlebags with fresh rations, the first columns were already on the move, heading towards the west.

Gerelma came towards me with a loving expression. I was not fooled; we were returning with gifts, after all.

I told her to see the keepers of the spoils, they would give her my share, amongst which were silver bowls and jugs worked with fine gold, pieces of silk, a fox fur and heavy wicker baskets full of rye. 'The *del*, the feather-and-pearl headdress and the young horse with a blaze are for Mother of Pearl Stream,' I added. 'Make sure she gets them.'

The silk *del* was printed with intertwined flowers between which flitted pink, purple and turquoise birds. It must have belonged to a Tatar noblewoman, as must the headdress in the form of a swan, its wings outspread and dripping with semi-precious stones. As for the little horse with the blaze, it was a piebald colt with dark markings on his back and flanks, patches on the skin that were almost blue and showed through his coat like indigo through milk.

Gerelma grimaced, shrugged, then went off muttering, 'Always every consideration for that Merkid. A slave who does as she pleases and wants him nowhere near her.'

I had Grey Ear saddled and behind the Blind Man on the leading-rein. After a short wait, Temüjin came up to us followed by Börte, who was holding the libation jug and dipper.

'Hey, Bo'urchu! Are you going to lead me behind your rump like a brat who can't stay in the saddle?'

'No, my Khan. But you know we haven't been able to make Grey Ear move.'

'You haven't. But I will. Do you want to lay a wager?'

'Yes.'

'Go on, I am listening,' he said, giving me a presumptuous look.

'If you can't master Grey Ear, you have to give me Yesügen.'

'Ah! Agreed. And what about you? What will you give me if you lose? One of your Merkid women. Mother of Pearl Stream? Or Queen of Flowers?'

He saw I was at a loss and quickly added, as he pulled himself up onto Grey Ear, 'I know, she's invisible. So let's say I choose her.'

I untied the leading-rein and handed it to him. He gathered it with the reins in his left hand and, with his right hand, pinched the black horse between the ears, then stroked its neck down to the withers.

'The Jürkin believe us dead. Let us go and give them a taste of the Blue Wolves' teeth. Shoo, shoo!'

As he said this, Grey Ear set off at a gallop, leaving me in his wake, dumbfounded.

The Jürkin were at the highest point of the Seven Hills in a bend of the Kerulen. Temüjin and I knew the place well from having lived nearby in the dark folds of the Red Mountains six springs previously.

Now the young khan was returning at the head of thousands of Mongols and although most did not have breastplates, all could boast two pairs of quivers full of arrows, one pair at the belt or slung across their shoulders, the other hanging either side of the saddle.

The Jürkin were bound to think that we had been weakened by the campaign against the Tatars. Not wanting to set them straight and risk them turning tail, Temüjin only deployed ten centuries in front of their encampments. Twenty more were put out of sight on the plateau of the Island of Grass, and a further twenty led by Qasar and Sübetei were to come by the north-west to cut off any flight through the Kerulen's narrow gorge.

We let the traitors organise their defences for a day and a night, while Qasar and Sübetei's troops took up their positions.

Then as soon as the peaks began to turn pink, the drummers on their great shaggy camels sounded the attack.

The light cavalry surged forward in waves, harrying the enemy's wings with their javelins and arrows. Then they scattered, shields on their backs, still loosing their arrows, to make way for the lances, maces and sabres of the caparisoned cavalry. Our first onslaught threw the Jürkin into disarray. By the fourth, their defences were in shreds.

The sun was not yet overhead by the time we finished off the last of them still fighting.

Protected by his personal guard of fifty courageous warriors and a further hundred archers, Sacha Beki had managed to flee up the Kerulen. Temüjin Khan ordered Jelme to ford the river and follow at a distance to make sure he did not escape Qasar and Sübetei. When Sacha Beki saw these two ahead of him, a sweeping glance was enough for him to realise he was lost. He chose to put down his arms rather than fight.

Bare-chested, his hands bound behind his back, he was thrown at the Khan's feet. Temüjin Khan studied him for a moment, then asked, 'Did you not swear loyalty to me? Were you not to be the first to fling yourself on the enemy and bring me their heads? Have you forgotten that it was the Tatars who delivered Ambakai Khan and your grandfather, his escort, to the court of the Golden King?'

Sacha Beki said nothing, only hanging his head a little lower at each question.

'ANSWER ME!'

'No, Temüjin, I have not . . .'

'KHAN! I am no longer Temüjin. I am the Khan, TEMÜJIN KHAN!' He lashed his face with his whip.

'No, Temüjin Khan, I have not forgotten,' resumed Sacha Beki, pitiful, his eye red with blood.

Sitting on our horses or squatting on our heels at their feet, we surrounded him and waited for his sentence to be pronounced. The breeze ruffled our topknots, the horses' tufts and the hanks of horsehair fixed to the throats of the lances and banners.

The Khan continued, 'My father used to say that our cousins the Jürkin were like lions. He thought himself fortunate to have them as allies. It has grieved me, Sacha Beki, to have had to fight them and kill those who protected you. You have not only broken your oath of loyalty, you have also incited your people to rob us. Giant was first. Then you disobeyed me by not bringing your ferocious warriors to fight the Tatars, and lastly, like the cowardly, skulking hyena, you pillaged my camp. Is that what you are, unworthy grandson of Kabul Khan – the loathsome hyena?'

The Jürkin prince nodded.

'Stretch out your neck,' the Khan commanded, drawing his sword.

Sacha Beki complied.

'By Tenggeri! May you be my slave for all eternity!'

The blade came down and Sacha Beki's head fell to the ground. Temüjin ordered that it be impaled on a lance.

'Now everyone will know that the Mongol princes and lords are not above the *yasak*.'

To underline this, he ordered that Sacha Beki's brother and two nephews be strangled.

For safety's sake, the remaining Jürkin were dispersed amongst the clans. They would have to prove themselves before they could be permitted to re-establish an *ulus*.

That same evening I rode out with Temüjin and Qasar along the banks of the Kerulen. At our back the Red Mountains had donned their coat of blue shadows; the river was a golden vein in the light of the setting sun and the distant horizon shimmered in the haze.

'I like this place,' Temüjin said. 'Doesn't it remind you of the throne of a giant who wished to touch Tengri's brow? Bo'urchu, do you think this grass will suit our horses?'

'*Anda*, in less than a moon they will not even need to bend their heads. It will tickle their ribs, green and crisp and curved like the edge of your sabre.'

Temüjin looked at his brother.

'You hear our friend? He knows what is borne on the wind. Plant our standard on the lip of that slope.' He pointed to a wave of grass which formed an amber border to the mountains' peaks.

'Raise my yurt there. Then I will be able to see the Kerulen from my threshold. Tell Belgütei and Temüge to set off now to bring back our women and herds.'

Qasar sped towards the crest, his powerful shoulders seeming to support the massive semi-circle of mountains. We heard his mount's hooves drumming the ground, his voice urging him on.

The steppe stretched before us, silent, soft and caressing. Languid in the late sunshine and the faint, dying breeze, Grey Ear and the Blind Man daydreamed, their eyes half-closed.

'Come,' Temüjin asked me. 'I will show you the best place to cross the Kerulen.' He stroked Grey Ear's neck with the handle of his whip and the charger moved off.

I was about to ask him how he had found the key to the black horse's heart, when he turned and said, with a radiant smile, 'It's a secret, Bo'urchu. I cannot tell you because only women and horses benefit from its charms. It is Temüjin Khan's caress!'

Chapter 29

The death of the Jürkin princes echoed far across the steppes. Was it not said when a young wrestler triumphed in his bouts that he was as strong and noble as a Jürkin?

Camel dealers, caravaneers, yak-drivers, artisans and bards spread the news. From west to east, horseherds, shepherds, berry-gatherers, fur trappers – all knew that young Temüjin Khan had killed his cousin at the foot of the Seven Hills for indiscipline and treachery, just as they all knew that he had previously punished Quchar, his elder cousin Altan and his uncle Daritai for their disobedience.

'Temüjin Khan is unbending,' said the elders around the fires. 'He is just and powerful and fears no one. He makes strong his khanate. Here is a leader who will be able to guide us and make us rich.'

And so, at the edge of the thousands of yurts that made up the young Khan's *ordo*, not a day passed without swathes of felt being stretched over fresh latticework slats and roof frames.

One fine day he called them together and said, 'Apart from stroking your horses, embracing your wives and fighting amongst yourselves, your hands are idle. We will give them something to occupy themselves.'

Never had the Island of Grass seen such activity. Everyone threw themselves into their work – saddlers and harness-makers, with their carved wooden frames, their dried grass, their squares of felt, hide and richly ornamented fabric, their silver studs; tanners fashioning the water bottles, leather lace and whips we took on campaigns, and cutting out scales of leather to pad the armour; furriers and weavers working side by side with shearers, as blacksmiths, armourers and tinsmiths, in a lather of sweat, filed, hooked and beat the metal to the same pounding rhythm. Everyone good-humouredly helped their neighbour or relative and the youngsters' laughter rang out, undiminished by the barrels of water they ferried to and fro or by the fleeces which turned their noses white and made them sneeze. The women wove and sewed, chewing pieces to soften them or treading the wet hides on the banks of the river, whilst the eldest made cheeses which they put to dry on the sunlit roofs, or prepared rations of meat which they hung in the spirals of smoke rising from the embers.

The men joyfully threw out their bare chests and Tenggeri shared in the merriment, his sky the purest of blues. However, one cloud remained in the Khan's eyes, a cloud whose name was Giant, the man who had wounded Belgütei in the shoulder during his investiture banquet. Temüjin had spared the life of this most famous of wrestlers and nothing indicated what was to follow. Nothing, that is, apart from a sign.

Lodged in Giant's maddened, shifty eyes, this sign was known as fear, that unimaginable canker of the soul I would recognise later on the faces of the besieged.

The Jürkin mastiff shrank into himself and stopped his barking, wishing himself elsewhere yet only managing to make his presence ten times more obvious. His frame would have blocked out a grown camel at two paces, yet he tried to be lighter than the field mouse as it scampers, panic-stricken, across the steppe.

One night when we were feasting, the Khan invited the men to wrestle. *Dels* and shirts fell to the ground and arms locked until the defeated rolled in the dust and the victors rose to their feet to circle in the dance of the eagle's flight.

Giant kept in the background, watching out of the corner of his eye and none of the Jürkin around him dared kindle his fighting spirit. The Khan revelled in the spectacle and seemed to ignore their group.

But then, as praises were being sung to the hundred victors who were to meet in the final contest, he addressed the council of judges: 'No wrestling tournament would be worthy of the Khan if the greatest of all wrestlers did not take part. Let the invincible Giant flex his powerful shoulders; I will find him an adversary to rob him of a little of his freshness.'

Temüjin waited until Giant was standing before him, bare-chested, then stared into his eyes. The wrestler grew more and more uneasy. He was about to speak when the Khan named his opponent: 'Belgütei!'

The latter started and exchanged a quick look with his half-brother. Then he stood up, undid the breastplate he wore at all times and, after practising a few feints, nimbly jumping from foot to foot, placed himself in front of his adversary.

A whisper ran through the rows of spectators: *Belgütei hasn't a chance, why didn't the Khan choose Qasar?*

Giant seized Belgütei's forearm and tried to secure his grip but the Khan's half-brother slipped away like a lizard. His second attempt seemed perfect – he had Belgütei lashed against his bull-like hip, and he never normally relaxed a stranglehold – but again Belgütei broke free. The crowd groaned with disappointment. What was happening to the Jürkin rock? Was he intimidated by the Khan's razor-thin eyes fixed upon him? Was this what made him so clumsy?

Clearly he was not giving of his best. Seizing his opportunity, Belgütei dived between Giant's legs, lifted him and threw him to the ground with a great thump. Then, in the same movement, he sprang on him, grabbed his forelock, pulled his head back and laid him flat, a foot in the small of his back. Giant had lost without a fight, his whole body buckling rather than just an elbow or knee grazing the gound. Belgütei glanced at his brother. The Khan parted his lips and sharply bit the lower one.

Straightaway Belgütei broke Giant's neck. It snapped with such a crack that all the dogs pricked up their ears and some got to their feet, their noses quivering. The victor dragged the body out of the wrestling ground and abandoned it at the edge of the plateau, whence it rolled down towards the Kerulen.

Which of the Jürkin would dare defy the Khan now? Deeply impressed by the lesson, a chief of the Jalair clan gave his two sons to Temüjin to be part of his personal guard, with these unnecessary words of advice: 'Let them keep to your threshold. If ever their attention strays, cut their tendons! If ever they prove disloyal, tear out their livers!'

And so the seasons passed between the Kerulen and the Onon, rhythmed by the arrival of the newborns and the departure of the elders who, if they did not ask a grandchild to suffocate them by jamming a sheep's tail down their throat, set off without a word to the mountains to breathe their last close to Tenggeri and offer their flesh to the animals. The shaman Kököchü had seen six of the sun's great cycles. In the year of the Jürkins' subjugation, Börte gave birth to a second boy who, when he started to walk and talk, was given the name Chagatai.

Two winters later, during the great cycle of the Horse, Börte's and the Khan's third son announced his arrival on a starlit night. He grew into a calm, strong boy named Ögödei.

In a sense their eldest son Jochi was the child I did not have. After all, his own mother wouldn't have been able to say whether his real father was Temüjin or the Merkid, Spirit Rabbit. When he was barely six springs, Jochi could hold a bow as steadily as a seasoned archer and steer a horse with complete mastery. Belgütei may have given him his first mount, but it was from me that he learnt how to listen to a horse and make himself understood. He followed me everywhere, saying that he wanted to fight at my side when he was old enough: 'We'll surround the enemy, crush them and deliver them to the Khan before he has even fastened on his armour.'

The youngster deeply admired his father. In his eyes, attacking one's rivals was the only occupation of interest. But, apart from this unshakeable conviction, Little Crumb, as I called him affectionately, was a very agreeable young companion. He did not talk constantly. On the contrary, he was quiet and watchful, paying attention to where he and his horse trod and to the direction of the wind, always careful not to give himself away to any animals which, in his imagination, were his father's enemies. Similarly, he did not ask thoughtless questions, but preferred to puzzle out the answers for himself, his little squirrel's nose upturned, his brows knitted. He did not like it when we made fun of his naive conjectures, but after our laughter was explained to him, he would pull down his fur cap and scratch the back of his head, relieved at having solved one further mystery.

When he shot his first field mouse with a wooden arrow, he brought it proudly to me so that we could share this trophy. I congratulated him: it was a clean shot to the brain and the grain the scamperer had been carrying in his cheeks was untouched.

'Tell me, Little Crumb, did you meet anyone on your way here?'

He thought for a moment, then gave a list of the people who had seen him with his prize: 'Old Sirtan, Bogdo and his two sons, Mergen and his sister who were collecting *argols*, Boro and then my mother with Not Him (his younger brother Chagatai's temporary name).'

'Is that everybody?'

'No, I saw Grandmother Hö'elün and her adopted sons too.'

'Fine. Let's leave aside the women and concentrate on the

hunters. That makes five. Do you know that one never hunts just for oneself and that one always has to give a share to those one respects?'

His face fell. 'There's not going to be much of the field mouse left. With you and me that makes seven.'

'I think you should forget about tasting your first spoils, but remember this as a lesson for the future. If you want the daughter of the Forest Spirit to be generous, you should make her a sacrifice of this pretty field mouse which seemed as wily and strong as a lion. But wisest of all would be to offer it to him who enjoys the pick of the hunts, the Khan, your father.'

He liked this idea. With a flick of his tongue, he scooped up the snot glistening on his top lip and went off to find Temüjin.

He had his mother's pretty eyes, and their fierce expression, which flared up at a trifle, could well have been inherited from his father. But he would never be as massive in stature as Temüjin, even if he were to wrestle every day, and his tall, sinewy frame reminded me of Jamuka. Was it possible that he had two fathers and that my *anda* had withheld the truth of that thorny subject from me? With Chagatai there was no room for doubt. Börte's second son shared some of his mother's features, such as her thin lips, but the handsome proportions of his face were the Khan's and his shoulders were curved like the roof of a yurt. As for Ögödei he was the spitting image of his father and when he started crawling over their felt carpets, the likeness was so striking that it felt as if we were watching the Khan in the first springs of his life. Moreover, until he was weaned, Ögödei's provisional name was The Other.

I remained childless: Gerelma was more sterile than a stone, and Mother of Pearl Stream gave birth to a stillborn. Gerelma threatened to take another husband, as she was entitled to because I had not made her pregnant, but the real purpose of her threats was to make me fear an eternal celibacy, a beyond where I would roam for ever without a wife on my arm.

Her relations with Mother of Pearl Stream were fraught. Although we had Merkid and Tatar slaves, she loaded her with chores of every sort and never missed an opportunity to mock her – her looks of distress, her groans under the strain, her princess's hands which had been spared labour and now were covered in blisters.

At first I had shielded my high-born Merkid wife from Gerelma's persecution in the hope that it would bring us closer.

But Mother of Pearl Stream was stubborner than a camel. Whether I allotted her the choicest or meanest cuts of sheep, whether I draped her shoulders and couch in furs and silks or forced her to sleep on the ground at my feet, she was always the same, never opening her lips or her arms to me or satisfying my desire to see her smile. Cold as the riverbed stone, she yielded but did not submit.

The day she lost her child I found her alone in front of the fire, her eyes shining with tears. I took her head in my hands and stroked her delicately slanting eyes with my thumbs. But when I tried to bury my nose in her soft neck, promising to cover her again at the next moon, she thrust me away.

'Haven't you understood yet? You can ride me until all my teeth are shaken loose, fill me with your seed until I suffocate, but I will never bear a child to the man who stole me from my beloved. Never!' Her whole being shook and her hatred pierced my heart.

'Your body on my back feels as heavy as the camel's, your kisses on my skin smell like the fetid breath of the hyena. How can you hope for a son when I shrink from your arms like hair from a branding iron? Your looks, your strength, your riches mean nothing to me and not a day goes by when I don't envy the birds in the sky. If only I could, I would fly away . . .'

'And I would become a bird of prey.'

'I would dive into a lake.'

'And I would become a fish hook.'

'I would let myself die and become a grain, dull and matt, blown by the wind . . .'

'And you would end up in my beak, since I would be a cock. Enough! You are mine and I will take you with me to my tomb.'

That evening, when I was neglecting my food, Gerelma said, 'Kill her now, because if you wait too long she will escape. That stinking Merkid would rather die by her own hands than by yours.'

An amulet was hanging from the northernmost roofpole of the yurt. 'Wear this round your neck,' she said.

'Who gave it to you?'

'The shaman. He swore that its powers would let you give me a child, just as you gave one to that sour-tempered Merkid. It is a silver birch root soaked in mouse's blood and the seed of a young hyena.'

Kököchü's authority over the clans was growing. Gerelma, like so many others, revered him.

'Kököchü says that it banishes grief as well.'

I said nothing, but the next morning I unhooked the amulet.

So I had no other child than White Cloud. By now my colt had grown into a strong horse. He had spent his first fifteen moons at his mother's side, always some way off from the other horses, but since then I had tethered him outside my yurt. White Moon had aged fast, as if her only child had worn her out before time. At least two or three other stallions had come sniffing round her crupper, snorting with desire, but she had never let herself be wooed again. Soon her fetlocks had sagged and her eyesockets, her mouth and the rims of her ears had taken on a sheen like old sheets grimed with fat. And the time came when White Cloud and I were the only ones to find her as attractive as ever.

Afraid of Bears' son listened and followed me around just like his father. Mischievous but receptive, he never left my side and skilfully performed all the tasks I set him. At first the Blind Man helped me and on his back I taught the colt to rhythm his stride, something to which the Blind Man was perfectly suited since, although his trot and gallop were not the quickest, they were strong, regular and unflagging. So White Cloud acquired an endurance few other colts his age shared. And when he galloped, his balance was superior to our finest horses – another reason I was glad to have delayed breaking him in. How many times did I not marvel at the sight of him galloping at my side, stretching his neck in the last rays of the setting sun, his withers poised, his back as taut as a lance, his muscles sleek, a bold look in those black eyes? It was as if I had a stork flying beside me.

All that remained now was to master his back.

One evening I let the Blind Man rejoin the herd. He stood snorting for a moment, before racing off down the flower-covered slope. I led White Cloud by the leading-rein towards the south. Before we crossed the Kerulen, a whinny rent the air. The Blind Man was saluting us. We walked shoulder to shoulder under the sapping sun and carried on under a starlit sky until at last we reached the steppe, a near desert, bare and empty apart from a few parched copses. We lay down, exhausted and in my case, aching because I had never made such a journey on foot before, and together relished the distance we had travelled, the seal of our complicity.

The following days we spent watching the great herds of saiga and the big cats that tracked them, searching the hazy mirages for the wounded, weakened or fledgling antelope. At night we watched the stars and listened to the breeze slipping past high in the sky, the vole scrabbling nervously at the threshold of his tunnels, the hyenas' yelping. And when the moon showed herself, we could make out the predators' silhouettes criss-crossing the endless plain with their constant back and forth. But next day it all seemed like a dream – in every direction not a shadow drew the eye and only the buzzing of the flies kept us awake.

It was there, in those solitudes bordering the great desert, that I mounted White Cloud. He showed no surprise at first, only contenting himself with listening to me and showing his profile. I urged him forward.

He moved a forefoot, then a hindfoot, then started off at a gentle pace, occasionally looking back at me over his shoulder. It was not until some while later, after we had drunk at a spring and surprised a jackal lying in wait for six terns, that he grew bolder. His thirst quenched, White Cloud lengthened his stride, blew hard at his hooves, and swayed his neck as if he was singing to himself. He broke into a trot, then a gallop. Intoxicated by the speed, he plunged his nostrils to the ground and let himself go, jumping and capering like a sheep and lashing out with his hindlegs. When he had run through his repertoire, he sped off, his neck straight as a pole, towards the Red Mountains.

By the time we reached the camp, the saddle and bit no longer worried him – he even seemed proud to wear them. Now his apprenticeship as a warhorse could begin. But as we were starting, a herdsman came to tell me that White Moon had lain down like a sick dog. Several days before, she had turned her back on the steppe to stand in the lee of a cliff, her muzzle down, her weary eyes half-shut. The herdsman led us to her. The white mare was lying on her side, her nose pressed to the wet ground soaked by the run-off of a spring. I bent down to her head and saw in her eyes my reflection and that of her colt's nose at my shoulder. She tried to express her feelings, but a death rattle prevented her. I soothed her, stroking her jaw. She was colder than a frozen river. In her dying eyes I saw her final message: 'Now I am galloping to Afraid of Bears. I am going, my spirit at peace, leaving behind me two sons, two accomplices . . .'

At any rate that is how I liked to interpret her last breath, which faded without further suffering.

I stood up.

White Cloud went up to the body, sniffed it for a moment, then pressed his nose into my hands. In the distance, in front of the line of tents stretching across the plateau, some men were galloping after a stallion, laughing as he deftly eluded their *ourgas*.

Lying along White Cloud's neck watching the chase, I was suddenly swept up by the immensity of it all, as if my horse's forehead joined me to Tenggeri. Everything became clear and my decision was made – I would not make White Cloud my lead horse, my companion in bloody conquests, always harnessed and waiting outside my yurt. The two of us were becoming one, like the *ourga*, the lasso-pole that is the symbol of love. This feeling of harmony would have to suffice.

It was true that that wily stallion in the distance, so skilled at using his herd to trick the herdsmen, would not have foiled us for long if we had concerted our efforts to catch him. White Cloud was my pole and I was his lasso, and I was in no doubt that he would have become a fearsome warhorse, with furious bursts of speed and a taste for the shock of the fray. But why risk the life of this sole heir? To see him proud and gasping and drenched in blood, to have him savagely trample his kind as they writhed in their death throes, to hear the bards sing his praises? I was convinced of his bravery. I had no need for it to be confirmed. All I wanted was his happiness, as surely as mine went by the name of Queen of Flowers.

I promised to plait him a garland of the most graceful fillies. All he had to do in return was sire colts, colts as white as clouds and as dazzling as lightning.

The Second Part

Chapter 30

The sky was white-hot, like the lid of a cauldron thrust into a fire. Yet still a vulture had taken to it and was wheeling in great circles, a speck no bigger than an eyelash. We say that that carrion-eater will never fail you if you trust it as a guide and, right enough, it was thanks to it that I spotted the man we were looking for. A blur in the heat haze, he emerged in the middle of the great sands that curved away below us. His body seemed to dissolve in the shimmering light and then reform, like a mirage. Tumbleweed blew past him, borne on a dry, burning wind.

He was leading a horse, or the horse was leading him, and high above the pair of them, the scavenger was floating on the hot air currents, saving its strength.

Just behind me nine riders waited in line, their horses, restless from the flies and sweat, running their heads along each others' necks. I sent two messengers, one to the west, the other to the east, to inform the rest of our detachment that we had found our man. Earlier we had set off south with five centuries in rainbow formation and spread out as we went. When each century was almost out of sight of its neighbour, we had split into groups of ten: that way we had kept in step and contact as we advanced along a front that would have taken at least twenty days to ride from end to end.

Now I was watching the man and his horse. They were struggling to make any headway. When the man sank to his knees, I steered the Blind Man towards them through the sandy gullies.

He did not hear me riding up, for he was too busy trying to drink the blood of his fellow unfortunate, whose milky blue eyes showed genuine blindness. His clothes were a mess of tattered rags, his boots worn through to the soles of his feet; the man was almost naked. A few strips of cloth were wound round his head. I tossed my water bottle at his feet.

'Spare your comrade's blood; he'll need it.'

He started and swung round towards me, wielding a thigh bone carved into a crude sabre. He was in such a pitiful state, his eyes so clogged with pus, that I almost failed to recognise him.

'Pleasure to see you again, To'oril.'

'Who are you?'

'The pathfinder.'

'Bo'urchu? Temüjin's faithful companion?'

'At your service.'

What had become of the Kereyid king's arrogant looks? Bizarrely, of his two eyes, the blue one, half-shut by a sabre wound long ago, seemed in the better state. Gone was the black beard which he loved to boast was as soft as the fleece of a newborn lamb; its remnants were white, patchy, lice-ridden. The skin on his face seemed literally plastered to his skull and with his aquiline nose he looked like a vulture that had been soaked in a downpour.

'Take my horse and we'll climb up to the plateau.'

'Have you seen my horse's eyes?' he said, groping around for my water bottle. 'Mine are the same; they can't see any plateau. I planned to head north to Temüjin, but if I've managed it, it's only thanks to the sun.'

He found the bottle, pulled out its horsehair stopper and, throwing back his head, drank in greedy gulps, milk running down his beard. When it was empty, he tossed it away and said, 'To get this horse, I had to behead . . .' That was all he could manage before he vomited up the milk and then belched.

'Mount up,' I said.

'. . . a couple of peasants who lived to the south of this accursed desert, and spent every waking moment of their lives bent double over their pitiful plot of soil. I had to break their daughter's jaw as well – she was a scrawny thing but she made quite a nuisance of herself – anyway, this horse . . .'

'Come, we mustn't keep Temüjin waiting any longer.'

'This horse laboured from dusk till dawn too, trudging round a well and trampling the grain under his twisted hooves. Knowing that the wasteland of the Gobi lay ahead and that my provisions wouldn't last, I earmarked him for my stomach and took their lousy camel as well – that scum, it was almost the death of me. Believe me, Bo'urchu, this horse you see at my side is worth a hundred of that rotten camel and if I'd known, I would have killed and eaten it the moment I saw it. May its soul roam the desert for all eternity!' He tried to spit but he did not have a speck of saliva left.

'Come on,' I said to stop him talking, 'let's go and find Temüjin. He has raised an army and scoured the desert looking for you.'

'Look what that stinking grain-crusher did to me! May all the demons under the earth burrow through his anus and suck out his brain!' He pulled away the rags covering his side.

A vast wound spread from his ribs to his hip and the strips of his *del* which he had used as a makeshift bandage were black with congealed blood.

In a flash flies were swarming round that putrid bite, which looked like the work of a great wolf.

Then To'oril collapsed.

The Kereyid king tried to open his eyes. We swabbed them with milk, and when he made out Temüjin standing before him, he clasped him in his arms.

We had lain him across the laps of four horsemen riding abreast. Now he wanted to continue in the saddle, the Kerulen being only four or five days' ride away, but only after eating and drinking. Any of us who could gave him a share of our provisions. He brought up his first mouthfuls, then wolfed down more of the cheese and dried meat. Then he wanted to tell us what had happened to him: 'Temüjin, have I told you about my brother, Erge?'

'The one who sought refuge with the Naiman after you had rid yourself of your two other brothers?'

'Erge never had anything to fear,' stormed the ragged king. 'I killed my two elder brothers because they were cowards, as false as serpents, always mocking me in front of my father. When he was gone, I crushed them under my heels because I knew they could knife me at any moment. Wasn't it the same for you with Belgütei's brother?'

'I understand,' replied the Khan. 'You've no need to justify yourself.'

'Two summers ago, the Naiman king died. His two sons quarrelled badly over one of his wives and were constantly at each other's throats. It seems the royal throne was too cramped for the two of them. So they divided up the Naiman territories. Tai, the elder, took the plains and Buyiruk the mountains. It was with Buyiruk's army that my brother managed to drive me out of my kingdom. I got away with a few of my faithful – no, that's not the right word: I thought them liegemen but many were just fickle hearts who spread confusion and slowed me down. I killed some of those turncoats, the others ran away on a moonless night.'

The ousted king was thirsty again. Temüjin gave him his water bottle. He drained it in one go, then continued, 'Climbing the Orhon valley and then up over Mother Earth's pelvis, we crossed our mountains with Erge in pursuit. We may have the same father but the same blood can't run in our veins because he couldn't catch me on our ancestral lands. To the south we crossed the great golden mountains, the Altay, drawing our sustenance from our horses' veins. After the desert came the barren plains, where we set course for the setting sun again and the land of the Black Khitai – because their king, the Gür Khan as his subjects call him, had once been my father's ally. We had to cross unstable, shifting mountainsides, treacherous rivers of mud, hostile lands where many of my men faded away. As for those who stayed with me, their only motive was the spoils I could give them. So, my son, you can imagine the relief I felt when we spotted an isolated yurt, even if our booty might be only ten rawboned goats, a shepherd, his wife or maybe his dog. To our stomachs, that was a blessed windfall.'

'A starving horse doesn't turn up its nose at meat,' cried Qasar.

'Very true,' To'oril agreed, making strange noises that were so violent that we feared we would see his soul leave his body. But he reassured us that it was only his bowels emptying and continued, 'As we came near to the Black Khitai's lands, we were surrounded and taken to Balasaghun, the royal *ordo*, Gür Khan's high-walled city of clay and stone. In remembrance of his relations with my father, the Gür Khan gave me a tent outside the walls to rest in. But he forbade me to enter his fortress and refused to recognise my title or yours, either, when I told him that you were my son. There is only one khan on earth, he said, and I am he, the Universal Khan.'

'Why didn't you try to reach me?' asked Temüjin.

'I did. I was counting on your support just as you once had mine. I even sent my own son to inform you. But Nilqa never returned: the Naiman patrolling between our kingdoms must have stopped him. Either way, I told the Gür Khan of our victory over the Tatars and of the merits of your wolves,

Temüjin. He flew into a rage. "Those Mongols are only good for robbing each other," he yelled. I said he was mistaken, that a great many of the Mongol tribes had rallied to your standard. His braying laughter grew even louder, "They are maggots; they'll tear each others' guts out in the end. Just like you and your Kereyid, they've always been the Jin's playthings."'

'This Gür Khan is a fool if he thinks himself mightier than Tenggeri,' Temüjin said. 'But I admire his hatred of the Jin: it was the Jin who drove his Khitai ancestors from their native lands.'

'That's as may be,' To'oril said, sceptically. 'At any rate, I felt I shouldn't stay long because every time he saw me, the Gür Khan would mention the Steppes of Hunger. He said there was no more miraculous place on earth, that I should let him escort me there, and he couldn't help nervously fingering the handle of the long dagger at his belt as he spoke. So one night I fled and worked my way up the River Chu. After nine days' trot, the river split a chain of mountains in two and fed into an enormous lake on the other side. I rode around its edge and slit a shepherd's throat for the sake of his meagre flock. But I hadn't even eaten the sheep I'd killed before I had to surrender it, and the whole flock, to some bandits. I had only one burning obsession: to reach you, my son! I followed the high mountain passes with their howling winds, their glaciers, their deadly cold; and when finally the vastness of the Gobi Desert filled the horizon, believe me, Temüjin, I was almost happy. Not that it lasted: I had to walk for almost a moon's cycle before I found water – and that was a salt lake! Thinking myself doomed, I fell asleep and my spirit roamed across the desert. Tenggeri must have heard my lament because when I woke up I was with those wretches who farmed along the river, the only one to cross that land of dust, scorched rocks and dunes. Its blue vein was enough for them to work the soil, and its coolness clad the slopes in tender green. It seemed as if they'd been there for ever with their blind horse and that good-for-nothing camel.'

'So, to thank them for saving your life, you took theirs,' I said, disgusted.

To'oril wiped a tear of pus from his cheek and searched for the Khan's face. Temüjin was stroking his goatee thoughtfully.

'Is it that gleaming breastplate that has made your Bo'urchu so magnanimous, or have all your Blue Wolves grown precious now their flocks are fat and their children grow in peace?'

'No, my faithful Bo'urchu has not changed. He is only wondering if your exile has so affected you that you have forgotten the meaning of gratitude. Bo'urchu has a high opinion of honour.'

'How could you doubt my loyalty?' cried To'oril, indignant. 'Did I not hurry to your side when—'

'I said nothing of the sort! Don't think that by coming to find you, I imagine that I have wiped out all my debts. I've saved the life of the great soul who launched his army for me, who was like a father to his son. I will give you a place in my *ordo*, I will give you horses, arms and warriors and I will demand from each of my men enough of their possessions to do justice to the dignity of your rank. And yet I will still be in your debt.'

Appeased, the Kereyid continued his story, painting it an even blacker hue. 'My benefactors were subjects of the Xixia and I quickly realised that to them I was just a slave who could earn them money. I was afraid that other toilers from further upriver would pay them a visit. So I cut off their heads before they could impose their will on me, saddled up the camel, loaded it with provisions and hurried away through the dunes, steering a course between the north wind and the rising sun, and giving thanks to Tenggeri for the winds he sent in my wake. After a few days the blind horse was showing its shortcomings in the sand. The camel wasn't much more vigorous.'

Qasar gestured derisively: 'Settled people's mounts are as soft as down.'

'True, my son. And you've no idea what cowards they are! I managed to get us through the sand and steered for the tip of the Altay range, pulling my blind one by the bit with his poor tail tied to the camel's halter. I headed straight for what I thought was an oasis, but the closer I got, the more my two beasts balked, nervous and stubborn. A thin thread of water flowed among a clump of sallow-thorns and a few figs before evaporating. I gathered the precious liquid and was bringing it to my lips when the wind suddenly got up and, with a great racket, stirred up a flurry of glinting, bone-dry leaves. That damned camel can't have ever seen a tree in his whole pathetic life because he broke free and took off as fast as he could in the direction we'd come from. My blind horse was thrown into a panic as well, but luckily I hung onto his halter and chased after that hunchback. But the mangy villain wouldn't let me near him. I implored, cajoled, called out endearments, cursed, but still he ran from me.

Ah, my friends! You'd have laughed seeing me like that. I knew my chances were bleak without him and the last of my provisions he was carrying. Eventually my horse ran out of breath and slowed down. In front the camel did the same and tossed his head. I brought the blind one to a halt; the camel stopped too. Do you know what was wrong with that idiot?'

Qasar laughed uproariously. 'Your camel thought you were fleeing from danger because you were going so fast. How could he know what you were really scared of?'

To'oril's tearful eyes had a half-astonished, half-sheepish expression. 'Don't mock me, Qasar: when hunger gnaws at the stomach, your mind grows drowsy and loses its way. Yes, I admit it, I was scared of losing that loathsome cud-chewer; from then on I tied his halter round my waist. One night a panther came so close that he scraped all the skin off my arse before I could stop him. If the blind horse hadn't been tied to my arm, he'd still be galloping, dragging my bones after him. The next day hyenas terrified him. As I had tethered him to a rock, he hurled himself on me and bit me in the side. We couldn't stand each other a moment longer. I hadn't eaten for days and I would have devoured a—'

'CAMEL!' Qasar burst out laughing.

We all joined in, To'oril included.

'Exactly, my son! I see you're beginning to put yourself in my position. Well I had no chance of bleeding him to quench my thirst. The moment I went near him he opened that horrific mouth. So the morning I found a gorge and managed to hobble him close to the edge, I pushed him over. Second stroke of luck: there was a natural staircase in the rock. But the ravine was deep enough to have kept a thick layer of snow at the bottom and that's where he lay, his legs broken, labouring over every breath: I still had to finish him off. As I was raising a huge slab of rock over his forehead, he sank his teeth into my wound. I set about him furiously, battering like a madman as he hacked away at my stomach. I managed to drag myself away marvelling at how tough camels can be. Up top, I chose a fine piece of rock and threw it over the edge. It smashed his spine. The second struck his skull, just above the eye. He started braying furiously, his head raised towards me, and I could see the rancour glinting in his remaining eye through the gloom. I shouted that it was the Naimans' fault. The third rock smashed one of his humps. The walls of the ravine groaned. The fourth hit the same spot. I was beginning to miss my bow and arrows when the fifth broke his neck. He became still and barely made a sound. A final rock convinced me that he was ready for the knife.'

'Lucky your horse was blind,' said Qasar. 'Otherwise he'd have pushed you over.'

As we burst out laughing, To'oril slumped forward onto the neck of his horse and then fell heavily to the ground.

Qasar jumped down and turned the old warrior over: his eyelids were slack, his chapped lips open over a purplish tongue. Our merry friend poked his nose closer.

'Well?' asked Temüjin.

'He stinks worse than his camel in the ravine.'

'Is he breathing?'

'Like a wild sheep,' answered Qasar, looking up at his elder brother. 'When he's eaten one of ours, he'll be farting like a camel colt in no time.'

Chapter 31

After two moons King To'oril was his old self again. Kököchü had watched over him in person and predicted that with the Sky's help he would cure him. And, as promised, Temüjin had given him tents, flocks, women, slaves and a personal guard. From that moment on every day saw an improvement in the Kereyid king's condition. Only his beard, the hair on his head – both as white as snow – and a slight limp remained as testimony to his ordeals. From his circle of tents we could hear him day and night yapping like the dog that gives itself airs. Qasar was his boon companion and their favourite pastime was getting drunk. His yurt never stood empty. There, more than anywhere else in the camp, people played, talked, sang, and, as may be, picked fights; and the *yasak*'s rulings on silence carried no weight in the deposed king's sphere. Naturally, there was also much speculation as to when he would recover his throne. Temüjin Khan was already at work. Spies were in place in To'oril's former lands amongst the entourages of the two Naiman kings – as our khan loved to say, lice had been put down the enemy's collar.

In the Year of the Oxen, Börtei had her fourth son, who would be known as Tolui. At the same time, To'oril learnt of the wheareabouts of his son. Nilqa had managed to reach Jamuka's *ordo* with a thousand Kereyid soldiers. To'oril went to spend the summer with him, then returned to Temüjin.

Nilqa's intention, it seemed, was to reconquer the Orhon with Jamuka's help. The prospect delighted To'oril but held little appeal for Temüjin, for whom Jamuka still hung like a shadow over his plans. My *anda* thought of the people of the Blue Wolves as a huge, unbreakable chain. And as he laboured slowly, stubbornly and secretly to assemble that chain, Jamuka always emerged as the missing, broken link, without which there could never be unity among the Mongols. If Jamuka managed to restore Nilqa and To'oril to their throne, then his cause, already supported by the Sovereigns, would be strengthened and there would be nothing the Kereyid could refuse him.

'Think of it, my son!' To'oril said to him, elated. 'With your Mongols and Jamuka's, we'll have twenty thousand warriors.'

'You know the resentment I bear towards Jamuka . . .'

'He fought against you, killed one of your brothers? So? He was simply avenging his own. Since then he has stayed quietly with his flocks.'

'That horse thief wasn't his brother; he was just an excuse. Jamuka only has a half-brother, Qorchi, and he follows me.'

'Don't be bitter,' the Kereyid went on. 'Isn't it you who always says that the Mongols should unite like the blue sky and be as one?'

'Yes, but there is only room for one sun in the sky. That's what Jamuka would like to be. But he doesn't just shed light: he's more like the moon, two-faced, and I know his dark side too well.'

At the start of the Year of the Tiger, Temüjin gathered together his army, realising that he couldn't risk leaving Jamuka to engineer To'oril's reinstatement singlehandedly.

But he laid down a condition: that he stipulate the campaign's strategy. Jamuka and his *tumen* would enter the Orhon valley from the south. Coming from the east and north with another *tumen*, we would take the enemy in a pincer movement.

At a council of the princes, nobles and commanders of the centuries, the Khan explained his plan. Straightaway he told us that To'oril's brother was of no interest to him: 'Erge hasn't even got three thousand soldiers. When he sees Jamuka's army he'll flee north to the River Tamir, which is the best pass through to the western slopes and his ally, King Buyiruk. We will pursue him, making sure we keep ahead of Jamuka's elite and he will lead us straight to Buyiruk. Then we will march on the Naiman army and take their lands.'

Our army moved off, each of our soldiers equipped according to the *yasak*'s decree with two bows, three quivers, a file for sharpening arrowheads, a hatchet, a knife, a pair of ropes, two gourds and a light leather float which they could tie to their horse's tail and use to transport material dry across rivers.

When we reached what had been To'oril's summer camp,

Jamuka and Nilqa were already in position and Erge, as anticipated, had bolted for the River Tamir.

Enraptured to be back in his beloved Orhon valley, To'oril was already planning celebratory hunts and banquets when Temüjin said to him, 'Your brother Erge has sought refuge with the Naiman. If we do nothing now, they will return. It is time to swoop down on them and restore your kingdom to the position of strength and respect it held before.'

Each soldier had three horses at his disposal. Our mounts were replaced and at the start of the Moon of the Cuckoo's Dance, we rode up the Tamir at the foot of the Khangai mountains. With Jamuka's squadrons following two days behind us, our army comprised almost twenty-five thousand impatient but disciplined men. They advanced in silence, lulled by the rustling tread of the horses in the grass and the jingling of their harnesses.

When we saw the Peak of Happiness cleave the horizon, Temüjin sent messengers to Jamuka. He proposed that we split up at that high snow-capped sentinel which stood alone in the middle of a vast, barren plateau. As we marched on Buyiruk's ordo, the Solitaries would take up position further to the east, on the Rolling Dunes, and block off access to the steppes, which were turning green with the season's first grass. Jamuka would take charge of the remounts so that they could graze and restore their strength.

Temüjin knew that the bulk of Buyiruk's troops were at the foot of the Altay range. He planned to drive them back against its high walls and seal off any exit from the east to the southeast. Three great lakes at the base of the Peak of Happiness reflected its sheer, ashy blue sides. We rode alongside the waters of the Black Lake and saw how in the distance, rising above their mighty foothills, the Altay's soaring peaks tore open the skies.

At dusk we dismounted and, squatting down on our heels, waited at the edge of the marshes until night had unfurled its cloth of starlight. The frogs croaked or, seeing the wing of a wading bird, left rings on the surface of the still water, and the mosquitoes buzzed infernally. Those were our first real assailants, tireless and countless, and by dawn any of us who couldn't protect ourselves had bloody faces. The Khan loved that: 'The Naiman know we smear our faces with our enemy's blood. So now when they see us, they'll think that a host of their clans have already fallen to our arrows.' But there were few tents near the Black Lake for us to throw down. The ground was stony with patches of sand, and its tufts of thin, scrawny grass could only give satisfaction to flocks of goats.

I went into one of the isolated yurts as the first rays of sunlight flashed off the Khan's breastplate. I found a toothless old woman churning her milk.

Without taking off my quivers I sat in the master's place. She handed me a bowl and said, 'It's a good omen to have a stranger cross one's threshold when the morning milk is boiling.'

A lamb followed her everywhere, winding itself around her legs, and whenever she looked at it, it would bleat and drop its pellets on the beaten earth. Suddenly a swallow landed on the edge of the smoke-hole and began its song. The old woman showed me its nest between the poles of the roof.

'Every spring we come back for her. My husband's furious. He says it's too hot here, the lake water's turning to poison, the grass is bad, the mosquitoes have made it their kingdom. And it's all true. Every morning he's out on the mountain looking for the horses. But a swallow in your home – doesn't that mean great good fortune?'

She had no way of knowing how true this was. My resolve to kill her as I crossed her threshold evaporated at the swallow's appearance. I stood up and asked her where Buyiruk's camp was.

She led me outside and didn't seem surprised to see her forbidding surroundings black with our men. She looked me in the eyes, saw that I would do her no harm and pointed to a thick cloud fraying above the ragged foothills. 'The winds off the Altay are driving that cloud. Soon it will spread out and when the sun reaches its height, its edge will cover the river where Buyiruk's flocks drink.'

They were good, the old woman's directions. The cloud moved across the sky until it took on the shape of an enormous, grey-bellied crab suspended over a thousand tents criss-crossing the banks of a muddy river at the base of a mountain. Buyiruk's ring of tents was a short distance apart from the rest, surrounded by a stone wall. Great poplars brushed against the cliff walls, but otherwise the site of his camp, a huge, steep-sided, stony basin studded with pyramids of eroded rock, could not have been less like an oasis. Red dust swirled and blew in every direction. Soon the sun was swallowed up and our drums rang out.

Buyiruk and his elites immediately climbed towards the

summits. Did he think looking down on the fighting would enable him to direct his troops better? It was a crass mistake. His defences reeled under the first waves of our archers, then Qasar's *tumen* scattered them. Without real leadership, the Naiman spun in circles, harried and riddled with arrows, and the great amphitheatre became a trap in which they were easily surrounded.

Long before finishing with their useless tents, we made inroads into the five centuries left by Buyiruk to protect his flight towards the clouds. And after bitter fighting, we managed to trample them beneath our horses' hooves and launch ourselves at the Altay, our faces smeared this time with the blood of the dead.

Jelme was assigned to escort the prisoners and the booty to a high, well-watered plateau which the scouts had discovered. We would join him there later.

Night fell suddenly from a stormy sky, forcing us to halt. We thought fortune had forsaken us, but resuming our course at first light after an infernal night under the relentless attack of the cold and the wind, we realised that Tenggeri was still watching over us.

It was hard to believe that Buyiruk could have reached the shoulders of the Altay and then slipped away by the other slopes for, as we followed his trail, we came across the chronicles of his night-time misfortunes. Where snow had thwarted his advance, horses were sunk up to their bellies and frozen to death. At other places the ground had simply fallen away, carrying off whole columns. Higher up, a corps of fifty or so soldiers clung to a great rock face. Since daylight had revealed the drop, they hadn't dared move. Higher still their companions were dotted among the snow, their faces blue or black, asleep and lifeless.

Temüjin called off the hunt. We turned back and took with us what we could, even a few prisoners whom we discovered when we quartered the horses' carcasses. The men had taken shelter in their mounts' stomachs after the animals had died – or perhaps they hadn't waited for their deaths to start disembowelling them.

We caught up with Jelme after two days' march, at dusk, under a sky flecked with fluffy clouds and a setting sun that stained the long necklace of peaks to our left with a phantasmagoria of greens, blues, reds, browns and apricots. Every peak was distinct from the others, pure and unique, and together they melded into a dazzling mosaic. Streams merrily flowed down the slopes towards a larger torrent which wound, glinting gold and silver, between the great grey fans of rockslides belched forth from the summit. In the distance, the mass of the Thousand Ornaments shone pink under a crown of austere clouds. The prisoners gave us surreptitious glances, dropping their eyes as soon as we looked at them. The women and the children were not so quick, and we saw strange fern-coloured glints shining in their eyes

When the mountainsides glittered iridescent in the last rays of the sun, we ordered a Naiman slave to sing, and in the purple shadows, her eyes feverishly aglint, she sang her tremulous, nostalgic song:

> Altay, Altay, lofty Altay,
>> From where the winds take flight
>> And the storms gather their shafts of fire
>> Spare our flocks
>> Spring undoes your white robes
>> Hangs your breast with a thousand flowers
>> Your forehead shines forth to the ocean.
>
> Altay, Altay, pure Altay
>> With cooing birds
>> Such joyous springs
>> Gather in our loves
>> Venerable and ageless
>> Why can't I, like you,
>> Hide my tears in the clouds?

We fell asleep under the crystals of the night. By morning, they had settled on our bodies in a thin, translucent layer.

We set off for the Thousand Ornaments, To'oril staying behind to wait for Jamuka and Nilqa's troops.

Seven days later, as we came out into the arid valleys dotted with salt pans, a large contingent of Naiman blocked our path. We instantly sent messengers to To'oril. That evening, when our troops were in battle formation, they returned with the Kereyid king's message: 'We will be in position tonight and will light watch-fires to the north. A host of fires. That way, my son, you'll know where we are and the Naiman will be terrified by our number.'

In the first glimmering of dawn, it was we who were terrified:

there wasn't an ally in sight. Apart from the wisps of smoke rising from their smothered fires, every trace of them had vanished in the night. We could turn and look wherever we wanted, but we were still alone and outnumbered by the Naimans. So this was To'oril's gratitude, the double-dealer. But the Khan said bitterly. 'It's Jamuka, that snake. He wanted our heads, and it's the Naiman who are going to give him them.'

Chapter 32

We managed to break out of the Naiman trap, but only with heavy losses. We were miserably beating a retreat when an emissary of To'oril caught up with our defeated troops. The Kereyid king's treachery had done him no good. Just like us he had fallen into a Naiman ambush as he was returning to his lands through the Tamir pass. He begged Temüjin to help him and, to our amazement, the Khan redirected his army of wounded towards him.

'Are we going to finish the rogue off?' I asked him.

'No, we're flying to his aid. He's our safeguard, just as we are his.' Temüjin explained that if old To'oril lost his kingdom or died leaving his son to succeed him, the Borjigin would be crushed by Jamuka's and Targutai's Mongols. To'oril was our only ally. Our survival depended on his life.

We arrived just in time to save To'oril and his son Nilqa, who had been driven back with a hundred of their men against the sides of the pass; the rocky incline was so steep that as they tried to retreat their horses lost their footing and rolled over and over, smashing their limbs.

To'oril apologised profusely and begged for forgiveness. He claimed that Jamuka had tricked him into thinking that Temüijin wanted to rob him of his Kereyid throne. 'He told me to be wary of you, that you had plotted with the Naimans of the south to ensnare me and that the fighting in the north was only a decoy to put me to sleep. So yes, when you sent word that the Naiman were arraying their troops where the Altay opens into its valleys, I believed Jamuka. I was afraid of a trap. I lit the watch-fires that told you we were there and then moved off before it got light. When we fell among the Naiman later as well, I didn't know what to think; that's why I called you again, my son. If you hadn't come to my aid, I wouldn't have discovered either Jamuka's baseness or the purity of the heart beating in your breast.'

As a special reward for having saved Nilqa, his father gave me ten gold cups and a mound of white silk carpets and columbine-coloured cloth. I passed these presents on to my khan because, if I had been acting of my own accord, I would not have saved those who the day before had been wishing for our death.

Our suspicions were allayed at a great feast on the banks of the Tula. Pledges of loyalty were made and sealed with the exchange of gifts. To'oril gave one of his nieces to Temüjin and he in turn gave her to his brother, Qasar, who, along with Sübetei, was the most famous of his commanders and an invincible fighter, although perhaps he lacked Sübetei's ingenious judgement. It was decided that, once they had recovered their strength, Kereyid and Borjigin – Mongols united – would march against the Naiman again. To'oril swore he wouldn't let himself be tricked by Jamuka or Nilqa a second time, and when the moment came to part company, he even confided his anxieties: 'I am growing old, Temüjin. Who will reign over my people when I am gone? I have no brothers any more. My son Nilqa? No, nothing turns out right for him. Be my eldest son, Temüjin: lead my men into battle and let Nilqa watch over my hearth.'

But in the semicircle where the king's and Prince Nilqa's wives sat, heavy headdresses shook with indignation.

Still, this lull did not satisfy Temüjin. He wanted to be convinced of To'oril's support once and for all, and the desire was even more urgent because, for his part, the implacable Jamuka, furious at not having been able to prevent To'oril and Temüjin's reconciliation, was preparing his ground.

The chief of the Solitaries could count on the Sovereigns, but this alliance alone was not enough to overcome the Khan. He needed other forces. So with cool clear-sightedness Jamuka turned to those we had fought in battle, the defeated of yesterday: Tatars, Merkid, Naiman. He had no difficulty in convincing the first two, who were only small, dispersed clans. But he needed almost eight seasons to catch up with the chief of the mountain-dwelling Naiman. Buyiruk had worked his way round the Altay and found valuable hosts in the Oirat, a small tribe on the far shore of Lake Ocean, whose lands faced what had been the Merkid kingdom until they themselves had been driven further north.

All these rebel tribes gathered on the borders of the Mongol lands. They sealed a pact of alliance and with the sacrifice of a white stallion, they crowned Jamuka 'Gür Khan', the Universal King.

The chief of the Solitaries sent a messenger to Temüjin to inform him of his elevation. This title of Gür Khan didn't amount to much in my eyes, but Temüjin took the business very seriously. According to him, Jamuka was preparing for battle.

'He always schemes,' the Khan said, 'but never leaves himself open to a direct accusation; he hates that. This message, for instance, puts us on our guard. So if he wanted to fall on us while we slept, he thinks it places him above suspicion.'

Another frustrating piece of news came at the same time: Altan, Khuchar and Daritai had left us for Jamuka's *ulus*, or perhaps Targutai's. The three princes had never forgotten their humiliation at the Khan's hands when he had confiscated the Tatar spoils and withdrawn certain of their prerogatives.

Temüjin decided to strengthen his relations with To'oril by giving his young sister Temulun to Nilqa. Children would be born to the union and a blood alliance would be the surest of guarantees. Or so he thought.

But Nilqa spurned the beautiful, gentle Temulun and doubled the insult to Temüjin by claiming that she was not of noble enough blood. Bitterly offended, my *anda* vowed that one day he would hang Nilqa's balls round his horse's neck.

A moon later, however, Nilqa – or rather his father – reconsidered. A Kereyid marriage-broker arrived one morning bearing the following message: 'I, To'oril, King of the Kereyid whose power knows no bounds, convey my apologies to you for the arrogance of my son. He will marry your sister, for such is our wish. With this belt as a token of his deference, he sends you his most abject regrets at having offended you.' The belt was of silver and inlaid with great oval turquoises.

'When is the wedding?' the Khan asked.

'King To'oril will expect you on the first night of the new moon.'

And so it was that we set off towards the Tula again. In a cart drawn by four white oxen, Mother Hö'elün consoled Temulun. Many springs had passed since that day when, as the Merkids gave chase, Temüjin's little sister had declared her passion. Now

206

she was a grown woman, but her grief, undisguised by her long hair, made her look like the tender, mischievous young girl I recognised so well. In all those years, she had never stopped looking my way but, knowing my heart was elsewhere, eventually she had stifled her desires.

When I looked into her great eyes and saw the welling tears, I told her that her marriage would secure our relations with the Kereyids, like the horsehair ropes that keep a yurt's felt walls from flying away in a storm.

We made a halt at Münglig's camp, that venerable shaman who was Kököchü's father and had been Yesügei's friend. He lived with two other families in the middle of the steppe – a place so remote it could just as well have been the middle of the sky.

'I was waiting for you, Temüjin,' he said, clutching a sheep's shoulder blade.

That evening he burnt another and, in the glow of firelight, examined it intently.

'Don't go there. A trap has been laid across your path.'

'How is it that your son has said nothing to me?' Temüjin questioned him.

'I don't know . . .'

'Isn't he the most powerful shaman of all?'

'Yes, yes . . . He must have studied the signs, but . . . I beg you, do him no harm. Quick, get away; you are in great danger.'

We set off back to our camp with a delighted Temulun, who swapped her cart for a horse's saddle.

When we arrived, a horseman was waiting for the Khan with a message from Qasar: 'Beware my brother, your ally To'oril's court has been in a great state of agitation for the last few moons. I am no longer allowed to attend their councils. Jamuka, with Nilqa as intermediary, is conspiring with King To'oril. Rumours are circulating that you want to disinherit Nilqa and that you have tried to strike up an alliance with the Naimans. Don't turn your back on anyone.'

The next day, as we set about striking camp in order to move to the great eastern steppe, Kököchü burst into the royal yurt.

'What is happening, my khan, we're on the move and I know nothing about it?'

'The cracks in the shoulder blades told me that the enemy was planning to slit our throats as we slept.'

'I saw nothing to suggest that!'

'You must be getting old, unless Tengri's favour has deserted you.'

When we failed to arrive at the new moon, the Kereyid moved out as well.

We were ready, watchful: the ground had been carefully studied, the wagons with the women and children and all our riches had been sent to Lake Kölen. But when our scouts reported that the great plateaus to the west were growing dark with thirty thousand horsemen, we all became lost in thought: our army was three times smaller.

Once in sight, they spread out and deployed their chequered squares of archers. They were all there: To'oril, Nilqa, Jamuka, Targutai and a horde of petty kings without kingdoms, Merkid and Tatar mainly, with an additional division of Oirat. The Sovereigns formed the vanguard, the Kereyid one wing, the Solitaries the other. They blocked off the great Uldja valley and extended onto its heights, their lances and banners seeming to slice into the low, baneful sky.

Night strode past and messengers galloped between the lines: it was agreed that battle would commence at dawn. Temüjin listened to the various reports of our scouts but did not say a word. From time to time he praised his horse for being as calm as he was, but even then he kept his eyes fixed on the troops' movements on the horizon. Like an eagle on a high perch, he watched and assessed, his tall silhouette outlined against the mass of clouds, his waist spiny with arrows, bow and sabre, as the downy feathers on his helmet twisted in the wind.

When all the *tumen* commanders had gathered behind him, he beckoned them closer.

'We are going to do what surrounded wolves do. Sübetei! Jelme! You will attack first. Fire three volleys to goad the enemy into breaking ranks and pursuing you. Then draw them out of the valley and, as we charge the centre, circle round and come back at their flanks. Be unsparing, and soon they'll lose all their composure. If Jelme has to yield on the left, Sübetei, you must drive into the right straightaway. Watch over each other and pound away at their sides in wave after wave so that they have no chance to counter our frontal attack. Jurchedei! I entrust the vanguard to you. Let your brave Urut smite the enemy as a storm flattens the grass.'

Quyildar, chief of the fearsome Mangkud, demanded to

speak. 'I claim that trust as mine and I challenge Jurchedei to see who will be first to bury his standard in the Sovereigns' backs.'

The Khan granted him this honour but insisted that Targutai be left to him. 'I want to castrate that traitor alive.'

The dark, motionless enemy lines were slowly revealed at dawn. They were grouped in squadrons of five hundred. The front two ranks were mounted on horses caparisoned from neck to knee and they carried wicker shields.

But To'oril and Jamuka's troops still hung back under cover of the hills. One of the Solitaries' messengers rode up in the pale light with these words of Jamuka's to Temüjin: 'Just as we were about to attack, To'oril relinquished his command and gave it to me. He says that I and his son have brought about this confrontation. At first I refused his demand, but he threatened to turn away from me. Isn't he just like one of those skittish horses that recoil at the sound of the drums of war? O my *anda*, if you do not wish to acknowledge my power and lay down your arms, then at least avoid our arrows, for you have nothing to fear from my sword. O my *anda*, how could I harm you without harming myself?'

'That's just like Jamuka,' said Temüjin. 'He'd fall out with his own shadow. Let's attack while they're squabbling like rooks on a branch.'

With this the Urut and Mangkud launched themselves at the enemy, bellowing their terrifying war cry: 'UKHAI!'

When the first hail of arrows struck them, they split in two, flowing to the right or left depending on which shoulder their horses wore their shields, and returned fire. The Sovereigns gave chase. Temüjin ordered five *tumen* to attack, one in the centre, the others on the heights to counter any reinforcements or overspill on the wings which the Urut and Mangkud were tearing to pieces with each of their sallies. Jamuka retaliated with To'oril's elite, the Tubegen and the Goshawks, but if one of our men was hit, five of theirs fell before he died. And the relentless tide of men sent into the fray by the Khan brought the Sovereigns to their knees. Temüjin had promised a hundred women to whoever led him to Targutai's personal guard and, like all my comrades, I spared no effort.

Wracked by remorse and the loss of his bravest warriors, To'oril tried to withdraw. This only enraged his son the more. He hurled himself upon us at the head of his men until an arrow shattered his jaw. In a flash the Kereyid had surrounded him and carried him off.

It was then that the Oirat shamans acted in concert to summon up the celestial powers. Gathering a brown bezoar-stone from a horse's stomach, they hung it from a willow branch which they had driven into the riverbed and chanted invocations to Tenggeri. In no time the sky had torn itself apart and a raging, frozen torrent was pouring down on our heads. We had fought our way through to Targutai's private guard when the storm plunged us into its depths and scattered us so that, with no idea who we were sabring – Sovereigns or allies – we had to fall back.

Kököchü immediately instructed us to cut the stomachs of the enemy's horses open and search them for those concretions of animal matter. We found every sort of bezoar: large, small, yellow, red, green, purple, round, gnarled. He chose one, the largest, which was the colour of half-digested grass. He tied it to his horse's tail and set off along the crests of the hills that were sunk into darkness, as the storm thundered and swirled about him.

When there was a lull, we flung ourselves on Targutai again. Temüjin was about to strike when his horse reared and threw him, an arrow embedded in the small of its back. I was holding out my hand to pull him up when my horse whinnied with pain and fell to its knees as well. Another arrow with identical featherings had hit him in the eye and blood was cascading down his nose. I looked around for the skilful archer, but the Khan was still driving forward and I followed to give him cover. In the melee he was almost on Targutai and I was sabring harder than ever when I felt an arrow shear off my neck guard. The Khan gave a cry of surprise. I turned, he slid to the ground and I sliced off Targutai's forearm just as he was about to split Temüjin's skull in two. Then, once again, we were plunged into utter blackness as the sky rent itself in twain, roaring and howling as only it can.

The massacre appeared to me in frozen, pallid tableaux. The lightning lit up lances and seemed to set the horses ablaze. The swords and blood-spattered animals clashed and bucked, and terror-stricken faces swept past on the ground which was now a muddy torrent. I saw my khan's face between my hands, his eyes half-shut and his mouth wide open, his quivering throat red with spurting blood and pierced by an arrow. Panic-stricken horses stampeded in the rout and I protected his beloved body with mine, then hailstones the size of my thumb whistled in the hurricane and would have drilled through us if I had not had my shield on my back.

At last Tengri's wrath played itself out. I took off the Blind Man's breast guard, covered Temüjin with it, and carried him on my shoulder towards the heights, my sabre in my hand, stumbling over the corpses.

Blood was churned into the mud, then night came, pitch-black, and it moved to the rhythm of death rattles and the gurgling of prone bodies. To my ear, the Khan's breathing sounded thinner than a horsehair and, as I held him, his body as hot as boiling milk, his bowels melted.

Chapter 33

The night's intimacies became plain in the first light of day and I was struck dumb. The small valley's floor was covered with the half-devoured corpses of men and horses. A hundred wolves were feasting. A little higher up, on the slope to which I had dragged him, Temüjin was lying in his own blood, an enormous wolf two paces behind him. My bow and arrows were next to my *anda*, my clothes were keeping his body warm and I was more naked than a newborn between its mother's thighs.

I dropped the leather bottle of milk, which I had left the Khan's side to fetch, and ran, brushing past two wolves squabbling over a man's arm. Our gentle-looking hills are hamstringers. I was only halfway up the slope when the wolf was already sniffing the Khan's throat. One bite from that maw would have been fatal. But the animal contented itself with licking the wound. I was reaching for my bow when the Khan gripped my wrist. The wolf peeled back its slack lips to bare its fangs and scarlet gums.

'Where were you?'

The Khan's eyes bore something crazed, questioning, besides that feline glint which always lurked in their depths.

'Looking for something for you to drink. Last night, when you were delirious, you told me you were thirsty.'

He reached for his neck. I told him not to move. I said his wound had stopped bleeding and that there was a wolf right by us staring at us strangely.

'Don't be afraid,' he said. 'He is our guardian.'

Looking at the beast, I thought I recognised the wolf from the Blue Lake. A white scar ran the length of his muzzle. If the fur around his eyes – yellow slits set in black velvet – had not been lighter, I would have sworn that it was the very same. But we were far from the Blue Lake and still further from our first meeting. Twenty springs had passed since that day. Could his soul have reincarnated already?

'Whose is all this blood?' Temüjin asked, looking around him.

'Yours. I cleaned your wound until late into the night and sucked out the clots in case they suffocated you.'

Pools glinted in the grass, their colour a gamut of reds and blacks from carmine to cured horsemeat by way of corn-poppy red, vermilion and crimson. His face was smooth and as pale as the moon. In his eyes two horses seemed to shuffle restlessly in the void.

From the end of the valley, which wound between wooded hills, we heard the sound of Sovereigns' voices.

'Temüjin, we have to go now.'

I pulled on my shirt, breastplate and boots, buckled my belt and, running to fetch the milk, poured it into his mouth drop by drop. I told him how I had been able to slip through the Sovereigns' rearguard in the dark. In the battle's chaotic wake I had found the bottle hanging off the broken shaft of an abandoned wagon.

'They'd have tortured you if they'd found you.'

'That's why I went naked. I could have passed myself off as one of our prisoners and escaped at the first opportunity.'

'You cleaned my wound, saved my life, risked your own. I will not forget this, Bo'urchu,' he said, his voice hoarse with emotion.

'Come,' I said, helping him to his feet. 'Let's be like wolves and rejoin our own before the Sovereigns find us.'

A little way on I found a horse standing in the shade of a tree. He was waiting for his rider, who lay beside him on the ground, his body riddled with arrows. We rode for as long as a rectangular, ermine cloud takes to glide from one horizon to the other, then came upon one of our centuries under Jochi's command. We saw them below us as they came out of a twisting gorge.

My Little Crumb was now a strikingly handsome warrior of nineteen springs: a skilled archer, valiant heart and thoughtful soul. Seeing his father in my arms, his head lolling against my shoulder, he offered him his horse, a docile gelding. Feeling too weak, Temüjin refused. Jochi's face clouded over. Nothing wounded him more than a refusal from his father. Ever since his hair had been cut for the first time, when he was just a little crumb, just a little child who would rush around bringing the lambs to heel, he had been like this, and I felt him locked in his emotions, torn between anger and distress.

The Khan was impartial. He never showed special favour to any of his children, except perhaps Tolui, eight years old at the time, who was a little dearer to him because he was the youngest. Jochi thought the opposite, however, and often pointed out to me his father's pride in one or other of his brothers. Jochi was also the subject of these displays of fatherly affection, and if he did not know that, it was simply because Temüjin never complimented his sons in their presence. But despite my reassurance, the eldest son remained convinced that he was the least loved. Whenever he did or said anything, he watched the Khan's eyes, hoping to see approval there. And as the beloved face never showed anything, Jochi interpreted this impassivity as disapproval.

His sadness made my heart bleed, but I could do nothing about it. 'You don't understand,' he always said; 'my father showers you with affection while treating me as a stranger.'

Did he know the doubts surrounding his paternity? I did not think so, but sometimes I would watch Temüjin with his sons and occasionally it would seem to me that Chagatai, Ögödei or the orphans brought up by Mother Hö'elün did enjoy the attention Jochi longed for.

We rode east in search of our wagons. Temüjin slept in my arms. His wound had not opened again.

'Your father will live,' I said to Jochi. 'He will live because he is eternal. That is Tengri's will.'

'I would have loved to be by his side last night. For it to have been my mouth that kept him alive.'

'What difference does it make whose it was? You would have done just the same.'

'Does he know that?'

I did not answer but wished that his words would lull the Khan as he slept, because in the young prince's eyes shone everything that is striking in a son's love for his father.

The rain beat down on our retreat towards the Great Khingan mountains, shrouding the dismal steppe in a thick grey cloud. We had recovered the wagons with our wives and children, our tents and livestock, and we rode in mournful silence, shoulders bowed, defeated, even though the battle had had no victor.

The count of our men stopped at two thousand six hundred. We reckoned our losses at eight thousand, and even if the enemy's had been double that, we would not have been consoled. We had fought like wolves but now, afraid that we would be found at any moment, we hoped for nothing more than a lair in which to bandage our wounds and praise our dead. Why weren't they pursuing us? It would have been easy for our opponents to finish us off.

Yet one feeling gave us heart as we retreated: Tenggeri had stood by our khan. Admittedly it was Kököchü's powers that had turned the storm back on the enemy, but I was not alone in thinking that he owed his success to Tenggeri, protector of Temüjin Khan, his chosen son.

I personally had another cause for satisfaction: my determination to become a father had born fruit, and it was now growing and wriggling in Mother of Pearl Stream's womb. I had arranged for two sturdy wet-nurses to watch over the expectant mother day and night.

We feared for our khan's health, especially when we heard that Ögödei and Borokul were amongst the missing. His third son was barely fifteen springs; Borokul, the little Jürkin entrusted to Mother Hö'elün whom he loved like his own son, was twenty.

'Those two wouldn't have wanted to be separated in the face of death,' he said, looking sadly at the sky. 'They must have perished together.' Then he beseeched Tenggeri to give back his two children.

Three days later, a black horse with a white muzzle approached our camp. Borokul was on its back, clasping in his arms Ögödei, who was as white as snow but alive. Like his father, he had been hit in the throat by an arrow and the tip had broken off in a vein. He had lost a lot of blood but Borokul had done everything to keep his wound clean and suck out the poison.

When he saw his children, two tears fringed the Khan's eyelids. He picked up Ögödei, laid him gently on the ground and heated his dagger to cauterise the wound. The wounded boy twitched under the knife. His father pressed his lips to his forehead and made obeisance to the ground, then the sky as Jochi watched, his face grave, his eyes dry and cold.

Chapter 34

We withdrew to the green uplands of the Great Khingan Mountains. Quyildar, the chief of the Mangkud, died when a stomach wound reopened while he was hunting a stag. Others followed, the rot spreading through them from where the rain of sword blows had fallen.

One evening. Mother of Pearl Stream disappeared into the larch woods, holding her womb, which was again swollen and stretched as taut as a yurt. I told the wet-nurses to go after her.

When they returned in the pale dawn, I understood from their looks of anguish that something tragic had happened. Their great black, staring eyes streamed with tears; they sobbed and tore at their cheeks, as they tried to tell me their horror. The moment the little steaming body lay on the carpet of moss, the wet-nurses had rushed forward to snatch it from its mother. But Mother of Pearl Stream was more nimble: she had clasped the child to her breast and run off through the shadows.

Their mutilated bodies were found at the bottom of a ravine, still joined by the indigo cord.

Regrets are sterile, but I knew that Tenggeri was punishing me for not being brave enough to give the beautiful Merkid her freedom when I knew she was in love with another. I may have sacrificed my childish self-interest once, by sparing White Cloud the torments of battle, but Heaven was showing me that there was more to wisdom than communing with a horse's soul. Of women's souls I knew nothing.

Being in no state to risk surprise attacks that winter, we rode down the river Kalka to the lands where Börte had been born. When we reached the plains, Temüjin planned to obtain the support of the Onggirad who, despite the many conflicts, had skilfully maintained their neutrality. Börte's father, Dei the Wise, had died. No doubt this made it easier for Temüjin to phrase his proposal of alliance. 'Either you submit to our banner and ensure your own good fortune or we destroy you down to your very last man.'

Were the Onggirad overawed by the Khan's emissary, Jurchedei, riding at the head of his valiant Urut? Or did they not know the truth of our numbers? Either way they chose to submit and we set up camp beside the river Tungg.

While we were there, Temüjin's uncle, Daritai, left Altan, Khuchar and Jamuka and returned to make amends, swearing never to disappoint the Khan again. He told us what had happened after the battle, which helped us understand why we had been able to flee undisturbed. First Nilqa had been gravely wounded, which prompted To'oril to recall his troops and return to his lands. Then, frustrated at the spoils that had escaped them, the Merkid, Tatar and Oirat clans had turned against Jamuka and Targutai and, once the storm had passed, initiated an incredible round of raids and quarrels. On top of that, Altan and Khuchar had clashed with Jamuka and finally Jamuka, under attack from all sides, took advantage of Targutai's decline – his severed arm had become infected – to make a bid to subjugate the Sovereigns.

In the new Year of the Dog, Temüjin Khan sent messengers to To'oril, Nilqa, Jamuka, Altan and Khuchar. He reminded each of them of their treachery. Kököchü, our emissary to the Kereyid court, took the most comprehensive message: 'Did we not say to each other that we wouldn't let anyone interfere with our alliance? But you have let the envious come between us. You led your army against mine. You struck terror into my women, my children and my flocks. Did you want to kill me like your two brothers? Have you forgotten how my father restored you to your throne after freeing you from slavery? Have you forgotten that I did as much? Did I not come looking for you in the Gobi, where, more parched than the dung of a toothless nag, you were reduced to bleeding a blind horse? I gave you the protection of my camp, I healed you, I fed you, I made sure you recovered your dignity. Did we not fight side by side? When you abandoned me on the dawn of fresh battles against the Naiman, was that the behaviour of an ally who claimed to be my father? Despite burying that dagger in my back, you begged me to save you when you were surrounded by the Naiman. Did I rebuff your plea for help, did vengeance make me deaf? No, I respected our ties of blood and came straightaway. Is this how you see fit to thank me? Together we enslaved the Merkid and the Tatars. We took their tents, their flocks and I gave them to you. What more do you want that is not already yours? Qasar! What have you done with him? Take care of him because I miss him and I have great need of my brother.'

Temüjin sent this message to Jamuka: 'When we were children, we used to have a game to see who could drink from my father's blue cup first. Most often I was up at dawn and I would drink the milk before you. That's why you were jealous of me. But you always found the cup half-full because I left it so for you. If you happened to get there before me, you never left a drop of that precious drink.

'Later, when we met up again, we renewed our pledges of loyalty, we shared the same *ordo*, the same blanket even, and still you envied me, who had less than you. And now here you are again, seeking to be the only one to drink from my father's cup, my adoptive father To'oril. Will Nilqa be as loving and patient as I have been?'

To his cousins Altan and Khuchar, he said, 'You chose me to be your khan when I had refused that honour, considering that it should rightfully fall to you. Can you have forgotten this? Were we going to leave the Khanate to Jamuka whose clan is of less noble blood than ours? You did not want that and you elected me. Now you have disobeyed me and turned your backs on me. Is this the devotion you swore to show? At least see that no one sets up camp at the source of the three rivers, on our ancestral lands.'

Lastly Temüjin adressed these reproaches to Nilqa: 'Our father To'oril wanted two sons. I am the adopted son, you are the longed-for one. What have you to fear from me? Why have you been jealous of me, who only wanted your good, who was a younger brother to you? Orphans are a gift from Heaven. Were you worried I would bring danger, when it is an auspicious act to welcome an orphan into one's family? You have driven me far from To'oril. Spare him any more torments. Calm your passions night and day and so long as To'oril is still alive, forget your desire to be king.'

As the omens foretold, the geese's early departure for the southern lands brought a layer of snow in the Moon of the Rutting Argali. Winter followed: white, long, doleful and silent, interrupted by brilliant blue days overlain with pink-tinged mists. Riding camels as shaggy as bears, we spent our days attending to our meagre flocks and crossing the pallid wastes in search of wild yaks, stray saigas or carnivores out on their murderous forays.

The yak hunts on camelback brought us great joy. Rather than shoot them with arrows, we preferred to give chase and run them through with our lances. This noble creature's sudden changes of direction earned us some fine skids and amazing falls which made us roar with laughter; camels can gallop on snow marvellously well, but manoeuvring them is a real test. Swathed in our furs – wolf, bear, fox or sable – in no time we would be bathed in sweat with beads of ice standing out on our moustaches. What delight we found accompanying those yaks at full tilt! Their skulls were so heavy they seemed to bore into the earth. Their thick black coats waved like garlands, their hooves threw up a shower of snow at every stride and their hoarse breath preceded them in two great columns of steam. When we were right on top of them, we would drive our lances with both hands into the fleshy hump to shatter their ribs and puncture their hearts. Sometimes the lance broke, snapped by the flying beasts. But if the lance held, the animal's jerking convulsions would shake our caps down over our eyes and strip our arms bare. And still the lance would keep vibrating with a life that refused to give in, and like lightning in a blue sky, it would give us an inimitable shock of pleasure that would last until the beast had collapsed and its blood drained out into the snow.

We'd throw ourselves on our heavy-maned prize, crush its skull if it was still alive and immediately collect its blood in our gourds and bowls – warming nectar which we drank down fast. Then we'd remove the most succulent parts, unfurl them in a steaming string on the snow, fillet the meat and arrange it so that it would freeze quickly whilst we ate slices of the heart and stomach. When we left, crows would be hurriedly pecking at the large red circle around the skeleton as, in the distance, a wolf's silhouette on a knoll heralded his arrival for the banquet.

The first echo of the Khan's embassies reached us as the grasslands began to flower with buttercups, columbines and forget-me-nots – white, pink or sky-blue – and as the wading birds built their nests on the boggy ground at the edges of the lakes.

After a winter spent at the Kereyid court, Kököchü returned

with To'oril's response, a lament which went, 'I am nothing but an ingrate to have broken away from you. I rejected you and my heart breaks, my sight blurs ... When I had no children, the shamans petitioned the spirits every day to allow me a son. My prayers were answered because Nilqa came. And then you appeared, like a second son. Both of you have been wounded and I almost lost you. I do not want to risk your lives ever again. From now on, O my son, if I nurture so much as a single bad thought about you, may all my blood run out ...' Taking his arrowhead file, our shaman cut his thumb until he drew blood and said, 'I saw To'oril cut himself like this and say, "Have my son drink this blood; then a little of my soul that has seen the light will flow in his veins."

He handed the Khan a birch-bark flask filled, he said, with royal blood.

'Open it.'

Kököchü uncorked the flask.

'Is it To'oril's blood?'

'I can't say for sure,' replied the shaman.

'You said you saw him with your own eyes.'

'He could ... have deceived me.'

'Is it human blood?'

'Most certainly.'

'Then drink it!'

'I am your shaman, not your food-taster.'

'What about me? Can I drink it?'

'Nothing is stopping you, except mistrust or fear.'

'The Khan fears nothing apart from Tengri's anger.'

'Well, pay heed to me, Temüjin, because I am the ear of Heaven.'

'And I His sword, His arrows and His will.'

Their eyes challenged each other for a brief moment before Temüjin indicated to the shaman that he could go.

Then he called for Ravenous Dark to be brought to him. This fighting dog was as broad as a ram but far taller. He was short-haired and black-coated apart from a blazing ruddy stripe that ran from his throat to the parting of his thighs. None of his opponents had escaped alive. A tongue so dark it was almost black hung perpetually from his wide mouth. And in his slanting eyes a small flame flickered in time to his charged, edgy breathing. Out hunting he had proved that he could open a yak's throat or tear out its innards through its balls with one snap of his jaws and that nothing, not even the dying animal's full weight on him or its vicious kicks, could make him relax his grip.

With two sweeps of his tongue, Ravenous Dark licked up To'oril's blood. Before darkness fell, he had howled and scrabbled at his ribs and spun round and round and finally lain down on his side, foam framing his mouth like a beard, his eyes red with pain. Poison. To'oril, that traitor, had never once kept an oath. As we were looking at the mastiff's corpse the Khan said, 'The Kereyid are feeding up their horses and it will not be long before they hoist their battle standard. They know where to find us and that cockerel Nilqa, who thinks I want to rob him, will be at their head. Open confrontation would be fatal for us. Let's leave the Onggirad. Let's make Nilqa think we're giving all our lands to him . . .'

My *anda*'s eyes were hard and implacable, like a sword drawn from its sheath.

'And then, when he thinks he's got rid of the Blue Wolves for good, we'll rise up as he sleeps and pluck his two cloves of garlic!'

'Whose delicacy will they be?' Temüge asked mischievously.

'Your sister Temulun's,' replied the Khan. 'They're hers, since he thought her unfit to be his wife.'

Chapter 35

Leaving our wives and children with the Onggirad, we moved off the great steppe, crossed the clear-flowing Argun and made for the Miry Ponds, a desolate country cherished only by mosquitoes. When we arrived there, iris, arrowheads and bullrushes were flowering in the marshes. Less than a moon later, all the colours – yellow, blue, purple, white, pink – had evaporated into the hot skies, and the water had followed.

We wandered like an army of shadows, searching for clumps of yellowing grass or the humblest watering hole. Soon we were reduced to exposing the pond mud on hurdles and squeezing out a few drops of the precious liquid.

The water, thus collected and drunk, caused terrible diarrhoeas which brought us to our hands and knees, and laid our horses on their backs. We scoured the bullrushes for white bryonies and spiked purple loosestrife, whose bulbs have soothing properties.

There were no more marsh birds to hunt, no more coypus, not even those black foxes that venture far from their forests to steal the last clutches of the year. Our horses leaned into us as we stroked them, their heads heavy, their eyes shut against the flies. We ate the weakest and the mosquitoes swarmed over this paltry supply of fresh meat. The thought of White Cloud and his herd with the Onggirad was heartening. But it was scant consolation . . .

We were a ragged, thin, grimy-faced band, but we were all armed and alert, ready to fire a child's arrow at the smallest lizard or field mouse that were everywhere now we had killed all the snakes. One day when we had collected enough of that brackish, gut-churning water for all of us, Temüjin Khan passed his cup round his faithful – me, Jelme, his generals and clan chiefs, Sübetei, Muqali, Borokul, Chila'un, Jurchedei. When we had drunk, he thanked us for sharing his ordeals and promised never to abandon us. 'May Tenggeri turn me into this muddy water if I break this oath.'

We felt far from Tenggeri, as if He had deserted us. And yet, whenever we were at our lowest ebb, something happened: a shower of rain, as short-lived as it was precious, a herd of gazelles, a visitor, such as the old man from one of the Sovereigns' minor clans.

He led a camel loaded with the poles and felt of his yurt and four equally burdened horses, around which crowded his women and children: a venerable grandmother, two fairly elderly women and two young girls.

A young warrior of twenty-odd springs had helped them come this far.

'Who is he?' the Khan asked the old man.

'A valiant soul whose arrows cannot be stopped. He wishes to put them at your service because his clan no longer exists. You dispersed his tribe; now its remnants have started quarrelling and fighting again.'

The archer was bare-headed and he wore a half-breastplate. At the sight of his quiver filled with arrows, I burst out, 'My *anda*! This is the Sovereign who killed our horses and hit you in the throat. I recognise the feathering of his arrows.'

The officers surrounded him immediately.

Temüjin approached him and asked if it was he who had shot him and his beloved charger, Grey Ear.

'I shot at the Khan from the top of the hill,' he answered without hesitating. 'The Khan can kill me if he wishes; what does it matter if I rot here or elsewhere? But if he shows me his favour, how happy I will be to gallop before him, smashing the stones under my horse's hooves and fighting his enemies.' He glanced furtively at Temüjin's scar and then looked up to meet his eyes.

'If you'd wanted to kill me, you wouldn't have come here to boast about it,' the Khan said, returning the archer's gaze. 'There is candour in your eyes and you do not disown your feats of arms. I like that. You deserve to ride with me. What is your name?'

'Jebe!'

'Well then, Jebe, since your arrows killed my warhorse and that of my right hand Bo'urchu, and hit me in the throat, I will call you Jebe the Arrow.'

Later three Sovereigns, a father and his two sons, came to us and confirmed that their people had been routed. 'Targutai cannot hold himself in the saddle,' explained the father. 'One of your men cut off his forearm. Feverish and bathed in sweat, he had to flee from Jamuka. My sons and I were the last of his escort and we thought of bringing him to you. We hoped to win your protection and reward, but on the way, our courage failed us. Hadn't we fought for him? What glory could we gain from a prisoner like that, a chief who dragged himself along the ground? So we released him and have come to offer ourselves to you.'

'You have done well,' the Khan said. 'If you had handed Targutai over to me, I would have beheaded all three of you because a man who raises his hand against his master deserves no trust, only death. Let that be added to the *yasak*!'

The days and moons passed and all we had to cheer our wretched existence was these drifting men searching for the Khan's army or pitiful families fleeing the looting amongst former allies. They preferred to join us and share our destitution than remain in the midst of the bloody clashes orchestrated by Jamuka.

Everyone told of the stubborn hatreds, the constant pillaging, the rapes, the massacres . . . Everywhere our steppes, our valleys, our woods had been laid waste and abandoned and everyone lamented not having realised Temüjin's goodness earlier.

The Kereyid had taken advantage of the chaos to occupy the west of our lands. Now their tents stood between the Onon and the Kerulen.

'And the Mongols?' stormed the Khan. 'What have they done to prevent this? And your arrogant Gür Khan, the seditious Jamuka? Is this how he protects your land?'

Rumours had it that the Chief of the Solitaries was with the Naiman. 'He'll have made some deal with Buyiruk,' thundered the Khan.

In fact Jamuka had, like so many others, quarrelled with Buyiruk. So he had gone to Buyiruk's brother, Tai, chief of the Naiman of the plains and Buyiruk's enemy. What were his plans? To gather reinforcements to challenge the Kereyid, to exterminate us or to form an alliance solely to do away with Buyiruk and take possession of his lands?

Temüjin understood now why our isolation had been so peaceful. The fire returned to his eyes and in the glow of its flames the prospect of conquest reappeared. He called us together.

'Nilqa and To'oril are convinced they have destroyed us. The squadrons they sent to the Onggirad lands came back empty-handed. Börte's tribe respected our ties of blood. They told them we had fled over the Great Khingan Mountains, crossed the Jurchet lands and settled on the marshy plains of the Amor river. But when they're threatened, my Wolves don't flee or lie down or even turn their backs to the enemy. And if they give that impression, it is only so that they can sink their fangs deeper into their victims' throats.'

He observed us, his face tensed, his eyes sharp.

'The Mongols are on their feet! Their breastplates gleam and they are invincible because my standard, the eternal banner of the Borjigin, flies in their front line, – this is the message you will carry to the scattered Mongols. Rebellion is fermenting in their hearts. They will arm themselves at our side and our horses' hooves will set the steppes on fire. But let's give the Kereyid a little more time. Soon they will grow drowsy, weighed down by fatty sheep and lulled by overconfidence. Then we will shed their blood!'

One morning, I was watching the arid steppe when I heard the bleating of sheep carried on the wind. The plaintive calls were so far away I could not work out where they were coming from, but there were so many of them that my mouth watered in anticipation.

I told Temüjin, and when the sun had reached its height, we saw the white and brown shapes of a vast flock appear at the lip of a plateau. There were more than three thousand animals flanked by a few men on powerful camels.

The leader of the caravan was a Moslem who said he had come from Önggüd country south of the Gobi. 'My name is Hassan. My master is Ala Quk Tegin. He is the ruler of a kingdom that lies between the wall of the Jin and that of the desert. On his orders I am going to the forests of the north to trade his flock for furs. Unfortunately the watering places we knew of are dried up, so we have had to detour from our usual route.'

Temüjin demanded half his flock for crossing his lands. He had nothing to lose by asking – we were going to slit the caravaneer's throat and take his flock anyway.

'They're yours if you tell me where we can drink.'

Surprised by this answer, the Khan studied the man, who was dressed in baggy trousers and a voluminous shirt with a pointed hood. He told him he knew a place and led him there.

Once his flock had been watered and rested, the Moslem divided it in two.

'These are yours.'

'Do you know who I am?' asked the Khan.

'A great Mongol leader,' answered the caravaneer, before adding in a level voice, but with a look of admiration, 'Perhaps the greatest of all.'

'And you don't fear me?'

The Moslem's eyes opened wide in astonishment, like two yurts on the horizon.

Temüjin Khan stood before him, hands on hips, legs splayed, jerkin torn from so much service, and everything about him was so black it was as if he radiated light. Only his belt with oval turquoises and the weapons tucked into it provided any contrast. His skull was the colour of burnt bark. Despite his forty springs, his face had only two lines at the corners of his eyes, each as thin as a horse's hair.

'Why should I be terrified of a lord who is just and upright?'

'You are clear-sighted, Hassan,' said the Khan. 'You realise I can't compensate you?'

'It does not matter,' answered the Moslem. 'I can read in your eyes that you are not the sort of man who forgets a friend. And that is the only debt that matters. I will for ever be grateful to you for being our guide and protector, and I will tell my master.'

Hassan stayed half a moon before setting off for the dense forests. Apart from the sheep he left us a creamy-white camel which was half a head taller than ours. 'Now,' he said to Temüjin, 'when you set off to win back your lands, you will be able to sound your drums as you go. They'll carry far and wide.'

We rode five days' march closer to the River Onon, because we needed to fatten up our horses before the arrival of winter and find a sheltered place with plenty of game in which to face its hardships. The further we went, the more the news of Temüjin Khan's return preceded us. In every *ayil*, at the mention of his name, men came out of their tents, quivers and arms at their belts, mounted their horses and joined our columns, followed by their wives, who sprinkled milk on the tails of our mounts and performed libations to the sky and earth as their children ran up to hand them leather bottles, gourds, bundles of provisions, shields, neck guards and any other implements they might need.

As we were riding along the winding edge of a ravine, far above the glinting thread of water that flowed below, a man burst out of a crevice, shouting, 'Temüjin! Temüjin!' It was his brother Qasar, so emaciated and ragged he was barely recognisable, his clothes and face covered with clay.

He clasped us to his breast. He had escaped from To'oril's *ordo* six moons before and had been looking for us ever since, surviving off the flesh of carcasses on the steppe. He told us that To'oril had set up a circular camp to the north of the Magpie Cliff beside the Kerulen. 'Between the source of the Three Rivers and the Ingoda valley, I met many Mongols who were unhappy with the Kereyids' presence. Some gave me shelter and fed me. Many fought against us with Jamuka, Altan, Khuchar and Targutai. But those four have either fled or died and the Mongols regret your exile, my brother. Let us go to the Spreading Tree, the Flint tribe are waiting there along with the Sovereigns, who lament like orphans.'

'Where are your wife and the little ones?' asked Temüjin.

'With the Kereyid. Their shaman, Iturgen, has them prisoner. That deceiver took advantage of a night when I was drunk to put a *cangue* on me. He tied my legs together, cuffed my hands to my chest and made me hop everywhere, hunched over under the collar. He fed me worse than a dog, left me to soil myself and forbade Metekna to clean me. That cur even gagged and chained me so he could take my wife in front of me. I see blood when I think of it.'

'Calm yourself, my brother. There's a way we can turn my situation to our advantage, and if my idea works, you'll have plenty of time to wring that shaman's neck.'

The Khan planned to send Qasar back to the Kereyid.

'You'll tell them: "I searched for my brother in the remotest corners of the land; I crossed mountains and rivers, looked under every stone and sniffed every scent; I called but I did not find him. All that time I slept under the stars with a clod of earth as my pillow. Now I am cold and hungry." They'll take you in and hand you back to Iturgen. Then you'll say to him that you did in fact find me but that I spurned you as a Kereyid spy. And when he has promised that no harm will come to your wife and sons, then you'll tell him where I am and that I have no more than two hundred men with me. Iturgen will come with a thousand, perhaps two, and we will kill him.'

Temüjin's prediction was correct. Accompanied by Qasar and his family, Iturgen came, but at the head of only two centuries, because Qasar had dared to say the Khan's entourage was just thirty-six strong. When the shaman saw the white swell of our tents at the mouth of the valley, he understood and tried to turn back. Too late. He was surrounded.

The members of his guard were killed one by one while he was bound and led to the Khan who, without even looking at him, ordered that he be handed over to Qasar. Qasar had promised himself that he would shatter Iturgen's eardrums, cut off his eyelids, rip his head off and spit – just for a start – down his neck. He'd talked about scalping him, using his long plait as a cloth for his arse, driving a knife between each of his fingers and filleting his hands up to the wrist. He'd said he'd flay him alive, all of him, patiently, strip by strip, and if that wasn't enough, he'd cut a few nerves. So there were a lot of curious onlookers when Iturgen was brought to Qasar and all of them were astonished to see the Khan's brother run the Kereyid shaman through the stomach with a single thrust of his sabre, grab his neck, drive his dagger four times into his ribs and then shove him away.

It was so quick.

Qasar could have wept: he had spoken so eloquently of his desire to prolong the traitor's torture. Instead of which he had killed his tormentor with five thrusts of the blade – typical Qasar, that great oaf always swept away by his emotions.

Still, at least the shaman had been taken care of. Our shaman Kököchü had protested and predicted terrible scourges if we killed someone of his rank. But his indignation wasn't as vehement as it could have been. No one in the Khan's entourage had forgotten Ravenous Dark's death. And everyone wondered if there was a connection between what Qasar had suffered at the hands of the Kereyid and Kököchü's role as envoy. Hadn't he said on his return, when Temüjin asked after his brother, that Qasar was living like a king?

The scouts confirmed To'oril's position. The Kereyid king's great, golden tent had been pitched and he was preparing to feast, without a care in the world. We assembled our forces in the little valleys which run among the hills bordering the Plateau of the Giants.

Temüjin and I occupied the winter pasture of my childhood, the valley of the Red Throne, with a detachment of a thousand men.

On an icy night we set out. It was dark, but the land was so familiar to me that I could have found my way to the meeting point with my eyes closed. We cut through the Blue Forests with half the detachment, while the other half detoured around to reach the west bank of the Kerulen. Their journey would be easier, but I'd calculated that it would take us the same time to reach our respective positions of attack. From the scouts, we knew that Temüge and the Onggirad were approaching by the gully upriver. With their help, Temüjin Khan could muster almost thirteen thousand warriors. According to our estimates, the Kereyid were occupying our lands with between fifteen and eighteen thousand men.

My horse was called Black Tail. He was honest, brave and even-tempered. Temüjin rode White-Mouthed Bay, a valiant steed who, despite the heaviness of his breast and rump, was considered one of the most agile horses we had. My khan had had to part with five mares for him. But he wouldn't regret it, because White-Mouthed Bay could justify all our expectations: his faultless manoeuvrability was allied with the fiercest determination.

When our right wing had drawn up in battle formation on the other side of the Kerulen, we tore down the slopes without drum rolls or war cries. Only the snapping of the banners under the grey skies and the clanking of the breastplates echoed our chargers' hooves as they rent asunder the stillness of dawn.

The enemy thought we were on the borders of the earth, more than a season's march away and here we were, sending up sprays of water at their feet! Surprise gave us wings. We struck in perfectly coordinated waves, giving them no respite, and the great Kereyid camp convulsed and succumbed in place after place.

The fighting continued as evening spread its shadows and mist. The Kereyid chiefs suggested that battle be postponed until the next day.

'Out of the question,' roared the Khan. 'We have them under our boots. Either they surrender or we crush them!'

They threw down their arms and submitted unconditionally,

apart from the honour of serving the standard of Temüjin Khan's Blue Mongols. The presence of their wives and children must have purged them of all thought of rebellion.

As ill fortune would have it – and it remained a mystery how it happened – To'oril and his son Nilqa escaped. They must have fled at the first attack and abandoned their warriors to their fate. Temüjin decided to push on to the *ordo* of the Black Forest on the banks of the Tula and then to To'oril's 'city of tents' on the plains of the Orhon, with its innumerable herds and booty from conquests and tributes imposed on caravans. Here, as elsewhere, the Kereyids put up only a scant resistance and three days and three nights fighting were enough to make their elites surrender. But there was still no To'oril. He had vanished without looking back or even stopping to empty his bladder, goaded on by his dread of Temüjin, whose trust he had exhausted. Qadak the Brave, one of To'oril's commanders, undid his belt and laid it and his weapons at our Khan's feet.

'When I saw my king's downcast expression,' he said, 'I couldn't bring myself to take him captive. The opposite: I helped him escape and fought to give him a head start. If I must die, then I will. But if Temüjin Khan is merciful, I will put all my forces at his disposal without reservation.'

The Khan admired the defeated man's loyalty. He took him with him and said, 'You deserve your name, Qadak. In Quyildar, I have lost another brave man. From now on, you and a hundred of your most faithful followers will take care of Quyildar's wives and children. To the first, give sons, to the second, give courage and happiness. May the children of his children for ever receive the orphan's generous share.'

In less than two moons we had crossed the ocean of grass and forests from the banks of the Argun to the source of the Orhon, and, in so doing, we had recovered all our lands.

Temüjin Khan stationed the bulk of his troops in the great Orhon valley and along the Tula river – the old heart of the Kereyid kingdom. To break up the unity of To'oril's people, he deported all of the Kereyid living in an arc from the Celestial Mount to the great bend of the Kerulen. Dispersed among our clans, they quickly blended in, especially since marriage with Mongols was encouraged. And the Khan judiciously gave responsiblity to several Kereyid chiefs.

To his loyal followers, who had fought at his side or had worked in secrecy, spying on the enemy, the Khan gave To'oril's golden tent and the tents of his wives. The royal treasure consisted of hundreds of embroidered triangular or oval yurts; dresses, headdresses, pearls, jewels, silks and furs, the softest wools, dishes incrusted with gold, silver and precious stones, weaponry, finely worked leather saddles with silver-chased engraving, cruppers, tiger or panther-skin saddle rugs – Temüjin Khan let his faithful have all these wonders. What's more, he ennobled those who had shown courage and devotion in battle and every adversity. And so simple shepherds or grooms became entitled to wear arms at royal banquets, to drink from their own cups in the Khan's tent and to keep any prey they killed in the great hunts – a host of privileges which I already enjoyed.

For having cleaned his wound for a whole night and slipped through the Sovereigns' lines to quench his thirst, my *anda* gave me thirty Uighur carpets and thirty pink-lipped grey mares.

Temüjin wanted to spend the summer on the Isle of Grass, then the winter with the Onggirad. I wanted to return to the Plateau of Giants and the valley of the Red Throne, where Afraid of Bears' mother had been taken by the forest's claws, and where we had gathered for our surprise attack on the Kereyid.

Our respective journeys meant we were to part where the River Tula winds round the Camel's Jaw, that sublime hill hidden by high natural walls – I to ride back up the Tula, he to rejoin the Kerulen.

'While my flocks grow fat,' I said, 'I will build a wall around the valley of the Red Throne and apart from me, your eternal guardian, no one will be allowed within that rampart.'

He decided to spend the night on the Tula's banks and, while the men tethered the horses, he asked me to go with him up to that great jawbone suspended above the endless green steppe. We crossed the river with its round stones, climbed up through the pine and larch, past the jagged, twisted boulders and at last we reached the short, light grass set in its jewel case of giant rocks. Polished smooth by time, those enormous stones and cliffs reared above our heads like a necklace in the sky and each bore the shape of an animal. Wherever an animal had been killed with respect and regret, its soul gathered here in the dark.

The great herds of clouds gliding through the azure sky added to the majesty of this phenomenal place. Eagles floated on hot-air currents as we walked across the velvet carpet, looking at the serrated forms pointing skywards and the round, sensual ones disposed on the ground according to Tengri's whim. One of the rocks, ten times my height and twenty times the span of my shoulders, was shaped like a tortoise; another looked like a lion's paw resting on a mound of tender grass.

Temüjin Khan startled me from my reverie. 'This place is yours, if you wish it.'

I looked at him, flabbergasted, and was about to say that no reward could give me more pleasure, when he continued, 'From the banks of the Tula to those of the Tereli a short trot from here, under that cloud which looks like a rearing horse, I give you these divine grasslands. That's not all, Bo'urchu! Look to the right of the gorge at that herd flying across the slope.'

I saw the herd immediately. It was following a white stallion which was leaping towards the heights, his neck arched, his mane dazzlingly defined against an orange-coloured cliff, his step buoyant, joyful. He did a final leap, pawing the air with his forelegs, and whinnied so that his greeting echoed all around.

White Cloud . . .

At his heels the herd stopped and formed a half-circle, a jumble of thick coats. I thought I recognised Black Coat, Blue Heart, Isabelle, the Roan with the Dragging Fetlock, White Lips, Shining Brow and then the Bay with the Smiling Scar . . . No, I wasn't dreaming . . . It was my favourite herd, White Cloud's!

'This is not a gift to thank you for your devotion, my sworn *anda*. They were yours already. I have just had them brought here and added a few mares and colts – the objects and fruits of White Cloud's desire.'

I was in transports of happiness; I could have flown if Temüjin had asked me to.

At the mouth of the gorge, a rider in a white *del* was trotting towards my herd. Her long hair danced on her mount's back.

'Her beautiful smile which inspires your horses is my second gift. Take her as your wife. When you see her, you will know her and you will realise how much I think of you as my own flesh. Go, Bo'urchu! Go to her.'

He rode off enigmatically, leaving me staring at the horse-woman.

Queen of Flowers? My everlasting, my beloved, my love, my all! My sweet . . .

Chapter 36

I reached her side, my heart chiming like a bell. She turned her chin away, hiding her face. I leant forward, caught a lock of her hair and tugged it gently. Head bowed, she glanced at me anxiously, blushing. I gaped open-mouthed for a moment, then said her name: 'Temulun...' My disappointment must have been blatant, because I saw she was on the verge of tears.

'Come,' I said, taking the bridle of her horse. 'Let's go and see the herd...'

White Cloud came up calmly and nuzzled us in greeting. Behind him his clan grazed peacefully, their flanks rounded.

As I looked at my stallion, Queen of Flowers' face danced before my eyes. Behind me, Temüjin's sister choked back her sobs.

Despite his age, White Cloud seemed little changed. His neck was thicker and more arched from his many coverings and, examining him more closely, I noticed that his hocks were slightly wizened. But there was still a harmony to even his slightest movements, a harmony which I saw echoed by many of his children. His candid, round, full eyes were still full of spirit and shining with satisfaction. He drummed a forefoot, shook his mane, and lifted his head high, ears pricked towards his herd. Then he gave a short, strident whinny. His mares looked up, some coming a little closer to fathom his desires. He wanted to draw my attention to his fresh conquests. I noted a tall bay with legs, mane and tail as black as ink; another with a cocksure air and a coat the colour of *argols*; another a uniform shade of fermented milk with ivory hooves and, at her side, a creamy-blue colt. Then a younger mare, two springs old perhaps, with a coat as golden as apricots and a forehead lit up by a patch of light hair that ran the length of her nose like a frayed piece of fabric. Had White Cloud had time to cover this youngster? I would have to wait for winter to find out. But he could be proud of his mares. They shone with the light of a thousand fires and their eyes blazed with confidence.

It was a long time since the silk purse containing one of Temulun's milk teeth had hung around White Cloud's neck. But she had protected and loved him no less. Now we had found each other again in this cradle of mountains, would he be glad to see me take her by the hand and smile into her eyes?

I halted my mount to wait for Temulun, then put an arm round her waist, another under her thighs and lifted her onto my saddle, her cheek against my shoulder just like that day when, as we fled the Merkids on Afraid of Bears' back, she had declared her child's undying love.

I chose a grassy ledge as our bed for the night. Tall, billowing plumes of cloud gathered over the distant, purple hills, their underbellies flushed by the setting sun. On the edge of our perch, flowers stretched out their bells into empty space. We watched my pretty herd far below between the deep blue of the firs, moving over the delicate green grasslands to the slow, delighted rhythm of their appetites.

Our hearts were dizzy and it had nothing to do with the height of our refuge. We did not say a word.

We stayed like that, shoulder to shoulder, looking to the south and listening to the quick, light beating of our pulses. When the sky pinned on its brilliant jewels, we lay down to watch the stars shoot across it like arrows, her hand in mine. I had banished Queen of Flowers from my thoughts. My despair had been so great that I realised I had to give up any hopes of her return as lost.

It was just before dawn that I bent over Temulun's face and looked into her great brown eyes spangled with gold. I touched her eyelids with my lips, traced her mouth with my forefinger and told her she would be my wife. 'The first of my wives, for such is the Khan's wish.'

'And mine, more than anything else,' she added, rubbing her little nose, cold with the dew, against mine.

All the simple ingredients of happiness were suddenly in place. I'd been blind to it, like an ermine chasing after a titmouse, its head in the air, when the plumpest of field mice drowses at its feet. Without Temüjin making my idyll possible by taking Gerelma to the camps in the east of my lands, I would have walked straight by . . .

There was nothing extraordinary about that time: the moons

still succeeded one another without alarum, the streams still sang more prettily in some places than in others. Yet nothing could compare to this feeling of fulfilment. I was happy and carefree because a woman loved me: there, that was the wonder of it. She was the first and she would be the last, the only one.

Since the day the Khan told me to go to the woman he was giving me as my wife, two summers and two winters had spread their velvet coats across the land.

We had pitched our tents near the Tereli and its giant, green-trunked birches. It sang loudly, that fast-running river, and great bronze fish spawned among its bends. We had splashed through its many joyful branches and played among its stones, red, garnet and blue, almost purple. Naked we had rolled in the tall grass, dried ourselves on the sandbanks and, clasped in each other's arms, drowsed against the tree trunks polished smooth by the current. We had gorged ourselves on redcurrants and strawberries and chased after the willow and tamarisk catkins, laughing as they blew on the breeze.

During these two great cycles of the sun, when we migrated between the Camel's Jaw and the Red Throne, our horses had grown fat, our stores of milk and meat had exceeded our needs and our men had never come back from the hunt empty-handed.

Great-granddaughter of Kabul Khan, Temulun was the perfect wife. Dawn never caught her asleep: she was always the first to rise and kindle the fire, to prepare the meal and warm the yurt and my heart. Like a bee that knows its days are numbered, she was always busy and never turned away from me or abandoned me. Attentive, gentle, calm and loving, this princess with simple aspirations never raised her voice, always showed the same level good humour, and if the initiative in lovemaking was left to me, she was always willing and always able to fill me with joy.

Her looks, her caresses, her actions were prompted by love alone and quietly, day by day, my love grew until when we were apart I only needed to picture her for my heart to leap with delight.

Her face had neither the aristocratic beauty of Mother Hö'elün nor even Temüjin's proud cast. She looked most like Temüge, the youngest of Mother Hö'elün's sons, whose oval face was distinctive simply because it was candid and merry. Temulun was beautiful because she was in love. And seeing her alive, watching her deck the poles of our yurt with flowers or helping her milk the mares gave me even more pleasure than holding her naked to my chest and smelling the nape of her neck, her armpits and all those nooks and crannies where the imagination loves to burrow.

One day Temulun was fitting me with a wool and silk-lined waistcoat and a supple cuirass of leather-covered iron scales which she had just made when a sentry announced that a great cloud of dust was rising in the east.

That evening, Jochi and Chagatai rode out of the gorge of the Camel's Jaw at the head of a hundred horsemen. Behind them the standard-bearer held the trident's three curved blades and underneath flapped nine yak's tails – black, the colour of war.

'I never realised a handful of warriors could kick up so much dust,' I remarked.

With a broad smile Little Crumb said that he would never forgive himself for scaring a friend. His brother, brows knotted, explained, 'Ten thousand of our men are at the base of the cliffs on the left bank of the Tula.'

'Has your father lost his taste for long journeys? Are they just for snotty-nosed brats now?'

'Joke away, Bo'urchu,' said Jochi. 'But he'll be standing in front of you before the end of this quarter of the moon. He is following with Ögödei at the slow pace of the wagons and the remounts. Our uncles will not be far behind. Qasar has taken the right bank of the Onon, Belgütei the River Khurkhu and Temüge is coming by the south of the Lutulun Mountains.'

'So I was right to sharpen my arrows?'

'Absolutely. And fasten your quiver firmly to your belt because Tai, the Naiman king, has vowed to recover the Kereyid lands and invade our country.'

'Where did you hear this petty king's bragging, Little Crumb?'

'You remember Hassan, the Moslem who drove his flocks by the Miry Ponds when we were there? He stops at my father's *ordo* every spring now. The Khan has already reimbursed him twice over for the beasts he gave us. You remember his master was called Ala Quk Tegin . . .'

'And lived near the Jin's great wall?'

'That's right. Well this Ala Quk Tegin is the chief of the Önggüd and the King of the Naimans asked him to form an alliance – as fellow Nestorians – and attack us in the rear. Through Hassan, Ala Quk Tegin warned us immediately and sent word of the Naiman queen's opinion of us. She's like a snake lurking under a stone, that witch: she calls us monsters, evil-smelling from our hair to the holes in our arses. The Mongols fornicate so much, she told the Önggüd chief, that their red-faced children swarm over the steppe like the lice that crawl over their skin. Let's drive them far from our kingdoms, those ugly, filthy quarrelmongers.'

'And what did your father say?'

'He promised to sit his divine buttocks on this Gürbesü's face – that's her name. She's Tai's mother and his wife at the same time.'

Temüjin Khan arrived at the head of ten thousand warriors. My *anda* welcomed me in his tent where he was holding council. His face coppered by the sun, his smile as lustrous as moonlight, he seemed younger than ever, his chest firm, his shoulders broad and full under his black *del*.

All his faithful attendants surrounded him: Sübetei, Jelme, Muqali, Jebe the Arrow, Jurchedei, Qadak, his younger brother Temüge, his sons Ögödei, Jochi, Chagatai and young Tolui, who was not yet old enough to address a gathering, and Mother Höelün's adopted sons, Kuchu, Blackbird and Borokul. The shaman, Kököchü, and his six arrogant brothers were there too.

'Come close, Bo'urchu, my blue courser, my trusty companion. Can you still let fly two arrows before your horse has completed its stride?'

'Yes, my khan.'

'Well then, the Naiman king's shields will be no help to him. Now, with Jebe the Arrow, I have my two best archers. We will roll up this Tai like a tattered rug!'

We moved out in squadrons of ten thousand across carpets of bellflowers with the Tula in sight and the dunes that accompany it like a pink spine.

Armour-clad, their faces swarthy, our soldiers' slow, silent progress was a radiant sight. Formed up in a broad chequer-board formation bristling with lances and silk banners, we sailed under a blue sky veiled with pearly cloud and, like deadly men-of-war, followed every pitch and roll in the ground without a single gap appearing between our ranks. Striking away from the bends of the river, we climbed into the gentle succession of rounded hills studded with buttercups, thyme and scabious, which rustled with the sound of a thousand fluttering wings.

So, we were just barking dogs, were we – quarrelsome,

stinking scavengers? Eaten up with their own conceit, those warriors of the west would soon see our battle array. They'd face the quivers that they boasted they'd seize and empty on the ground. We were coming with our lice, our stench, our hideous faces and blood-red eyes – so they said. But in those eyes they'd soon see a murderous light, a hunger for massacres, women, riches, feasting and fresh meats, which they'd never forget.

The scouts reported that the enemy had deployed roughly fifteen thousand men on the heights of the Orhon valley. Counting their reserve troops, the royal guard and some crack elites, we estimated their strength as 25,000 fighters. King Tai had assembled his whole army.

The Naiman we had enslaved during the campaign against Buyiruk gave us valuable information about Tai. According to them, Buyiruk's younger brother was a coward who preferred to go hunting with a falcon and a few noblemen than to rally his warriors for great, meticulously organised hunts. Conducting distant campaigns was a source of annoyance for him, and he was loath to embark on draining, uncertain expeditions. It was as much as he could do to drive the mercenary tribes back over his borders. When he could have come to his brother's aid, his horse had remained tethered in front of his great stone tent.

The Khan immediately sought to take advantage of the Naiman sovereign's reputation. He ordered dummy riders to be made of felt and strapped onto each remount with girths and willow switches so that the enemy would believe we had eighty thousand men in the mountains, when in fact we were not even twenty thousand. Half of our army went down into the Orhon valley to set up encampments, each man taking a dummy with him. The other half stayed on the heights to watch over the other decoys, five per man. Dusk picked out our silhouettes and when night fell, we lit fires and had the remounts march past to sustain the illusion. Thinking that the hoax would make the Naiman turn on their heels, we were just waiting for that moment to fling ourselves on their backs.

They may have been agitated, but still they did not leave their positions. Did that mean that eighty thousand Mongols did not terrify them? Were their archers so numerous that they did not fear us? Would the fear we planned on spreading amongst them turn against us?

Inspecting our men was enough to convince me otherwise.

Scanning those faces: round or angular, emaciated or fat, crooked, seamed with scars or the pox; with their flat or bulging brows, long plaits worn from the crown or thin braids at the nape, thick lips or mouths that stretched from ear to ear – all those faces expressed impatience for battle, a hankering after destruction, pillage, massacre and dismemberment. And in their sharpened eyes shone that exalted gleam, that dazzling boldness, that muffled, miscreant restlesness that anticipates murder. Who could doubt these implacable warriors, this mixed-breed army? They were already in the enemy's midst, slicing open their bellies and galloping over the mess of their entrails.

In fact, what we did not yet know was that at Tai's side stood his counsellor, the shadowy Jamuka, that inveterate intriguer, who had been enlisted in this campaign as tactician. Temüjin's diehard rival didn't believe the Naiman scouts' reports about the size of our forces. He knew, from having instigated it, that the fighting of those last years could not have spared more than forty thousand Kereyid and Mongol of fighting age.

'Even if he'd rounded up all the remaining Tatars, Merkids and Onggirad,' the Chief of the Solitaries explained, 'Temüjin couldn't have assembled that many men.'

'They have as many campfires as there are stars in the sky,' repeated Tai.

The Gür Khan without kingdom suggested they retreat. 'We'll see how many follow. Their horses are tired; this will bring them to the last stage of exhaustion and then we'll be able to pick them off on the western slopes of the Khangai Mountains.'

The King thought this sound advice and passed it on to the army's commander, his own son, whom he asked to prepare the retreat. But his father's request so aggravated him that Staunch the Thickset flew into a rage in front of his generals.

'Our king's shaking like a leaf because he's seen more Mongols out there than in all his nightmares put together! But how could he have seen any in his life, when he's never ventured further from his yurt than a pregnant woman going to piss? Like a bottle-fed lamb he doesn't dare cross the threshold of his tent for fear of finding the world full of starving dogs! How many Mongols are there really facing us? Haven't they just come with their wives and brats to try and frighten us? Didn't Jamuka say that more soldiers followed his standard than Temüjin's? And isn't he with us? So what game is he playing, terrifying my father at the moment of attack? We will launch ourselves at them at dawn before my craven father can go and cry on his mother's shoulder.'

Learning of his son's resolve, Tai asked Jamuka how to defuse the situation. But the Solitary, now getting the full measure of his ally's cowardice, took a malicious delight in alarming him: 'Temüjin is the slyest of all adversaries. But his wiles would be nothing if his fearsome warriors were not like starving lions, hard as iron. Even when they're streaming blood and riddled with arrows, they pursue their prey impassively. Your son puffs out his chest like a capercaillie, but when they charge and he feels their breath, you had better hope that he doesn't falter, because when a Mongol speaks, his words are always made good.'

Staring into space, his eyes wide, the Naiman king made his decision: 'Since every life must end in death, let us join battle.'

It was utter carnage. As the enemy advance guards began to ride down into the valley, ours advanced on fast-moving geldings in compact little groups, like clumps of thorny scrub on the steppe, and goaded their flanks, broke up their order and then left the ground to the bulk of our army, which launched itself at them like an arrow. We were like a blade that cut deep into their lines and spread out as we drove forward, crushing them in a single wave, trampling them underfoot, riddling them with arrows and hacking them to pieces. Those who escaped dared not rally and outflank us, for they were deceived by the silhouettes of the troops led by Temüge and Ögödei, the sixty thousand dummies that looked down on the battle. We advanced without yielding a scrap of ground, driving the Naiman back up the foothills and valleys of the Khangai, breaking them into isolated groups so that our light cavalry could pick them off on the crests or put them to flight. Their horses rolled down the slopes through the tall grass dotted with cornflowers and poppies, shattering their necks and legs. Few got to their feet to return to the fray.

As we pushed forward, King Tai retreated up the mountain. He watched the fighting and asked for the names of the protagonists: 'Those five noblemen pursuing my braves, nipping at their horse's hocks – who are they?'

'They are Temüjin's wolves: Bo'urchu, Jebe the Arrow, Kubilai, Jelme and Sübetei,' answered Jamuka. 'They feed on dew and human flesh. They are so fierce the Khan tethers them. But turned loose on the days of battle, they ride on the wind's back straight at the archers, their mouths open, drooling with joy.'

As his guard was set upon by our men, King Tai wanted to take shelter above a small valley that ran across the path of our assault.

'And those Mongols rushing to encircle my guard, gambolling bareheaded, scornful of danger – who are they?'

'They are the Urut and the Mangkud, the trophy-takers. They seize lances and sabres with their bare hands, slash throats with their nails, and tear off their enemies' plaits and topknots!'

The Naiman leader urged on his horse to a higher promontory. 'And who is that man behind them with the white-crested helmet who swoops down on my men like a ravenous hawk?'

'Ah! That man!' said Jamuka breaking into his finest smile. 'Study him closely, because he is my *anda*, my sworn ally, Temüjin. The Khan of Khans. His entire body is cast in brass; your warriors won't find a chink for their arrows, not even one that the point of an awl could penetrate.'

'Quick, let's climb to the top of the mountain!'

'Steady, my lord; you've taken fright. Didn't you boast you'd seize their quivers? Come now, look at that one to Temüjin's right. His arrows are on his back. Go and take them from him! That's Temüjin's brother Qasar, a true tiger. When he was a dribbling brat, Mother Hö'elün used to feed him last because otherwise there would have been nothing left for her four other children. He needs a whole horse every meal; his body is stronger than three breastplates. His long arrows can cut through four men in a row at five thousand paces.'

Then Jamuka ordered his equerry to send whistling arrows to the chieftains of the clans under his banner. They carried two messages. One – 'I am withdrawing' – was for the Solitaries. The other – 'You are in command' – was for his four hundred or so allies – Qatagins, Salji'uts, Dörben and Sovereigns who, once free to choose whether to continue fighting on the Naimans' side or not, came over to us.

Night fell as the Naiman regrouped on the heights of the Khangai. We broke off the murderous revels and surrounded that part of the mountains we knew from having hunted there with the Kereyid. Our opponents tried to escape under cover of darkness. It was a grave mistake: they stumbled on the scree, the ground gave way under their feet and at least a third of their squadrons were hurled over the precipices, piling up at the bottom in a bloody pulp of bone, flesh, hooves and iron.

We caught up with them again in the morning as they tried to reach the southern slopes. King Tai had been badly wounded in the head by a hooked lance. His generals formed a circle round him and begged him to return to the struggle. But the top of the king's skull was split wide open and it made no difference his men telling him that Queen Gürbesü had arrayed herself in all her finery to see him fight; Tai stayed on the ground, as motionless as a piece of dung.

Then his commanders returned to the fray to fight to the very end. Like heroes, they refused to surrender and all died sword in hand.

From the Altay to the Khangai, the vast Naiman lands were subjugated. Gürbesü was brought before Temüjin in his great azure tent. She was a strong, tall woman with a pleasing although austere face, who appeared even more stately in her heavy robes and plentiful jewels. She was ordered to kneel.

The Khan was eating. He asked for the scarf of gold thread which the conquered queen wore across her shoulders, wiped his hands on it and dropped it at his feet. Was he going to humiliate her further – undress her, give her thick black-and-gold brocade robes to his men and sit his royal backside on her pointed nose?

'You thought us ugly and evil-smelling, isn't that so?'

She tried to reply, but a guard stopped her, explaining that she was not to speak directly to the Khan – an official would relay what she said to our master.

Surprised, Gürbesü apologised profusely. 'All I sense here is the cool wind that blows unceasingly across the sky, and the sight of you is more radiant than the white clouds that cross those infinite expanses.'

The Khan then told her that she'd have to get used to his couch, since he was taking her as his wife.

From now on Temüjin reigned from the western slopes of the Altay to the western slopes of the Great Khingan, and to travel from one end of his kingdom to the other would have meant a journey of seven million paces. He shipped many of the Naiman off to the east and dispersed all their craftsmen amongst our clans, particularly the blacksmiths, whose work was of high quality. He retained King Tai's chancellor, a level-headed Uighur by the name of Tata Tong-a. This scholar could read and write

Uighur, Jin and Khwarezmian, as well as speak certain Mongol, Naiman, Khirgiz and Kereyid dialects, and Temüjin gave him high responsibilities. He was to be the first to transcribe the *yasak*, which he did in Uighur. He was also made responsible for the education of Temüjin's sons. So Jochi, Chagatai, Ögödei and Tolui learnt to read and write Uighur, and the youngest – whose name meant Mirror – then aged eleven springs, proved to be the most gifted. The Khan took Tata Tong-a as his personal interpreter, and he asked him to devise a language that would be common to all the vassal tribes.

Queen Gürbesü gave Temüjin a man's skull. Set in white gold and chased with emeralds, it was in two parts, the crown having been sawn off and fashioned into a drinking cup. Gürbesü the Cunning, as we called her in private, said this artefact was all that was left of To'oril. 'One of our patrols came upon him drinking at the Nekun stream. He looked like a runaway, so the guards didn't believe he had once been the Kereyid king and put him to the sword.'

'He can't have been alone, can he?' asked Temüjin. 'He fled with his son, a few princes and at least a detachment of archers.'

'Our border guards assured us he was.'

'Then Nilqa must have abandoned him!' the Khan exclaimed in amazement. 'My adoptive father has been richly punished for leaving me.'

He looked at the cheekbones which shone with a thousand emerald-green facets. A fine scar marked the left eye socket, a wound which had only seemed skin-deep when he was alive. Each of the teeth had been set in silver, so that he seemed to be giving a fantastic grin, a frozen rictus of joy.

'From now on, his skull will be my cup,' the Khan said. 'That way he will continue to give me succour.'

Queen Gürbesü told how once, when she was offering libations to To'oril's head, the jaw had opened and the teeth had chattered; her son had been so terrified he had swept it to the ground. It was said that this foretold great misfortune for the Naiman king. Did his fatal head-wound not confirm the portent?

Temüjin said, 'Milk, meat and most of all women, gold and silver, always made King To'oril's teeth chatter with excitement. Why should death, his great concubine, have brought any change?'

We received news of To'oril's son, Nilqa, from the lips of his own squire who had abandoned him in the Gobi Desert. The traitor described his master's flight to our khan. Prince Nilqa had left his father at Mount Kongor when To'oril's mount had slumped to the ground, lifeless. Then he had crossed the valley of the salt lakes, the Altay Mountains, where he had hunted argali and ibex, and finally the great desert expanses by which he hoped to reach the Xixia. When Nilqa had been creeping patiently towards a herd of *dziggetai*, the wild donkeys of the desert which are preyed upon by gadflies, the squire had deserted the prince, taking their two horses.

'What do you desire as a reward?' asked the Khan.

'To serve you, O Kha Khan!'

'What would you say to serving the greatest of my squires, the master of my herds?'

As the squire kissed the ground in thanks, the Khan bit his lower lip and added, 'Ah, well then, so be it! Serve my faithful Bo'urchu and be sure to make a good pillow for him when death comes!'

As he straightened up, I seized the kneeling man by the arch of the eyebrows, forced my fingers into his sockets and froze his shout by slitting his throat. Such was the fate of shiftless souls who dared appear before the Khan hoping that treachery would be met with gratitude.

So, Nilqa was wandering the desert. Jamuka and his hundred Solitaries must be doing the same, along with Tai's stubborn son, Staunch the Thickset, who had managed to flee as well. But under that blazing summer sun, I barely spared a thought for our adversaries, so impatient was I to return to my *ulus* at the Red Throne and, most of all, to my greatest joy, my gentle wife. As each of my horse's strides brought me closer to her, so my body and my spirits soared. I could feel the approach of a great happiness. The happiness of a warrior sated with blood and starved of love.

Chapter 37

The sun played through the leaves, patterning Temulun's smooth skin with pools of gold and black silk. We had just made love and now, lying on the mossy carpet of a hollow amongst the larch and silver birch, we were both in that state when desire has been satisfied but love only blazes up the brighter. I was at the peak of happiness. My hand glided over her rounded stomach, the gentle bulge that made us a loving trinity.

As soon as I returned from the campaign against the Naimans, everything about her had told me of this new richness: her forehead clear as light, her diamond smile, her knowing wink, her songs of fox cubs, her silences, full and shared. She didn't say anything but waited to be naked to see in my eyes the effect of this tenderly cradled treasure. She wasn't showing much, but from the way she walked in the firelight as if following her womb, or stayed on her feet only a step from our bed, I finally realised: I was a father.

Mongols do not cry. But that night, my nose pressed into Temulun's pert belly button, my arms hooped round her waist, I doubted I was one.

That day when I caressed Temulun's belly, all desires slaked, laid the foundations of our bliss and heralded days that were sweeter than any other. All around our mossy bed irises observed us, their violet-and-yellow heads and upturned collars caught by the shade. The sun was sinking and its watery light, our only finery, was fading. For a moment, falling through the leaves, it lit up my wife with eye-like spots of light, transforming her fine-grained skin into leopard's fur. When it sank in the west, setting the trunks of the larches ablaze, it cast a final ray on her belly button.

'It's a boy,' she said. 'I can feel it, I know. Look how bravely he stretches out his little fist to meet your fingers.'

The last of the sun flashed on the satin-smooth peaks, while higher still, Tengri's blue was as dazzling as ever. I tilted back my head and closed my eyes, my heart beating a trot, whispering, 'Thoya, Thoya . . .'

Thoya was a girl's name meaning Little Light, and if the child was going to be a boy as his mother claimed, it would throw the evil spirits off the scent. A little light but a very brilliant one, like that last luminous droplet of sun that flickered on Temulun's belly. When it went out, a wave of melancholy swelled in my chest and quickly dissolved. I looked at Temulun, at her long, loose hair on the moss, her relaxed smile etching two arcs of contentment across cheeks as white as boxwood. Her forehead smelled so sweet that an ant never grew tired of exploring it. In the silence we whispered endearments. And in the vice of my temples, the words kept repeating: Temulun and Thoya . . . Thoya and Bo'urchu . . . Temulun, Bo'urchu, Thoya . . . Thoya, Thoya, Thoya . . .

Temulun wanted to return to the Isle of Grass where Temüjin Khan had established his *ordo* for the winter. Mother Hö'elün was there, now so old she could no longer leave her yurt, and Temulun wanted her to share the gift of being there at the moment our child appeared.

We arrived at daybreak. The Isle of Grass was black with tents, from which the steam of the day's first milk rose gently into the air from them. This mass of tents made the plateau even more imposing, set in its great cradle of mountains. Each group of yurts formed a circle crossed by two diagonal paths, at the centre of which stood a chief's tent – the tent of a father and patriarch. Along the edges of these circles ran even broader thoroughfares, crowded with waggons, pyramids of *argols*, roaming lambs, goats and dogs, and horses waiting for their masters. The largest, most colourful and best-laid-out circles belonged to the Khan and his many wives, whose tents fanned out around his, which was white, rounded and swollen like the full moon. Only the shaman's *ayil* could rival the Khan's, and Kököchü's azure tents with their gold or silver braid glittered more dazzlingly than even those of Temüjin's own brothers.

At that moment when the sun stained the high reliefs pink, purple and cinnabar, the herds of horses were making their way to the distant escarpments.

As I crossed my *anda*'s compound escorted by ten of his guards, I saw that he had more tents then I had ever known one man to have. He had a dozen wives and at least twenty new children. The number of his slaves had multiplied by ten, his exclusive guard accounted for five hundred warriors, and more than two hundred and fifty tents surrounded his own like petals.

He received me in the tent where he took his meals. It was ten paces wide, and apart from the cooking utensils and three large *airag* skins, it was decorated purely with his and his first wife, Börte's, saddles and harnesses. Each was finer than the last and I admired the finely worked wood and leather, the studs set with precious stones, the silver medallions depicting flowering branches, snakes, wolves or does; the saddlecloths with their brilliant, hypnotic patterns, the tiger-skin and leopard-skin sweat flaps, the winter cushions of blue wolf, sable or ermine fur, and the cruppers and breast collars spangled with coral, pearls or turqouises as fine and gleaming as the stars in the sky.

'Come to me, Bo'urchu, most faithful of my faithful. Come and sit at my right and drink the auspicious morning's milk; it is thanks to you our horses are impervious to exhaustion.'

At the Khan's side were his sons, Jochi, Chagatai, Ögödei, Tolui and Mother Hö'elün's four adopted sons. Opposite him were Börte, the mother of the four princes, the young wives of Temüjin's three eldest sons and a bustling swarm of serving women. The floor was covered with embroidered rugs, some showing hunting scenes, and thick cushions that served as backrests.

'How are your herds? Are your grasslands still lush?'

The Khan wanted to know if I had had an agreeable journey. I told him how eagerly the Mongols had ridden up to meet my caravan, how they had fallen in with me and reported all the goings on of those past few seasons, all the news that spread from *ayil* to *ayil* and would eventually reach the Khan's ears as highlights. All these horsemen had bade me convey their goodwill to the Khan.

Three days had passed since he had been told we were on our way. So I estimated that our messenger had needed nearly six days to reach the Isle of Grass. It struck me that the Khan could improve his network of sentries and messengers.

'What do you suggest?'

'A larger body, better organised, which would spread across our lands like a spider's web. Those riders would gallop hell for leather over short distances and then pass on their message to

247

the next in line. That way you would have heard from me the same evening.'

'It's a good idea, Bo'urchu, as long as the message is short and straightforward. The more complex the message, the more intermediaries that hear it and tongues that repeat it, the more confused it will become. In that case there must be only one voice relaying it, like a single arrow aimed at its target. But you're right; success will depend on the horses. Fetch Tata Tong-a.'

When the Uighur arrived, the Khan asked him to enter a new law in the *yasak*: 'Every 40,000 paces between *ayils*, a herdsman shall keep a relay of three fresh, well-fed horses, permanently saddled and kept at the disposal of the Khan's messengers, princes, noblemen and leaders of his army. Every man appointed to this task who does not make sure it is carried out to perfection will prove unworthy of my trust. If he fails in his duties, his kneecaps will be broken.'

The Khan had conceived a network of links which once given a structure would become a marvellous message service, comprehensive and methodical. However far his conquests took him, he would never be entirely cut off from his principal *ordo*, the city of tents on the Isle of Grass.

Tata Tong-a read out what he had written as Qasar, Belgütei, Temüge, Jelme, Jochi and I smiled with delight at seeing each other again. When the scribe had finished, he was sent to assemble the Khan's messengers and the officers responsible for implementing his edicts. Then we drank and ate to celebrate our reunion and I paid little attention to Kököchü or his contemptuous brothers who winked at each other and cast quizzical looks at my weapons as if I was too lowly to be entitled to wear them in the royal tent.

Once we had eaten, we mounted up. Temüjin wanted to show me the *ouiaa*, his horses' hitching rope. It was not far south of the camp towards the Kerulen – a long arrow would have reached it if shot three times. Qasar claimed the rope was twenty thousand feet long. Knowing his taste for exaggeration, I halved its length, but that still left room for three thousand horses. Each end of the rope was fixed into the notch at the top of a tall stone pyramid; it was as thick as a fist and made of plaited horse and yak's hair. A thousand of Temüjin's mares were tethered ready for milking.

'Go ahead, tether yours,' said my *anda*.

I had brought about twenty mares with me and gave instructions for them to be put next to the royal mares. Then we rode up through the Seven Hills to the grassy heights of the Red Mountains – game country, where we hunted stag. We had separated one of them from its herd when a scout asked to speak to the Khan. He said that six men – Solitaries – had been captured near the banks of the Kerulen. The hunt was called off: the news must be important.

They were kneeling, bound together by a vast wooden collar and guarded by a line of archers. The leather covering the iron scales of their cuirasses was threadbare, unstitched or ripped open, and they were covered from head to toe in wool grease and dust.

Temüjin ordered that one of them be released. He ignored the other five, villains so weary of wandering and their leader's misfortunes that they had handed him over to the Khan in the hope of a better future. The favoured one dragged himself over to his benefactor and kissed the ground at his feet.

'This release is only conditional,' said the Khan. 'When you have given me proof of your allegiance – and we will be old by then – perhaps it will be definitive . . .'

'How could I go on living at your side? Or dare to look at you?'

Despite his battered armour, his shirt in tatters and his sombre, ravaged face, I recognised the sly expression of the great, the handsome, the arrogant Jamuka.

'We lived together, shared the same blanket, the same bowl, dreamed of the same joys. And then I turned my back on you. Despite our pact, I fought you blindly and stubbornly. Three times you opened your wings to me and I refused their warmth. Now you offer me their shelter again. I feel black jealousy. Would you see me red-faced with shame? No, Temüjin, you have surpassed me; you have united four hundred Mongol tribes; you have annihilated our enemies; you have conquered me. You have countless followers, tents without number, fat herds. I have nothing, and sometimes my loneliness is so acute that I turn to see if my shadow still follows me. All I long for is death. Grant me this favour: kill me. But do not shed my blood. And first kill these so-called companions, these traitors of the worst stripe.'

Temüjin thought for a moment before speaking. 'You are indomitable, Jamuka. And arrogant. To my company you prefer

249

death's. I never want to hear your name again. No child may bear it and no one may utter it. Tomorrow at dawn I will grant you your wish.'

He pointed to the other five. 'Behead them!' Then, as the guards seized the prisoners, he made for his tent with us following. Jamuka struggled, shouting, 'My *anda*! I must die by suffocation at your hands!'

Temüjin slowed his pace but did not turn around. Again we heard the former Gür Khan call: 'You alone can deliver me . . .'

Then Temüjin said to me, 'Take him and twenty men and set off for the Red Mountains. Let him chose his burial place and at sunrise, suffocate him in the felt.'

'He wishes to die at your hands, my khan – not at mine.'

'It is impossible, Bo'urchu! He is my *anda*; the sacred ties forbid it.'

He fixed his eyes on me and I thought I saw a flash of panic there.

'Granted he set himself up to block my path and hoped for my fall, but he never wanted my death. Tenggeri would never countenance my killing him. Go, Bo'urchu! Help him return to the blue of Heaven and do not shed a single drop of his blood.'

I understood why he refused and accepted that he was delegating the task to me, the most faithful of his followers. But still I was anxious.

'I will come with you half of the way,' he added. 'Then I will take Yesüi to the Lakes of the Islet.'

He went into the great royal tent and I clasped the eastern pole of his threshold with both hands to ask for the protection of the kindly spirits.

Chapter 38

Temüjin and Yesüi broke away from the column as agreed. Jamuka swung round to me, vexed.

'Calm yourself,' I said. 'He's just going to distract himself with his favourite because his duty is painful and weighs heavy on his mind. He will be back at dawn.'

'What joy that princess must feel. The Khan grants her her every wish, sings hymns to her beauty; his eyes cling to her like silk . . .'

'But he'll tear himself away from her armpits – even though they smell of petals – to kill you.'

My retort left him quiet for a moment. Then he seemed to decide to open his heart, and his words rang like a declaration of love.

'Yes. At last he is going to embrace me. I must die, but when he bends down to give me peace in the other life, I will feel his breath, the first breath for me . . . Ah, Bo'urchu, believe me, I will relish the moment of my soul's flight for Heaven . . .'

He was watching me out of the corner of his eye and drew his own conclusions from my silence. 'Don't look offended, Bo'urchu! You're wondering what more I could want from my *anda* when I have shared everything he has, even his wife?'

I said nothing. He grew furious.

'His recognition, Bo'urchu, his recognition – that is the only thing that has ever mattered to me. When I realised I'd never get it, I challenged his power, coveted his property. It was thanks to me that he was able to recover Börte, to avenge himself on the Merkid, to recover his own people. And yet he never allowed me a share in his future. I could not hope for a more insidious revenge than to give Börte a child! And to make no attempt to hide it. He has three treasures which make him strong which he'd never share with anyone, even his own sons – Börte was one, she was there, within reach and I had to be recompensed.

He couldn't ignore me after that. Now, every time he looks at my son, Jochi, his eldest, he knows that I have been paid what I was owed.'

Intrigued, I asked him which were the other two treasures Temüjin would not share.

'Power, Bo'urchu, power,' he said rolling his eyes. 'He wants to rule alone. I took his wife in my arms and he did not kill me. But when I tried to divide the leadership of the Mongols between us, I saw havoc and anger flare up in his eyes. Then I realised that he would get rid of me one day, just as he had done his half-brother Bekter and the princes and so many others, and just as he will do with any whose eyes stray towards his throne.'

'What is the third treasure he never shares?'

'Horses. Seeing any hands but his own on his mares drives him mad with jealousy. Touching them is as great a sacrilege as looking at his wives.'

'That cannot be right. He entrusts his horses and their secrets to me . . .'

'I know. But weren't horses the cause of your first meeting? If you hadn't been in his path when he was chasing his meagre herd of geldings, who knows if he would have survived. Bo'urchu, you are the Great Keeper of Horse, the Ideal Anda. You owe him nothing and yet act as if you owe him everything. You are more precious in his eyes than his favourite mount. I envy you, just as I envy that Tatar princess who at this moment must be trembling beneath him, as all tremble when the Khan looks at them.'

We rode over the hills looking for a site. Jamuka decided on a broad, soft ditch that was almost circular and grown with tall grass. While we hobbled the horses, the Solitary went to the edge of the drop and contemplated the grass on the plateau below, rippling in waves under a cloak of shadow. As a backdrop to his silhouette, a necklace of dazzling mountain peaks soared into the sky.

We put the heavy felt carpet down next to the ditch and then moved away to eat our rations of dried meat – me, my twenty men and three archers from Temüjin's personal guard. Jamuka stayed standing as night fell; it seemed as if he was amongst the stars.

I went over to him in the first glimmerings of daylight and told him to take his place.

'I'm waiting for our Khan.'

'He's here, but he won't come any nearer until you are ready.'

'I want to see him.'

'You will, when you're lying on your back.'

'Let us wait for the first ray of sunlight, Bo'urchu, the last one I'll ever see . . .'

When the sun had loosed its first arrow, Jamuka agreed to lie down.

'Why did you refuse to live at my side?' he asked, his face bitter. 'We would have saved ourselves great torment . . .'

'I am not tormented . . .'

'You hate me!' he said, with a little laugh.

'No, but living with you would have made me sick to my stomach.'

I gave the signal: the men lifted the felt. Jamuka sat up, his eyes boring into me.

'I am the one, the Khan's right arm,' I said, throwing myself on him. My men rushed forward to pin him down.

'Wait, Bo'urchu! I'll give you a reason to hate me.'

I was strangling him, but he struggled and his mouth twisted as if he was trying to tell me something – a name, which suddenly I understood.

'What are you saying?'

'You heard,' he said, coughing and spitting. 'Queen of Flowers.'

'What do you know of her?'

He smiled. I jammed my fingers in his nose and pressed my knife against his ear. 'SPEAK! SPEAK! Or I'll spill your blood!' Waves of murderous desire flooded over me.

'She's been mine all this time,' he said. 'I took her and I made her pregnant. That should be enough to win your hatred, Bo'urchu, shouldn't it? Or does it need more? Wait, I haven't finished: Temüjin agreed to me taking her . . .'

If my arm had been wrenched out of its socket, I couldn't have felt a more brutal pain.

Swifts darted in and out of the dappled light, hunting. I faltered for a moment, as they called shrilly to one another.

'Where is she?'

'Ask him; he's the one who tells you his secrets . . .'

I stood up slowly, chose four of the strongest horses and ordered that his wrists and ankles be tied to their girths.

When he was hanging off the ground, face up, I sent one of my men to the Red Throne and told him to rally my troops – almost two thousand men – and meet us at the Pass of the Ash-Grey Birches. I told the three archers of the Khan's personal guard who were about to return to the *ordo* to take this message: I had not failed in my mission, but Jamuka had expressed another wish – to die in the presence of a Mongol woman with Merkid blood in her veins.

We headed north-west.

Jamuka didn't say a word. We pushed our horses into a trot. Little by little his body became slacker, his head lolled further back. I instructed the four horsemen carrying this strange plough shaft to whip their horses so that they pulled against each other and tore at the Solitarys' joints with all their might.

By the end of the day, our mounts were drinking from the River Tula. His face peony red, Jamuka tried to speak. 'You can rip the flesh off my bones, Bo'urchu . . . and you can find her . . . but she'll still come running to me . . .'

'Hold your tongue or I'll cut it off and throw it to the crows.'

'I took her . . . sabred her . . . till the blood spilled! But the truth is' – he struggled to get his breath – 'she became as yielding in my arms as curds . . .'

I kicked him in the face.

'I vomit on you!' he shouted, his nose and lip split open, his eyes sparkling black. 'She gave me three little ones, three sons.'

'You'd love to be that proud! Is that why she ran away back to her own people?'

'Wake up! It was those Merkid dogs that stole her from me.'

So, at last he had told me where to find her.

'Ah well, they'll be delighted when they see what I've brought them, won't they?'

'You can't let them kill me,' he screamed. 'The Khan must deal the final blow.'

'Tell me where she is and you will die as you desire.'

Jamuka held his tongue, still brimful of arrogance despite his wretched condition.

I ordered that he be tied to four fresh horses and that they be kept moving all night. That way he would get no rest. I heard him groaning, but his lament assuaged neither my rage nor my need for vengeance.

In the early morning I untied him for a moment. He tried to stand, wincing horribly, but couldn't.

'Don't break me bone by bone, Bo'urchu. Kill me,' he begged.

'Where is she?'

'On the banks of the River Uda.'

'Whose prisoner is she?'

'Broken Stump's, that Merkid pig, heavier than any camel's load.'

'How big is his *ayil?*'

'No more than three hundred of fighting age.'

If we hurried, we could reach the Uda valley at the furthest corner of the Merkid lands in ten days. I sent a messenger to the Khan to tell him our destination and we set off immediately, carrying Jamuka still tied as before.

After crossing steep mountains dotted with black larch forests and sheer-sided valleys, we finally reached the Uda valley. From its crests, taking care to keep under cover, we spotted Broken Stump's camp. Jamuka had been delirious for three days, calling each of my men by my name. His face was greenish, like stagnant water. As I bent over him, he opened his eyes slightly and said, 'You won't see any regret in my eyes. I was all over her like a mongrel and if I had the chance I'd crawl to her thighs to drink my fill again.'

I cut the straps tying him. His head hit the ground first. His arms were longer by a fist and when the blood started circulating through his purplish, bloated joints, he writhed with pain. His hands, and halfway up his forearms, were blue.

Without waiting for the agony to wear off, I stamped on his parts as viciously as I could.

Under cover of the night's mists, which were still hanging low in the valley, I set off at dawn for the Merkid tents, taking five hundred of the men we had met up with at the Pass of the Ash-Grey Birches. The rest of my troops stopped halfway down the slope and fanned out like a garland above the camp.

Silently we darted in amongst the tents. My men had their orders to kill purely to prevent noise, when they had no choice. Twenty dogs, two geese and six men had tasted our blades by the time I pulled back the doorflap of Broken Stump's tent. While my bodyguard tied up one sleeping figure, I rushed to the couch in the northern corner, tore off the chief's felt blanket and jammed my knife against his throat. I felt a body under my foot. I called for the fire to be rekindled and saw a young girl, no more than twelve springs, curled up naked and shivering on the rug by the couch. Another girl just like her, dark-skinned and terrified, was in Broken Stump's bed, wedged between his back and the tent wall. The Merkid leader had huge thighs and a huge arse and a vast, taut belly under which the purple helmet of his sex stood upright. I kicked the girl onto the floor and gestured to the other to make herself scarce.

I forced Broken Stump to his feet and tied his wrists and ankles to the yurt's latticework frame. There was no sign now of his presumptuous little churnstaff; it had shrunk away, an absurd flaccid thing under his drowning cow's belly, curled up like a snail in its shell.

'Is one of your wives called Queen of Flowers?'

He nodded.

'Who did you take her from?'

'The Solitaries betrayed us . . .'

'Who from?' I repeated, jabbing my sabre into his belly.

'Ja . . . Jamuka.'

'Where is she?'

He nodded to the next-door yurt and tried to add something, but I sliced his groin open from hip to hip; as his life poured out in a single gush of blood, he said nothing, too stupefied to speak.

I had barely crossed Queen of Flowers' threshold before I froze, paralysed by what I saw: kneeling on all fours on a couch, gripping the wooden tent frame, a woman had her back to me. Her broad, quivering buttocks were split by the bloody, purplish head of a newborn.

The four women helping at the birth drew back. Jerky, convulsive ripples ran along the deep furrow of the mother's back. She turned and saw me.

Twists of black hair were plastered to her face and shoulders with sweat. Her mouth was slightly open and she was breathing in short stabs, and her eyes were wide with surprise and pain. But the light they bore was just as it had been so long ago – wild and luminous. My heart beat like the hooves of a thousand charging horses. She stared at me, her body shuddering. Thin lines stood out on her forehead and a little twisting blue vein throbbed between her eyebrows; she began to sob in silence.

The women went back to their places. In a spurt of frothing, golden fluids, the child was pushed out and wrapped in the cloth blessed by the shaman. The baby was fatter than any I'd ever seen, as bloated and hideous as its father.

I went over to the mother, who was lying on her back, clutching her face in her hands. I looked at her full-lobed breasts, heavier than before. They swung to the rhythm of her sobbing, and her sex, once smooth and silken, gaped wide, snaggle-haired and fanned out towards her thighs.

I covered her with a blanket and took her in my arms. Her tears fell twice as fast whilst she hid her beautiful face. I pressed my lips into the hollow of her throat. She smelled sweet, of warm moss, damp clover, the first milk of the year and the blood of her placenta.

My lips moved back up to her mouth, lingering on the silk of her lips, the dune of a cheekbone, the wings of her nose, the two little pools of her eyes beaded with sweat, and I drew deep into my lungs the smell of her dripping hair clinging to her forehead as her misbegotten child bawled.

'I've come to fetch you. That fat dog will never curse you with child again.'

She bit her lower lip, rolled her eyes, then cried out. The midwives pulled off the blanket: her pelvis was split by another bald little head. Despite all its mother's efforts, this second crumpled visitor hesitated on the threshold, until it had to be pulled out of her fertile womb. Not as strong as his predecessor, still he was a sturdy boy – or he seemed so, anyway, until the matrons gave him a smack with a bunch of willow twigs. Nothing: silence, and soon he had stopped breathing. The women rushed about, shooting me black, reproachful looks.

I took my beloved's face in my hands and traced her cheekbones with my thumbs. Her eyes were deep-sunken, which only made them glow more like burning embers. Her bloodless, chapped lips whispered, 'Oh! Bo'urchu ... Bo'urchu, so you have not disowned me? You have come at last ...'

'Yes my flower, I'm taking you away and no one will be able to part us again. But first I have to go – just while you breastfeed – and kill the man who stole you away from my kisses, who took my sun ...'

'Broken Stump?'

'No, Jamuka.'

Her eyes flared wide. 'He's alive? Here? Don't do him any harm, I beg you. He ... he ... loved me.'

Her face white, almost translucent, she began to wince, more and more convulsively, her hands holding her belly, her wrists digging into her hips. Suddenly she arched her back, screaming.

The women rushed forward and pushed me out of the tent: a third newborn had just announced its arrival.

It was light outside. My warriors had the Merkid penned in

their yurts. I tethered my horse in front of Queen of Flowers' tent and called out that it was hers from now on. Then I took off the gelding's leading-rein and climbed alone to the hills where the rest of my troops were waiting in groups.

The men I had left in charge of Jamuka said that he had lost his mind. I asked for him to be brought to me. His face was grey, stubbled; he stank and his eyes were shut. His soul was departing. He was laid on the ground and I had ropes tied to his wrists and ankles. Then I ordered that four horses have the docks of their tails wrapped in wet bandages. The rest of their tails I coated with a mixture of tow, twigs, and pine needles and backed them towards each other until I could tie Jamukha's four limbs to their necks. Then I set fire to their tails and whipped their rumps: the horses pulled in all four directions, struggling against each other, rearing and kicking so that a final scream was torn from the Solitary. The flames licked at their thighs and soon their collective panic tore out his arms and carried them off at a furious gallop, as the rest of his body careered away in the opposite direction.

My men's sport was to give chase, because they had all laid bets as to which of Jamuka's legs would give way the first. They whipped up the two horses, forcing them to pull apart until they had got their satisfaction; then, laughing and arguing, they calmed the animals and patted out the flames on their scorched tails. I walked up, cut the last rope, straddled him – no worse humiliation – and shouted, because I wanted him to see me kill him, 'JAMUKA! You vile scavenger!'

He fainted. With one thrust I drove my sabre into his chest up to the hilt. His eyelids shot open then went limp, but in that reflex of terror, before his last, fetid breath had filled my nostrils, I saw his black, miserable spirit dwindle and fray like a piece of old cloth.

I drew out my blade: a jet of blood spattered me. Blood bubbled in his open mouth.

I wiped my sword and walked away alone into the forest. I remember walking over carpets of red needles, crossing streams with mossy banks and clearings dotted with orange, pink and yellow poppies. I remember climbing amongst the larches, scaling rocks and finding, thanks to a young stag suddenly jerking up its antlers, a rocky ledge on which I crouched down and made a libation to the earth and sky, not with milk but just with the sap of my eyes.

Then I prayed to Tenggeri so intently that my spirit rose up, high, so high into the sky that its everlasting blue became opaque, black and endless.

Somewhere, eagles screamed.

Under my fingers the rock was scalding hot, yet I was cold. The forest was alive, rustling with a thousand noises. That night the wolves went out on a great hunt.

Chapter 39

'Sain baina uu, Uncle Bo'urchu!' Jochi's joyful greeting coincided with the sun's first rays. 'May winds and women always smile on you. Have you slit the throats of a hundred sheep to leave such a bloody trail behind you?'

It didn't even surprise me that he'd been able to track me down without me suspecting anything, and in such a short time.

My first impulse was to tell him who his father was. But . . .

'I killed Jamuka.'

'You did well. Wasn't that what he wanted?'

'I killed him in the Jin manner, cruelly. Worse, I spilled his blood and disobeyed your father.'

'He unloaded the responsibility onto you,' retorted his eldest son. 'He won't blame you for anything. Jamuka refused his mercy, so the Khan turned his back on him. You took possession of his soul – what of it? All he had to do was live faithfully at our side. Forget him! Instead be pleased that I am here.'

I realised then that I had only been in those parts since the previous day. Jochi, who had come with his brother Chagatai and four thousand men, explained their haste: the moment Temüjin's archers reported that I was riding away with Jamuka, the Khan had commanded that we be followed.

'But when he heard your second message, he gave a more specific order: to scour these lands and kill every Merkid we found.'

'I haven't the heart to fight.'

'You are exempted. The Khan orders you to return to the Isle of Grass as quickly as possible because Aunt Temulun is missing you. If you dawdle, your brat will arrive before you do.'

My Little Crumb screwed up his almond-shaped eyes, a mischievous grin on his face.

'Did you say every Merkid?' I asked.

'Well, every man at least.'

I was worried about Queen of Flowers. Before galloping off to my wife and our child, I had to tell Jochi what had made me tear Jamuka to pieces. I told him everything.

'I recognise my cunning father,' he said when I'd finished. 'He knows how to choose the agents who will carry out his plans and in so doing keep himself safe from the consequences.'

'You don't understand,' I burst out. 'If he has wanted to deceive me all this time – me, the most faithful of his wolves – how can I fight his enemies?'

'Because! Because he demands it. Whether he was complicit or not in Jamuka kidnapping Queen of Flowers, it is by what you hold most dear that he truly measures your devotion. You belong to him. Body and soul. And he will not let a Merkid woman, even one with three-quarters Mongol blood, come between you.'

Jochi's remark was perceptive: the Khan's methods were treacherous. I did not know how I would respond.

Concerning Queen of Flowers, my decision was made. Despite the wild longing I felt to be with her, to take her as my wife, I did not wish to wound Temulun, my sweet spouse.

I asked Jochi to go to Queen of Flowers straightaway. He could not mistake her: my horse was outside her yurt and she would have newborns in her arms. I told him to take her and watch over her and her children. Temulun must be kept in ignorance for a little while longer . . .

Temüjin's eldest son assured me he would do all this and keep it secret; then I slipped away into the forests and the ravines.

I was trotting towards the Isle of Grass when arrows whistled past my helmet. Three hit me, two badly: one in the arm above the elbow, one in the knee, and a third, the most painful, in the fleshy part of my chest. Two others hit my mount in the neck and at the base of the shoulder. A Merkid ambush.

Luckily those rotten, brainless lard-guts were bunched all together on the same part of the slope, up ahead of me. I forced my horse to the right through the larches. The ground fell away suddenly and soon he was going too fast to keep his footing. We clattered down, smashing into trunks and stumps. A fallen tree broke my fall four or five paces from the drop over which my poor horse fell, sawing the air with his hooves. It seemed like a whole lifetime before he hit the ground with a terrible crash.

I crawled to the edge of the cliff. Below I made out a vast pond which looked as if it never gathered anything more than rainwater. Ripples spread out in circles on its surface. In the middle I made out the sad sight of my horse's spine.

The Merkids came closer, laughing. I pulled the broken arrow out of my arm. The one in my knee was too deep.

'Mongol!' shouted one of the Merkid. 'We're going to cook your bulbs!' He drew his bow; I jumped into space, dreading the black sheet that came towards me at staggering speed.

The daughter of the Spirit of the Forest must have been satisfied with my mount because I didn't break my neck – only my knee – as I hit the water and then the bottom almost simultaneously. It was thick mud, which cushioned my fall and allowed me to crawl away on all fours underwater. Then, hiding in the reeds, I leaned against the bank and bit hard on the green turf, so excruciating was the pain. I was barefoot and my trousers were yanked up to the top of my thighs; the arrow wasn't in my knee any more; nor, it appeared, was my kneecap. It didn't seem the best idea to go back and try to find it in the mud. But it's what I did. And regretted. I'd been crawling about like a crayfish for ages in the unlikely hope of finding the piece of bone when I felt hands pull me up by my plaits.

Dragging me back onto the bank, they disarmed me, thrashed and stripped me. Something like a pebble fell out of my trousers. I recognised my kneecap. In my dive the arrow must have prised it off and it had got caught in the folds of my clothes. Scant consolation: they wanted to scalp me. First they pissed on me, then shat, then forced their filth into my mouth.

Until that moment the prospect of dying hadn't crossed my mind. Now my hands were tied to my ankles, it struck me in all its voraciousness, imminent and implacable.

The Merkid made a pile of branches, *argols* and dry grass under my arse. It looked as if they were going to carry out their threat. 'You've got fat balls, Mongol!'

'And we're going to cook them up nicely.'

They split their sides laughing, which did not stop one taking a flint out of his belt. The fatal moment was approaching.

My knee hurt so badly that I was in a hurry for it to be over. I shut my eyes . . .

'Let's get out of here!' shouted one of them.

I opened an eye: they were dashing to their horses like sparks flying from a fire.

From the other direction, twenty horsemen were galloping towards them. Standards floated behind them and further back, a convoy of waggons appeared at the edge of the forest. Soon I made out the insignia: a wolf's jaws against an azure-blue backdrop, and nine black tails under a trident's flames: the mark of Temüjin Khan. The waggons were drawn by oxen, one of them was carrying one of the Khan's tents and Ögödei led the caravan. My *anda*'s third son was thought to lack ability; that wasn't my opinion.

He told me that his father had split off from the convoy five days before to go to the Celestial Mount and curry Tengri's favour. When the horse sacrifices were finished, he would rejoin Jochi and Chagatai's troops.

Üsün, of the Ba'arin tribe, happened to be riding with Ögödei. This old man was an excellent shaman who had barely had a chance to minister, so overwhelming was Kököchü's dominance. Of his many gifts, his talent as a healer was the greatest.

He treated me first, applying herbs and ochre and green powders and unguent the colour of black honey to my wounds; then he made a flexible splint out of reeds and willow branches. He also gave me some kay's blood to drink, drawn straight from the muzzle, and a piece of bark to chew.

When I refused to lie in a waggon for the rest of the journey back to the Isle of Grass, Ögödei gave me one of his geldings, Deaf Magpie. I was helped into the saddle. Üsün checked the splint and said, 'Be careful when you dismount.' Then he gave me other sachets of powder and roots and small dried bulbs to fight the pain. I urged on Deaf Magpie, as the old man raised his prayers to the sky and ten archers fell in close behind me.

When I reached the plateau of the Isle of Grass, the sun was gliding slowly to the west and the country sweltered under a shroud of red dust. The air was muggy and thick.

Temulun received me with a beaming smile, huge, bearing our Thoya with marvellous grace. Her joy radiated such a light that I forgot the agonising pain in my leg.

I was laid on my couch and washed. Once we were alone, I tenderly took her two plaits adorned with turquoises in my hands. Her eyes rested on my face like two stars.

'Aren't you hungry?'

'I'm not going to eat until our little terror has let out a bawl.'

'It's the new moon,' said Temulun. 'More than nine have passed.'

'Ah! Thoya . . .'

'Shush!' she said, putting a finger on my mouth. 'The spirits have very sharp ears. I've been waiting for you. Now you're here, I will go and bless the steppe with my waters.'

I drew her to me, nuzzling her with little darts of my nose, sniffing her, whispering that she was fuller and more beautiful and more richly adorned than the royal yurt of her brother the Khan. She let my hand slip under her clothes and sang as I traced the swell of her belly. Her voice lulled me as I played with Thoya, who kicked against my hand. Despite my swollen leg, which I could not move, I felt as if I had wings.

Through the smoke-hole I saw the sky grow dark, not with night but with great banks of cloud that seemed even more forbidding when a faint glow in the distance showed their extent. I pressed closer to Temulun's milky body, and it soothed me better than all of old Üsün's herbs, far better.

In a whisper I began the lullaby my father used to sing me and, before I could finish, I fell asleep thinking of a beautiful cluster of fawn-and-brown coats with shaggy manes gambolling over the sunny grass. And my spirit escaped into a dream . . .

The colts were being herded by a small boy on a gleaming chestnut. Face tanned like a ripe date, the young horseman was smiling, his *ourga* proudly tucked under his arm. He seemed to be my son and I was overwhelmed with pride, until I realised which horse he was riding: Afraid of Bears!

The portent startled me awake. I shivered, my throat as dry as if I had swallowed the fire's ashes. A bolt of lightning struck close to the yurt, outlining the smoke-hole in blinding white light. Temulun stood up to pull across the felt cover. Outside, the storm rumbled and echoed terribly. It felt as if I'd barely closed my eyes.

I emptied a pitcher in one draught but that did not quench my thirst. Temulun wanted to go and milk one of our mares tethered to the Khan's hitching rope.

'Haven't we got enough servants?' I asked, trying to dissuade her.

'My husband's home,' she said, catching my chin and rubbing her nose against mine. 'I'm not going to let anyone else take care of him.'

'Have you ever heard of a wife milking mares without her husband being there, helping?'

'Well, I'll just have to tell them that your spirit is there. They love you so much, you'll be able to feel them nibbling at the sleeve of your *del*.'

'I won't let you. Come on, that's enough; let's go back to sleep.' Which I did.

My sleep was troubled, nauseous. In a hazy, half-conscious state I sensed someone outside the yurt. They were untying the gelding. I sat up on my elbow. Temulun was gone. Furious and moved at the same time, I imagined her riding into the gusting winds despite her rounded, taut belly.

My tenderness gave way to anxiety. The mares wouldn't be tied up, the Khan's groom was bound to have turned them loose as the storm was coming. Would Temulun be able to get close to them? Mightn't her waters break if she chased them? What sort of husband was I not to have stopped her? And what sort of warrior to be so heavy-limbed? Questions assailed me. Why such a thirst, such a wound, such a dream? What did it foretell? Milking on a night like this was madness. And it was so easy to borrow a jug; otherwise what was the good of being surrounded by thousands of friendly tents?

I got up and limped to our slaves' tents. Twice the wind knocked me over. I raised the alarm at the first tent, scaring the occupants, who all jumped to their feet.

I ordered them to wake the camp and send all able-bodied men out searching, starting at the Khan's hitching rope.

Soon Temüge was at my side. As the youngest brother, he was the guardian of the fire and the *ordo*. He put the men in rows and they climbed down towards the hitching rope, all tied together by *ourgas* because the darkness and rain made it impossible for them to see their neighbours in line.

That night, the endlessness of the *ouiaa* seemed nothing compared to the endlessness of passing time.

The men climbed back up the slope at daybreak. The storm had died down and their tired silhouettes stood out against the great strips of cloud that hung in its wake. The women ran to them, moaning. Anxious dogs, their fur standing on end, danced around them barking. Soon the charcoal head of Temüge's light-tan horse crested the slope, then its chest, and a prone body in the rider's arms, legs hanging down slackly either side.

I raised my eyes, my throat choked. O Tenggeri! Why have you taken her from me? She was so gentle ... Didn't I, if anyone, deserve your punishment? What have I done to provoke your wrath, your bitter determination to cut me off from the people who are my whole life? Who has sent this devastation? Jamuka, because I slaughtered him? Queen of Flowers, because I broke the taboo by bursting into her tent when she was giving birth? Gerelma, for having rejected her?

I set out the marks of mourning in front of my yurt to stop anyone coming in; then I lay down on my empty couch, with nothing in sight but the circle of sky that I hated and with grief overflowing my heart.

Days passed without bringing me sleep. The Khan's army returned. I sent for Jochi. He was a long time coming and when he finally entered my tent, I understood his reluctance. He was crying – not for his aunt, but for the second tragedy he had to report.

Barely had I left him in the forests of the Ulda valley before Chagatai's troops had set about putting Broken Stump's camp to the sword. When Jochi reached it, there was nothing left.

'What have you done with Bo'urchu's horse?' he asked his brother.

'Over there with the others,' answered Chagatai.

'What about the woman in the yurt?'

'Ashes, burnt with the wet-nurses and the brats.'

Jochi protested that the woman was under his charge, that his brother had no business commanding the men in his absence, but it made no difference. The Khan's second son told him, 'It's not for you to give me orders. The only ones that count are our father's. I followed them.'

Little Crumb also told me how furious his father had been when he found out that I was going to the Merkid kingdom with Jamuka. He had snarled, 'Ever since a Merkid laid hands on my wife, they have been like lice on my collar. The Khan of Khans cannot leave a corner of the sky to them. Lay their country waste! And if they tell you you have taken all they possess and ask what more you want, tell them: your women. And when you've taken those, kill them! All of them! And their children.'

As if I could hear it myself, that fatal voice sank straight to my heart and rotted it and left me paralysed like a helpless old man waiting for death. My eyes remained dry, staring: I was nothing but a great teardrop, with no hope of a ray of light to melt me. O Implacable Blue! Why don't you take me? I curse you.

Temulun was buried under a sad, low sky. I stayed in the half-light of my tent as the lamentations bore off mother and child:

I am Temulun, princess of the Borjigin

266

Daughter of Mother Hö'elün, sister of the Great Khan Temüjin.

I grew without cares
Faithful to Bo'urchu
Bent on giving him a little one

Never again will I hear the sap rise
See the sun climb or the lamb feed
Heaven's wrath has carried me off with my eldest.

Despite the silence in which my tent enfolded me, the camp's worst gossips talked and I learnt what had happened that night. As I thought, the mares had been turned loose at the first sign of the storm. Not being able to see them, Temulun had wandered till she had found one with full teats. Had she had time to squat down, to get milk? What difference? – the lights in the sky had terrified the skittish mare. Just one kick had been enough to carry off the most adorable of wives. Amongst the gossip that disturbed the lonely peace of my yurt, there was one piece of news that made my grief doubly acute. The old woman telling it thought she was whispering. But to me it seemed as if she was yelling at the top of her voice: 'It was a boy, a fine, strapping lad.'

The name of that son pounded in my head like a hammer: Thoya . . . Thoya . . . Thoya . . .

Woe is mine for having had such hopes; woe is mine, the orphan damned to live without offspring. I am Bo'urchu! Bo'urchu the ill-named!

Chapter 40

Winter passed without me paying it heed. The universe shrank to the walls of my yurt, my cocoon, and the smoke-hole flap hid the circle of sky I did not want to see any more. Stretched out on my couch, I was like a chrysalis. Even the ashes of the hearth remained cold. As the days and nights passed, drab and frozen, my strength wasted away. So, I had to be alone: Tenggeri had decided. But even that tortured me less than the idea of never being able to move like before. My severed kneecap was a constant reminder. It never left my hands. I kneaded it constantly, saying to myself that I'd end up being called Bo'urchu the Lame, that my arrows would no longer be unerring, that on horseback I'd have to rule out manoeuvres and feats I loved; I'd have to camouflage my weaknesses, perhaps even fear the enemy. What pleasure would there be in waging war like that? And for who?

Leaving my tent seemed a pointless waste of effort. Nothing, nobody could rouse me to that ordeal. Qasar, Belgütei, Temüge and good Jelme tried, but I was like a stone. Then Jochi came. He clasped me in his arms, talked to me, lectured me even, when he was not sitting quietly in the shadows. His presence affected me like a song, an unguent on my burns. He was like the rain, the wind, the slap of a hoof that starts rockslides. I responded and stood up to limp round my tent. Then Jochi left to fight the Xixia with Chagatai and Ögödei, at the head of six thousand warriors. Qasar, Belgütei and Sübetei rode at their flanks, while Jebe the Arrow and Jelme, each with two thousand men, formed the rearguard and oversaw supplies and reinforcements.

While Jochi was away, his young son Orda was given the task of watching over me. Every day the little boy pestered me to walk. He couldn't understand how a Mongol – a chief what's more, the Great Keeper of the Khan's Horse and his father's mentor, could be disabled. This little squirt was no taller than a ram, but he rode a horse with his chest so puffed out it was as if he'd wrung a bull's neck. And for him, a man was one of two things: on his own two feet under Tenggeri, or dead! Servilely bedridden, I was no example for him, who was so impatient for us to go hunting together.

So I got up and one fine day, when a tit was singing at the top of his voice on my roof, I went out. The sky dazzled me. I shut my eyes for a moment before carefully cracking them open a chink. The sky was a limpid blue, infinite, and the steppe was covered with a thin, sparkling layer of snow. Realising how much I had missed these two was marvellous.

Two moons passed before we celebrated the return of our squadrons. They had led some fine raids amongst the oases of Kansu, burning crops, destroying irrigation channels and feeding the harvests to their horses. They had routed the Xixia troops, brought back plenty of spoils – mostly from caravans – and gathered valuable information. Most importantly they had discovered watering places and pasture because Temüjin's wish was to conquer this kingdom on the threshold of the Jin empire.

Temüjin erected a statue on the very spot where Temulun had died. I avoided it for a long time. But one evening when a storm was brewing, I saw its grey shape and steered my horse towards it. As broad and tall as me, the figure was almost manly: she wore a dagger and a canvas roll at her belt, and she had one hand on the haft of her weapon, the other raised aloft holding a snuffbox. Her beautiful oval face was slightly tilted forward, silent. The almond-shaped eyes were serene, almost joyful. I rode away, taking care to keep in their line of vision.

Soon after the festivities celebrating the campaign, we left the Isle of Grass for the region of the Three Lakes. This migration of the Mongols was a gripping spectacle. First came the armoured columns three deep and in staggered rows, stretching endlessly ahead. Then the convoys of waggons carrying the tents and baggage, great colourful, creaking mountains. Then the vast herds whose number could only be guessed by the fantastical clouds of dust they stirred up. Anyone wishing to see this exodus in its entirety would have had to stand watching for three days, and the pastures in its path were ruined for a long time. Clouds of smoke mingled with those of dust as the herdsmen lit fires to enable the grasslands to rejuvenate in the future.

At the front Temüjin was radiant. Surrounded by his brothers,

269

his sons and his generals, he led his people whilst at the same time watching over every detail of his caravan. A perfect harmony and assurance emanated from his dense, powerful presence, like that of an eagle hanging in the azure sky, its wings outspread.

He had won, or was on the verge of winning, all he had ever hoped for. The Mongols were united. Enemies and disaffected tribes had thrown their lot in with them. Rebels had been disembowelled and left to die where they had fallen; any who still resisted would soon stretch out their necks to his blade. Temüjin now reigned over a deadly ocean of archers. He was the supreme ruler and he intended to make his triumph known to any still ignorant of it at a great *quriltai* when he would be invested Kha Khan, Emperor. The date had been set for the last quarter of the Moon of the Cuckoo's Display, when he would enter his forty-fourth spring. Eighty messengers had set off for the other kingdoms to proclaim the news.

This fresh coronation may have thrilled him but the true cause of his happiness was our destination: the Three Lakes, where Mother Hö'elün had given birth to him.

This venerable grandmother travelled with us, crippled with pain, and bedridden in her great tent mounted on a waggon drawn by twelve oxen. To stop her being jolted too much, forty slaves on camelback stretched taut the thick horsehair cords that cushioned the waggon's platform. Temüjin remembered the country around the Three Lakes, the Borjigin's former winter pastures, as a magical place.

'You'll see, Bo'urchu, the grass is silky, undulating, dotted with flowers of every conceivable colour and cooled by tender streams which spurt from the ground like milk from breasts. The mountains there are gentle and topped with light forests, but from their summits the view stretches in every direction.'

The Khan was telling the truth. The meadows succeeded one another, luminous, bordered by tall forests of larch, red pine and chalk-white birch. Our horses' hooves stirred up a powerful smell of thyme, and across the translucent sky glided cranes, swans, herons and pelicans. We pitched camp. The royal tents were pitched next to the largest of the Three Lakes, which the Borjigin called the Eldest Son. Its waters were reputed to heal all ailments. The Khan's yurt was pitched exactly two hundred and eleven paces from the bank, on the exact spot where he had been born. At dusk, the animals came out of the forest on the opposite bank to drink, and the appearance of a lynx, a bear or a wolf nosing its way through the undergrowth, golden in the setting sun, always drew an attentive audience of hunters.

Kököchü came here on moonless nights to converse with the spirits. He threw sculpted bits of wood into the water, where they immediately burst into flames.

Drinking from the 'bottom' lake healed stomachs; the 'top' one cured liver and kidney pains. There was also a marsh which healed eye ailments. It was in the deepest heart of the forest. If a man with failing eyesight wetted his forehead, neck and the back of the head three times a day with its waters, he would recover the use of his eyes. But he must take care not to get his eyes wet; if he did so he would be blind for ever.

One evening Temüjin sent for me. I walked through the cedar wood where women and children were chattering and playing in the cool shade, crossed a great expanse of grass bright with forget-me-nots and clover, and entered the royal tent.

The Khan was sitting crosslegged on thick white felt carpets. He was gazing at Yesüi on his left, who was having her plaits oiled. At his feet were pyramids of food on silver trays.

'Come forward, Bo'urchu.'

I bowed, ignoring his favourite's bare shoulders.

'Make sure your horse is ready, because at dawn tomorrow we set off together to ride for three days over the land of my childhood. We have matters to discuss!'

We rode down through the little valley which wound its way past his tents to an *obo*. We walked round the cairn three times, adding a stone each time before laying our offerings on top: a handful of white horsehair from me, a blue silk belt from him. A few steps away, a spring welled out of a hillock, fed into a pool and then flowed by different channels amongst a copse of willow.

'This is where we used to come to fetch our water. Our tents were down there on the edge of the forest. Do you see that fallen tree?' Temüjin pointed to an old, rotten trunk covered with mould.

'Temulun was still on the breast when it fell by our yurt and Mother Hö'elün used to say that it had lain down so that she could feed her and keep an eye on our flock at the same time. I can still see her, my mother, beautiful and proud, undoing her blouse and freeing her breast in the blue shadows. She would pick up Temulun, sit down and sing softly as she fed her.'

'Why did you want me to marry her?'

He looked astonished.

'Was that wrong of me? She became yours when I could have given her to any one of a hundred princes by way of alliance. You are more than a brother to me, my *anda*! I wished yours and my family's blood to be forever mingled . . . She did as well. My sister loved you! Have you forgotten?'

'How could I? She is like my shadow . . .'

'Do what I do,' he roared. 'Walk straight into the sun and never look back!'

He remounted and put his horse forward, still heading westwards. I followed. His tall, broad form seemed to affect everything it passed; the grass bowed, the wind became heavy with the scent of wormwood, the horizon opened up and the distant, cloud-crowned mountains took on more depth and grew as black as the expression on his face.

When we had skirted the larch forest, he said, his face coppered with sun, 'Look at this plain. This is where I took my first gallops with my father.'

Golden grasslands stretched away, bordered with ochre mountains to the west. To the north they came to an abrupt halt at a ravine which gave onto the River Balj.

In the distance we saw the black, sharp-edged forms of old gravestones. Then we plunged into the larch woods of Rich Mountain, the sacred mountain, untrodden by any woman. It was deathly silent among the trees.

We came out into a clearing which was dominated by a great ten-point stag. He stared at us, his antlers hidden in the branches of a solitary apple tree. Then in a few bounds he disappeared into the forest. Another stag pressed against the low branches of the tree, but this one was wizened, its skull worn away by the elements. All that was left of its antlers was two stumps of bleached bone.

'That is the first stag I ever killed,' Temüjin said. 'And as you see, he lives on.'

Keeping to the edge of the wood, we reached the summit, tethered our horses and dropped to our heels. We could see a large part of the camp and, all around us, the mountains receding in gentle waves. The sun shone down from the vault of the sky, enveloping the country and transforming every unshaded patch of ground into a furnace.

We stayed there in silence for a long time, gazing at the floating haze, until grass fires began to send up thick columns of smoke to the east. Seeing them, he said, 'When the horses are fattened up, we'll set off for the Xixia lands again. We'll pillage their caravans, sack their villages and, once his fortified city has no more supplies, their king will have no choice but to bring out his army. Then we will take Ningxia, dash its battlements and its stone houses to the ground and enslave the Xixia! I want you there, by my side.'

Troubled, I answered, 'Look in front of you, O my Khan! If you wanted to see your kingdom's frontiers, you would have to be able to see twenty times further than this! No human eye could do that. Your prestige, the people who have rallied to your banner – it is all more than your eye can comprehend. Isn't that enough for you? If we had two hundred times as many flocks, we'd still have enough grazing lands to feed ten times more! You are feared! You have united four hundred tribes! There is no empire that can rival your wealth! Do you think you won't be able to enjoy it, that you'll grow bored?'

'I am feared because I deserve to be feared,' he growled, getting to his feet. 'All the kings of the world will learn that! Not a single drop of Mongol blood shall be shed without the blood of ten men being shed in payment! I have sworn this oath before Tenggeri! The Jin shall pay for their crimes against our ancestors, as all shall pay who do not bow their heads before me, their khan, Heaven's chosen one!'

I looked at him, dumbfounded. He was beside himself, as if he had been transformed by some strange, dark spirit which sprang from the deepest core of his being.

'Isn't the sky in harmony?' he asked, furiously. 'Isn't it at peace? It is so, because it is one! And it has chosen me to establish the same concord here on earth. Every Mongol who refuses to fight is a traitor to Tenggeri. I will personally spill their blood on the ground!'

'Is it treason to live in peace under Him as I plan to?'

'Yes, because first we have to convince the other peoples of the benefits of respecting the *yasak*. Their faces, the colour of their eyes, their gods, their idols – none of this matters. The only thing that matters is that they have one khan. Only then will lasting harmony be possible from east to west. As for us two,' he continued, 'so long as you refuse to banish the shadow that slants across our hearts, misunderstanding will always blacken our days.'

'Whose fault will that be?' I cried, feeling as if I was throwing myself into the void. 'Since the day you charged me with killing Jamuka, that shadow has weighed on me because he revealed your complicity in Queen of Flowers' abduction.'

He started to put his foot in the stirrup, disappointment and irritation etched on his face.

'We promised not to let a third party confound us. If the grounds of our affection were thrown into question, we would establish its transparency face to face. How could you believe such lies? The spiteful cur who told them only wanted to drive us apart. You suspect me of chaining up your happiness, when I have always sought to set your heart free. If anyone else had torn Jamuka's body to pieces when I had ordered that there be no bloodshed, he would have had his hands cut off. But I didn't punish you. By luring you into the Merkids' ambush, Tenggeri did it for me. And if He carried off my sister, it was to reproach you on my behalf. Don't you understand? There, I have spoken!'

He mounted up and tore off down the slope.

At the foot of Rich Mountain the floor of a birch wood was strewn with the skulls of sacrificed horses, their empty sockets turned to the sky as the sun threw leaf shadows on their shattered foreheads. I stayed among those bones, waiting for it to grow dark, and it seemed that their dust-dulled maze of cracks echoed the hideous despair that pounded in my chest.

The Third Part

Chapter 41

Silver in the brilliant sunshine, the steppe glittered in my sleep. I was naked and moving as fast as the wind but with no part in it, as if a bird was carrying me on its wings. I had no control over my invisible mount. Streams, swamps and rocks loomed up before me and were gone. I was as close to the ground as if I was on horseback and my breakneck speed made my stomach churn at every fold and hollow. My soul was flying without a harness. Was it racing to Tenggeri? Was He who ordains everything taking me back?

A mountain darkening the horizon to the south drew me towards it. It was broad and perfectly flat at the summit, like a yak asleep on the sand. Spirals of cloud massed above it. I flew past its midnight-blue faces, swivelling to keep them in sight. The clouds were swelling, stretching, twisting: the Khan's face appeared, enormous, wild, majestic. He looked at me, his jaw clenched tight, and the sombre, reproachful look in his eyes tore open my stomach like a poison . . .

The vision grew blurred as the lowing of the cows penned up for the sacrifices broke into my dream.

I was lying on my bed. Outside, children were running and jostling and clapping at the head of what sounded like a convoy of camels with little spherical bells hanging from their harnesses; they jingled to the rhythm of their padded strides and their rings grew shriller the closer they got . . . I came to: it was the eve of the Great Day!

Tomorrow Temüjin would be crowned Kha Khan! An extraordinary honour. None of his ancestors, not even Kaïdu and Kabul who were named Kha Khan out of deference, had held this role. Sovereign of all the Mongols, he would reign over an empire and his splendour would illumine kingdoms far beyond our frontiers.

The sun was already high in the sky and flushed the edge of

the smoke-vent gold. Large crows passed overhead in a flutter of wings, unsettled by the tumult of the camp.

A freshly shaven head with laughing eyes poked round my door. 'Bo'urchu! Bo'urchu!'

It was Orda, Jochi's eldest son. He was wearing a brand new sky-blue *del*, with a festive purple hem. He was six springs old now, with a scar on his right cheek as a memento of a riding fall, and he exuded the most irresistible zest for life. His great black eyes shone with excitement.

'What is it, Littlest Crumb?'

'Quick, Uncle Bo'urchu, there's an animal going down to the river which is as big as a mountain! It's got two big bows and two huge shields on each shoulder and instead of a nose it's got a great big willy that drags on the ground and there's a funny yurt on its back.'

'Are you sure you're awake? Are you sure it's not Qasar riding one of his great white camels?'

'No, Uncle Qasar is feverish; he drank too much of the strong milk. My father's trying to freshen him up and get him dressed. Come on!' He dashed out, pushing past the serving woman who was bringing me my food.

I pulled on my boots and blue shirt, buckled a bright-yellow belt and, limping heavily, set off through the camp. Hordes of laughing children were charging about on horseback without giving any warning, closely attended by a retinue of overjoyed dogs and terrifying any lambs, kids and tethered horses in their path. The women shouted vainly after them.

We had been preparing for the great day for almost three moons. Forty thousand Mongols had descended on the banks of the Onon and others were still flocking from far-flung corners of our territories, the former kingdoms of the Kereyid, Naiman, Tatar, Khirgiz, Tumat and Oirat.

The city of tents reached as far as the crests of the surrounding hills – a span of half a day's ride – and the brown cloud hanging over it testified to the number of campfires perpetually alight. From morning to evening, oxen-drawn waggons shuttled between the forest and the camp with their loads of wood. There were so many people and such a commotion that the mud lanes were permanently jammed with horses, poultry, dogs, drunken men, dung and detritus of every sort. There people gutted their sheep and talked – and sometimes argued – endlessly, whilst above their heads, on the incredible horsehair web strung between the tents' roofs, saddlecloths and lashes were put to dry, game was hung and provisions were stored: quarters of meat, sinews, hides, cheeses, herbs and sheep's stomachs.

Set predominantly on the valley's gentle slopes, the vast *ordo* also occupied the level ground bordering the Onon, despite the risk of flooding. As for the islands in the river, they were reserved for the foreign princes, noblemen and ambassadors who were still arriving with their caravans laden with gifts. They came from the Lob Desert, from Dzungaria, from Uighur country, with panthers in diamond necklaces at their camels' sides, white-skinned, exhausted, bare-armed slaves, fine-boned horses like gazelles, with foam-flecked mouths and bulging veins, and so many other treasures . . .

One of these caravans which had crossed the Altyn Tagh mountain range and the Gobi was undoubtedly the one Orda had told me about, because I could see a huge animal's backside swaying between the felt roofs. And it was carrying a strange yurt on its back and going down to the Onon.

A huge, joyous crowd in their best clothes had thronged to the prime crossing place and were avidly watching the parade of wonders. The river there was not so deep, but just as treacherous as elsewhere, and underfoot the current swept away rocks which were at least the size of a human skull.

The man sitting on the elephant's neck – that was the name they gave this venerable animal – made him kneel until his stomach touched the ground. Then the two passengers in the yurt – an astonishing wicker saddle shaded by a parasol – slid down a rope. They wore close-fitting tunics and silk trousers – the younger-looking's ivory-coloured, the other's black and green – and delicate coils of fabric adorned with a feather on their heads. One of them was the son of a king, the other his tutor. They were fragile-looking and sparkled like two jewels. Our men quickly surrounded their mount, debating how to unsaddle the beast.

Everyone exclaimed as the elephant stepped into the river to bathe. He sprayed himself with his nose, making terrible noises of impatience and contentment, then rolled up that mighty appendage and waded through the waves in a cauldron of foam, his mouth open and his ears spread, before rolling over onto his side. The children laughed and the adults were stunned into silence by the size of the beast: the water instantly built up behind him as if he was a dam.

Eventually his rider, the Indian who also seemed to be his master, rubbed him down with branches. He walked right up to him, seemingly unafraid of being crushed. Energetic and attentive, he talked to him constantly as he worked and, after stroking his forehead a few times, asked him to stand up and follow him back onto the bank. The elephant calmly obeyed.

The great saddle was put back on and its girth done up, this time to even louder laughter and comments. Then, to our boundless joy, the prince and his tutor ascended their moving throne with perfect dignity and crossed the river.

The great tireless tusked one, as some called him, fuelled our conversations for the rest of the day. The species was mortal, we learnt: of the three elephants the Indian sovereign had sent, two had died on the way, one on the high plains of Tibet, the other between the Lob and the Gobi. Intended for our khan, all that was left of them was their harnesses, the great wicker baskets with their silk awnings and the thick, richly decorated cushions.

The Indian caravan went to find a place in the shade of the tall willows and settled for sandy ground not far from the Önggüd ruler, Ala Quk Tegin, who had been there for a moon already with his faithful shepherd, our friend Hassan the Moslem, and a hundred camels and ten times as many sheep.

We stayed on the bank chatting, walking up and down and looking at the strangers on the other side, especially the female slaves who came down to the river with jugs on their hips. We made fun of their timidity, their diaphanous robes which snagged in the clumps of tamarisk and their breasts which spilled out as they bent over and were caught by the shimmering light reflected off the choppy waters.

Above the treetops, the khan's royal tents stood high up the slope in the first folds of the mountains. They were three times fuller and more rounded than usual yurts and their white was three times more brilliant. His wives' tents, twelve in number, stretched out to the east, those of the princes and the shaman Kököchü's family to the west, and together they formed a great crescent. Before each of them was planted the standard, with its three bronze flames and nine silver yak's tails. A row of armed, breastplated men barred entrance to the compound. A little below, other vast, rectangular tents which were open to the south, lined a plateau and swelled in the breeze. The largest was white with an azure border. This was where the investiture would take place. As he waited to be crowned Kha Khan,

Temüjin had chosen a place in this valley from which he could look out on his city of warriors. At his feet, through the trees bordering the Onon, he could see those who came to pay him homage and hoped to conclude an alliance. Even more importantly, he was near the Celestial Mount, that mountain which had saved him more than once, which he worshipped each moon and where he prepared himself before every campaign. The Onon rose there and from his eagle's lair Temüjin could see the spine of that adored massif which, he used to say, echoed Tengri's every command.

The Kerulen and the Tula also had their sources on the Celestial Mount. The first was known as the River of Disputes, in memory of that far-off time when it was a border of the Tatar kingdom. As for the second, it mingled its waters with those of the Orhon, then the Selenga, before plunging into Lake Ocean which flowed out to the North, the direction of the dead, the south being the source of life and the home of birds and souls.

As the sun set Temüjin appeared, the crest of his helmet glinting golden in the low light. Behind him, a thousand horses grazed right up to the peaks of the mountains, watched by armed herders.

He looked at the Onon, that dark serpent that winds between the mountains, eating away at its banks, heaping up shingle and sand as the sinuous mood takes it, spitting out water-sculpted trunks, and causing branches and animals to bow their necks.

The elephant is the only animal I know that has no need to bend its neck to drink. In the evening we heard him pulling at his chains, and rummaging in the ground. His boredom stirred up a thick layer of dust. It rose above the leaves and swirled in endless spirals, caught by the wind.

On the day of the coronation, the hordes of horsemen began to cross the Onon's twin branches at dawn, in a boiling, muddy sea of foam. Their number was so great that the banks repeatedly gave way and, as they climbed towards the Khan's tents, pressed together leg to leg, the grass disappeared under an impenetrable forest of horses' limbs. Some carried one or two children in front of them, others even more, with the eldest sitting behind on the crupper. Those youngsters too small to hold themselves in the saddle followed with the women, bundled together in baskets swinging by the side of the camels; they clung to the ropes and sucked their thumbs, looking wide-eyed all around them or grabbing at the forelocks and reins of any horses they could reach.

The men had put on their breastplates, greased the shoulder straps, coloured their shields, and polished the gold or bronze of their studs, rivets and everything else that catches the eye. The plumes of their helmets fluttered above the neckpieces, their quivers bloomed with arrows and their sharpened lance points flashed like silver wounds in the blue of the sky.

The accents of a hundred tribes entwined: guttural for the Kereyid, sing-song for the Mongols of the Three Rivers, staccato for the Tatars, harsh for the Naimans whose jerky delivery was full of clipped emphases. The different dialects ricocheted back and forth, and to make themselves understood, faces exaggerated expressions and hands gesticulated as booming laughter burst from gleaming chests. They spoke of their battles, their horses, their master; they displayed their wounds, their arms, their jewels.

As the clans filled the space, each gradually became aware of what was happening. A nation was being born! And before the majesty of this event they fell silent. There were a hundred thousand on horseback, their eyes blazing brighter than their standards. They took off their headgear and, bareheaded, their throats dry, their mouths slightly open, panting almost, they waited more silent than statues.

Among their close-packed mass a straight avenue the width of a waggon led to the rectangular tents. As the drums began to beat, noblemen, chiefs and high dignitaries began to walk down it, their names on every tongue. The murmur grew louder when it was the turn of Sübetei, Jebe the Arrow, Jelme, Muqali, Kubilai or me, one of the Khan's faithful companions, his generals, his ferocious wolves. A triple row of footguards protected the terrace overhanging the valley. They held lances adorned with fluttering pennants and the front two rows faced the people. Behind them, the elites took their places. Tata Tong-a, who was in charge of protocol, made sure foreigners did not commit any errors, such as pointing the soles of their shoes towards the royal tent or resting their elbows on their knees.

Temüjin sat enthroned on thick white felt carpets. To his left sat his wives, their faces like a pearl necklace: first Börtei and Yesüi, separated by Mother Hö'elün: then Yesügen and the other princesses, who may have been less beguiling but nonetheless, just like the favourites, wore heavy headdresses embellished with precious stones and coral and sparkling *dels*. Such artistry and wealth – and rivalry – had gone into their finery that they dared not move an eyelash: they sat frozen, a fixed, faraway look in their eyes. The shaman was to the Khan's right, then came the Khan's brothers and sons in order of age. A long ivory-coloured carpet stretched out from my *anda*'s feet. Kököchü strode around the edge of it until he was standing opposite the Khan in full sunshine. He took off his stockings, walked to the middle of this circle of cleansed, fulled wool, shook his drum three times, brought it to his waist and then let it go. The instrument carried on shaking but didn't fall: it was floating! The metal pendants and little cymbals jangled, the ribbons fluttered, and the stag's rutting cry rang out, softly at first then more and more regularly, a clear, deep bellow; the spirits were working the drum. The shaman spread his arms and threw back his head; his feet left the ground. The crowd started and laughed in amazement.

When he was perfectly horizontal and hanging a cubit off the ground, Kököchü began making incomprehensible noises. Then he chanted, or at least – because his lips were only quivering faintly – a voice possessing him chanted, 'Genghis! Genghis! Genghis! . . .'

Drummed out quicker and quicker, this name that means Ocean sounded vehement, like a reproach.

Squinting, his eyes shining more than gold, Temüjin observed the shaman. It was as if he was lifting Kököchü with the brilliance of his eyes alone.

The shaman fell heavily to the ground: the spirits must have broken off their conversation. Fanbearers rushed forward to give him something to drink. He struggled to his feet and, white as a silkworm, pronounced, 'For three dawns now Tenggeri has appeared to me wearing the blue coat of the blue tit. Every morning this bird has alighted on the same tent and called three times: Genghis! Genghis! Genghis!

'Then it has risen into the air and, as the sun spreads its rays, the arc of a rainbow has entered the tent through the smoke-vent. That tent is our khan's. Tenggeri's sign is like a mountain stream flowing across rocks, crystal-clear, irrevocable: it shows me the chosen one. Temüjin is no more! Let Genghis, Heaven's will on Earth, come forward.'

Temüjin complied, walking to the edge of his tent's immaculate white awning, then stopped dead. Qasar and Temüge followed suit, on either side of the carpet and a step from it.

283

'Let any who dare, enter his white abode,' continued Heaven's intercessor. 'The witless, the coward, the sworn adversary – let them know how Tenggeri watches over his son! Let them see what form His anger will take!'

The shaman seized a slave, pushed him into the middle of the sacred circle and pointed his staff at his heart. The wretch instantly burst into flames. He started running, beating at his shoulders and thighs and screaming. The lance-bearers killed him before he had reached the rows of dignitaries.

Kököchü took three steps and, raising his arms, continued, shaking with suppressed rage, 'Genghis will cross the highest mountains, breach the thickest breastplates. No army will withstand him because his mandate comes from on high.' And speaking directly to Temüjin, he said, 'If you are this man, do not be afraid to step forward. Nothing and no one can deceive you. We will raise you above us all.'

The Khan unbuckled his belt, hung it round his neck, bared his head and stepped out of the shade. Within six strides, he was standing on the disc of white wool.

The crowd did not react for a moment, too full of wonder at the fact that he had not caught fire. The first to kneel were the freed slaves. Then all heads bowed. Qasar and Temüge went down on one knee and lifted their eldest brother on their shoulders, and Belgütei and the Khan's sons immediately joined them. Thousands of arms waved and threw their caps and helmets into the air. Then they took cups from their breast pockets and emptied their gourds, performing joyous libations to Genghis Khan and the sky, the earth, the eight directions and to their horses, drenching their manes.

My *anda*, everlasting Tenggeri's jewel, paraded like the sun over an ocean of bare skulls and radiant smiles, his blue *del* merging with the azure sky. The ring of standard-bearers framed his resolute face. His eyes scanned the throng of beaming faces. Our eyes met and he saw the prodigous happiness his glory gave me. But he didn't blink or give me the faintest smile of complicity or acknowledgement. Then he vanished amongst the banners, imperturbable, hieratic.

Temüjin was no more. What grievances did Genghis Khan have against me?

Chapter 42

Gerelma sniggered.

'So this is your *anda*! On the day of his investiture he honours and rewards all his faithful and you are the only one to come away with nothing.'

This was the first time she had shown the cutting edge of her tongue since our tents had again been pitched side by side. She had learnt to hold her peace, but that her husband, the Khan's right hand, should return empty-handed was too much for her to bear. Outside, the great camp echoed to the noise of the celebrations entering their first night on the banks of the Onon. The fires shot their sparks up to the stars.

'Be quiet, fool; you don't know anything!'

'The Khan cited all his brave officers and made them rich. Those who once were nothing but simple shepherds have heard their exploits sung by his divine voice. Are you less than they, worse than a ram-flogger, for him to brush you aside like this?'

She was right. I had been present at Genghis Khan's eulogies and heard the list of rewards. Only one man had been forgotten: me.

'What does it matter! I don't need praise to serve the Khan. I should tear out your tongue.' I went out.

Five members of the Khan's personal guard were waiting outside my yurt, the tips of their helmets and quivers dark outlines against the red sky.

'What do you want?'

'The Khan is surprised you are not with him.'

The one who spoke was nearest my yurt; he was leaning his elbows on his saddle and he seemed to be smiling.

'Tell him how happy I am. He need not worry, I'm not leaving – quite the opposite: I am going to join in the celebrations.'

'Take care, Lord Bo'urchu, that the sun does not find you carousing; Genghis Khan expects you tomorrow at daybreak.'

They pulled their horses round and galloped towards the Onon, disappearing into the fireglow.

I had planned to flee the commotion and go to my pastures at the Red Throne half a day's trot away. The Khan's summons put paid to that. I spent the night staring at the Milky Way and finally drowsed off like the heavy-eyed elephant, chained and alone.

I had to wait with the Khan's personal guard while I was announced. A pungent smell of wildcats floated on the breeze. It came from the cages of intertwined branches north of the tents, where they constantly paced back and forth, shooting menacing looks through the bars. All the Khan's gifts were collected around them. Panthers and leopards side by side with peacocks, monkeys and other strange animals; parrots and nightingales which would soon be released from their diamond cages; pyramids of carpets embroidered with scenes of hunts, battles, investitures or marriages, which were piled amidst a cornucopia of jewels, fabrics of every colour, intricately wrought weapons, dishes and bowls in pewter or silver or white or yellow gold. The Khan had also been given two hundred slaves, mainly female, and six wives, who compensated for their looks with their noble blood. One of them came with two dark-skinned eunuchs, whose eyes were as round as rubies. There were pedigree horses, some with thick coats and sturdy limbs, others as delicate as gazelles, slender and full of fire but with bellies too high off the ground, which would not stand the rigours of the steppe and would have to be sent south of the Gobi. I liked the camels. They were grouped by origin and their coats succeeded each other like sand dunes of every colour, from milky white, sable, orange, brown and henna red to black. The wool at their necks was a cubit thick. The handsomest had come from Ala Quk Tegin's studs. They were enormous and looked like clouds sprawled on the grass. Only the constant working of their jaws and their great jet eyes reminded one that they were anchored to the ground. But for the Khan, the most touching presents were those on larch perches a hundred paces long and two cubits off the ground. Sparrowhawks, falcons, goshawks, merlins of every sort gripped these rails next to golden eagles and ospreys. Most of them were hooded, and they turned their blind heads from side to side and opened their wings to cool themselves.

By the time a breach opened in the ramparts of the Khan's

guard, the first rays of the sun were caressing the royal compound.

Sitting in the middle of his family, the Khan stared at me thoughtfully and smoothed his moustache. He was wearing a sky-blue *del* with a crane in courtship pose finely embroidered in gold thread on each face, and on top of that a long pearl-grey tunic. He wore a silk turban with an emerald brooch clasping three tern's feathers in its middle. Börte sat to the left of his great throne the size of a bed with its back covered in silk and gold brocade; she was the highest and her headdress was level with her husband's shoulders.

I knelt. The Khan got up from his throne. His cup-bearer, who stood next to a low table holding pitchers and basins of precious metals, handed him a bowl. He took it, came forward, raised me to my feet and gave it to me.

I blessed the sky and earth with the foaming milk, then drank.

Genghis Khan did likewise before he spoke: 'Last night, as we feasted, my wife Börte reproached me for failing to reward one of my braves. How could I have forgotten the most valiant of all my comrades, Bo'urchu! When I was nothing, he left his family in order to follow me. Ever since then he has always ridden ahead of me into the fray. His body is my shield, his arrows my judgement.'

He listed my actions, recalling how I had saved him in the battle, shielded him from Targutai's sword, sucked clean his wound, quenched his thirst . . .

'Yesterday I pretended not to see you. I knew the envious would mock you and I also knew that, even when forked tongues poured scorn on you, nothing but honey would flow from your lips at the mention of my name. I have learnt that I was right. So now I wish everyone to pay heed!'

He stepped forward, unsheathed a short, silver-handled scimitar and slowly looked around. 'Bo'urchu, son of Naqu, is my ferocious wolf. He is my precious *anda*. He would kill himself for me. You Mongols! Be like Bo'urchu! Let no one plot against him or covet his property, otherwise' – he raised his scimitar – 'I shall see to it personally that their traitors' heads roll in the dust! Bear witness to what I say and spread word of my decision to raise him above you all!'

The thousands of foreheads bowed. I saw Orda at the far side of the royal tent next to the sons of Qasar, Belgütei and Temüge. Eyes sparkling, he smiled at me as he scratched his cheek.

His grandfather continued, 'You are on my right, Bo'urchu.'
Then, shouting to the crowd, he proclaimed: 'He is on my right for all eternity!'

Chapter 43

The huge Selenga valley opened up as we came out of the dark forest. Our horses picked up speed, eager to reach the evening's halting place, and the grass's intense green in that sudden, brilliant light was reflected in their eyes.

'Tchoo! Tchoo!'

My mount's ears swivelled as I urged it on. Four springs old, this was his first campaign. He had a squirrel-grey coat and a merry, determined, attentive temperament, although yet to be fully formed. Son of White Cloud, he reminded me of Afraid of Bears, his grandfather. I wanted to make him my lead horse. But he would have to thicken out before he could go into battle, and so I was followed by three remounts.

The season before, when I'd gone to fetch the colts out of the herd to begin their training, I hadn't been able to find him. I had searched for three days until finally I found him at dusk. He was standing stock-still, looking south, and he seemed to be hitched to a strange waggon. When I got closer, I recognised the body of the elephant. That animal had been too sick to take his master home, so the Indian prince had given him to the Khan, apologising for the state of the only survivor of the original three. The driver had stayed to ease his loneliness, but the elephant had not survived another moon. One foggy morning he had stood up and set off south, at such a slow pace that his rounded silhouette could still be seen in the distance at sunset. His keeper had followed him on foot, chanting a threnody of farewell. They had continued like this for five days until the venerable giant sank to his knees in a pool of mud. By dawn of the sixth day he had stopped breathing and his friend was slumped against his trunk, weeping.

I had found my colt dreaming between those tusks adorned with horsehair and prayer flags, and when I saw that great skeleton picked clean, my horse's name came had come to me:

Babei Ikedzan, Great Solid Elephant. It was apt, because my colt was surefooted and sturdy across the shoulder and his stamina enchanted me.

'Lucky your elephant hasn't got a trunk,' Jochi said as he rode beside me. 'He's going so fast it'd get tangled under his feet.'

'Mock away, my handsome lord. You won't be laughing when he beats your coursers at the games.'

'Ah, Bo'urchu! You don't really think Babei is the best of White Cloud's sons, do you?'

'I know every one of them. They are my blood!'

'Then you should know I have the fastest since you gave him to me at Orda's first haircut.'

'I grant you that Pearl Grey is agile and swift as an arrow but he hasn't the heart to stay the distance.'

'Well, while you're exhausting Babei, Orda is working Pearl Grey into a sweat. He will ride him at the great spring games.'

His announcement saddened me since, with no children of my own, I had hoped his son would ride Babei. Jochi saw my upset.

'I was only joking, Bo'urchu. Orda will choose the mount he thinks is strongest. It will be his first horse race, I want him to win it.'

'I do too.'

That evening, as we sat near the circle of sixty or so standard-bearers round the fire, he drew me aside and said, 'If I don't come back, I want you to take my wives and my two sons into your yurt. It is my wish that they stay together if I die.'

I was speechless, because Jochi was doing me a great honour. Custom in such cases dictates that the dead man's youngest son claims his father's wives, apart from his own mother, who goes to the youngest of the uncles. Admittedly his sons Orda and Batu were far too young to take care of their stepmothers. But that still left his brothers Chagatai, Ögödei and Tolui who could each claim his wives, their role being to oversee the dead man's estate so that it could be restored to him in the hereafter.

But my Little Crumb paid no attention to family protocol. He smiled at me, visibly satisfied with my surprise. My heart brimmed over at such trust; it distressed me that tomorrow we would be parted.

We each had twenty thousand men at our disposal. Genghis Khan had ordered me to subjugate the remaining Merkid: a few implacable tribes had sought refuge in the Barkun Mountains at the far end of Lake Ocean. Jochi's mission would take him to the country west of the lake, to master the forest tribes, the Oirat and Tumat. Muqali rode with me while Jochi had the experience of the inflexible Sübetei to draw on.

Jochi also confided in me about a different matter and added another request. During the last campaign, Jochi had struck up a friendship with a Merkid. 'He was my prisoner, but seeing his youth and skill as a bowman I could not kill him nor did I want to hand him to my father, so I let him escape. His name is Blue Quiver. If he gives himself up, don't kill him. Bring him to me.'

Sweeping down from the peaks of the Barkun Mountains we encircled the bulk of the Merkid tribes and drove them into a raging river, staining it red with their blood as far as the shores of the great lake. Blue Quiver was found, disarmed and spared as Jochi had asked.

My tent stood on a promontory above the lake. The young Merkid was brought there and a few days later I gave him back his quivers to see how skilful he was. His rudimentary arrows fledged with a falcon's feather and tipped with bone carried huge distances and always reached their targets. Jebe was the only archer I knew who could rival him. In the rays of the setting sun, which made the lake blaze like a copper shield, I never grew tired of watching him fish.

He stayed with me all the time I was there and told me he did not know who his true father was, since he had been conceived when a Kereyid had abducted his mother. Raids had reunited him with his tribe but that had not tempered his hatred of his Kereyid father: 'To him I was nothing but a bastard!' he said, thereby revealing the profound grounds for Jochi's attachment to him.

Some Merkid harried our scouts, forcing us to pursue them north of a wall of mountains. Blue Quiver confirmed that they were Sure-Footed's clan.

We were marching in divisions of a hundred when a scout informed us that one of the centuries had flushed their caravan out of hiding. I trotted to it, guided by the smoke of the fires lit by our men.

When I arrived I saw the convoy and its beasts of burden straggling the length of a narrow vale that wound amongst hills. The ground was littered with dead – old men, for the most part – and in their midst, on the slopes or in the stands of fir, my warriors were raping women, each more brutally than his neighbour.

I ordered that the mayhem stop immediately.

They looked at me amazed, and seemed to have trouble understanding why I was angry. Hadn't the Khan said we should take prisoners unless we met resistance? My men knew this, but it didn't change the fact that all I saw were their haggard eyes and open trousers. In their slovenly disarray, they looked like wildcats who had tried to put on human clothes. I was their commander, the Khan's voice.

'You're behaving like dogs! These herds, these tents, these skins, even the humblest wooden dish – everything here belongs to Genghis Khan. What right have you to touch these women? Can't you wait for the spoils to be divided up?'

I gave the order to reassemble the caravan. As they obeyed, I heard the sound of panting coming from behind a bank. I put my heels to Babei and saw a woman trying to escape from one of my soldiers. She was bare-breasted, on all fours, and he was dragging her by the ankle. I saw that he was one of my finest archers and was wounded in one arm, a recent wound that hampered his movements. The woman's face smashed into the ground. As it did so, he heaved himself on top of her and pinned her legs down with his shoulders. Both of them were black with ashes and sweat. With his good hand the archer grasped at the Merkid woman's clothes, which were rolled down to her hips. He tried to pull them off but her belt was too tightly buckled. He was reaching for his knife when I ordered him not to move.

The girl got to her feet, trembling. Despite the grit blackening her face, I saw she was young. Our eyes met. She lowered hers and covered her breasts.

The man sat down, panting, swearing and wincing.

'Did you defile her?'

'I tried my hardest, but you came . . .'

'Is that true?'

The girl lifted her chin, her great gazelle eyes fixed on mine. Her attacker's life depended on her answer.

'Yes, he didn't touch me. I am the same as the day I was born.'

I felt a fierce desire to kill him. A hooked lance had nearly torn his arm off above the elbow.

'Are you Rank the Bowman?'

He nodded.

'From now on, you will be responsible for the maintenance of the lead waggons. Go get that arm amputated if you don't want to lose it all.'

I was about to let Babei have his head but . . . I had never seen such pretty shoulders, such graceful arms. She saw me looking at her.

'What is your name?

'Qulan!'

'Go back to your people, Qulan. And if anyone asks you, tell them you belong to Genghis Khan!'

After putting some of the Merkids to the torture, we found out where Sure-Footed and his men had retreated to. Muqali took charge of the expedition and I returned to our camp at Lake Ocean.

It was no hardship not having to fight more. We had carried out our mission. The Khan would be satisfied. But I felt lighthearted for other reasons that I didn't understand. Something was keeping me there.

One evening I was told that the Merkid girl had dared to ask to see me. I gave permission for her to come to my tent. When I pushed back the rectangle of felt, I knew the source of my attraction.

Immaculately dressed, with her hair glistening like black snakes on her white *del*, she was smiling a majestic smile, her cheeks flushed, her great eyes resting on me. It seemed as if she had materialised from the blue mists rising from the ground. She said that she had brought me something.

'Come closer.'

She bowed respectfully, approached and handed me her present: a white tiger-skin cap with a mink lining and a purple tassel.

'To thank you for your timely intervention, my lord,' she said, bowing again.

'Who are you?'

'Don't you remember my name?'

She was not yet twenty springs, her breath was a child's, fragrant like the steppe after a storm, and I could have devoured her. She turned away with short, measured steps.

'Qulan!' I cried.

She stopped, showed her profile over her shoulder with the hint of a smile on her lips, then carried on walking.

The days passed, the sky drew on its canopy of blue and I felt as if a colony of nightingales were nesting in my chest.

Muqali soon returned to find me smiling placidly and laughing for no obvious reason. Sure-Footed accompanied him, having laid down his arms without a fight when he was surrounded. The last of the rebel chiefs justified this surrender by exhaustion. 'The hostility between the Merkid and the Borjigin dates from Yesügei's abduction of the fair Hö'elün. We made amends by taking Börte, the Khan's pure-hearted wife. That was a bad mistake because ever since he has hounded us as if he wanted to kill us down to the very last man. But Merkid and Borjigin come from the same blood, that of Blue Wolf and Fallow Doe. I want to save my tribe and my children. If they die, if my bone is severed, who will honour my ancestors?'

'What have you to give the Khan in return for his protection?'

Sure-footed stared at me, his shoulders thrown back, a reddish gleam floating in his eyes like that which lit his hair.

'My most precious possession, my daughter.'

'Where is this treasure?'

'She is here, amongst your men. She was taken with my caravan in the Vale of the Winding Brook.'

I ordered that his daughter be brought before us.

She came followed by two warriors, the locks of her hair playing in the breeze, her hands clasped under the sleeves of her white *del*. Her silhouette undulated between the caparisoned horses and I watched the delicious roll of her hips. When she was near enough for me to see her eyes – huge, matchless, the eyes of a gazelle – I murmured involuntarily, 'Qulan.'

'Sure-Footed! Haven't you well-fed herds and furs as soft as silk?'

'In my eyes nothing rivals my daughter,' the Merkid chief replied haughtily. 'My herds are scrawny, and your khan won't even glance at my cloth and jewels once he has my daughter in his arms. As I crossed your camp she threw herself at my feet to tell me she belonged to Genghis Khan. She is ready to marry him to save us from oblivion. Qulan, tell them this is your desire.'

She stood before us, disconcerted, her eyes going from mine to her father's.

'Genghis Khan has countless wives,' I stammered, 'each of incomparable beauty.'

'Sure-Footed's daughter surpasses them all!' These were General Muqali's words. He was on his feet, staring at Qulan, literally drinking her in, struck dumb by her wondrous face.

So, Qulan was a princess. Smeared with ash and soot, I had taken her for some sable-hunter's daughter.

'The Khan cannot marry her,' I shouted, louder than I would have wished. 'One of our men has defiled her!'

Sure-Footed sat bolt upright, his aggrieved face questioning his daughter.

I suddenly realised that when I had spoken in the Khan's name she had thought I was him. I continued, 'I, Bo'urchu, the most faithful of Genghis Khan's faithful, saw with my own eyes your daughter being taken by one of my archers.'

The moment that followed seemed as long and turbulent as the steppe. Her father and I waited for an answer. Qulan bowed her head. Two tears rolled down her cheeks, then she looked at me intensely before acknowledging it to her father by blinking.

My legs went weak; with this lie this peerlessly beautiful woman was declaring her wish to live with me. Never, since the day I set eyes on Queen of Flowers, had I desired a woman so much.

There were three of us who knew the truth: I, she, and Rank the Bowman. That night I stole to the one-armed man's grassy couch and slit his throat.

For a long time I regretted not having been able to find the words to stop Qulan leaving the night she gave me the white tiger-skin cap. But I had an even keener regret: that of giving the Khan the idea of using relays of horses for his messengers. With these the fearsome net of his cohorts of spies had been drawn tight. Now the Khan had ears everywhere. It was almost as if our horses' ears strained to keep him informed.

We had performed our mission. Genghis Khan ordered me to return immediately to the Isle of Grass.

Chapter 44

'Be careful, Bo'urchu: the Khan wants to be in control of everything nowadays; it's like a madness.'

Qasar hung his head.

I had just reached the Isle of Grass. Finding Qasar in the camp was surprise enough in itself, let alone seeing him so downcast. What had become of the joyful tiger, with his roars and wild gallops? Hearing his story, I understood his distress. His elder brother had repudiated him. Had he flouted the *yasak*, stolen from or killed a member of his family? From what he said, he had only protested against Kököchü's privileges.

'We can't enter the Khan's presence without an escort any more. Only the shaman and his brothers are exempt from this absurd protocol. They come and go without being announced, walk in on any family gathering, debate any matters they please and complain the whole time about not being properly rewarded.'

Was the Khan being taken advantage of by the man who had enthroned him? Did he fear the shaman's powers, the wrath of Heaven? He certainly never opposed Kököchü, whose influence grew from day to day.

Qasar had been the first to react. 'In the past we never had cause to complain of you,' he said to his elder brother. 'You were just. But now you have become Genghis Khan, you impose duties on us that the shaman and his brothers completely ignore. They request and are given offices that others would fill far more suitably. Who are they, what have they done, to be more highly regarded than your own brothers?'

'Hold your tongue!' ordered Genghis Khan. 'They are the children of Münglig and the grandchildren of Charaqa, the only one who didn't abandon us when we were banished by the

Sovereigns. The old man paid with his life for it. His descendants will move freely among my lands and my tents.'

Qasar's indignation came to the attention of Kököchü. From that moment on the shaman determined to avenge himself.

Idleness did not agree with Qasar. A skilful archer, as strong as a bear and a wonderful warrior, he always had to be fighting or hunting. Periods of rest saw him sink into endless bouts of drinking where the only reason for him to get to his feet was the prospect of an identical welcome in another *ayil*.

So Kököchü had no trouble enticing this good-natured soul into his yurts. Nor much more warming him up and then provoking him. I never found out exactly what happened that night. But one thing was for sure: Qasar got a thrashing from Kököchü's brothers. His nose was split from cheekbone to cheekbone, his eyes were as swollen as two plums and his shoulder was dislocated.

Although they were strapping lads I could not believe that Kököchü's brothers could have won a fight with Qasar that easily. When he was drunk and as clumsy as a seal, he could still snap a bull's neck. Perhaps he had been afraid to lay a finger on the shaman's brothers? You can defy an army and death but no one, not even Qasar, can live in fear of Tengri's retribution.

Hoping for understanding and justice, he asked to see the Khan.

'May that be a lesson to you,' his brother had said dismissively. 'From now on, keep to your place!'

Shaken by the verdict, Qasar withdrew.

He should have let the storm pass, but as he emptied pitcherfuls of the fermented mare's milk that makes heads spin and tongues fork, he was compelled to pour out his feelings to each of his many hosts. He took delight in recalling how the shaman had once plotted with the Kereyid and tried to poison the Khan. Some of his companions tried to reason with him; others urged him to rebel. When he Khan got wind of the affair, Kököchü had turned it into a raging tempest. A threat had appeared to him in a dream, he told Genghis Khan. 'The Sky will give you the whole earth. It will send its lightning against those you will conquer. But as I slept, I saw Qasar blowing dark clouds towards your shoulders. If you don't take precautions, your brother will riddle your empire with arrows.'

Qasar was seized and forced to his knees in front of the Khan, who stripped him of his helmet and belt. When she was told what was happening, Mother Hö'elün had two white camels hitched to her waggon and arrived in the middle of the cross-examination. Her two eldest sons were facing each other, one on the ground, humiliated, the other framed against the sky, unmerciful.

Two slaves supported the emaciated old woman. She walked forward without glancing at the Khan and placed herself between him and Qasar. Picking up Qasar's belt and helmet, she restored them and his dignity to him, touched his cheeks with her bony, gnarled hands and then, leaning on his powerful shoulders, painfully heaved herself upright. Her face was bathed in tears. She undid her blouse and cupping her wizened breasts, said to Genghis Khan, 'Behold the breasts that nursed you! What crime has Qasar committed that you should want to destroy my flesh?'

Ashamed, the Khan did not say a word.

'When you were little you suckled at one of these breasts, and Khach'iun and Temüge at the other. But Qasar drained both of them to the last drop. He was the terror of wet-nurses. You, Temüjin, inherited cunning and daring, Qasar strength and dexterity. He has put all his strength at your service; he has run your enemies through. Now he has conquered your adversaries, do you want to rob him of his shadow?'

As his mother's eyes bored into him, the Khan turned on his heel and strode into his tent.

The dowager ordered that Qasar be untied.

Two moons had passed since then.

'Believe me, Bo'urchu,' Qasar continued, 'the Khan isn't the same any more. If Mother Hö'elün hadn't intervened he would have tortured me until I'd confessed to some plot I'd never had anything to do with. He may not have dared touch this helmet again, but he has taken away my command of a *tumen* and stripped me of many privileges. The shaman has a great hold over him; he fears him like the plague.'

'Who wouldn't fear Tengri's intimate who can rise up into the air and set bodies on fire?'

'That show at the investiture was just a masquerade,' he said, breaking into a bitter, scornful smile. 'Didn't you smell the stench of that slave? That wasn't just burning flesh. Kököchü had anointed him with some secret substance. People say I'm an idiot, but I'm not so stupid as to be taken in by his conjuror's skills.'

The next day the Khan returned from the hunt. The convoy of shields and richly brocaded saddles had not crossed the Kerulen before one of the messengers came to announce that I was to wait by his tent. He rode up on Bay with the White Mouth, flanked by his standard-bearers. A press of noblemen and elite archers followed, their sun-drenched faces split in broad mother of pearl smiles.

Amongst them I saw Yesüi's face, standing out as white as the moon. Grooms rushed towards her. She shot me a sidelong glance, then dismounted.

'Sain baina uu, Bo'urchu!

'Sain baina uu, Kha Khan!'

He let go of the bridle and put his hands on my forearms to raise me from my bow.

'Don't flatter me, Bo'urchu. No grand-sounding titles; Genghis Khan is enough. Come inside, we have matters to discuss.'

I gave him an account of the campaign. He listened in silence. The features of his amber face were clear and emerald splinters glittered in his eyes. Surrounding us, drinking from silver bowls, were his sons Chagatai, Ögödei and young Tolui, his brothers Belgütei and Temüge, his uncle Daritai, and the shaman Kököchü and his six brothers. When I had finished, he handed me a bowl, visibly pleased with the news that the Merkid had been all but wiped out and the meagre remnants brought to their knees.

'Drink! My brave one.'

He gave orders that freed men be sent to settle on the former Merkid lands and then, in a level tone, he asked me straight out, 'And this *dziggetai* Sure-Footed wants to give me – is she as beautiful as they say?'

'Hmm,' I replied, almost choking. 'That whore is pretty, yes, I suppose . . . Let's say she's not obviously tainted. And that's enough to impress those Merkid boors.'

'Why didn't you bring her to me?'

'One of my archers raped her,' I said, my voice cracking. 'I didn't know she was Sure-Footed's daughter. Anyway, I stepped in too late. But don't worry, O my Khan; that Merkid's looks wouldn't threaten a single one of your wives.'

'Pity. Sometimes, you know, Bo'urchu, I grow weary of Yesüi.'

I feigned surprise, then raised the bowl of frothing milk to my lips to mask my discomfort. But like the marmot who knows that an eagle is above its run, I felt his eyes on me.

'Where is this archer? I must punish him.'

'He has paid for it, my *anda*! He is dead! His soul escaped his body thanks to a terrible arm wound.'

'His name?'

'Rank . . . Rank the Bowman.'

Genghis Khan straightened up, gave me a strange look and snapped his fingers.

Under the awning of the tent a silhouette appeared. It was missing an arm.

'Step forward so we can see you,' ordered the Khan.

The man took a few steps forward. I recognised Rank the Bowman, the very one whose throat I had slit in the high, distant Merkid lands. He looked at me without any animosity, almost as if he was intimidated; his severed arm was heavily bandaged. It was not his double or his spirit; in my haste I must have killed one of his neighbours that night.

The Khan stood up and went to the threshold of his tent, followed by his entire retinue. Before disappearing, he shouted, 'Quench your thirst, Bo'urchu, just as you quenched mine that night when Jebe's arrow hit me. Now we are even!'

His voice was cold and hollow, without any anger but with an undertone that reminded me of the yelp of a wounded wolf.

Chapter 45

In the year of his investiture, 1206, which for us people of the steppe corresponded to the great cycle of the Tiger, death struck the Khan's entourage three times. On three occasions, Genghis Khan, without needing to reach for his belt, was the instigator. They all took place during the Moon of the Argali in Rut, when the birch leaves turned yellow.

First Jochi returned from his campaign against the peoples of the forests. The Khan's eldest son had conducted it to perfection. The Oirat and Khirgiz had been subjugated, and the former had even fought at our side against the Tumat.

He brought back waggons filled with princesses and furs, and the men of those parts who asked nothing but to serve his father numbered almost thirty thousand.

Well satisfied, the Khan rewarded his son richly and decreed that the conquered lands would henceforth be his dependency, his *ulus*. This operation had, however, brought tragedy: Borokul, one of the Khan's adopted sons brought up by Mother Hö'elün, had not survived a Tumat ambush. The Emperor loved Borokul and was very affected by his loss. So when Jochi asked for an additional favour – that Blue Quiver, his young Merkid friend, be able to live with him – the Khan flew into a rage.

'You should have killed him already!'

'He is loyal, a wonderful shot—'

'Enough! Not a single Merkid male shall outlive me. Kill him!'

'I can't, Father.'

'You dare defy me?'

'Your eldest is right,' I interrupted. 'This Merkid is brave—'

'Silence! Don't forget, Bo'urchu, that you have exhausted your credibility. Borokul was loyal and brave as well. He would never have talked behind my back. Now he is dead, my heart is in pain and this Merkid must pay. Kill him, Jochi; I order you.'

It made no difference my suggesting to Little Crumb that it

was better he suffocate Blue Quiver with the thick felt and thereby preserve his soul, than let the Khan slit his throat. He still resigned himself to implementing the cruel sentence with weary shoulders and eyes flooded with rage and tears.

Once his father's order had been carried out, the handsome features of Jochi's face grew dark and were never to grow light again, tortured by a sort of convulsive, permanent anxiety.

Mother Hö'elün died without a sound. The amber glow of her eyes faded daily until one morning she was found lifeless. But even her eyes bore the pain of having seen her eldest sons at each other's throats. Despite her intervention, she thought their discord was incurable and she was right. The peace may have held between Qasar and Genghis Khan since then, but mistrust and suspicion lay in waiting.

Qasar wanted to escort his mother's funerary waggon with his thousand warriors, but Genghis Khan gave this privilege to Mother Hö'elün's three adopted sons, to whom the old woman had transferred all her affections in the last seasons of her life.

The earth was on the verge of freezing and her burial place was a long way away. Her body was quickly taken there and henceforth the Khan decreed it forbidden ground.

Despite Genghis Khan's omnipotence, one man always escaped his authority. That man was Kököchü.

The shaman's prestige now reached the borders of our lands. Not a day passed without him receiving gifts from distant dependencies and often the scale and value of them exceeded those given to the Khan. He now wished to be known as Most Celestial. But not content with this magnificent title and the schism he had opened in the imperial family, he continued to extend his influence over the Khan's closest attendants and brothers. With adept manoeuvres, gifts, trades and privileges, he seduced them and secured their votes at the assemblies. And so it was that in just one day he was able to lure away virtually all of Temüge's vassals. When the Khan's youngest brother charged one of his faithful to recover his men, Kököchü and his brothers beat him, tied a sadddle on his back and sent him back like that to his master. In answer to such an affront, Temüge strode into the circle of Kököchü's tents. The shaman ordered his guard to force him to his knees and apologise for having trodden the sacred ground of his compound without permission.

In the dead of night, Temüge demanded an audience with the Khan. When the Emperor had listened to his brother in silence, Börte jumped out of bed and cried in a fury, 'It's time for action, Conqueror! Since when have you allowed him to raise a hand against your brothers? Yesterday it was Qasar, today it's Temüge; will it be you tomorrow?'

'He wouldn't dare . . .'

'Riding roughshod over Temüge, the guardian of our hearth, is a test. If you let him do what he pleases when you're alive, what will he do to our children when you're dead?'

'I won't die . . .'

'Don't be stupid. Act before he kills us!'

The Khan heeded his wife's arguments. As youngest brother, Temüge was the guardian of his hearthfire and so of his kingdom. This was not merely a symbolic role: when the Khan was on campaign, Temüge saw that order was kept in the royal *ordo* and protected our lands. To challenge him was to challenge the Emperor, and the Emperor had not forgotten that twice already the shaman had all but delivered him into the jaws of the Kereyid. Confrontation was becoming inevitable. He had to respond quickly. He looked at his young brother and said, 'When Kököchü comes here at sunrise, do what you will with him.'

Next morning Temüge watched for the shaman's arrival. As usual Kököchü came with his brothers, and, on this occasion, his father. Temüge followed them into the Khan's tent. He threw himself on the shaman when he had just sat down, seized him and pulled him to his feet.

'Yesterday you were cock-a-hoop. Why don't you pit yourself against me directly this time.'

Most Celestial struggled. His brothers tried to intervene but the Khan, and then their father, stopped them with a wave of the hand; the two men fell to the floor.

'Outside!' shouted the Emperor.

They got up. The shaman tried to explain.

'Outside!'

In a tremendous rage, the shaman followed Temüge. He had barely walked round the side of the tent before Rabid Mastiff, Heavy-Jowled and Black Glut, three of the finest wrestlers enlisted by Temüge, jumped on him and broke his neck, his shoulders and, last of all, his spine.

Alerted by the terrible sounds of bones cracking, two of his brothers shot out of the tent; the wrestlers were already dragging the lifeless body out of the way. The brothers ran back inside, yelling that the Khan had murdered Most Celestial and threatening him until they were seized by guards.

'Take them away!' Genghis Khan ordered. 'You, Münglig, stay!'

'I have always been loyal,' said the old man, his face haggard with grief. 'O my khan, pardon my sons.'

'You have brought them up poorly. If you don't muzzle them, I will get rid of them. Their shadows must never darken my path. Do you understand, Münglig?'

I often wondered if Mother Hö'elün's death influenced the most dangerous and unlikely decision Genghis Khan had to take: to eliminate Tenggeri's intercessor. True to his usual self, he had let his younger brother carry out the task. But what difference did that make? Heaven cannot be tricked. Eventually I accepted that his awesome love of power had compelled him to take that step. Jamuka, Jochi and, more recently, Qasar had told me: 'Women, horses and above all, power, are the three things the Khan never shares!'

The shaman's body was put in a tent. On the Khan's orders, the door and smoke-hole were sealed up and three rows of the old guard were put to watch over the tomb. He shut himself away for three days with his counsellor, the efficient and discreet Tata Tong-a. At dawn on the fourth day he broadcast his version of what happened. 'Despite Tengri's disapproval, Kökö-chü used his powers against the prince's family. So Tengri broke his bones and took his life. The Sky appeared to me in my sealed yurt, in utter darkness. It told me who our great shaman was to be. His name is Üsün. Henceforth he will be at my right.'

Üsün knew all the plants, all the animals, all the stones, all the streams. It was he who had first tended my wounded knee. His wisdom was as deserving of respect as his great age.

And yet the Khan found no peace of mind. He spent the winter in seclusion, receiving only a few of his dignitaries. Admittedly he was preparing campaigns, discussing the reports of our spies, hatching designs in secret. But his isolation hid a stubborn anxiety, that of having incurred the disapproval of Tenggeri, just one of whose bolts could transform the Emperor of Emperors into a louse-dropping.

Chapter 46

For three moons not a single bird enlivened the icy sky.
Countless animals froze on their feet. The royal *ordo* spent the
winter on the banks of the Onon, buried away in the heart of the
mountains, sheltered by their slopes and mantle of larches.

I was on my lands at the Red Throne, two days' ride
downstream; every day I would go out on camelback after my
herds and drive them further afield because I was afraid they
would give up trying to graze, disheartened by always finding
the soil as hard as stone. If one of my horses dozed off, I would
rush to him because it meant that the underground spirits were
playing, lulling him to sleep. But all my urgency was futile that
winter: Tenggeri had given the spirits permission to feast.

Encased in a coat of blue mink and rocked by the camel's
rolling gait, I would sometimes drift off, hunched over the
warmth of the heated stone at the bottom of my breast pocket.
And invariably my dreams would set me down on the same
shores: in Princess Qulan's great eyes; on the verge of her lips; in
the dimples of her smile or the wings of her arms.

The more pitiless the season became, the more I warmed
myself at the memory of the beautiful Qulan, and desire swelled
in me so painfully that I had to face the truth: I could not
conceive of life without her. I had to find her again.

The rocky mass of the Red Throne now had its outer wall, as I
had promised the Khan. But I was the only one to see it. Often I
climbed to its western edge. On that side it followed the ridge of
a hill which was studded with great ochre and grey boulders of
indecipherable shape. From there one looked down at the giant
larches on the slopes, moaning in the wind, and across to the
ocean of blue mountains. A pathway twisted between the rocks
up to the summit and led to a little terrace, a balcony suspended
over a sheer drop. Those great boulders were arrayed around it
in a circle, as if they were deliberating. But its most striking

feature I called a flame-red pine, which was what it had been before it was struck by lightning long ago, perhaps even before Khabul Khan's reign. Now there was no trace of burning. All the bark had been stripped from its trunk which had been bleached white and snapped in two. The part still standing was as tall as a man, but far broader; the rest must have fallen, burning, into the void at its feet. It had suffered horribly: its roots, even at the base of its trunk, didn't just writhe in the ground but reared up, trying to gain a better hold further away. Likewise two low branches, one on each side, stretched backwards, like two misshapen arms trying to anchor themselves better lest their beloved trunk be pushed over the edge. Alone at the tip of the cliff, its ribcage split open, defying the wind and lightning, it was the leader of the pack, intractable. It seemed to be hiding a double-edged wooden sword blade behind its back, a branch which, long ago, had grown up flat against its trunk. The tree was dead, and yet it gave the impression of being able to turn around at any moment and walk between the rocks, dragging its long buried roots after it with great swings of its shoulders, marching towards some battle. Standing bolt upright and facing Tenggeri, it defied the passage of the ages. Far away to the south lay Temulun, to the east Afraid of Bears, to the west Queen of Flowers. My pine would never bend its shattered brow to expose the few bare little branches, snarled by the wind, which sheltered at its nape. So from its stubborn silhouette, I drew the strength that would allow me to fly to Qulan, who was to the north and who was . . . alive.

It was Jochi's visit to my *ulus* at the Red Throne that precipitated my act of daring.

Blue Quiver's death had only sharpened his resentment towards his father. Genghis Khan's inflexibility, he said, could not simply be explained by his hatred of the Merkid. We had lost count of the number of captives spared for bravery, and clever young Blue Quiver was easily as valorous as our most faithful lieutenants. For the first time, I shared Jochi's dark feelings: the Khan blamed him for being another's son, even though he was the only one responsible for that possibility.

Jochi told me I was deluding myself if I hoped to be with Qulan: the Khan was impatient to see her.

'All the reports testify to her extraordinary beauty. Riders are leaving tomorrow for Sure-Footed's camp. They will order him to present himself with his daughter at the imperial tent. You are not meant to know the purpose of this mission.'

'Little Crumb, this isn't revenge, is it?'

'No, Bo'urchu, I am angry because you have been like a father to me. You are the only one to have served the Khan immaculately. He orders us to dry up the well of Merkid blood, but when one of their women catches his fancy, he takes her and despises us, crushes us and the chance of happiness we could have snatched ourselves. What are you going to do?'

'I was about to set off,' I said morosely. 'Now that's hopeless. Unless . . .'

'Unless?'

'I go right now – that's my only chance to reach her before the Khan's patrol.'

'Ah! The Bo'urchu I know! That's how to act. Go! Fly to her! Take her far from the Emperor's bed, Mother Börte will be grateful.'

I untethered and mounted Babei.

'Did you come alone?'

'No, I am with Flayed Wolf and Bata and a dozen high-spirited archers. They are at the mouth of the valley in your horse-herder's tent.'

'Good, listen: tell them that you couldn't find me. That way, when Genghis Khan suspects – and he will do – he'll be told that you missed me. He won't think you've warned me.'

'Why hide the truth from him? I'm not afraid of facing up to him any more.'

'Don't! Not yet . . . The wolf never lets himself be tickled, especially not his balls.'

He nodded; I smiled and dug my heels into Babei's ribs.

I picked up ten archers at the edge of my *ulus* and we sped into the night towards Lake Occan.

At the tenth sunrise, Sure-Footed's handful of tents was in sight. I sent one of my men to order him to strike camp immediately, saying this was the will of Genghis Khan.

From a hill I watched their hasty preparations, proof of the Merkid chief's submissiveness. Horsemen cantered up into the hills to fetch the herds; the tents were thrown on the ground then folded and bundled onto the waggons or tied to the backs of their yaks. Soon the bleating of sheep drowned out the clatter of tent poles, and finally Qulan got into the front of a waggon. My heart listed so violently I had to check Babei's girth hadn't come undone, but he was standing as firmly as ever, not having even batted an eyelid.

I followed their progress along the crests. There were only twenty of them and they must all have been part of Sure-Footed's family, half women and children, the other half men, two of whom were elders. On reaching a clearing, they swept the snow from a stream and set up camp. The snow and dwindling light turned the countryside blue. I crept closer to spy on Qulan's great dark eyes and, far away as I was, her long lashes seemed to stretch out of the fur hood encircling her face. Her breath condensed in long, pallid plumes. She lay down on the waggon; her father made a frame of four poles over her and stretched a great rectangle of felt over them as a wall.

I could not take my eyes off this bed, where I dreamt of curling up.

Eyelids closed like half-moons, she was smiling in her sleep. Cloaked in hoar frost, she seemed like a star come to earth to light my nights. Behind me Sure-Footed was the first to get to his feet.

'Who are you?'

'Bo'urchu, Genghis Khan's *anda*. As soon as your daughter wakes up we have to leave; it's not safe here.'

'I am ready.'

Qulan was sitting up, observing me with an expression of amazed delight. I had never seen a more spellbinding gaze: calm and frank, the pure, honeyed reflection of a transparent heart.

'Then let's go! Bandits are everywhere here. I will take you to the royal *ordo*.'

The following days were as marvellous as they were sad.

I had no trouble convincing Qulan to give up her waggon for the back of a red-roan with one blue and one bronze eye who was as watchful as an owl. I knew that he would keep her warm. We rode with a gap of a few paces between us, not daring to say anything, constantly looking at each other and continuing to sneak glances even when we pretended to be absorbed by the horizon or distracted by our thoughts.

I was as awkward as that first time, thirty-two springs before, when the daughter of a friend of my father's had chased me. I was twelve then; she was two springs older. She was called Hazel and her boldness made me realise that love is not satisfied by stolen looks alone. Hazel had knocked me over and hugged me.

She was sweating hard and her smell of sage had an acrid, insidious edge which only much later I attributed to her desire. I stupidly took fright and we had fought about how to play our game. Then she had had to go with her father and I was left there like a stupid little pup in thrall to my virgin's excitement.

At Qulan's side I reverted to this silly little boy. What could I do? I loved her and this feeling overwhelmed me, scared me, as much as it transported me, until I felt I wasn't my own master.

With the advent of Genghis Khan I had lost my brother Temüjin. I feared his anger but not enough to kill this mad hope that had me riding along the edge of this terrible abyss; nor enough to cancel the beauty of these moments that I relished like a condemned man granted has a sudden, miraculous reprieve.

Our horses imperceptibly drew closer to each other until our stirrups kept touching with a clinking sound that thrilled me like birdsong. She was wearing a white ermine fur and wolf-skin boots. A smell of warm ash and soft leather came from her clothes.

The next day I drew her up the slopes and along the crests of the hills while our convoy continued along the valley floor. We swapped horses and her tongue loosened. She thought Babei's back was more spacious and comfortable than the downiest bed, expressed her joy at being liberated from her father's waggon, wondered how many horses I had, where my limp came from, was saddened to learn it was the doing of her people, then asked about the Mongols – our customs, our games, our khan, the number of his wives, their characters, the order of precedence. She asked about countless details, was surprised, blushing sometimes and dazzling me with her smiles. Her voice was as melodious and flute-like as the black warbler's song when it knows it is loved.

'If only this journey would never end,' she blurted.

'I doubt that's what the Khan would want.'

'Despite all the horrors I'd heard associated with that name, and despite thinking you were him, the moment your eyes landed on me, I felt myself dissolve. And that feeling was stronger than my fear.'

'O Qulan, if there is one moment when I will envy my emperor, it is the one when he holds you in his arms.'

It wasn't long before Sure-Footed's little convoy was stopped by the Khan's scouts. They were puzzled by the tortuous route we had taken, but they quickly set off again for the Khan's encampment.

We watched from a hill crowned with a fir wood.

'Our escapade will soon be at an end,' I sighed.

Feelings wove their web across our eyes.

Night found us propped against Babei's shoulder, with her curled up in my arms. It was bitterly cold and in the pallid moonlight against the snow-covered ground our lips were blue. She would bury them in her fur hood but then reveal them, quivering, as if they were burning to tell me something. Yet we stayed mute, entranced by our faces that whispered the exact same thing.

A song gnawed at me:

O Qulan
I am Bo'urchu
One of the Mongols who subject peoples
With the noise of their drums alone
Now the drums of my heart beat in vain
Because I have won what I cannot have.

In the days that followed we became lost in the Kentei Mountains, lost as we longed to be and wilfully made sure we were. Until then my men and Sure-Footed's convoy had been saw us every day. They met up with us in the evenings when the beasts were tethered, or in the morning before they were saddled. But we did not want to see anyone any more; we were self-sufficient, amazed by each other as we were.

Our disappearance was dangerous – Qulan knew that. She hoped the Khan would disown her. I, that he would give her to me.

An illusion – the fact we had to disappear proved that – but this period of grace, intensely experienced like no other, obscured the inevitable outcome.

Our eyes met and danced with the same passion; we walked over the icy ground and it was as if spring bloomed where we trod. We slept entwined in each other's arms under our furs, inhaling our scents until we were delirious. There was no milk as soft as the skin of her neck, no mane more like silk than her hair, no music more exquisite than the sighs of bliss that set her ribs heaving at my touch. We felt that delicious, tantalising agony of not being able to yield to our desires. I had to fight, I had to resist my princess of love and honey, although it felt as if my heart would break and as if my lance would shatter.

Despite my suspicions concerning Queen of Flowers and the way Genghis Khan had wormed Yesügen away from me and claimed her for himself, I could not bring myself to betray my *anda*. To try to control my burning desires, I started dreaming that he would prefer to give up Qulan rather than risk losing me.

For a whole night she listened to me tell the story of my life at the Khan's side. My praises revived my admiration of him. I passionately described the man he was, told of his feats of arms, his intelligence, his goodness, his courage, as if I had to be convinced.

Had I sung my *anda*'s praises too eloquently? As dawn approached, the gentle *dziggetai* said, 'If women were allowed to marry more than one man and if he is as you say he is, then I could submit to his will so long as I was allowed to love you unreservedly.'

'It's inconceivable. He wouldn't allow it and I don't know if I'd agree to sharing you.'

Her charms made me dizzy, intoxicated, but by drowning in her great scarab eyes, I managed to restrain myself and not pluck her flower. There was only one breach of our truce. It was at the coldest point of the night. Qulan's whole body shook; I told her I knew a remedy for her discomfort. She asked what it was.

Our horses were standing, frozen silhouettes under the moon. I took her face in my hands. It was smooth and more luminous than the seven fiery stars that we had watched toppling down the sky. My lips caressed her lips. Cold as stone, she became burning hot. She wasn't breathing. I crossed her mouth's threshold with its rims of silk and lapped against her mother of pearl teeth. Her full throat quivered like the ribs of a dove caught in a trap; her hands felt for me, stroked me like a squirrel its fur. We kissed, more tightly woven in each other's arms than ever seemed possible. Her hips started to tremble and then jerk so violently that our teeth clashed. When our lips agreed to separate, I saw glowing in the jewel case of her eyes that same feeling I felt more than ever before: ecstasy.

Dawn took us by surprise, pressed against each other, our fur coats undone, unnecessary. Our love was still virgin.

It had been a harsh test: Genghis Khan could not have a surer proof of loyalty than this one.

Admittedly the eyes he had vowed to gaze on when he looked

at his wives had changed. They shone with a troubling light, and their lids were heavier, smoother and more majestic than the wings of a swan landing on its beloved lake.

Qulan touched the amulet hanging around my neck. I opened it and gave her its contents, my kneecap.

She shook her head with alarm. 'I don't want it. If you died without that precious bone, you wouldn't be able to be reborn.'

I took her right hand and put my knee's little canopy into it.

'If I'm never going to see you again, I don't mind whether I'm a wolf or a bird or a stone or a flower or a tree. What does the rain matter and the sun and the moon and the sound of horses and the hunt and the wild delight of flying in the sky . . . if I am far from you? Take this and keep it round your neck, between your breasts. Then I will always be at your side and I will perfume your nights. Yes, look after it as it will look after you until we see each other again. If Tenggeri decides otherwise, I know you will bring it to me in my resting place.'

Her fingers closed around the flat bone. She pressed her cheek against my chest and swore that nothing and nobody would separate me from her.

'I love you, I trust you.'

Those were my last words.

Breathing as deep as I could, I stored the smell of Qulan's hair in my memory. Then the Khan's warriors rode towards us, driven by an ineluctable order.

Chapter 47

'By order of the Khan, follow me!'

'Whooah, Chagatai! Does the Khan order you not to greet me either?'

'My uncle would be wise to save his spit. He'll need it.'

'Princess Qulan is under my protection,' I said, challenging him.

'From now on she is my responsibility; I will ride with her.'

'Then the two of us will, if you insist.'

'The Khan insists.'

'By my arrows! Does he entrust you with watching over his wives? That's a great honour for a second son!'

'I am the first son. Ögödei is the second.'

'And Jochi?'

'As his name suggests, he is my father's guest. Nothing more.'

I did not say another word until we reached the royal *ordo*.

When he saw Qulan, I knew he would not show me any favours. If all the blue of the sky had taken refuge in his eyes, they could not have been more luminous.

The Emperor's black, terrifying silhouette stood straight-backed in the light, superb in its arrogance, and his gaze crushed all before him. He approached and walked round her, his head high like a stallion seducing a new, sinuously beautiful mare.

Everyone held their breath: warriors, the shaman, his adepts, Sure-Footed and his kin, the men of the imperial family. The Khan stroked each point of his thin moustache in turn, already relishing the pleasures of the nights to come. Qulan would be his! He would make her his favourite because her beauty surpassed all understanding and because the Khan's thoughts, transported by this divine apparition, now no longer rose above the belt.

He pointed a finger at me.

'You despoiled her! You dared do that! You! YOU WILL DIE! On your knees!'

Stunned, speechless, I shook my head.

'ON YOUR KNEES! Throw that dog to the ground!'

Ten of them ran at me, but before I was surrounded, I drew my sabre and threatened the Khan.

'Kill me then, if you think I'm guilty!'

'Why have you taken so long? Why did you break away from Sure-Footed's convoy? His daughter is pledged to me; she is my wife! I know how much you resent it, Bo'urchu. You wanted to take your revenge and deceive me by violating her.'

'You are wrong, Temüjin . . .'

'Are you defying me?'

'Yes, because since Temüjin has passed away, Genghis Khan behaves like the great wolf that suspects the males of his pack of covering the females behind his back. He is blind because I am the most trustworthy of all his lieutenants.'

'So be it. We'll see if you confess on the Liar's Wheel.'

I almost fell to my knees.

The Liar's Wheel was a torture instrument made of two heavy flat stones. A horizontal lever wound the top stone down until it touched its twin. Two yaks were harnessed to this lever and their slow, inexorable circuits ended up crushing the victims. The site of this Jin invention had become the dogs' favourite place. As the yaks walked round, they ran up, moaning, their mouths watering at the cracking bones and spurting jets of blood. Sometimes the bravest plucked up their courage and tore away a hand or a foot.

There was a disturbance in the crowd behind the rows of archers. The guards parted and the Khan's wife, followed by his cortège of brides and slaves, came onto the square.

'O my spouse, what has happened? Why do you roar like the storm?'

'Bo'urchu has deceived me.'

'Speak, Bo'urchu,' Börte encouraged me, her expression impassive.

'The Khan accuses me of sampling the Merkid princess.'

'Calm yourself. His appetite is great, as you know. Where is she?'

She followed my gaze, studied Qulan at length, then said in a low voice, as if to herself, 'What dead man would not be reborn at the sight of that girl?'

314

'Come here, you whose beauty has sowed trouble in the royal tent before you even arrived.'

Qulan obeyed.

'Did he despoil you?'

'May Tenggeri strike me down if I lie, but all this man did was protect me. I am just the same as when my parents brought me into this world.'

'We will see about that. Woe is you if you are lying; I will not be able to check the Emperor's wrath.'

Genghis Khan left the square, wrestling with a shame like that he had felt when Mother Hö'elün had taken Qasar's part.

While the female shamans, healers and wet-nurses went with the royal wives to examine Qulan, one fear oppressed me. What if, having seen the Merkid princess's beauty, Börte wanted to be rid of this rival? She only had to tell the Khan that Qulan had been defiled and it was the end of me. And of Qulan too.

But the Khan's first wife was upright and staunch. She told her husband that the Merkid princess was a virgin, the same as the day she was born.

When the Khan said nothing, Börte added, 'Her waist is as slim as the weasel's and her skin is so soft only Heaven can know its secret. This time the Emperor will leave me for good . . .'

She sighed and went away.

I waited in that cursed place for him to vindicate me. In vain! When all it would have needed was a word, a gesture, and all the fervour of my devotion would have been rekindled.

Granted I still had my belt and the cap on my head, but he had humiliated me and wounded me worse than any sword and, if Börte had not intervened, wouldn't he have killed me? Like so many others. All our promises, our ties of blood, my marriage to Temulun – all of it had been wiped out in a moment. Because of a woman! A woman we both desired more than anything in the world.

O Qulan! Genghis Khan will taste you, gather the pollen from your orange blossom, enter your gate on sheets as soft and precious as your skin. Between your arms and perfumed hips he will be a glistening necklace, a miraculous river. What a gift I had given him! I swore through teeth clenched so tight they almost shattered, that it would be the last present he ever had from me.

The light of the setting sun was receding as I galloped across the plateau, which was bathed in the cruellest red glow. I kept to the shadows at the foot of the mountains.

We had ridden for two days and two nights. Brave Babei never once flinched and when I bayed all my torment at the sky, he shook his neck as if to tell me not to be in pain.

I dismounted on the level ground by the Blue Lake, the exact spot where Genghis Khan had first been crowned. At that season the place was deserted; the nearest yurts were half a day's trek away. I walked alongside the dismal, black waters, then left Babei in a clearing to crop the colourless grass and went into the forest of firs. They grew so close together that the undersides of their branches were dry and bare. They whipped my face and snapped with sharp cracks as I pushed my way through. I heard foxes yapping very close and chasing each other between the trunks.

I wanted to merge into the darkness and not see anything ever again, but I had to keep an eye on Babei. I retraced my steps and lay down in the clearing with a patch of heather under my back. My courser was grazing calmly, meticulously, wreathed in blue mist. Suddenly I felt a presence and, looking around, eventually made out a pair of wolves eighty paces away. Their coats the colour of rocks had stopped me seeing them before. The male was watching me as the female raised her nose, her eyes half-shut. She was pissing on the ground, preparing herself for the great loner. She was young: it must have been her first coupling.

I thought they were going to go away, but the male sprang on the she-wolf and licked her withers. She threw back her head, showing her throat, her hindquarters arched. His legs shaking slightly, he entered her with one thrust. She moaned and twisted. Digging his fangs into the fur at her neck, he held her tight against his loins. They stayed like that for a long while, unmoving, until the she-wolf grew calm and invited him with an almost imperceptible swaying to continue. Then he accompanied her movements. The more she howled, the more savagely he thrust into her.

Their lovemaking lasted until the middle of the night.

Just before darkness swallowed them up, the male stared at me and in his arrogant gaze I saw Genghis Khan's eyes. They were pitiless, devouring. I remembered what he had said one day about war: 'The most exciting thing is not the men we kill or the herds we take, but the women we make pregnant. Humiliating

our enemies like that is the greatest pleasure battle can give a
man.'

Chapter 48

Fifteen years passed before I was given the chance to see the Khan again. I may have been young Temüjin's lucky star, but Genghis Khan, the Son of Heaven, had no need of me on his conquests.

Shut away in my *ulus* at the Red Throne, I was nothing in the new dispensation. He was everything and everywhere, loved and feared, the supreme ruler and preparing to conquer the rest of the world.

I had companions to cheer my reclusive existence. Qasar, Belgütei and Jelme visited me. But my tent's most regular guest was Jochi, who used to tell me about Genghis Khan's incomparable, insolent successes. It is thanks to my Little Crumb that today I am able to retrace his father's exploits as follows:

Not long after I had left the royal *ordo*, a Jin embassy had arrived to announce the death of their emperor and the identity of his successor.

According to Jin protocol, we Mongols should have bowed down before them. But fifty thousand of our men were drawn up on the other side of the Kerulen river in order to overawe the visitors. Genghis Khan received the ambassador not in his tent but thirty paces away, where his throne had been set up. And it was the King of Gold's representative who had to kneel and deliver his message in the attitude of a vassal, stammering terribly. Chancellor Tata Tong-a acted as translator.

'The Prince of Wei is khan of the kingdom of the Kings of Gold?' Genghis Khan repeated in surprise. 'Aren't the Jin emperors chosen by Heaven? Tenggeri can't have nominated such an imbecile.'

Then he stood up, and as the Jin delegation were made to kneel, he spat towards the south – to the ambassadors' stupefaction – and sneered, 'The Prince of Wei!' Any emperor treated so disdainfully would have raised his army to avenge the insult. But not the King of Gold. He went to ground in his capital and none of his troops ventured beyond the Great Wall.

Every summer since his investiture, the Khan's squadrons had plundered the gardens of the Xixia. But in that year, 1209, they turned on their fortresses, although with little success.

'Those walls that protect their towns were difficult,' Jochi explained to me. 'We couldn't scale them or force the gates, because the inhabitants shot at us from the ramparts and smashed our ladders. Our archers covered us, accurate as ever, but still we lost many more men than we killed. We laid waste the surrounding fields, trampled their orchards, slit their peasants' throats, but still they wouldn't come out from behind their walls and we didn't know what to do next. Defeat would mean only fighting on ground that suited us in the future, and admitting our inferiority in the face of fortifications. This the Khan couldn't tolerate. "Those walls that bruise the earth and offend the eye," he told his officers, "are only for cowards. They cower behind them like lambs in the pen; but let's be patient. If they don't want to fight, we'll make these walls their tomb."

'Something that inspired a greater terror in them than us would flush them out. But what? It was as we were watching the vultures circling above the garrison town of Wulahai that an idea took shape. We promised the inhabitants we would lift the siege on one condition: that they gave us all the town's birds. Thinking they were getting off lightly, they emptied all the nests and gave us whole colonies of swallows, pigeons and sparrows, a pair of swans, chickens even – thousands of birds pecking and calling in every imaginable type of cage – and so, with our strange cargo of aviaries strapped to our saddles, we pretended to lift the siege. But the following night we returned. We'd wrapped the birds' feet in oakum, and when we were within sight of the walls, we set fire to them, opened their cage doors and they flew in a great thunder of beating wings back to their nests. In no time Wulahai was ablaze and spewing out its inhabitants onto our sabres and arrows in the early light. We massacred that garrison town like fire itself.

'Then our elites with Genghis Khan at their head marched on Ningxia, the Xixia capital on the west bank of the Yellow River. The country was rugged, the march hard going, and many times we had to work our way around chasms that gaped like open wounds in those grey lands ridged with high ochre dunes.

'Protected on one side by the Yellow River and on the other by the Ala-Chan Mountains, Ningxia was a very different proposition. We didn't know how to make a start on those black stone walls looming up against the sky. It didn't seem likely that the ruse of the birds would work a second time: spies had told us that many canals ran through the city. Instead the Khan set about diverting the Yellow River to flood it.

'This colossal undertaking cost many slaves their lives. But we were making slow progress until the autumn rains swelled the river, swept away our dyke and washed away our camp.

'The Khan was debating whether to retrace our steps or settle down to wait when a Xixia delegation approached to negotiate. Our harrying raids had destroyed their oases and cut off the caravan routes. Now we were to reap the rewards: mighty Ningxia's reserves had run dry. The Xixia king, who called himself the Celestial King, kneeled before the Khan and accepted all our conditions. He recognised our suzerainty and immediately paid a tribute – which was to be collected each spring – of a hundred white camels, falcons trained for the hunt, fabrics, gemstones and weapons. He pledged his loyalty and troops to the Khan. As a token of alliance, he also gave him the most beautiful of his daughters and a hundred chosen men from his guard.'

Jochi described the banquet that celebrated the end of this campaign and the Khan's delight. He could be well satisfied: with the Xixia under his suzerainty, his authority now stretched to the frontiers of the Jin kingdom. Our ancestors must have been clutching their sides with joy.

At the start of the year 1211, Genghis Khan assembled the princes, nobles, chiefs and vassals of his empire at a grand *quriltai*. Barchuq, the Uighur sovereign, Buzar, King of the Almalik and Arslan, ruler of the Qarluk, came to pay homage to the Son of Heaven.

The Khan was not indifferent to these shows of allegiance by three tribal chiefs who had travelled far, but he took particular pleasure in the alliance officially concluded with Ala Quk Tegin, the Önggüld chief, since the purpose of the *quriltai* was to decide whether to invade the Golden King's kingdom.

The vote was unanimous: the time had come to avenge Ambakai, the Mongol ancestor impaled at the Jin court.

'One moon later,' Jochi told me, 'the black silhouettes of our vanguard were in sight of the Great Wall that protects the Jin empire. At the Summits of the Wild Foxes the enemy soldiers had a foretaste of our anger. We put them to the sword so savagely that they swore never to cross their endless stone serpent again. But another year of bitter impatience passed before we were able to overcome this obstacle.

'The opening came from the east when a Khitan prince rebelled against the King of Gold. He sent word that he could raise a hundred thousand allies. The Khan immediately dispatched Jebe the Arrow to the easternmost corner of the Great Wall. Together the prince and Jebe worked their way around it over the frozen rivers and then laid siege to Liaoyang, a powerful citadel barring entrance to the kingdom of the Golden Kings. As elsewhere, they couldn't breach the fortifications: it needed a trick from Jebe the Arrow. First he made it look as if he was breaking away from the Khitans. They stayed a few days longer, tried to storm the walls once more and then also seemed to give up the fight. Galvanised by this easy victory, the Jin streamed out after them, convinced they were about to finish them off. Their first surprise was when the Khitans did an about-turn and they were suddenly outnumbered. They tried to withdraw behind their fortifications. Their second surprise was that the fortress had been taken by Jebe. After that they had no reason to be surprised because they were all massacred.'

The clever archer used this tactic again at the pass of Chü-yung-kuan, a defile overshadowed by precipitous heights which it would have been suicidal to attempt to negotiate. He sent an advanced guard which turned back at the first sight of the enemy. The Jin set off in pursuit and by the time they realised that they had been lured into an ambush, they were surrounded by the armies of Jochi and the Khan, who had linked up with his cunning general.

Then the two of them made a clean sweep of the passes and fortifications leading to Zhongdu, 'the central metropolis', and, as Jochi said laughing, the Jin corpses were 'piled up like argols'.

'The Khan pitched camp on the Terrace of Dragons and Tigers; before him lay the great plains and the golden towers of Zhongdu.

'The city seemed vast and impregnable, but Genghis Khan's generals champed at the bit to take it by storm. He thought a siege would cause overly severe casualties and drag on interminably: "My starving wolves have better things to do than watch their hair turn white."

'He left a large garrison at the city gates and set off south-west into a region of cultivated plains that seemed never-ending. Its paddy-fields, sorghum and maize fields, orchards, gardens, harvests, dykes and irrigation canals were destroyed, burnt, flooded, ripped up. We hunted the villagers and peasants, put them in chains, and when a fortress appeared before us, it was them we drove against its ramparts to help us storm it and take its inhabitants, weapons and women.

'The Khan spread terror as far as the Yellow River, which was so wide in that part of the Jin kingdom that he had to abandon the idea of crossing it. Then he drove east until he reached the ocean. Tolui was with him commanding the army of the centre. I was leading the right wing with Chagatai and Ögödei and we did likewise west of the T'ai-Hang Mountains. Qasar, on the left wing, ravaged the provinces to the north-east of the capital and subjugated the Jurchen lands beyond the Sungari river.

'The booty was colossal. We entrusted it to our Önggüd allies and then, in the spring of the Year of the Dog – three years after the start of the invasion – the Khan brought his armies together before Zhongdu again.

'Great confusion reigned in the Jin court. The Prince of Wei had been assassinated by one of his generals and replaced by a new emperor: Hsüan-tsung. Genghis Khan sent him this message: "By the will of Tenggeri all your provinces have fallen before my horse. Here you are alone, shut in your golden city, surrounded by my irascible warriors. The climate of your kingdom infuriates them, the walls of your city are like grit in their eyes. They feel a great wrath towards you and each of them hopes to hang your head from his lance. I am ready to have them withdraw to our steppes, but what will you give me to appease them?"

'Next day, when the sky and earth were golden in the sunshine, huge quantities of precious metals and silks were piled at the city gates. With them were vast sacks of salt, tea, black sugar, nutmeg and a host of other spices we did not know how to use. As tribute they also gave us a thousand young women, including a princess of the blood, a thousand young men and three thousand horses.

'Then Genghis Khan left the city to return to the royal *ordo* beyond the Gobi, but not before leaving spies and propagandists throughout the conquered lands because the Jin empire, ravaged by our hordes and weakened by intrigues and discord between ministers and military leaders, was wracked by uprising and conflict. The Khan hadn't lost hope of occupying the imperial city one day; only wisely, and trusting his intuition, he preferred to wait for more opportune times.

'The Emperor Hsüan-tsung was not fooled. Despite his capital's high walls, formidable garrisons and arsenal, he knew he had had a narrow escape. With a certain wisdom inspired by the terror of hindsight, he retreated from Zhongdu to take refuge in his southern capital, Kaifeng, on the opposite bank of the Yellow River, the Jins' natural ally. He left his best generals to defend the city, enjoining them to fight to the last drop of their blood should the Mongols ever return to put them to the siege.

'This withdrawal was a mistake,' Jochi told me. 'Left to watch over the central metropolis, cut off from more than two-thirds of their army and abandoned by the court, the Jin garrison became demoralised. Many of the battalions accompanying Hsüan-tsung to Kaifeng turned back in order to camp near the frontiers and wait until our troops returned so that they could surrender to them.

'Genghis Khan's reaction was instantaneous: in the first days of the Year of the Pig, he launched an army corps at Zhongdu which was intercepted. The enemy outnumbered us ten times over but most of their troops had no experience. As for those who were professional fighters, they were unable to survive outside their stone fortifications and were commanded by incompetents. We swiftly rolled them over, and their lifeless bodies were tossed onto the bones of their pig brothers who had ventured out of the city in previous seasons.

'When we appeared before Zhongdu, one of the city's generals threw himself from the ramparts, and he was followed by thousands of women holding their children in their arms. Others tried to hang onto the legs and tails of the horses of a troop of fleeing horsemen.

'Our allies, Khitai and Önggüd, and the even larger battalions of Jin rebels swelled our dark array bristling with banners and lances. Then the besieged saw heavy catapults being drawn up at our rear towed by a hundred slaves apiece, which they themselves had successfully used against their southern neighbours, the Song.

'The imperial city was ripped open two moons later. The Khan left the business of sacking it to Muqali. He headed northwards again in search of cooler mountain air at the foot of the Great Khingan chain.

'Zhongdu was not one but four cities. We took them each in turn, methodically killing and razing everything that dared stand upright under Tenggeri. The palaces and gardens of the King of Gold were ransacked, revealing such riches that the tribute paid three seasons before by the Jin emperor to see us leave seemed derisory and humiliating.

'A whole moon was needed to collect the bodies and count them. And the city burned for another moon still, creating such a stench that the scavengers kept away.

'Genghis Khan returned to the banks of the Kerulen, leaving Muqali with an army of 40,000 men. His mission was to obtain the surrender of the King of Gold, who was still sheltering in his southern capital. After two seasons marching and fighting, Muqali bypassed the Yellow River by the west and saw the walls of Kaifeng. He could not get close since Jin troops stronger than his were massed around the town. So he concentrated on recovering the citadels we had captured and the enemy had retaken after we had gone. Everywhere our army found hordes of naked, emaciated civilians roaming the desolate lands. Fear and horror flashed in their eyes. We enlisted the strongest. The others, if they did not die on the way, tried to join the Redcoats, an insurrectionary army rebelling against the court of the King of Gold whom we recruited as well.'

Genghis Khan had spent this time savouring his victories in the north of his empire, at the sacred source of the Three Rivers or on the Isle of Grass. But the treasures accumulated, the storehouses of grain, the gold, the jewels, the fabrics, the women, the horses, and the slaves in chains gave him only limited pleasure. He had distributed everything amongst his wives, his men and his allies, keeping nothing for himself and saving the rarest marvels for Qulan, his favourite. He was passionately in love and devoted all his time to her. He had confided in his shaman that there was only one thing he feared: divine wrath. In his eyes the illustrious beauty of Qulan eclipsed that of the Sky. Mightn't his love arouse Tengri's jealousy?

That was my dearest wish. But it had been so long since Tenggeri had answered my prayers that I despaired.

Chapter 49

In 1218 the royal *ordo* was pitched on the Kereyid's former pastures. And it was there, in the rich Orhon valley, that the Khan first showed an interest in the lands of the west, the kingdoms of the Moslems, and in Khwarezm in particular, from where the great caravans travelled to the Xixia's lands. He decided to become part of this trade, all the more so since his storehouse, the Jin empire, now gave him an excellent bargaining position.

Jochi told me that the Khan assembled a caravan laden with gold ingots, jade, ivory, Jin silk and wool spun from the hair of Yellow River white camels. He put three Moslems in charge and sent it to Mohammed, the Sultan of Khwarezm, with this message:

'I have brought the Jin to their knees and subdued all the tribes who live in the north of their empire. My country is a mine of silver and an ant-heap of warriors. I have no need to make a show of my power: to live in peace is all I could desire. I know the vast extent of your empire. You in the west, I in the east – that is how it should be. O my son, let us live in harmony and foster trade between our people and countries.'

Mohammed questioned the caravaneers about the Khan's achievements, then sent them back with an evasive response which committed him to nothing. A proud soul, what he wanted most was for Genghis Khan not to think of him as his son: he was no one's vassal.

Jochi told me that Staunch the Thickset, the Naiman prince we had defeated long before with his coward of a father, King Tai, was still alive.

He had been able to escape us over the western slopes of the Altay and, after crossing Dzungaria and Qarluq's fiefdom, the land of the Seven Rivers, he had taken refuge in the capital of the Black Khitai, Balasaghun. He had married the daughter of the

325

Khitai king and dethroned the old man soon after. Then he had made enemies first of the peasants by ravaging their harvests, then of the Moslems who were the majority in those countries. Sultan Mohammed had threatened him but not actually done anything.

When Staunch the Thickset crucified the imam of Hotan, we were about to embark on our campaign against the Jin. The Uighur, Qarluq and Almalik kings, former vassals of the Black Khitai, had come to the Khan's *quriltai* to ask for our protection. Genghis Khan had assured them that once the Jin had been brought to their knees, he would send an army. While we were taking Zhongdu, the King of Almalik had been caught out hunting by the Black Khitai, and Staunch the Thickset had killed him. As soon as the Khan returned to his native land, he put Jebe the Arrow in charge of the affair. He was to concentrate on the Naimans' armies alone – no pillaging, no rape – because our reputation in those parts, spread by caravaneers, was of bloody warriors, sowers of chaos and horror. Jebe the Arrow scrupulously respected his orders. He sped without stopping to Balasaghun which Staunch the Thickset had abandoned. The inhabitants barely had time to see our troops' impeccable order before they had set off again in pursuit. Loyal Jebe reached Kashgar. The fugitive had left the city the day before, driven out by the hostility of its Moslem population. He hoped to reach the Pamirs, but Jebe was always at his heels, ready to launch lightning strikes. Jebe left him no respite, decimated his rearguards, hunted him over the sheer passes, driving him ever higher until the Mongol wolves pinned him back against the foot of the giant glaciers. Jochi confirmed that Staunch the Thickset had been beheaded, and so had his troop of a thousand men methodically and unwaveringly.

Jebe returned by way of Kashgar and Aksu. At each stop, he proclaimed his victory and declared that by order of Genghis Khan whoever persecuted Moslems would suffer the same fate as Staunch the Thickset. This won him great renown.

On the banks of the Orhon, the Khan feared for a moment that these successes would go to the head of his loyal lieutenant. But when Jebe arrived, driving before him a thousand brown horses with white muzzles, the Khan's favourite colouring, he was reassured. 'There could never be a perfect double of Grey Ear which you loved so and which I killed with one of my arrows,' Jochi said kneeling, 'but I have brought you this herd, O my Khan, to help ease your pain.'

Genghis Khan had, in the meantime, sent another caravan to the Sultan of Khwarezm with five hundred camels carrying gold, silver, silk, fur, stones and leather. The caravaneers were again Moslems, but this time they were accompanied by an ambassador whose mission was to meet Mohammed. All the Mongol nobility had given him money to buy the most remarkable luxuries to be found in Khwarezm.

'The convoy reached Otrar,' Jochi told me, 'a frontier town on the banks of Syr-dar'ya. The governor shut his gates on us and when night fell, he stormed out to pillage the caravan and put our soldiers and ambassador to death.

'At this terrible news, the Khan shed tears of rage. The drums beat, the banners were raised, the arrow-messengers sped across the empire. Every man of fighting age was to assemble on the Altay immediately. Only the divisions engaged in the Jin lands were left to continue their mission.'

Genghis Khan paid heed, however, to his new counsellor, the sage Yelü Chucai. According to Jochi, this Jin subject was a remarkable man. A Khitan aristocrat by birth, he had faithfully served the Kings of Gold as advisor. He was lean and tall, almost a head taller than the Khan; he wore a long white beard and was adept in many arts, including astrology, divination and medicine. The Khan had brought him from Zhongdu along with a thousand craftsmen and scholars. Unlike his compatriots, Yelü Chucai wasn't afraid to confront the Khan and he refused to denigrate his former masters. Such loyalty pleased the Khan. So, when Yelü Chucai told him that it would serve no purpose destroying the Jin plains to turn them into vast grazing lands – it would be more useful leaving them to flourish so they could provide higher returns than the tribute already levied – Genghis Khan gave him his attention. And now the army was regrouping to avenge our ambassador, he was prepared, despite his fury, to give the Sultan of Khwarezm one last chance.

'Let's suppose,' he said to Yelü Chucai, 'that this governor massacred my people and pillaged my caravan without the Suttan's approval, as you say. Well then, I will ask Mohammed for the head of the guilty man. We'll see if he gives it to me and which of us is right.'

'Might as well ask a gelding to cough up the grass he's just eaten,' I said to Jochi.

'Wait, uncle; you won't believe what happened next. Two Mongols and a Moslem immediately set off for Bukhara where

Mohammed received them. When they asked for the head of the governor of Otrar, he put the Moslem to death and sent our men back with their heads shaved.'

The Sultan did not know the significance of his gesture or the consequences that would flow from it. Like teeth and nails, a man's hair is witness to his inner health and essential in the fight against spirits. Robbing him of it makes him vulnerable. By flouting this taboo, Mohammed had signed his death sentence.

When he saw the shaved skulls of his envoys, the Khan swore that he would never permit anyone to lay a hand on his ambasssadors again. He summoned the scribe responsible for the *yasak* and decreed that diplomats, of whatever provenance, were untouchable. Whoever disobeyed this law would be executed.

During the summer of 1219 the Mongol army gathered and organised itself by the upper reaches of the Black Irtysh, under the snowy peaks of the Altay range. It numbered two hundred thousand warriors and more than a million horses, more than any one chief could unite.

But still Genghis Khan was uneasy about venturing into the vast, hostile, distant lands of Khwarezm. He sought reinforcements from the Xixia, reminding the Celestial King of their agreement.

'You swore to be my right wing. The moment has come to put your forces in my hand.'

The Celestial King replied that his men couldn't undertake such a hazardous expedition. He offered to double their annual tribute instead and sent us a thousand white camels with manes like lions. The Khan sacrificed them to Tenggeri and vowed to tear out the tongues of the Xixia people because they did not keep their word.

He was furious at not being able to carry out the sentence immediately, but first he had to avenge the Sultan's insult. He sensed it would be a long campaign. Three years, five years, ten years? Well then, his revenge against the Xixia would have to wait that long. But what filled him with dread was being separated from Qulan. A moon away from her already seemed like an eternity to him. Would he see her again?

This fear must have shaken him to the core because he took two decisions, each as major in his eyes as the other: Qulan would go with him on his invasion of the Moslems' lands. Then he called the imperial family and his generals together to nominate his successor, the future khan.

His previous behaviour suggested he knew of the rivalry between Jochi and Chagatai, but he certainly hadn't imagined how much those two loathed each other. That assembly gave him the chance to guage the distance between his sons. It seemed like a gaping abyss, without sides or edge.

Chapter 50

Before the Khan's ravening wolves swept down on the west, Jochi came to my tent. With his expressionless eyes and long face, he did not look like someone about to fight in new lands. He observed custom and drank the milk of brotherhood, but his heart was elsewhere.

'The Khan appointed his successor at the last *quriltai*. Guess which of us four he chose?'

I thought for a moment then said, 'Ögödei!'

'You knew?'

'No, but if you had been chosen, you would have blazed with the light of ten suns when you entered my yurt. It couldn't have been Chagatai, otherwise your fury would have set the roofpoles shaking. It couldn't be Tolui either, because as the youngest son he is already the guardian of his father's hearth and his inheritance is assured. Only Ögödei was left. Of you four he is the least demonstrative but by far the wisest and he most resembles your father. He is like his reflection; he embraces all his plans. The Khan couldn't nominate you or Chagatai without risking the empire one day reverting to what it used to be, divided and dazed by quarrels. Ögödei will be able to maintain unity. And he will see to it that you and Chagatai keep your distance if you are still at each other's throats.'

'Stop dreaming!' Jochi blurted. 'The Khan wants us to fight side by side.'

'Tell me . . .'

When he had explained the purpose of the assembly, Genghis Khan had turned to Jochi who, like all present, was expecting to be recognised by the tradition of birthright. But suddenly Chagatai had broken the silence: 'He's your guest, not your eldest son! I am the eldest son and I don't want a bastard on the throne.'

Jochi had hurled himself at him and the Khan's attendants had had the greatest difficulty prising them apart.

'By what right do you claim the throne?' Jochi had shouted. 'What feats entitle you to think you could rule over us? You're no match for me with the bow or on the wrestling ground, let alone in battle. Let us fight and we will see once and for all who is worthy of this honour.'

Paralysed by the hatred of the two brothers and unable at first to make his voice heard, the khan had adjourned the council. Did he listen to the moderate Börte that night? However that may be, next day he had said, 'What use is it my building an empire if my sons cannot live in it in peace? When I married the woman who bore you, the Mongol tribes were like you two: they rose up against each other, pillaged each other, killed and weakened each other. I united them around my standard. They are a single block now, solider than the Altay. What example will you give them if you behave like this? When brats squabble on the threshold of a tent, the master's dogs become so worked up they end up tearing each other to pieces. To avoid the empire being split up, I have chosen Ögödei. When I am no more, he will be my voice, my will, the guarantor of the *yasak* and its continuity, the Khan. And you his brothers must obey him. Chagatai, let me never hear you speak about Jochi like that again. Both of you, I forbid you to belittle and harm each other. You will fight side by side and support each other shoulder to shoulder. If you disobey me, I will hamstring you.'

The two brothers had knelt.

I asked Jochi what he intended to do.

'Obey him, fight the enemy and prove that I am better than Chagatai. In the bitterest heart of battle, I want the Khan constantly to receive word of my exploits so that he will finally know I am worthy to be his eldest son.'

Jochi had described the Khan's great army to me with such fervour that I could not resist going to watch it from the heights of the Altay. I found a breathtaking spectacle. It stretched from the gently sloping foothills to the mists on the horizon and from east to west like an infinite border to the blue forests and the snowy peaks, barbed with lances and banners and budding with the grey felt of thousands of covered waggons. The gentle breeze carried the thousand and one smells of this ocean of manes and tufts, from which glinted the countless flashes of sharpened sabres.

I felt nostalgic observing that multitude. My chest heaved with pride because I could imagine how powerful a commander must feel with such an army before him. Its organisation and discipline were the work of the Khan, vivid proof of his foresight. They were founded on the ancestral decimal system: ten men formed a platoon, ten platoons formed a century, ten centuries a division and ten divisions a *tumen*, or ten thousand men. One man was placed in charge of every ten men; of the ten platoon leaders in a century, one was chosen to command the century; of these ten, one was a divisional commander, generally a nobleman, and of these ten lords, one commanded a *tumen*. All advanced as a single close-knit unit, each dependent on the other, and on this matter the *yasak* was definitive: no soldier could leave his group – whether of ten, a hundred or a thousand – even if it was to join another. Whoever broke this law was put to death, with the nine other members of his unit and its leader as well. If all ten in a platoon fled and their century did not catch them, the whole century was executed.

The Khan imposed this implacable system when the auxiliary troops were growing as numerous as the army's Mongol core. These troops were made up of subjugated enemy tribes, mercenaries, slaves – freed or not – volunteers and the forcibly conscripted. Among them were Tatar, Merkid, Khitan, Kereyid, Naiman, Oirat, Khirgiz, Önggüd, Xixia, Jin and Jurchen and even Moslems, the latter often being used as spies along the borders of Khwarezm. Each formation frequently answered to the authority of a Mongol. So in a century it wasn't rare to see ten Mongol lieutenants leading ninety staunch federates but, in this pyramidal structure, there was never a problem of race. All were treated the same, all obeyed the same, and all helped each other until death. The Jin slave and the blood prince were rewarded or punished in exactly the same way. Admittedly the divisional commanders were Mongol nobles, and those of the *tumen* were princes or the Khan's most loyal heroes, but their responsibilities did not give them the slightest leeway.

Pride may have welled up inside me, but very soon I felt a pang of bitter anguish as I screwed up my eyes to try and see the royal camp and Qulan's yurt in particular. She was there, Jochi had told me.

I had questioned him at length about what she felt for the Khan.

'When he stands before her, he is the sun and moon in turn. Sometimes he radiates light and sometimes he grows pale as if he is absorbing all her languour, crushed by the faintest of her sighs. But he recovers quick as a flash to raise her spirits with his laughter.'

Was she swayed by his affections? Did she love him?

Jochi couldn't say definitely. Or didn't want to.

'Either way, he devotes all his efforts to that outcome. He spoils her: she's covered with jewels and every day sees her adorned with new finery. Her drinking cups, pitchers and trays are damascened with gold and silver and if she gets bored, she can run her fingers through basins of emeralds, amethysts and rubies. Her roofpoles are made of ebony and encrusted with mother of pearl. In the cold season, her yurt is covered with three layers of white felt and its ropes plaited with the hair of the Khan's brown horses. The most beautiful sable and ermine winter furs will line her walls and four tiger-skins backed with Karakul lamb's wool will caress her feet. My father has also given her a thousand piebald mares and nine grey mares with pink skin, which at dawn or dusk or when they are bathing look like water lilies.'

As he listed all these splendours, my eyes travelled around the walls of my yurt. The felt walls were grey, the wattle cracked and stained yellow by mutton suet. The beaten-earth floor was black with ash. There was nothing bright, except perhaps the silver studs of my saddle and harness, the speckled or striped hides that lined my sweat flaps, the cruppers set with faded blue turquoises. There were my weapons, the quivers and sheaths of tooled leather; but none of that charmed a woman . . .

Seeing my downcast expression, Jochi had said, 'She hasn't forgotten you, Uncle.'

'Have you talked to her?'

'At the first hunt, when the Khan entered the melee to kill a tiger to adorn her yurt. Knowing we were out of earshot, she asked after you. I told her your grief, the pounding of your heart, the foundering of your life since she left your side.'

'What did she say?'

'Despite the Khan's love and her position, the envy of any woman, there isn't a day or night when she doesn't think of you, doesn't see your face. Your kneecap never leaves her side. Just before dawn, she brings it to her lips. Here! She gave me this for you.'

I had taken the lock of hair he handed me and unfolded it. A little clay horse hung from the end, swaying gently: it was as broad as three fingers and so detailed, it seemed to have been sculpted with a needle. The plaited lock of hair represented the horse's mane and tail, and then ran through a tiny loop on the withers. As I sniffed it, Qulan's milky fragrance had filled my nostrils.

Now I hoped to catch sight of her on the Altay's foothills. The army stretched as far as the eye could see and I longed to slip into it secretly. Not that the fighting and the sight of blood flowing like a river would have entertained me. I just wanted to see her, once, only once more, then die.

Chapter 51

As summer drew to a close Jebe the Arrow was the first to launch his troops. The two *tumen* of Jochi and Chagatai followed; then, in the next wave, those of the Khan, Ögödei and Tolui. Next Belgütei, Kubilai, Jelme and Sübetei set off, the formation growing ever broader like geese in flight. By the time the rearguard struck camp five days later with the supply waggons, flocks and reserve horses, Jebe was already entering the country of the Seven Rivers, the Qarluq's fiefdom and the army's agreed rallying point.

At the head of their armies, Arslan and the Prince of Almalik warmly greeted our general, who had avenged them by hunting down Staunch the Thickset. A few days later the Uighur sovereign arrived at the head of ten thousand men.

Mohammed, the Sultan of Khwarezm, had the advantage of numbers but he had scattered part of his forces along the Syr-Dar'ya river, as far as the Fergana valley, to warn of any attack from that direction. His mind must have been clouded with unease because he had distributed the bulk of his troops amongst his fortified cities, Samarkand, Bukhara, Urgench or, further south, Merv. Had he walled up his forces because he had heard of our invincibility on open ground?

I was the former Keeper of the Khan's Horse and I knew of only one way to make him retreat: force his cavalry onto their hindlegs by burning all the steppes between the mountains and the deserts. But just as he had shrugged off Genghis Khan's threats, so Mohammed did not think to prepare. Anyway, by then it was too late. One morning the Mongol troops fanned out in front of Otrar, the culprit.

The town governor who was responsible for our ambassador's death chose not to surrender: he thought he could save his skin by fighting. The siege lasted two moons.

Meanwhile the contingents led by Jochi and Chagatai moved

down the Syr-Dar'ya and took the citadels of Sighnaq and Jand. Other *tumen* drove upstream and laid siege to the frontier towns. The Khan penetrated to the heart of the Khwarezmian kingdom by skirting the Desert of the Red Sands. In the first moon of the Year of the Dragon he took up position in front of the high ramparts of Bukhara. Unusually for those parts, its citadel was outside the city and itself protected by walls.

Otrar fell and was razed to the ground. Its governor was delivered bound hand and foot to Genghis Khan. The Khan's bodyguard pinned him down as silver was melted over a fire, then the molten metal was poured in his ears and his eyes. This was how he died.

But our ambassador was still not fully avenged. Mohammed had sanctioned the crime, and had committed three others himself: one against the person of our Moslem ambassador, and two by laying hands on our envoys. He had humiliated us – that was the most serious of his crimes. Genghis Khan had sworn before Tenggeri that he would make him regret his acts.

'We will hang so many Khwarezmian heads from our saddles that that fool Mohammed will die of terror when we appear before him.'

Now the assault on Bukhara could begin.

It lasted three days; then the town's garrison of twenty thousand men waited for darkness before breaking through our lines and fleeing. Bukhara's citizens made no attempt to fight. The Khan forced them to dismantle their own walls to fill in the moat of the citadel in which half a division of Turkish mercenaries were holding out and shooting from the ramparts at those they should have been protecting. When the approach works were finished, catapults and battering rams were wheeled into position by the Bukharians, who were themselves driven forward by our whips. The citadel's walls were blown apart, its heavy gates ripped open and by then the Turkish garrison may have wanted to surrender, but it no longer had the chance: we massacred them all and took possession of the town, stripping its houses, palaces and mosques, killing any inhabitants we found, ransacking their coffers and carrying off their carpets, jewels, grain and wine.

The looting lasted seven days and Bukhara burned in a great conflagration. Following the course of the Zeravshan, Genghis Khan then marched on Samarkand. Sated with the women they'd raped and the riches they'd accumulated, his battalions flanked the winding columns of Bukhara's survivors.

From the north-east three other *tumen* joined the Khan, driving before them captives bent double with fear and pain. The Mongols had divided them into groups of ten. If one of them could not keep up, all ten were killed. Twenty thousand had been put to death on their journey south.

When the Khan reached Samarkand in the Moon of the Cuckoo's Dance, all the prisoners were dressed in furs, like us, and one out of every group of ten was given a Mongol standard.

Mohammed had fled. The citadel was held by his uncle with fifty thousand Turks. Samarkand's inhabitants formed militias and came out of the city to fight. Our troops drew them towards the river where the Khan's, Tolui's and Ögödei's *tumen* were waiting. Sabring those callow infantrymen was child's play. In less than a day, the emerald gardens were red with blood. Immediately the Khan invested the suburbs and the prisoners were sent to attack the city walls. Mohammed's uncle did not wait for them to be stormed but came out to surrender, as did his Turkish mercenaries, who hoped we would treat them as compatriots. They misjudged Genghis Khan and his contempt for cowards. Their women were raped, their children's throats were slit, then they followed. Just as at Bukhara, the city's inhabitants were orphaned by the loss of their garrison and they resigned themselves to abandoning their homes.

Meanwhile the contingents led by Jochi and Chagatai were bogged down under the ramparts of Urgench, the capital of Khwarezm. According to the reports regularly reaching the Khan, the delay was due to the poor relations between his two eldest sons.

Instead of destroying Urgench, Jochi was trying to negotiate, since he knew he would receive it as his dependency an edict of his father's had bequeathed all land conquered west of the Red Sands to him. Chagatai, on the other hand, naturally wanted to raze it to the ground. A river ran through the capital, so the two brothers agreed to occupy a bank each. This partition proved disastrous. Three thousand Mongols were swept away by the river as they tried to gain a foothold on the city's main bridge. In a fury, Genghis Khan immediately sent Ögödei at the head of reinforcements to reconcile his sons, overthrow Urgench and bring the two quarrelling princes back before their father.

Unlike Bukhara and Samarkand, Urgench put up a valiant

defence. So the three brothers concerted their efforts. Since the countryside provided no stones for catapults, they cut down the mulberry trees of the suburbs to make missiles. Then the prisoners, dead or wounded, were fired over the ramparts. Finally cauldrons of burning naphtha were launched behind the bastions. Only a few of the town's quarters were still untouched by flames, when the inhabitants begged to reconsider Jochi's offer. But, furious to see the furnace his bequest had become, he first separated the craftsmen, women and children who were fit to enter service, then put the rest to the sword, breached the river's dams and, after a yearlong siege, completely destroyed the town.

Genghis Khan spent the summer of 1220 south of Samarkand in the southern oases of Transoxiana. Jebe and Sübetei didn't rest: their mission was to hunt the Sultan.

'Wherever he goes, wherever he hides,' the Khan had roared, 'rout him out. Give him no respite. Wear him down, devastate any country that gives him refuge; I want him to be like a swallow over the ocean that grows tired and has no perch on which to alight.'

So the two valiant officers embarked on a phenomenal sweep through the lands of the west, beginning with Khorasan and Iraq-'Ajemi, the great vassals of the Khwarezmian empire. At every fortress, every oasis, they promulgated the Khan's message: 'Divine Tenggeri has given me for empire the lands that extend to the ocean, from East to West. Whoever shall submit shall be spared. The rest shall perish, and their wives and children with them.'

When the governor of Tüs met this threat with contempt, the Mongols entered his town and pillaged it. The next day they were in sight of Neyshabur, which Mohammed had just left. Their prey was within reach of their scimitars, yet he managed to draw them on to Rasht on the south-western shores of the Caspian. As they followed in pursuit, they turned and massacred the inhabitants of Damghan, Semnan, Amol and Shahr Rey.

Jebe and Sübetei pressed so hard on the Sultan's heels that he had no time to wait for the great powerful army raised for him by his Persian vassals. At Qazwin he met up with one of his sons, who had mustered a force of thirty thousand. His plan was to make for Baghdad, but he was taken by suprise at Qarun and only escaped us by a miracle. For a while we lost his track – the runaway had abruptly turned and headed back to the Caspian – but it was picked up again at Shahr Rey. He crossed the mountains of Mazenderan, losing his horse under him, and then undertook his final journey, to the island of Abeskum. On its shore he fell to the ground, his body riddled with our arrows. And that is where he died, after being hunted for nine moons.

Once our horses were fat again, the Khan marched on Balkh, the Sultan's former lair where he had hidden behind walls of beaten earth. On the way he destroyed the city of Termez. Balkh and Taleqan followed.

He sent his youngest son, Tolui, one of his sons-in-law, Toguchar, and a force of one hundred thousand Mongols, allies and prisoners to confirm Khorasan's willingness to submit. But despite the orders of Jebe and Sübetei, who had spoken in the name of Genghis Khan, the son of Heaven, the towns of Nessa, Neyshabur, Sebzevar and Herat resisted, along with lesser fortified towns in the vicinity.

The ensuring slaughter was absolute, methodical and pitiless. At Neyshabur, the Khan's son-in-law was killed. Tolui beheaded all the corpses. Every living thing – newborns, the old, animals – was massacred. Then he built pyramids of skulls so high that they could be seen two days' ride away and so nauseating that their stench reached the desert of the Black Sands.

When Chagatai and Ögödei presented themselves at the royal *ordo*, their father at first refused to receive them. Not only had they returned without Jochi, whom he blamed for the siege of Urgench lasting so long; but they had also divided up the town's booty amongst themselves, without setting aside a share for the Khan. After three days' disgrace, they were permitted to appear before the imperial tent. The Khan reprimanded them so severely that they swore never to deceive him again or they would of their own accord stretch out their arms for him to cut them off. They gave him all their booty and offered to bring back Jochi, by force if necessary. Genghis Khan said they'd be better occupied staying where they were, earning his forgiveness. Then the felt curtains of his tent fell.

Next day two of the Khan's messengers set off in the direction taken by Jochi's troops towards the Aral Sea. The order they carried was categorical: immediate return.

But Jochi flouted his father's command and kept galloping like a madman across the Kipchak plains north of the Caspian where he thought the Khan's voice would not reach. He was not running away; he was simply heading straight for the steppe, bareheaded, his standard trained at the azure sky, to subjugate the nomad tribes who ply that ocean of grass. Hadn't the Khan promised him the west of his empire? So, he would take all the lands from the north wind to the setting sun. And thus, of the Khan's four sons, gain the greatest khanate. For such insubordination the *yasak* did not decree thirty-six punishments, but only one: death!

Chapter 52

I was on the summit of the Turtledove's Beak, the smallest of the Seven Hills, patiently waiting for a magician to pass. Such a man couldn't slip by unnoticed. Temüge had asked me to fall in with him and see he didn't spin out his journey. The Khan's youngest son, the guardian of Mongolia, was probably afraid he'd vanish.

What was there about this Jin that made Genghis Khan, who was a hundred days' ride away in the thick of his conquests, so impatient to see him?

His name was Chang Chun and by repute he knew the secret of the elixir that confers immortality: perhaps this explained the Khan's interest in receiving him at the other end of the world. Yelü Chucai, the Khan's Khitan counsellor, had told him of the merits of this Taoist monk whom the Kings of Gold had long tried to make a part of their court.

Temüge had planned on sending him with a troop of captured princesses bound for the Khan's pleasures, but Chang Chun had refused to travel in such company.

At my feet the Kerulen flowed past the hill's rounded beak and it wasn't long before the sage's convoy was reflected in its waters. He was very old, as lean as a creeper and so light that his mount seemed to be riderless. He was accompanied by twenty Mongols and another, much younger, Jin, who was wriggling around so much in the saddle his arse seemed in pain.

They were too far away for me to be able to see their faces. I looked to the east. There was Temulun's statue, a black, upright shadow amongst the parched grass. Beyond it I could see the grey stones timidly rising up from the moss-covered ground, which was still a brilliant green despite the scorching heat. This ghost of a city was one of Börte's follies. 'Outside our empire,' she had exclaimed one day, 'the first wives of kings have their own cities. Well, my womb has carried the Kha Khan's offspring. Is it decreed that the steppe should not become my palace?'

The Khan had thought it a preposterous whim. But how could he quash it, when he was constantly on the move with his preparations to conquer Khwarezm and when he was taking one of his favourites with him for the first time? Börte ordered that the work begin. Three parallel streets started mongst the mossy banks of the sulphur-tasting spring and ran towards the amber vein of the Kerulen. On each side, low square walls stood two cubits high as bases for yurts. At each corner, great stone tortoises, part of the booty taken from the Jin, stretched their open mouths out over paved gutters. Pillars sculptured with hunting scenes and the emblems of the Mongol tribes rose from the middle of their backs. These pillars would support the roofs and ensure that the rain drained off through the tortoises' mouths. No doubt about it: this town was a woman's caprice. I wheeled my horse to keep up with the Khan's esteemed guest.

Dark forebodings weighed on me as I rode along, troubling images of Börte's city. I didn't like the scars they left in the earth. Apart from the rocks that naturally burst from the earth's innards, I associated stonework with souls' departing. The gravestone of Temulun, for instance, or those of the many Turks buried on our lands. The visible parts of these boneyards always gave me a feeling of anguish, which was even more painful because their slender silhouettes had something both unfinished and definitive about them. Börte's idea of a town gave off exactly the same stench of dereliction, sudden paralysis, fragmentation, collapse, ending . . .

The works would resume when the royal *ordo* returned. Yet something was going to waste away and destroy itself . . . I couldn't have said what.

After two days' march, as I was riding up the Tula valley, I met a detachment which had come from the the foothills of the Altay to give me a message from Börte: 'Faithful companion, shed your leaden grief for my sake and gird on your golden eagle's wings. You alone can save the most precious thing in the world to me, my own lifeblood. Be quick, my friend!'

Did this appeal have something to do with the Jin's journey? Was there some link the Khan had forged from Khwarezm? I had no idea, but knowing Börte's legendary composure, I didn't doubt its urgency and headed for the setting sun at breakneck speed.

Börte's silhouette had grown rounder with age. Her cheeks were flushed like two ripe figs and from the corner of her lips two veined furrows framed her chin. No doubt her headdress hid some grey hairs as well, but her emerald-green eyes spangled with gold flecks were as brilliant as ever, blunting the chisel of time. Her beauty was unchanged, even by her anguish.

'Bo'urchu, my friend, you are all I have to save him; all our other companions are far away.'

'Save him?'

'Jochi. He remains deaf to the Emperor's summons. Caravaneers and arrow-messengers have warned me: my husband is furious; he has sworn to trap him under the felt and trample his body to death. Find him before the Khan's hordes. He will listen to you . . .'

'He might, but his father?'

'Calm yourself. Genghis Khan knows the worth of his men. You are the only one who would give your all for his life.'

'Have you forgotten that he wanted to kill me, that he forsook me and left me to slink home like a dog sniffing its own vomit?'

'No, and he even less than me . . .'

'Stop, my queen! Ask me what you want. You do not need to convince me of what I cannot believe.'

'Listen, Bo'urchu. Of his faithful you are the one who knows him best.'

'I thought so. My reclusive life suggests otherwise.'

'Since Mother Hö'elün died, he has changed.'

'Since he has been emperor.'

'Only I know his torment. Even Qulan has no inkling. And I assure you that he suffers for what he has done. He knows all too well his injustice, his betrayal, his inability to be as unbending towards himself as he is towards others. But there, that is the truth of it! He betrayed his *yasak* for a woman and so lost his best companion . . . This is his punishment. He has too much pride to show you his sadness, but his favourite's face constantly reminds him of his weakness.'

As I stood up she added, 'He'd better not dare touch Jochi, because if he does I'll tear off with my bare hands the head of that woman who makes his spin.'

This further argument made me hurry to fill a sack of

343

provisions and set off west with the Taoist monk as my riding companion.

Chang Chun spoke little and always softly and concisely. He was a good man and although physically he was a frail, ethereal figure, he emanated a powerful aura of serenity. Before parting company in the famed orchards of Almalik, I asked him what he expected of his meeting with the Khan.

'I am a simple man from the mountains,' he replied. 'So I never expect a great deal: to remain under the great square that has no corners, to listen to the voice that utters no words, to look at the great form that has no shape and let myself be carried by the wind ... I think your master expects much more than me.'

'And what future do you see for him?'

'A short one, if he does take better care of himself.'

'So why this long journey?'

'One cannot enter a yurt with just one foot.'

Chapter 53

Otrar, the guilty city, was nothing but a mass of dust and rubble. As I followed the river to the Aral Sea, for landmarks I had demolished fortresses on one side and white pyramids of skulls on the other; and both teemed with rats. Sometimes I'd come across wretches in rags, walking skeletons with hollowed-out eye sockets. As I passed they'd huddle together and fall to their knees, whimpering, their foreheads pressed to the ground as they awaited death. I was alone and old, but there was no doubt that they saw a thousand Mongols at my shoulder.

I skirted the sea by the north. For days I saw nothing apart from herds of wild donkeys galloping in the shimmering light across the barren plains. I hadn't eaten for ten days until at last, when the Moon of the Rutting Antelope was full, I met one of our patrols. They guided me for five more days until we reached the banks of a river where Jochi's camp was pitched.

Near the prince's tent a woman's body was impaled on a waggon shaft. The sharpened point had ruptured her breastbone and her broken, heavy silver and amber necklaces hung sadly among her sticky hair. Perched on her rump, which had turned blue, three crows gaily pecked at her flesh.

Jochi's yurt bore the marks of illness. I was announced. Three shamans came out and I lifted up the felt doorflap. Little Crumb was lying naked on his bed, his eyelids edged with darkness, his face running with sweat, a pallid smile on his parched lips.

A bitch-bark dressing covered his crutch. He spoke in a hushed voice and his breath felt as hot as a cauldron on a fire.

'I've been on the other side of the Caspian Sea, in the kingdom of the Alans,' he said. 'It's not a sea; it's a lake, vast. Compared to it Lake Ocean is just a drop of water. I pushed the Alans back to the mountains that border their lands.'

'Did one of their arrows wound you?'

'No, mine was broken by one of their women. That bitch impaled outside is a princess I captured in the mountains and took by force. Look what she had hidden in her jade column.'

He showed me a small iron object, a sort of tube with tiny spikes at the end.

'The pain was terrible. It couldn't have been worse if a ferret had bitten me.'

'When did this happen?'

'Three days ago. Now my sex is like the head of a flayed camel. Pus wells out of it like water from a spring. One of my prisoners was a Moslem versed in the art of medicine. He told me that my only chance was to have my stem and bulbs cut off. I had his throat slit.'

He caught me by the sleeve and made me promise to kill the three shamans treating him if he did not recover. I reassured him and asked why he didn't reply to his father's messages.

'When I've conquered the lands to the north and west of the Caspian, I will send him word. Not before. But I will never return to his side. There are large grasslands on the upper reaches of these rivers, like these where we grew up. I want to establish my *ordo* here in order to campaign against the country called Great Bulgaria and beyond, amongst the peoples that ride horses as broad as elephants. They have great stores of gold, precious metals, furs and many other treasures. I will give them all to him.'

Jochi told me of Mohammed's death. Our troops then had no more reason to stay in Khwarezm. Yet the fighting had continued on all fronts. Jebe and Sübetei had pursued reconnaissance raids south of the Caspian. The governor of Tabriz, the capital of Azerbaijan, paid them a handsome tribute. Then they had marched on Tiflis, the capital of the Christian kingdom of Georgia. Faking a headlong retreat before King Giorgi III, they had exhausted his heavily armoured horses, and then suddenly turned about on a carefully chosen patch of steppe and decimated his armies. In the spring of the Year of the Snake (1221), they were in Persia again, at the westernmost corner of the former Khwarezmian empire. The cities of Maraga and Hamadan fell, their inhabitants, apart from a few craftsmen, were slain and everything that could not be taken was burnt. In the Moon of the Rutting Argali, when I had just parted company with the monk Chang Chun at Almalik, the Khan's two loyal generals had returned to Georgia, crossed the Caucasus Mountains and sowed panic amongst the Alans. While I was with Jochi, they were barely ten days' march from us.

For his part, Genghis Khan had spent the summer in the mountains of Bactria, where it was cooler, and in the autumn he had moved southward towards the high mountain barrier of the Hindu Kush. Jalal al-Din, one of Mohammed's heirs, had taken refuge in these mountains and by constant ambushes, had managed to surprise our scattered squadrons.

Our aim was to capture the Bamiyan valley, a haven of peace and plenty surrounded by forbidding cliffs and defended by a citadel reputed to be impregnable. Mütügen, Chagatai's second son, was killed by an arrow in a skirmish. The Khan particularly loved this grandson. Demented with rage, he ordered the attack. The Mongols scaled the rocks and walls like snakes and the Khan led the way, without even a helmet. Our losses were heavy, but once we had stormed the fortress, no one was spared in the massacre. The ruins we left behind became known as the 'Town of Sighs'.

When the destruction was complete, the Khan summoned Chagatai to his side. He accused him of not being as obedient as he used to be. Chagatai couldn't understand why his father was so angry. He knelt at his feet and swore that he would rather die than disobey him.

'Well then, I forbid you to cry,' the Khan said.

'If a single tear appears at the corner of my eye, kill me!'

Genghis Khan stared fixedly at Chagatai and when he was sure that he wouldn't falter, he told him of his son's death.

'Mütügen is no more. A Moslem arrow carried him off.'

Chagatai's jaw clenched so tight everyone present could hear the screech of his grinding teeth, as if they were going to shatter one by one. But still he mastered his grief.

The next day Genghis Khan marched on Ghazni, a fortress built on a spur of rock where Jalal al-Din had managed to rally 70,000 soldiers, mainly Turkish and Afghan mercenaries. Chagatai was at the head of the right wing, Tolui the left wing, and their horses were smeared with enemy blood. But the vanguard led by Shigi, one of Mother Hö'elün's adopted sons, was defeated by the Moslem mercenaries. For the first time Mongols retreated in complete disorder. Outnumbered and surrounded, they were riddled with arrows, sabred or driven over precipices into gullies. Any who fell into the mercenaries' hands alive were tortured: they were castrated, their chests and backs flayed; their eyelids and lips were cut off and their eardrums shattered, and then they were buried up to their necks.

When he arrived, Genghis Khan listened to Shigi's explanation of the battle and declared him responsible for the defeat. But he was lenient, saying that it would serve him as a lesson.

Jalal al-Din was no longer on the site of his victory. A large part of his troops had abandoned him after a misunderstanding between Afghans and Turks. We immediately gave chase; by forced march our army caught him up two days later as he was preparing to cross the River Indus.

Genghis Khan deployed his platoons and attacked at day-break. He had ordered that the Moslem prince should be spared. The fighting raged until midday. Driven back against the cliffs of the Indus, Jalal al-Din had only 500 men left. Making a last furious charge, he jumped his horse into the turbulent, yellow river, with his shield on his back and a handful of faithful at his heels. The Mongols wanted to follow suit, but the Khan, full of admiration for the Moslem's valour, ordered them to leave him be. Then he turned back, having first destroyed Ghazni. Jalal al-Din's brothers had their throats slit and his mother was deported to Mongolia along with thousands of artisans.

The Khan sent his army to Herat, Balkh and Merv, where our Moslem prefects had been killed and rebellion was brewing. These towns were visited by a second and more complete devastation. For a whole moon, everything was systematically destroyed: the dykes were torn up, the canals filled with silt, the orchards and crops burnt, the trees sawn down. Rivers flowed red with the blood of the victims. Then the winds and the sandstorms, which no longer met any obstacle, covered what had once been the gardens and oases of Khorasan and Bactria.

More than forty days' march from there Jochi was dying. His strength failed day by day, draining away like water from a forest after a storm. My friend was delirious, weeping with rage and weaker than a newborn. Each day we bled a horse to sustain him, but he did not improve.

He wanted me to take command of his army and for his sake effect the conquest of Great Bulgaria. When his skin became the colour of a stagnant marsh and his spirit began to curl out of his parched, open mouth, I went to meet Jebe and Sübetei on the

Kipchak steppes. I had no difficulty persuading them to carry out Jochi's plans. The Khan must have known the disastrous state of his eldest son's health.

We rode as far as a city called Kiev, which in Turkish means 'The Forbidden Fortress'. From there we sent envoys to the Russian princes whom we never saw again. The Prince of Kiev, supported by those of Chernigov and Galich, sallied out of the city at the head of 80,000 men. After skirmishing, the Mongols fell back to the south, drawing the Russians after them. The pursuit lasted nine days. On the morning of the tenth day, Jebe and Sübetei's columns spun around to face the enemy, their dark squares arrayed for battle across the whole steppe. Shoulder to shoulder with them stood the *tumen* of Genghis Khan's grandchildren: Guyuk, Ögödei's eldest son, Batu, Jochi's second son, Mochi, Chagatai's eldest son, and lastly Orda, at the head of his father Jochi's *tumen*. The prince of Galich, backed up by the Kipchak auxiliaries, did not wait for the Princes of Kiev and Chernigov to attack. We hewed his men to pieces, then we routed the infantry and Prince Chernigov's heavy cavalry which were exhausted by their ride. The Prince of Kiev barricaded himself in his fortified camp. He offered to pay a sizeable tribute in return for peace. His offer was accepted. When he stood before us, we suffocated him and all his people to avenge the death of our envoys. I took women, slaves, horses, cows, furs, gold, silver and chests full of gems and precious objects. I counted a thousand waggons of treasure, as many of women, ten times more of slaves and thirty princesses. All of it was destined for Jochi.

When we reached his *ordo*, black felt covered his yurt. He had been dead for two moons and his bones were already showing through his rotting flesh.

The three shamans responsible for his health were put to death.

An enclosure was erected around Little Crumb's tent, with stone pillars, and canvas-and-felt walls held in place by hemp ropes. In his honour a thousand horses were sacrificed, a thousand oxen, bulls and cows, flocks of goats and sheep and camels. They were arranged in the sepulchre, beside the slaves and princesses and weapons and tents and treasures. A thousand Mongols in armour and on horseback accompanied them. Then the sepulchre was covered with earth. A hundred guardians were entrusted with protecting this bare hill in the middle of the grassy steppe.

When dusk spread out its purple veil, the funeral laments rose up and one could hear the sobs in every voice before they were snatched away by the breeze,

> I am Jochi, Genghis's eldest,
> Famed for my Bravery,
> I have lived on earth,
> Now I am no more
> All is as it should be.

High up in the sky pelicans glided in spirals and then seemed to vanish, snatched away by the great void.

Messengers informed us that the Emperor was in Samarkand and had ordered the withdrawal of all his troops. He planned to conclude the campaign with a series of great hunts.

In Jochi's name I informed him that his son would join him on the way. I dreaded seeing him again, as the bearer of such tragic news. I would see his soul and I sensed that that would be a terrible thing.

Chapter 54

The sunshine flashed on the snow-capped peaks on the horizon leaving us blinking and screwing up our eyes in its brilliant, impeccable light. From the northern banks of the Aral Sea to those of the River Ural, Jochi's twenty thousand men had driven the game towards the Steppes of Hunger. Now to the south-east, between the Talas and Chu rivers, the Khan was waiting for the kill. A moon previously, his elite battalions and army near Chimkent had finished off the game Ögödei and Chagatai had driven from Bukhara where they had spent the winter hunting.

Jochi's scouts had gone ahead to tell the Khan that his eldest son was beating the game towards him, and that the duels to come promised many pleasures.

After two moons' march, we finally saw the first tents and, in the distance, riders bent forward over their mounts' necks, *ourgas* in hand, chasing at the heels of the scattered herds. Then we crossed the packed camps of Turkish and Moslem prisoners brought back by Sübetei and Jebe, to which we added our own. Their faces were as varied as they were exhausted. We brought Bashkirs, Kipchaks, Qangli and Bulgars, but also great numbers of Russians, Georgians, Orosud, Alans, Sergesud, Magyars and Sasud.

Two days' trek through the encampments was needed to reach the royal *ordo*. On horseback or squatting on their heels, the thousands of soldiers were bartering the spoils of their campaigns.

One of their commanders told me that our drive had been exceptional. The game was so plentiful and broken with tiredness that they only had to lean down from their horses to catch them with their bare hands and many of the animals had been set free. He also told me about the hunting accident the Khan had suffered the day before in the mountains. A wounded bear had charged him, and although the animal hadn't had a chance to get close to him before it was riddled with arrows and lances, the Khan had fallen heavily and was still in pain.

I had to leave my horse and continue on foot since horses were now barred from the royal *ordo*.

Sitting crosslegged on a broad gold throne with a purple step, Genghis Khan was waiting for me. At his side, as pale and light as a dove in full sunshine, sat Qulan.

The Son of Heaven greeted me: 'I am happy to see you, Bo'urchu.'

Almost as pale as his favourite, his moustache and goatee were completely white, but his eyes still blazed as they always had done, fierce enough to paralyse the boldest hearts.

'I heard of my khan's fall. Should I be worried?'

'My pride hurts more than my bones. The Taoist monk you rode with as far as Almalik told me that it is a sign from Heaven to remind me of my age, and that I would do better to leave the pleasures of the hunt to others.'

'You can open a blind man's eyes, but he won't see for all that.'

'That's just the answer I gave him,' he said, amused.

Then he did me the great honour of presenting the drinking cup to me before inviting me to sit at his side for the serving of the meat.

On a low table a few paces from him baskets of melons, apricots, dates, peaches and other fruits from those sun-drenched, well-watered parts were attracting clouds of wasps. Despite the speed with which two young slaves squashed the insects in their fists, they couldn't drive away the swarm. Great silver trays of mutton were circulated one after the other and the cup-bearer poured the fermented milk. The Khan carved himself and gave me the choicest bits, including a perfect fatty tail. The princes and I ate in silence under the Khan's impassive gaze. There was neither reproach nor benevolence in his eyes. I sneaked a glance at Qulan, since I sensed that she was surreptitiously watching me as well. Despite the whiteness of her complexion, she seemed more resplendent than ever and the beating of my heart left me short of breath.

Genghis Khan laboriously got to his feet and returned to his yurt, followed by his favourite. But just before she disappeared, she gave me a look in which I caught a glimpse, brief as a lightning flash, of a cornered tear.

When the sun had fallen behind the crests, the Emperor asked to see me. As he lay on his couch, staring at the sky, he asked, 'Why isn't Jochi with you?'

'He is dead.'

'Leave me!'

And in the ensuing silence, I heard the silk fabric rip between his fingers.

I rode back up the Chu valley in search of the great lake close to the river's source. An old man from Balasaghun had sworn that this was the season when it was visited by colonies of black swans, whose flesh tasted like chestnuts. I had not reached the pass that led through the mountains before a squad led by Jelme caught me up.

'Don't stray too far,' the faithful general advised me. 'The Khan wishes to see you again before you leave.'

'What does he want of me?'

'I don't know.'

'There he is again, looping his *ourga* round my neck!'

'Come now, Bo'urchu, don't be as suspicious as a horse that's just been gelded.'

'That's just it; scars on a body are a better writing than ink on parchment. You can't scratch them out or forget them.'

'I know that, my friend, but look at that rock over there that looks like a bending woman. Beyond it, a short walk for an ambling horse, is a forest of mulberries. And under those branches with their black and gold fruit is the Khan's favourite. Her surprise would be great and all her hopes fulfilled if she were to find you there.'

The warrior broke into a broad smile, pulled his horse around and rode away, singing at the top of his voice,

The scatterbrain may lose his head
Oh that's nothing compared to the lover
He forgets if he's alive or dead
Oh if his balls are his or another's.

At the place he'd pointed to the river split and meandered by different channels through thickets buzzing with insects. On the opposite bank a mulberry wood cast its shade over tall, thin grass. She was there among the bluish stalks, surrounded by her subjects like a flower in the midst of nettles.

She saw me and called for her horse. An umbrella-bearer

accompanied her, trying to keep up with her mount's hurried step, but unable to shield her from the sun.

I stared at her and marvelled. She was in the prime of life now, staggeringly beautiful, the perfect symmetry of her face tenderly emphasised by a white silk chin strap and two plaits coiled either side of her neck.

'I have waited for this moment so long,' she said, 'that my head is spinning.'

'Can't we be alone?' I asked, looking at the umbrella-bearer.

'You can talk freely; he is deaf.'

'Is he blind as well?'

'No, but if he dares look at me I can order him to be beheaded.'

'Well let's be rid of him immediately, because I can see in his eyes that they have already rested on you and that no punishment will deter him.'

The slave was dismissed.

Our horses pushed on into the shade, the grass up to their shoulders. Thrushes scattered before our approach, and a jay, chased by a pair of warblers, called out as it disappeared into the branches.

'I thought I'd never cry as much as the day the Khan separated us. But that was nothing . . . The night when I was stripped, tasted, possessed, becoming his treasure for ever, as he loves to tell me over and over, my sobs grew heavier. Since then my body has been made of tears. And they can never be staunched.'

She wanted me to speak. I shook my head. I was incapable, paralysed, my palms damp, my temples on fire, my stomach knotted as tight as sinew around an arrow. I struggled, fearing I'd break the spell . . . I had no words to express the chaos of my heart.

'O Bo'urchu . . . there hasn't been a single hill, thicket or river where I haven't hoped to see you. On the most desolate plains, the barrenest deserts, I scanned the capricious mirages that every time seemed to be dancing around your silhouette. But no matter how I searched, became drunk with hope and clutched at my bed in the darkness, I could not cling on to you. So then I had to mould my desires so as to imagine you always at my side. A rider in the distance, a breath, a cloud, a rock – everything was a pretext to conjure you up. In the Khan's eyes, under his touch, it was your face watching me, your caresses shaking me, and carrying me off under the starlit sky, because that was my most secret dream. So, Bo'urchu, like this, through all the marvels and horrors. I have loved you.'

Hadn't she adored Genghis Khan too? Be quiet, quiet, I said to myself; fight against your pride: hasn't your love just declared herself, when you're so old with your hair already white and despite all your bitterness you've never been able to resist the Khan either?

From around her neck she took the amulet which held my kneecap and brought it tenderly to her lips. In turn I opened my shirt and took out of my pocket the white tiger-skin cap with the purple tassel which she had given me on the banks of Lake Ocean, and the little horse woven into the lock of her hair which she had sent to me by Jochi.

She told me that she knew where to find me, that she was certain that one day we would be together for ever. Then she pulled up her mount's head and rode through the amber shadows to rejoin her umbrella-bearer.

I stayed there, following her with my eyes. Behind her the grass slowly sprang back upright, erasing the temporary path, and in the place where she had been a spider began unfurling its sunlit thread.

'Your horses, Bo'urchu, are known as the finest in the empire.'

'I no longer have the great herds of before, O my Khan. I have only kept a few heads, the descendants of Afraid of Bears.'

'I know that; it only makes your horses more precious. Do you know the one who caused my fall?'

I didn't. From his bed, his eyes sad and his colour drained, Genghis Khan observed me calmly.

'Subtle Gold.'

By his mother, Silken Muzzle, this horse was a grandson of White Cloud, and so a great-grandson of Afraid of Bears.

'This fall vexed me,' continued the Khan. 'But it also opened my eyes. I realised that I was tired, worn out by all the ground journeyed, the night-time marches without halts or sleep, these days without food or rest. I have avenged our ancestors and assured the greatness of my sons. All our companions are rich and feared. I have accumulated more riches than any people will ever possess. But I have lost my eldest son and I hold that against myself . . . Now I am weary. I need nothing; all that matters to me is to see our land again, live simply in my yurt, sustain myself with the wind, walk quietly, guided by the smells of the steppe, sit on a rise and follow the course of the clouds. The Jin I brought from so far away is supposed to know the secret of immortality. That's why I wanted him at my side. He told me he knew potions for longevity but none to prevent the final decline. He is very wise, that hermit. He taught me his religion. The search for Tao is a beguiling discipline and when he went home, I promulgated an edict on its behalf, lifting all conscription and tribute from those who invoke the Sky like him. In Bukhara I listened to the Moslems as well, and the Nestorians and the Buddhists and many other beliefs, often complex and contradictory. To all of them I have extended my protection. In return every day their believers pray that I will live ten thousand times ten thousand years.'

'About the number of men you've killed,' I pointed out.

'Whoever is afraid cannot stretch his bow,' he said. 'Those piles of headless bodies, those blood-red rivers, those levelled cities – all that was necessary. You know full well that if you have a chance to kill, it is a crime just to wound. Everything becomes simpler afterwards, in peace. But I haven't asked you to come here to talk about the past. Do you know how Börte is disposed towards me? How will she receive me after all these years spent away from her with Qulan? I am afraid to see her again and announce that Jochi is no more. Help me! Go to her!'

'On one condition.'

He sat up and stared at me. His eyes were a bird of prey's now.

'Never! Get out!' he ordered.

I complied, but added just before leaving, 'You'd do well to watch over your grandsons as closely as you do her, our favourite, because already they show tendencies like their fathers to strip each other of everything that gives them warmth.'

Chapter 55

Genghis Khan could travel freely from the Yellow Sea to the Black Sea. Yet he waited for Börte's prompting before returning to the banks of the Tula where the felt palaces of his wives stood.

Her message ran as follows: 'O Conqueror, on the lake with the reed-covered shores there are many wild geese and swans, too many for your arrows. Other delights have appeared on the lands of your fathers. In every tribe there are many young women as sweet as milk, too many to be counted. Saddle your courser and enjoy these delights, choose your due.'

After a year hunting and feasting on the banks of the Irtysh, the Khan, reassured by his wife's invitation, moved his *ordo* back to the Tula river in the autumn of the Year of the Cockerel. He enjoyed – in moderation – the delights Börte granted him unconditionally and, as soon as winter ended, he set off again with Ögödei and Tolui to fight the Xixia, those traitors who hadn't kept their word on the eve of the conquest of the Moslems. Before marching against the Khwarezmian empire, the Khan had called the Sky to witness that he would eradicate the Xixia on his return. Nothing was more important to him now than to fulfil this vow.

This time, however, he had to take Yesüi with him: the Tatar princess demanded redress, furious at having been usurped by Qulan in the Khwarezmian campaign.

As he was approaching the enemy's cities south of the Gobi, the Khan deployed his army for a great hunt. Some young troops no doubt needed to be put through their paces but, as far as the bulk were concerned, the Mongol army was the most powerful and pitiless there could be. The simple truth of it was that the Khan wanted to satisfy his unbridled appetite for the chase and bring to a more fitting close a hunting season he had thought wanting.

He was riding in front of the quiver-bearers and imperial falconers when a herd of *dziggetai*, quick as fire, shot out from behind the dunes. Three of them crashed into the Roan, his mount, before disappearing in a terrified clattering of hooves. Shocked, the Roan reared and fell on the Khan, who found it very hard to get back to his feet. When he complained of internal pains, it was decided to set up camp there and confine him to his bed.

The next day the princes and nobles were summoned to the imperial tent. The Khan had spent a troubled night, fevers and pain granting him no quarter. The generals were worried and wanted to go home and wait for him to recover before resuming the campaign.

'If we withdraw,' Genghis Khan protested, 'the Xixia will say we're cowards.'

'Let's give them an ultimatum,' Ögödei countered, 'and see what they say.'

His father accepted this plan, even if without enthusiasm. Then his old companions knew that their fears were well founded: he was more seriously wounded than he would admit.

The message for the Xixia was equally alarming: 'If ever you broke your word, I swore to shell your and your family's balls like nuts and make them into necklaces for my horses. Well, more terrified than a marmot about to give birth, you were not at my right to fight the Moslems. Now the moment to pay has come. Prepare yourself for my anger.'

Over the following days the Xixia ruler sent sumptuous gifts to the royal camp in multiples of nine. Appealing to the mercy of the Emperor of the world, he blamed his chief advisor for his desertion of duty.

The Khan's companions sighed with relief. They could withdraw with their heads held high, confident they'd return once the Khan had convalesced.

But then the Xixia chief advisor himself sent a message to Genghis Khan: 'If the Mongols want to measure themselves up to my warriors, let them come to the slopes of the Alashan.'

'Since we cannot withdraw any more,' the Khan said in a blind fury, 'let us fill their nightmares with blood.'

The advance guards went up the course of the Xi He as far as the oasis of the Nanshan range. Strapped onto his horse, my *anda* followed a day's march behind. The green caravanserais of Suzhou and Ganzhou were brushed aside. Then it was the turn of Liangzhou and Yingli. As planned, the Xixia chief advisor was defeated at the foot of the Alashan.

Our troops embarked on rampant pillaging, massacring and raping the inhabitants with the full blessing of imperial command. Only Ningxia remained, the tremulous sovereign's capital, the last defensive fallback of his vast kingdom.

Genghis Khan didn't wait for its surrender. He handed the siege over to his young generals and left to conquer the land between Kukunor, the huge blue lake, and the tributaries of the Yellow River. Harsh country, high plateaus fissured with impassable gorges and exhausting treks took a further toll on his health.

At the very start of the Year of the Boar (1227), he set up camp close to the River Wei He, on the heights of the Liupanshan. Despite his suffering, his hunger for vengeance against the Jin did not abate. In fact, I think the pain actually made his resentment keener, because he planned in the cool of autumn to go to high-walled Kaifeng where the King of Gold was still enjoying his reprieve. In anticipation, Genghis Khan had dispatched Ögödei at the head of a hundred thousand to attempt a breakthrough.

During that summer of waiting, messengers constantly attended his bedside to inform him of his army's gains. Ningxia was collapsing section by section, but holding out. To the southeast, nearly a moon's march from his summer lair, Ögödei was at the gates of Tungchuan, a near impregnable fortress flanked on one side by a river and on the others by sheer escarpments. The King of Gold's finest units were defending this strategic point, the key to the plains of the Yellow River and Kaifeng.

The young officers in command of the siege of Ningxia were threatened with punishment if they did not resolve it quickly. The delay preyed on Genghis Khan's nerves because he knew the end was near. His end.

His worn-out body left him little hope. He may not have thought twice about his first fall or the Taoist monk's warning that it was a sign from Heaven; it was quite different with his second. Those *dziggetai* with their huge staring eyes stampeding at him; the lather of their sweat on his *del*; the black hoofprints on his ermine hat; his body, bruised for ever – none of that was just chance. Above all he couldn't forget that in the Merkid language, the word for *dziggetai* is *qulan*. No matter that he'd wiped the Merkid from the face of the earth, the ancestral rivalry between Merkid and Borjigin was not finished. Souls yielded to the sword and abandoned their mutilated shells, but their demands for vengeance would not stop until fortune had been fairly distributed. And he was still heavily in debt. The time to settle debts was very near, and this only increased his anguish.

Meanwhile solitude rested like the thick padding of a horse's collar on my shoulders. Luminous skies followed one after the other as I rode my lands at the Red Throne, counting the game and rounding up the herd morning and night for milking.

I tried not to think of those who were dead: Queen of Flowers, Temulun, Jochi . . . News had reached me of Muquali's death in Jin country. The insatiable warrior had fought to his last breath. Jochi's children were far away, campaigning against the Xixia. My old friends Qasar, Belgütei and Jelme likewise. Gerelma, my first wife, that louse on my collar, had died in spring before my eyes, carried away by the river in spate when the herd knocked her off her feet as she was trying to lift the leather bottles of milk. This should have felt as if a thorn had been removed from my foot. Sitting my horse and holding my *ourga*, I had seen her disappearing into the water that boiled on that stretch of the river. I had ridden closer. An arm had shot above the surface, pointing at the sky and spinning round in the eddies. Just as she might have caught hold of my *ourga*, I had pulled it away. You cannot help those who are drowning without risking the wrath of the spirits. So was it her gaping mouth or her bulging eyes that had made me gallop upstream, racked with remorse?

Where the riverbed shelved I hooked her belt and pulled her onto the bank. She was dead; her face was bloated and she had swallowed part of her purple tongue. I pushed her back, begging the water spirits' indulgence for having taken from them for an instant what was theirs.

One evening I was sharpening my arrowheads in the last rays of sunshine, sitting on the Red Throne's broad, flat stones, when my loneliness bore down on me from the full height of my sixty-five springs; and it felt like the weight of as many winters, arid, cold, lifeless, each as white as my hair. I thought back to those happy days when I could imagine no other old age apart from in the saddle at my khan's side. Our wives' tents would have been in the same *ayil*, side by side, open to the sun. Drowsing dogs would have flanked our golden thresholds, their ears pricking up at the constant laughter of our grandchildren. Cruel, vanished peace . . . Alone and tired, sometimes I would listen to the wind. I liked that music which, when the arrogant wonder of that country seized me bodily, when the light scattered the shadows and I shivered in the emptiness of it all, brought salt tears to the back of my throat.

I was choking them back when I saw twenty horsemen crossing the clearing. They preceded a group of women, of whom only one enjoyed the attentions of an umbrella-bearer. They brought their mounts to a halt five hundred paces from the stone wall that ringed the Red Throne; then the woman shaded by the umbrella left them and came towards me alone and I could see that she was Tengri's most beautiful creation.

She threw herself from the saddle into my arms and we rolled in the grass, both of us crying and laughing, me nuzzling her hair, the rim of her pink lips; her tears which I drank mingled with mine and my heedless hands ran over her waist and her back, the silken armpits of her *del*, the hollows of her neck, her throat and nape, back to her waist and the curve of her lower back, her belly and her ribs, her ribs and her breasts, her breasts, her breasts and always her eyes gazing into mine.

Breathless, pushing me away and immediately clinging to me she said, 'Let's go behind those rocks; something terrible is happening.'

Sheltered by the Red Throne, which was purple in the dusk, I begged her to explain herself.

'I've been ordered to go to the Khan. I think he's dying.'

'Don't go! If you're right, he'll take you with him in his grave.'

'No, Bo'urchu,' she said, shaking, trying to untangle her arms pressed against my chest. 'He won't because . . . O my sweet one, be strong like the eagle in the sky; I will go to him and ask that he agree to my living with you.'

'You don't know him – what he's capable of. He'd kill his brothers – he did once already – even his children to keep you . . .'

Her eyes were so big the sky could have huddled away in them.

'He isn't what you say any more,' she protested.

'He told me he wanted to return to the pure way as well. But don't you understand that even dressed in rags, with no horse, no food, no people, he would never give you up because Qulan, my gazelle, my love, you are the marvel he cannot survive without.'

'Not to go to him would mean death for both of us – you know that. Nothing could shield us from his wrath. This is our only chance. If I fail, I will call your name as I kill myself.'

Then she fled.

In the shadows of the Red Throne, the galloping hooves of her departing horse merged with the beating of my heart.

I fell to my knees and started ripping up the grass we had rolled on with my teeth and nails. Soon there was none, so I stuffed earth into my mouth until my stomach rebelled.

Chapter 56

Protected by walls jutting out from the town's massive fortifications, the monumental gates of Ningxia trapped a host of our men. They left no room for our battering rams to work up speed and we were hacked to pieces.

In the middle of the Moon of the Rutting Stag, the western gate finally gave. The Mongol troops stormed the streets, houses and pagodas. At the other end of the city, part of the population tried to break out through the eastern gate. They were allowed to: it made it easier to slaughter them and turn the pink dunes into a charnel pit.

Genghis Khan wasn't aware of Ningxia's surrender. He had died south of the Liupan Shan mountains, in the middle of the Moon of the Roebuck, the hottest days of that year, 1227.

Nonetheless the Xixia king, bareheaded and without his belt, was still led to the royal *ordo*. Through one of the raised flaps of the tent he could see the Khan's legs. The interior of the tent was plunged in darkness. The fallen king apologised feverishly, begged a thousand pardons, offered gold, gems, camels, women, princesses. He would strip himself of all he had for the Khan's sake, he said, groaning, he would be his footstool. When he had nothing else to offer and was begging to kiss the Khan's feet, his head rolled on the ground, without him having seen or heard the son of Heaven. Nothing he held dear was spared.

Genghis Khan's death was kept secret until his return to Mongolia. The enemy was not to find out about this great mourning. His final journey lasted three moons.

In Mongolia it is considered lucky to meet a funeral cortège, since the dead are supposed to grant all their earthly joys to those who see it pass.

Onlookers on the Emperor's route were even more fortunate. They were all beheaded and so granted the great honour of serving the Khan in the beyond. Even the faint silhouettes of

363

people watching the army's columns from the distance were put to the sword.

Throughout those three moons, as the cortege crossed the plateau of the Ordos and the Gobi Desert, and witnesses were killed, the bards sang the Emperor's praises and the shamans implored Tenggeri to grant him eternal life. The bodies piled up to the rhythm of chants and the lashes of whips that permanently scarred the backs of the twenty-one oxen harnessed to the hearse. Every evening the noble beasts offered up their foreheads to the mallet, others took their places for the next day, and so it continued until the heavy wheels fell silent in front of Börte's felt palace.

Like all the empire's subjects, I did not know that my *anda* had died. The Moon of the Roebuck had very nearly been my last as well. Climbing the Red Throne, I had put my hand on a nest of vipers. Bitten on the forearm and the face, I had sworn viciously; the flat stones were seething with snakes. If the Khan had tethered his horses there as I had once hoped, they would never have been able to take hold.

A hideous old shaman with an undying face saved me but could not drive all the poison from my veins. From then on my limbs were always cold, my back hurt and I pissed blood. The slightest effort drained me and I barely ventured ten paces from my yurt.

In the Moon of the Ibex, the news of the Khan's death passed through the empire. His burial was fixed for the thaw. All that winter the Mongol people converged on his couch to pay a final homage. The steppe shook under the press of mourners; then they froze into a single, identical block, sealing off the horizon. All of them crushed under two pale, mournful skies, felt abandoned.

The following moon, Jelme came to my *ayil*. Since I could barely hold myself in the saddle, he wanted to set up my tent on a waggon to escort me to the funerary *ordo*.

'Genghis Khan would have so wanted you to be at his side,' he said, trying to convince me.

'I was at his side . . . I am still, and soon I will join him again.'

'Free your mind of care, Bo'urchu. Listen to this message he told me to give you just before he died.'

Then our old companion, the valiant warrior, who was balding and beginning to stoop, repeated word for word what my *anda* had said.

'Bo'urchu, my loyal Bo'urchu, now all is growing dark. My soul is rising by the smoke-hole towards the blue Sky, blue as the shirt you wore that first day when you helped me recover my meagre flock. Here we are reunited, thanks to Qulan, our *dziggetai*. Yesterday she begged me on her knees to restore her freedom so that she could go to you . . . I wanted to kill her, carry her away with me, keep her for ever. But in her distraught face, in those two eyes as vast as lakes glittering with starlight which mean everything to me, I saw your face, your goodness, your greatness, the brilliant blue of your shirt which dazzled me so much and has never ceased to do so, even if sometimes, blinded, I have seemed to turn away from it. Qulan . . . I saw how she loved you, how you loved her, how I was unable to love you both . . . until yesterday. The love she has given me is the love she feels for you; it is the love that belongs to you! As I return to Tenggeri I, Genghis Khan, swear this oath. May your horses carry you tirelessly wherever you desire for a hundred times a thousand more seasons. And may the woman we adore watch over the two of us, a hundred times a thousand more springs.'

Confined to my bed, old fogs and mists and bitternesses evaporated. I flew above the mountains, the clouds . . . Suddenly I realised that we had never been apart. Temüjin's arrows had never sought to wound me, or if so only to draw us back together.

'Where is she?'

'She is attending his burial and will oversee the death of the witnesses, once his sepulchre is closed and its traces erased. That was his last condition. Then she will join you.'

Work on the Emperor's sepulchre, a veritable palace of felt in a hollowed-out mountainside, would take another two or three moons. Its sacred location was to be a complete secret: all the slaves that gave their labour would be killed.

'Were those his last words?'

'No, he asked to see Ögödei and Tolui to tell them the strategy to use against Kaifeng and to complete the conquest of the Jin. Once he had explained his plan, the flames in his eyes stopped flickering and the black veil swallowed them up.'

Chapter 57

'Grandfather! Grandfather!'

I saw the troop of little children running towards my tent. They were Lame Bear's, the shepherd whose family had been looking after me for the past few seasons. That giant with one leg shorter than the other had twelve brats. Six of them were calling me, clapping their hands and jumping around outside my yurt.

I had just reached the rocky crest of the hill which spans the Red Throne like an amphitheatre and they couldn't see me.

'Grandfather! Grandfather! The first colt came last night!'

A seventh nipper, the youngest of those already weaned, was shouting at his brothers and sisters to wait for him. He'd fallen over and, bare-arsed and muddy-faced, was cursing them and throwing stones.

From my promontory they looked no bigger than flies, but their joy carried me to the centre of their dance. Spring was timidly showing its gentle face and my first colt of the year, the Year of the Rat, had been born.

I had witnessed his arrival before I started my climb. I still had the smell and blood on my arms. He had been born in the middle of the clearing as I was preparing to climb the Red Throne . . . for the last time. His mother, Twisted Forelock, had appeared at my threshold, stepping gingerly as if on hot coals, nodding her neck and swishing her tail, her feet hidden by the layer of fog hugging the ground.

She was a great-granddaughter of Afraid of Bears and delivered her first colt into my arms, half wrapped in his blue-and-red sac of life. I had gently set him on his glistening hooves on the ground and cleaned him. He had trembled, spread his forelegs like a camel drinking, wobbled for a minute on his hocks then boldly stepped over to his mother's teats without falling once.

I stayed with them until his coat had almost dried. It was silky russet, that burnt red that is the mark of the most sumptuous of golden chestnut stallions. He was a real little Afraid of Bears, with a frank, trusting gaze, full of mischief. Tying the cord round his neck, I told him I was going to join Genghis Khan in his tomb.

My russet colt signalled his agreement with his muzzle and in his eyes like two blue yurts I could see his pride.

He dived back under his mother's womb and I started my slow ascent.

Lame Bear's children turned back, angry not to have found me in my yurt. It had taken me all night to reach this crest, which would have been so easy for them. I had struggled up the slope, stooped double amongst the tall larches, blackened by thunder, which moaned mournfully from their full height.

I had to scramble over rocks before reaching the passage that wound between the boulders and led to this terrace with the flame-red pine. There it was, my tree, its old trunk split open by thunder, a living crown like a green parasol now swaying gently in the blue sky with the joyful insouciance of survivors. Similarly the once bare double-edged sword that reared up from its base now displayed four young branches green with fresh needles.

He was there too, sitting amongst the roots twisting among the stones, my wolf. The great white wolf I knew so well with the broad chest as full as the moon.

A black mark zigzagged the length of his muzzle above his mouth. It was definitely him – my wolf from the Blue Lake at whom I hadn't been able to fire my arrow, the wolf that had reappeared by the Khan, licking the wound in his throat. Only the colours of his coat had reversed. He must have been a thousand years old, and I knew it was time to take off my clothes.

I lay down, the white tiger-skin cap with the purple tassel beside me, the little horse and her lock of hair in my hand. The wind whistled between the rocks and the sky was blue as always.

I felt it being put on my chest, right against my heart. There was no need to touch it to know it was my kneecap. The thin body with full, warm breasts tenderly pressed down on it. Her long hair enveloped her kiss.

One dies very quickly when all is as it should be. Then time leaks away as it pleases.

It was the first time I had seen her from above, undressed, lying on top of me, and I had all the time in the world . . . The waterfall of her hair like a shroud over my old husk, her magnificent rump drenched with sun, and the beams of her legs darting like twin grasssnakes.

At our feet my wolf had his eyes half-closed and he was smiling, his great tongue twitching. The flame-red pine had changed into a woman who was wrapping her arms around his powerful shoulders. Naked and joyful she was the daughter of the Forest Spirit.

They were both watching over Qulan with me, as she sobbed on my corpse, and together we formed a whole, at peace.

Bibliography

Grousset, R., *The Conqueror of the World*, Edinburgh/London, Oliver & Boyd, 1967. *Le Conquérant du Monde*, Paris, Albin Michel, 1944.

Hamayon, R., *La chasse à l'âme. Esquisse d'une théorie du chamanisme sibérien*, Nanterre, Société d'ethnologie, 1990.

Hessig, W., *Les Mongols, un peuple à la recherche de son histoire* (trans. from the German by M.-P. Matthieu), Paris, Lattès, 1982.

Hoang, M., *Genghis Khan*, trans. Ingrid Cranfield, London, Saqi Books, 1990. *Gengis-khan*, Paris, Fayard, 1988.

Pelliot, P. and Hambis, L., *Histoire des campagnes de Gengis-khan* (incomplete trans. from the Chinese by P. Pelliot), Leyden, 1951.

Percheron, Maurice, *Sur les pas de Gengis Khan*, Del Duca, 1956

Pian del Carpini, Giovanni da, *Historia Mongalorum; il viaggio di frate Giovanni del Pian del Carpini ai Tartari* (ed. and with commentary by Giorgio Pullé), Studi Italiani di Filologia Indo-Iranica, Anno IX, vol. IX, Florence, Tipografia G. Carnesecchi e figli, 1913. *Histoire des Mongols* (trans. and with commentary by Father Clément Schmitt) Ed. Franciscaines, 1961.

Roux, J.-P., *Histoire de l'Empire mongol*, Paris, Fayard, 1993.

Faune et flore sacrées dans les sociétés altaïques, Paris, Maisonneuve.

La mort chez les peuples altaïques anciens et médiévaux, Paris, Maisonneuve.

Rubrouck, W. of, *Itinerarium. The texts and versions of John de Plano Carpini and Wm. de Rubruquis, etc.* (in Latin and English), 1903.

Secret History of the Mongols, The (ed. and trans. by Francis W. Cleaves), Boston, Mass., Harvard University Press, 1983.

Vladimirtsov, B., *The Life of Chingis-Khan* (trans. from the

Russian by Prince D. S. Mirsky), London, G. Routledge & Sons, 1930.
Le Régime social des Mongols (trans. from the Russian by Michel Carsow), Paris, Maisonneuve, 1948.

Various

Aubin, F., *L'art du cheval en Mongolie*: Production Pastorale et Société n. 19, Paris, Maison des Sciences de l'Homme, 1986.
Bogros, D., *Des hommes, des chevaux, des équitations*, Favre/Caracole, 1989.
Bourbolon, C. de, *L'Asie cavalière*, Paris, Phébus, 1991.
Frédéric, L., *L'arc et la flèche*, Éditions du Félin/Philippe Lebaud, 1995.
Gernet, J., *La vie quotidienne en Chine à la veille de l'invasion mongole (1250–1276)*, Paris, Hachette, 1978.
Jan, M., *Le voyage en Asie centrale et au Tibet*, Paris, Robert Laffont, 1992.
Jenkinson, A., *Early voyages and travels to Russia and Persia*, London, Hakluyt Society Publishing, 1886.
Legrand, J., *Vents d'herbe et de feutre*, Éditions Findalky, 1993.
Moreau, M., *La pensé mongole*, L'Ether vague/Patrice Thierry, 1991.
Shuduo G., Zhang, Y., Linggui F., Zhanghi, Z., and Shouyi, B., *Précis d'histoire de Chine*, Editions en langues étrangères, Beijin, 1988.
Soukhbaatar, T., and Desjacques, A. *Contes et récits de Mongolie*, Nathan, 1991.
Storey, R., *Mongolia*, London, Lonely Planet, 1993.
Tschinag, G., *Ciel bleu*, Métaillié, 1996.
Turnbull and Mcbride, *The Mongols*, Osprey Publishing.
Yule, H., *Cathay and the Way Thither* (trans. by Ter Sarkissian), London, Hakluyt Society Publishing, 1886.

Glossary

Aarul or **Arul**: wide variety of dried cheeses which could be kept for up to two years.

Airag: fermented mare's milk (also called koumiss, from the Turkish kimiz). Mildly alcoholic, this vitamin-rich drink has therapeutic properties. Distilled it produces a brandy of more than 30% proof, called Arkhi, an essential part of social and religious rites.

Anda: sworn brothers. The pact of friendship must be sealed with an oath and exchange of presents (and very often blood.) Once anda, the two sworn allies must support and help each other for the rest of their lives. The sacred union is generally inherited by the descendants, clans or tribes of the two anda.

Argols: Animal dung. Drying quickly in the Mongolian climate, argols are the main source of fuel.

Ayil: small group of yurts belonging to one family, answerable to a head or chief. Ayils were dispersed over an ulus.

Cangue: A wooden collar used as a portable stocks.

Del: coat dress.

Dziggetai: A timid, wild donkey.

Obo: cairn. This pile of stones is found in places that are either sacred (spring, summit of a mountain) or hard to get to (col, overhang). Every visit is marked by walking around the cairn three times, adding stones and making offerings of tobacco, a ribbon, a few drops of alcohol, or a lock of hair or mane, since an obo is considered the dwelling place of a spirit.

Ongon: Small felt or wooden idols, which are the vessels of spirits, particularly the ancestors', and the object of continuous family and clan observance.

Ordo: Imperial camp.

Ouiaa: Rope strung between stakes to tether horses.

Ourga: Lasso and pole to catch horses.

Quriltai: Plenary assembly of princes, nobles and clan chiefs. Attendance obligatory.

Tenggeri: the Eternal Blue Sky, the Sky God.

Tümen: Formation of 10,000 men, the largest of the subdivisions of Genghis Khan's army. The other units, all in multiples of 10, were the arban (10 men), ja'un (100 men) and mingan (1,000 men)

Ulus: Domain; well-defined tribal lands and the tribes living on them.

Yasak: Edict or prohibition. Legal code promulgated by Genghis Khan, inspired by the customs and beliefs of the Turkic-Mongol peoples. Initially transmitted orally, these laws were subsequently transcribed on scrolls in Uighur.

Yurt: The tent of the nomads of the Central Asian steppe. Nowadays Mongols call it a ger.

Acknowledgements

For their help, attentiveness, candour, spirit of collaboration and great kindness, a huge thanks to Jacky Gourlaouen, most faithful of all the faithful and my sworn Anda, and to Anne Dion, beloved sister.

My thanks go also to Gordana, my stream of flowers, who somehow patiently bore this long ride, and to her son Ilan Vuk, to Lhotsé and to all those whose advice, encouragement and help bore witness to their friendship: Ben and Brigitte, Michel Chemin, Jean-Louis Gouraud, Jean Claude Fasquelle, Aline and Hubert Honoré, Huguette Lebeau, Jacques Malaterre and, most especially, Denise Loridan and Brigitte Ollier.

Under no circumstances could I leave out Patrick Sabatier, who inspired me with his passion for Mongolia, Anne Mariage and the First Secretary of the Mongolian Embassy to France, Aniaghun Munhbat, who, from Boulogne-Billancourt to Ulan Bator, ensured good fortune shone on my journey.

My thanks to the many Mongolian families who received me with such affecting and genuine hospitality, emblematic of the noble souls of their people, as well as to the spirits of the forest and the steppe who spared me many dangers and, above all, lit my path with thoughtful guides. In particular Batbileg known as Bata, his brother Osko, but also Gansukh, Soumara B. Tsesen and Messrs Damdinsuren and Khaltar, who run the Khuduu Aral camp and stinted neither in their efforts nor in their great knowledge, which they so generously shared with me.

The translator would like to thank Roly Chambers, Rose Garnett, Emma O'Bryen and Philip Quarco for their expertise. Spelling of names and places has followed the conventions of Ingrid Cranfield's excellent translation of Michel Hoang's *Genghis Khan*, London, Saqi Books, 1990, with the exception that, for ease of recognition, Khan has been kept throughout and *k* used instead of the Greek letter gamma.